I0690430

DREAMING OF CHRISTMAS

JOANNE DANNON

CLARENDON 3
PUBLISHING

CONTENTS

COPYRIGHT

Dreaming of Christmas

Copyright © 2018 by Joanne Dannon

ISBN Kindle: 978-1-925450-32-3

ISBN print: 978-1-925450-52-1

ISBN large print: 978-1-925450-46-0

Dewey Number: A823.4

Edited in UK/Australian English

All rights reserved. By payment of the required fees, you have been granted the non-exclusive, non-transferable right to access and read the text of this e-book on-screen. No part of this text may be reproduced, transmitted, down-loaded, decompiled, reverse engineered, or stored in or introduced into any information storage and retrieval system, in any form or by any means, whether electronic or mechanical, now known or hereinafter invented, without the express written permission of **Clarendon 3 Publishing (www.clarendon3.com)**.

This is a work of fiction. Names, characters, businesses, places, events and incidents are either the products of the author's imagination or used in a fictitious manner. Any resemblance to actual persons, living or dead, or actual events is purely coincidental.

A MAGICAL CHRISTMAS IN
JERUSALEM

W hen falling in love isn't as easy as falling in love.

AUSTRALIAN PROJECT MANAGER Kiara Lonsdale is career focussed and determined to provide and care for the grandmother who raised her. Taking time off work to vacation has never been high on her agenda, but this year she's made an exception. She's helping her gran fulfil a life-long dream by accompanying her on a Christmas to the Holy Land tour.

JACQUES LENOIR and his extended family run tours in Israel and he's committed to their business. Jacques feels responsible for his grandparents' welfare since they risked their lives, and others', as operatives in the French Resistance, during the War.

· · ·

BUT OVER ROMANTIC dinners in the desert, camel rides, and mud baths at the Dead Sea, sparks fly between Kiara and Jacques. Will this only be a holiday romance or will a touch of Christmas magic make it last a lifetime?

DEDICATION

To my amazing family xxx

CHAPTER 1

For Kiara Lonsdale, Christmas was the best of times and the worst of times. Charles Dickens would be rolling in his grave at the desecration of his famous line, but every December Kiara was torn between enthusiastically hanging out tinsel and humming carols or hiding in her bedroom reading romances and eating pudding. This year would've been no exception except she and her beloved grandmother were about to land at Ben Gurion airport in Israel.

Her gran, June Lonsdale, gripped Kiara's knee hard with anticipation, her gaze drawn to the window. "Darling, we're here, we're here." Grabbing a hankie that had been hidden in the sleeve of her cardigan, she dabbed at the pools of salty tears in her eyes. "If only Ronald could've been here with us."

It may have been a year since her much loved grandfather had passed away from cancer, but a lump of pain still formed in Kiara's throat at the mention of his name. She had gazillions of happy memories of his cheery smiles and happy-go-lucky disposition. How many countless occasions had he served champagne? "Life is for celebrating" he always said.

Whether it had been a birthday, her finishing school, or winning a promotion, that night he would open a bottle of bubbly.

Her gran had certainly hit the jackpot marrying him and Kiara hoped to find a husband who'd be as wonderful and caring as her pop had been. "He's here in spirit with us." She forced a smile before her throat clogged again with emotion. The two women held hands as they descended and the pilot expertly skidded the giant plane to a halt.

"Welcome to Israel," a flight attendant announced over the system before giving out the local time and outside temperature. Kiara took a moment to peer out the window and take her first glance of the holy land. It reminded her of Australia: modern, clean, and inviting.

The reminder of what she'd left, in Melbourne, hit her in the belly. Her senior role in managing complex IT projects consumed her every waking moment; she couldn't remember the last time she'd taken a vacation. Yet, here she was accompanying her gran on an overseas trip instead of ensuring the rollout of the company's new customer service system was efficient and methodical. She hoped her replacement didn't botch up her eighteen months of detailed and meticulous planning. There was a reason she was sought after as a contracted project manager; she was really good at what she did.

Glancing out the window again, she took in the number of large planes, their wings and empennage decorated with international logos and colours; she still couldn't believe she was here instead of conducting meetings and making endless calls.

She and June patiently remained in their seats as the frenzied rush of passengers made their way to the exit, before they gathered their things and walked slowly to Immigration.

"Is the tour company meeting us before or after we get our luggage?" Kiara's eyes widened at the diversity of people walking around the airport.

"After. Apparently there is another family joining us to Jerusalem," her grandmother replied.

"Are you okay?" Kiara asked, unease nibbling her belly at seeing the shuffle of the older woman's feet.

June's hand brushed her concerns away. "Don't fuss. It's been a long flight and I'm not as young as I used to be."

Kiara stifled a smile then a yawn. Having spent the night in Hong Kong to break up the twenty-two hour flight had meant they'd been travelling for two days now and she couldn't wait to get to their hotel in Jerusalem. Australia really was at the end of the earth when it came to travelling to Europe or the Middle East.

They paused to watch the stream of visitors take their picture under the "Welcome to Israel" sign before they continued to Immigration.

June stopped walking and grabbed Kiara's hand, her eyes filled with determined revelation. "I have a good feeling about this trip. I believe something wonderful is going to happen."

Kiara's shoulders sagged with a strained sigh. "It's almost Christmas, this is a good time of the year."

June's face stilled with premonition and wonderment. "No," she replied with a determined shake of her head. "I mean, I just had this feeling, right now." She pointed to the ground. "We were meant to come *now*, something wonderful is going to happen to *you*."

Kiara brushed her lips against the older woman's soft cheek. She'd come on this trip to appease her grandmother, keeping her company on the long flights. With her bad track record of falling for the wrong guy and losing her parents at an early age, it was unlikely that her grandmother was right.

All those wonderfuls and happily ever afters were unlikely to happen to her.

Not wanting to upset her gran she joked, "We're here to do a biblical tour, *for seniors*, in the holy land."

"Don't be flippant." June's finger wagged in front of her eyes, but there was genuine warmth in her eyes.

Kiara gave June a warm smile. "We've already had a miracle happen here, albeit a couple of thousand years ago."

They resumed their walk to the airport's exit. "A Christmas miracle in Jerusalem, I like the sound of that." June sighed.

Kiara frowned. A Christmas miracle in Jerusalem?

Unlikely.

There was more chance of her gran tap dancing from the airport all the way to Jerusalem.

* * *

THEY RETRIEVED their luggage and after a refreshing iced coffee they made it to Jerusalem within two hours. Kiara's breath snagged in her throat as the road wound toward the beautiful, ancient city. All thoughts of IT and project plans disappeared and a powerful feeling of yearning tumbled in her tummy. She may not believe in something miraculous happening to her, but she did feel the energy and attraction of this ancient land. For the first time since June had raised the crazy idea of celebrating Christmas in Jerusalem, a realisation settled on Kiara. She was glad to be here.

Soon after, they were dropped off at their hotel, allowing them time to settle in and rest. Excitement wound through her belly and Kiara gave her bed a scowl. Sure, the room was inviting and lovely, but she wanted to be outside and play tourist.

June glared at her granddaughter. "You're bouncing off

7

the walls. Go and walk somewhere and leave me so I can lie down." She sat on her bed. Pointing to the door she said, "And don't forget your key."

A buzz of excitement and restlessness had her unable to stand still. Kiara grabbed her coat, hat, and scarf before virtually skipping out the door. "Bye, Gran. Love you," she called before the door closed with a "click".

Heading toward the hotel's front desk, not paying attention to her surrounding, she walked right into something, or rather, someone. Her bump caused a folder and sheets of paper to scatter in every direction.

"*Mon dieu!*" a decidedly male voice exclaimed. He tried grabbing everything off the floor.

"I'm so sorry," she apologised profusely before bending down to help retrieve the papers.

The papers all collected, she stood and turned to face the bloke she'd knocked into, and her lungs emptied with astonishment. He was handsome, really handsome, as in model handsome. With piercing blue eyes, defined cheekbones, tidy eyebrows, and dark brown hair, he had that very male edgy look that she found very appealing. But his cleft chin and two-day growth gave him a rougher edge that set her heart racing.

With shaky fingers, she handed him the papers and apologised again, the words tripping over her tongue.

"I'm assuming you're eager to get outside and see our beautiful city?" He lifted his eyebrow questioningly.

Her lungs remembered to breathe and she took a moment to admire his square-cut jaw and perfectly bowed lips. Despite her five foot eight inches height, she still had to look up at him.

A sudden urge to stroke the stubble along his jaw gripped her. Reprimanding herself, she clenched her hands into fists. That was really inappropriate. Just because he was a handsome stranger didn't mean he'd want a random woman trailing fingers across his face. She stifled an unintended giggle, thankful he couldn't read her thoughts.

"Again, I'm so sorry. I just arrived and I wanted to get out of the hotel." Blustery nerves made her blurt out exactly how she felt.

She shook his offered hand, loving the feel of his fingers wrapped around hers, firm but gentle. "Welcome to Israel." His lazy smile made her tummy dissolve into a pool of longing.

"Thank you." She paused. "Do you happen to know if I turn left or right, at the main road, to get to the Old City.

His stance was relaxed and informal. He wore denim jeans, which were moulded to his long legs, together with a thick woollen jumper. An anorak was held in the crook of his arm. "What do you want to see?"

She restrained herself from throwing her arms up in the air but she couldn't contain the excitement in her voice. "Everything, but I've only got a short time before the tour picks us up. I think the Tower of David is close enough to visit."

"Yes." He stopped to scratch his chin. "I have to go by there, why don't I take you? I mean" —he cleared his throat— "I wouldn't want you getting lost, since it's your first time here."

Sucking in a deep breath, she wanted to say yes, but a worm of concern made its way into her belly. Walking with a stranger, albeit a handsome stranger, in an unknown city was tempting, but probably not advisable. "I don't want to impose," she said, not wanting to appear rude.

He held out his hand. "Jacques Lenoir."

Taking his larger hand in hers, she replied, "Kiara Lonsdale." Not so flustered, she noticed a lanyard around his neck and her eyes opened in surprise when she read his credentials. "You're a tour guide?"

He shifted his stance. "My family and I run tours. In fact, we're starting one this aftern—"

"Lenoir Tours?" She gasped. "My gran and I are on your tour for the next week."

A smile spread across his lips. "I thought I recognised the name."

Kiara returned his grin and hope radiated along every vein. A gorgeous guide and she was going to see him every day over the next week.

Bursting with excitement, she pressed her lips together in the hope she didn't start a happy dance in the middle of the hotel lobby. Alleviated, she didn't have to worry about stranger-danger. Relief washed over her and she felt her heart ease with relief. "Well then, Jacques, I would appreciate you showing me where the Tower is."

He lopped his arm through hers. "It will be my pleasure."

Outside, her long, thick hair blew across her face so she pulled a hand-knitted beanie on, not only keeping her hair in place but her ears warm. The cold wind was biting and uninviting. "It's now summer in Australia so it's a bit of a shock to be walking around in winter." She shivered.

They strode together along the street, their pace in sync with each other. "So tell me, why did you come on the tour?"

"To be honest, it was my grandmother's idea. She always wanted to do it but my grandfather refused to fly. Something traumatic happened to him when he was enlisted in the Korean War. He never spoke about it and he steadfastly refused to get on a plane." She paused to catch her breath. "Gran always wanted to have Christmas in the Holy Land," she gushed, hoping she wasn't boring him. A quick check and she noticed he was looking at her intently, listening to what she was saying.

"And here you are!" Jacques replied, grinning.

His accent was an eclectic mix of Israeli, American, and… French? She couldn't quite place if he sounded more Israeli or European.

Walking along the cobbled streets that were modern and busy with cars, she couldn't help but look around and admire the beauty of the golden bricks.

"This is Mamilla Mall." His arm swung in the air toward the beautiful shopping precinct they walked past. "It's been rebuilt and very different to how it used to be." He took her hand to guide her to the side of the road. "Have a look at this." He pointed to numbers written on the large bricks. "With the plan of restoration, they determined how the original buildings would be rebuilt. This is how they did it, stone by stone, brick by brick."

"Wow, that's amazing," she gushed.

He flushed. "Sorry, I can't help myself."

"No, please, I'm really interested." And she was. He seemed to know everything about the city and she listened intently as he gave a running commentary on everything they passed. Before she knew it, they'd crossed through the Jaffa Gate and into the Old City. "You're talking, I'm listening, and I forgot to take a picture of me at the gate."

"I promise to make up for it over the next few days," Jacques said.

Whoosh went the air from her lungs as he looked at her with his gorgeous blue eyes, which you could figuratively drown in.

Her Australian candour and inability to stop had her blurting out, "Did you really need to come here?" She may be stumbling over her words but she desperately wanted to know why he was spending time with her. Because of her? Because he was a nice guy? Because it was his job? The idea he was doing it out of duty made her want to sulk like a petulant child.

He stopped walking, turning to face her, surprise etched across his jaw. "*Bien sur*. I was getting some pastries for my *maman*, there's the shop" —he raised his arm and pointed to the street ahead of them— "over there that has her favourite cakes."

Kiara's heart skipped a beat. Handsome, interesting, family oriented. Could this guy be too good to be true? A quick check on his left hand showed no wedding band, but then, not all men wore them.

They walked toward the shop and he continued to tell her interesting tidbits of every street and every place they passed, making her head spin.

He guided her to a small bakery that could only be described as a hole in the wall. "They make the best *menena*, which are shortbreads with a date filling. They are *magnifique*."

Her eyes opened in surprise. "You're French?"

"*Non*, Israeli. My grandparents settled here during the Second World War, after escaping from the Nazis. Our family has lived in Jerusalem ever since."

Her interest in him hitched up a notch. "Your family history sounds very interesting." She hankered to ask him a ton of questions of what his grandparents did, why were the Nazis after them? Why Israel? Why didn't they return to France after the war?

He brushed his finger across her brow. "Your forehead is creased with questions. I'll answer them, but for now, try a *menena* before I take you to the Tower." He held out a box full of tiny pastries covered in icing sugar.

She took one and nibbled it. "It's delicious."

"They are." His smile extended across his face.

"Let's go." He looped his arm through hers and led her along the cobbled streets.

Jacques walked her feet off, showing the Old City over the next two hours. Full of interesting commentary, he explained the fighting over Jerusalem over the centuries and the impact to the city. They could barely walk a few metres before there was yet another interesting piece of history to look at, take pictures, or talk about.

As they walked side by side he asked, "Tonight, we're having dinner as a group, but I was wondering if you'd like to see the Light Show at the Tower of David?"

She stopped walking, not having expected an invitation out. Was it a date? "It's not part of the tour?"

He shook his head. "We have too much to get through and often people see it after the tour has completed, however, I know that you're returning to Australia at the end of the tour so you may not have time to see it."

Confusion swamped her. Was it a date? Or part of his job as a tour guide? "What about my gran?"

His brow crinkled in disbelief. "But of course, she comes with us. Will you mind missing the official dinner tonight? We'll need to eat earlier." He extracted his smartphone from his pocket and typed away; after finding the web page he wanted, he read it then looked at her. "The show starts at eight o'clock. I can collect you both at six, which gives us time to eat before the show. You'll love it." He kissed his fingers in a manner that European men did. "It's *magnifique*."

She couldn't help the smile that stretched across her lips in anticipation, not just seeing the show, but also spending time with the gorgeous Jacques.

He returned her smile and she felt an uncharacteristic urge to giggle. She worked with plenty of good-looking blokes in her corporate career so the effect he was having on her was very surprising.

They started retracing their steps along the cobbled walk way. "*Bien sur.* Let's go back to the hotel and I'll see you at six in the lobby. I'll bring a ticket for both of you."

After a rest, hot shower, and a change of clothes, Kiara met Jacques in the lobby.

He kissed both her cheeks and looked around. "Where's Madame Lonsdale?"

She sighed. "She's very tired from the flight and apologised for not coming along."

Kiara had been disappointed yet selfishly and secretly delighted to be spending alone time with Jacques. Her gran was still tired from the travelling, despite the afternoon nap. "We have a busy few days," she'd chided her granddaughter. "I'm not sitting outside in the freezing cold watching a slide show."

Kiara implored her to attend, not wanting her to miss out. "But, Gran, it's going to be—"

June silenced her with a cluck of her tongue. "I'm looking forward to dinner in this very nice hotel where it's warm. We have a busy day tomorrow visiting churches, gardens, and the Mount of Olives." She yawned. "I need to rest."

Kiara had kissed her cheek before heading out to meet Jacques.

Looking at Jacques she said, "Don't you need to be here for the dinner?"

"*Non,*" he said. "My sister, Lucie, is in charge tonight."

"It sounds like the company is very family oriented," she said, her voice filled with longing. She couldn't help the wiggle of jealousy in her belly, she'd love to have such an extended family.

"It is." He placed his hand at the base of her spine to lead to her to the door. "I'll tell you more on the way."

Over the most delicious dinner of grilled chicken, hummus, tehina, salads, and pita, they chatted and she felt like they'd known each other for years, not hours. There was something reassuring about the way he listened and made her feel special despite the endless questions she'd badgered him with.

"This dinner is amazing," she said, before biting into a piece of delicious pita.

"They make their own bread," he said, tilting his head to the owners.

"I love it," she said. "Tell me more about your family business."

"We personalise our tours, especially this one over Christmas when travellers are away from their homes." He took a sip of water. "You'll meet the whole Lenoir family the day after tomorrow."

Surprise made her gasp at his casual mention of the get together. "That's Christmas Eve. Don't you want to just be together? I mean, as a family?" Surely the family would rather be together than with a bunch of strangers?

His eyes widened in astonishment. "*Mais non*. We always invite everyone on the tour to our home."

Nervous fingers fluttered to her throat. "Sorry, I think it's a lovely idea, I just thought…" She stumbled for the right words.

He didn't seem to notice her discomfort and continued speaking with his deep voice. "We offer options of attending Church in the afternoon or Midnight Mass."

"You really think of everything," she said, taking a sip of her water.

He leaned forward and she could see the genuine warmth in his eyes. "This is not just a job, it's our livelihood." He paused. "The business supports my parents, grandparents, my sister, and me. We specialise in a number of tours for seniors, teenagers, and families who want to come and have a tremendous experience here."

She admired the determination and self-assuredness outlined in the sharp line of his jaw.

Casting a quick look at his watch he said, "Finish up, we need to get going."

*   *   *

Two hours later, they sat together in a small café huddled over hot chocolates.

"That was the most amazing show I've seen in a long time," she said before sipping her hot drink. "Sitting outside in the cold was definitely worth it, thanks for taking me. I can't get over how incredible the imagery was. I mean, this afternoon you went through the city's history, but to see superimposed pictures of King David, the Romans, the Crusaders, and everything else was…" She waved her hand in the air, looking for the right word.

His hands cupped the mug for warmth. "I've seen it many times and I still enjoy it. Do you know they use twenty projectors for the visuals?"

She rolled her eyes in jest. "And of course you have to know that."

"*Bien sur*. Of course. But what I don't know is you. We've talked for hours but I hardly know anything about you. Tell me, Kiara, why did you come here? Was it to have a magical Christmas in Jerusalem?"

Her jaw dropped and tiny flutters in her throat made it hard to speak. *A magical Christmas in Jerusalem*. That's what he'd said. She was sure she hadn't used that expression with him, so how come he had? Was her gran's prediction right? Was something miraculous going to happen to her? Or did that only happen in the romance books and movies she loved so much?

CHAPTER 2

The following morning, after a delicious buffet breakfast, the tour group of twelve people met in the lobby. Unlike her, all the attendees were over sixty and either in couples or travelling solo.

The tour guide was Lucie, Jacques' younger sister, who appeared to be around the same age as her, twenty-nine. With efficient kindness, Lucie organised her tour charges. "Shalom, friends. I hope you enjoyed breakfast. Today, we're going to start with a drive up to the Mountain of Olives where we will see..."

Lucie's excited voice explained the day ahead and Kiara swallowed sharp pangs of disappointment. Jacques had told her he wouldn't be there for the day but she was still grumpy because of his absence.

Silly, really. She'd barely known him twenty-four hours and yet she already had a strong affinity for him, hoping to see him again. Pushing her fingers into warm gloves, she reminded herself that his friendship was unlikely to be "real". How many times had she travelled to Asia and met lovely people from Australia, New Zealand, America? When they returned home the friendship fizzled out. Some acquaintances only worked while on vacation, she reminded herself.

But despite her reassurances, she really liked him. Funny, friendly, family oriented. He ticked all the boxes. Except he lived in Israel and she lived in Australia where her well paid, executive job and California bungalow waited for her return.

Maybe he was just being kind, after all, she was part of his family's tour. Pushing aside all thoughts of his dangerously blue eyes, designer stubble, and dark hair that sat in fashionable spikes, she focussed on the outing.

Like her brother, Lucie was very knowledgeable and the day was spent site-seeing in Jerusalem. Kiara turned to her grandmother. "You chose well. This tour is very accommodating."

June sniffed. "You didn't think I'd book *any* tour, I spent time on the Internet researching," she said in her all-knowing voice.

Kiara brushed her lips against her gran's cheek. "You are so special."

The long day of walking and sight seeing ended with yet another delicious dinner of felafel, pita, dips, and salad.

* * *

THE FOLLOWING MORNING, nervous anticipation ricocheted in her belly making it hard to focus. She was going to see Jacques today. Trying not to behave like a love-struck teen, she went through the motions of getting ready but spent extra time applying light makeup and pink lipstick, to look her best.

After breakfast, she was the first in the lobby and catching sight of him made her heart flip flop. Seeing her, he strode over and kissed both her cheeks. "*Boker tov*, good morning," he said. "Did you sleep well? How was breakfast?"

"Great on both accounts," she said, unable to hide the smile stretching across her lips.

"You look beautiful this morning," he whispered in her ear and Kiara felt her face grow warm. Perhaps they'd bumped up the heating because she was suddenly decidedly hot. "We're going to Bethlehem today and this afternoon we'll be at our family home." He paused. "I want you there," he added in a low voice that made her tummy tumble in delight.

That afternoon, seated next to each other, the mini-bus drove them to a small block of units in the new section of Jerusalem. "When my parents got married, they bought an apartment in the building as well as one for my grandparents to live in," Jacques explained.

"You work together and live next to each other. Don't tell me you live there too?" she said in mock horror.

"*Oui.* I live here in one of the apartments but Lucie lives with Maman and Papa, and Gabrielle lives in Tsfat."

"Gabrielle?" she asked.

"My older sister. I'm the middle child and Lucie is the youngest," he clarified.

Lifting an eyebrow she playfully asked, "Gabrielle's the rebel of the family?"

He grinned in return. "Sort of, she's an artist and very talented. When she married, she moved to live in Tsfat—"

"Where's that?" she asked, since Tsfat wasn't on their itinerary and she didn't know much about the city.

He lifted the folder from his leather satchel and flipped the pages till he found a map of Israel. He pointed to it. "Tsfat is here in northern Israel. We go past there when we visit Galilee." His finger indicated the lake and areas around it on the map.

He continued, "Tsfat is beautiful, a spiritual home for religious Jews, but Gabrielle loves being around other artists.

Her husband works in a restaurant." He paused. "There aren't many Christians living there so she always comes down to spend Christmas with us. You'll meet them this afternoon."

The bus stopped outside an older-looking building with carefully tended gardens. He pointed out the ground floor apartment. "We entertain in my grandparents' apartment because not only is it the largest, but it has the easiest access."

"And your clientele is…" she paused, "…older."

He touched her nose. "We do have younger people on our tours but we love our older guests."

"I saw that yesterday and today," she said. "You're very accommodating for those travellers with plenty of rest stops, cups of tea, refreshments."

"Come on." He tugged at her hand. "I want you to meet my grandparents."

The warmth of his hand holding hers made her grin widely. The day was getting better and better. Not only was he sitting next to her, but he gave her smiles when he thought no one was looking. But her gran had noticed. She'd been delighted and had told her so at lunch.

It took time for everyone to alight from the bus and make their way into the apartment. The room was warm and inviting and since they were the first to arrive, Jacques introduced his grandparents to her. "Agathe and Jacques Lenoir."

"Lovely to meet you," Kiara said, shaking their hands. After exchanging pleasantries, she turned to Jacques and whispered, "Another Jacques?"

"The tradition in our family is for the first born son to be named Jacques. Papa and *grandpere* are also Jacques."

She threw him a cheeky grin. "That should make it easy in remembering everyone's names."

A buffet table had been set up and Kiara admired the huge array of Middle Eastern delicacies as well as the French inspired *petit fours*. Her mouth watered at the delicious scents of buttery pastries, rose water, and sugar.

"You must try everything." Jacques's hand wavered over the magnificent array of afternoon tea goodies. "My grandmother made them and she is quite the cook."

Kiara rolled her eyes in feigned apprehension. "Do you know how much I'm eating? Everything tastes so good, I won't be able to fit in my jeans soon."

He chuckled in reply.

A knock on the door announced more arrivals and Kiara was shocked to see *more* people arriving, at least fifteen with grandparents and children.

"Who are they?" She didn't recognise anyone as they hadn't been on the tour.

"Family friends," he replied.

"You invited friends on top of the tour group?" Bewilderment made her question sound snappy rather than curious. She didn't mean it, but she was shocked to see the Lenoirs hosting not only the tour group here but others.

It was very different to what she was used to in Australia. Often her colleagues complained about having *one* family over. Here, the Lenoirs had the tour attendees *and* extras. It made her head spin with wonder at how the older Lenoirs had done it. In addition, she couldn't help but feel in awe at the kindness extended to everyone in not only being invited but feeling included. Despite them being in an apartment, furniture had been moved, fold out chairs brought in to accommodate the number of invitees.

Kiara watched as the newly arrived guests greeted and kissed Jacques's grandparents. There were hugs, kisses and... tears? Warm emotion filled the room and Kiara could see there was a strong affinity between the two families.

The children scooted off into another room and the

guests were encouraged to help themselves to the large array of food, drinks, and tea.

Conversation flowed and the noise level rose, a mixture of French, English, and Hebrew spoken.

"Excuse me," Jacques whispered into her ear.

She watched him walk to the kitchen and tried not to admire his butt and long legs clad in jeans. A minute later he returned with a bottle and shot glasses and after filling them, the guests were encouraged to take one. Unlike the tour guests, there was no apprehension by the others enjoying the clear liquid.

Shouts of *l'chaim* filled the room as they enjoyed the shots.

Not partial to alcohol like vodka and gin, she was reluctant to drink it. Taking a sniff, the pleasant smell of aniseed filled her nostrils. Under the encouragement of Jacques, she drank the small amount of liquid before it slid down her throat burning it as it made its way to her belly. Her eyes widened. "Wow, that's nice but potent," she said.

"It's Arak." Jacques lifted the bottle. "Another?"

She shook her head. "I think one's enough, it's warming me up."

Once he'd ensured everyone had enough Arak, he took her by the hand and organised chairs next to his grandparents.

"Kiara is interested in your story, why you came to Israel," he announced.

A number of pairs of eyes looked at her and she squirmed in her seat, flustered at the attention. "You didn't have to announce it," she muttered.

The guests clapped and one of the older gentlemen looked at the Lenoirs senior with tears in his eyes. "Jacques." He raised his glass of Arak to the older man. "While you celebrate the birth of Christ, we're celebrating the miracle of

Chanukah. But for us together, we're celebrating the miracle of your survival, your unbelievable courage, and your fortitude in facing adversity and doing such good during a time of evil."

The determination in his words made the air whoosh out of her lungs. After taking a moment to look at the guests, a feeling that something momentous was about to happen settled on her. It was both comforting and exciting knowing she was going to be privy to something very special between these families.

Turning to Jacques, she asked, "They're Jewish?" They'd mentioned they'd celebrated Chanukah and now she was interested why a Jewish family was here on Christmas Eve. It didn't make sense.

"*Oui*," he said. "Listen up. Every year we spend this time together and remember the best and worst of humanity." His warm hand held hers, comforting her.

Kiara sat immobile in her chair, desperate to know what had happened to draw these Christian and Jewish families together. The noise level dropped and Jacques's grandfather started to speak in his heavy French accent.

Silence filled the room as he transported them to 1941 when he and Agathe were newly-weds living in a small village in Vichy France. They were in love, wanting to be together and start a family, but the world was at war and the Germans had taken over their beloved France.

"We joined the Resistance, eager to help France in any way we could. We may not have been involved in reconnaissance but we did pass on any information that we could." He paused. "And then the Germans came after the Jews. We had Jewish neighbours and we'd always got on well with them. One night they came to us, desperate, asking for help. We didn't have money but we took their two children and another two from another family and hid them in our cellar, behind a false wall I'd built, to protect them. We kept them underground for a few weeks and then…" His voice cracked and he lifted a glass to his lips to drink.

Kiara's eyes widened seeing the shake of his hands. She swallowed away the fear, dreading what she was about to hear.

Clearing his throat, he said, "Both sets of parents disappeared."

The silence in the room was deafening, everyone's attention was focussed on the older man and his deep, accented voice. "The four children, bless them, remained in the cellar but we struggled to feed them. We barely had enough food for ourselves, let alone four extra mouths." His breathing picked up a notch and his wife gently placed her hand on his in a calming motion. It seemed to work and his breathing seemed less laboured. "I hunted and stole food and we pretended to be yet another young couple caught up in the war. And then a friend warned us, a neighbour had informed the Gestapo we were part of the Resistance."

A few people gasped, including Kiara, her hand flying to her mouth.

"That night we took the children and left the village to find refuge. Thanks to our contacts in the Resistance we hid in barns and walked hundreds of kilometres to get to the coast. We didn't know where to go. Italy was aligned with Germany and there were rumours of Egypt falling to the Germans." He stopped, took a hanky from his pocket, and wiped his wet eyes. "We joined and blended in with other refugees and by boat came to Israel, Palestine as it was known then."

Agathe continued the story, "The British were here and although the borders were closed it wasn't hard to get in. We came to Jerusalem and stayed in its safety for the remainder of the war," she said. Like her husband, Agathe's English was heavily accented.

"What happened to the children? To the parents? Do you know?" Kiara desperately wanted to know more, awestruck by the bravery of this elderly couple seated in front of her.

"We returned to France, to our village…" Agathe stopped and Kiara could see deep pain etched in the lines around her eyes. "So many dead. It was awful. But by God's help, we found the parents of two of the children. A miracle, since most of the French Jews had been killed by the Nazis. The parents had miraculously survived and so had their children."

Tears sprung to her eyes and Kiara couldn't imagine the joy and gut-wrenching of that reunion.

"We cried and hugged when we found them, quite unable to believe they'd both survived thanks to the bravery of the Resistance." She took a deep breath. "Many of us Christians were killed or tortured for standing up to the Gestapo but…" she paused, "…I'd still do it again."

A deep voice then interrupted. "Because of your bravery we wouldn't be here today."

A sob caught in her throat as Kiara looked at the man who was in his mid-thirties who'd spoken.

"Thanks to you, you saved my father and my aunty, and for every day while I am on this earth I thank and praise you," the man continued.

Kiara couldn't stop the tears slipping from her eyes, looking at Agathe and Jacques, then to the Jewish family. "Because of you, they're here?" She gasped.

Agathe smiled. "*Oui.* We even raised them Jewish."

Laughter broke out around the room breaking the heaviness that shrouded everyone after the tale.

The youngest Jacques in the room then said, "Not only did they save the lives of Jewish children, something they could've been executed for. But they raised two of them as observant Jews in their Christian home."

A few of the devout crossed themselves and Kiara found her body sagging with gut-wrenching emotion, against Jacques, still amazed at the incredible story of his grandparents.

"You're Christians and yet you raised them in their own religion?" Kiara's voice came out in a hush.

Jacques's grandfather gave her a warm smile. "Of course. It's what their parents would've wanted. God rest their souls."

Tears sprang to Kiara's eyes. She'd never come face to face with people who'd faced such adversity. They'd risked their lives for children who weren't even theirs and stood up to the Nazis, defying them in a heroic, confident, and strong manner.

"And your own children?" Was Jacques a descendant from them directly or had the Lenoirs adopted more children? A young married couple would've had their own children, especially before the ready availability of contraception, but there had been no mention so far.

Agathe's eyes brightened and she held her husband's hand tightly. "Our first child was born soon after the war." She breathed out a long breath. "For many years, I wondered if I couldn't have children but now I know that I couldn't get pregnant till I felt safe. I felt safe here." She pointed to the ground. "And this is where our Lord blessed me with a healthy pregnancy, not once, but many times."

"Amen," many, in the room, responded in a low voice.

"This is our home both physically and spiritually. It's where our Lord was born and where we happily raised our six children." She turned to the Jewish family, her face filled with love and kindness. "Two may not be biological but I love them as much as if I had birthed them."

A sob exploded from Kiara's lips and Jacques placed his arm reassuringly around her. "It's okay, *cherie*."

Kiara dug into her pockets till she found a crumpled tissue to mop her eyes. "You should've warned me, I need a box of tissues."

He handed her a clean, white handkerchief. "I was a boy scout," he said, smiling.

The eldest gentleman stood and raised his glass of Arak. "To the Lenoirs. May God bless you and keep you."

"Amen," the room responded.

CHAPTER 3

Soon after, Jacques and Kiara stole out of the apartment, rugged up, to the bitter cold night.

"I don't know what to say," Kiara said, pulling her beanie over her ears. "The bravery, the incredible journey your grandparents took."

"They are the head of our family. We are here because of them." He took her gloved hand in his as they walked along the street. "Our business supports not only us but them. It's our duty to keep them in their apartment and pay their bills."

"Of course, I see that," she added in a reassuring voice. "But you love what you do."

He turned to her and smiled. "I do too. As the son and grandson, there is a heavy weight of responsibility for me to ensure the business remains viable for not just my grandparents but also my parents."

"Have you ever wanted to do something different?" she prodded.

"For sure," he said before adding, "But I would never do anything that would take me away from my family."

"Your happiness isn't important?"

He shook his head slowly. "It's not like that. You've heard the story, you can see how important my grandparents are. They deserve the best of everything. What they did, what they achieved is nothing short of miraculous."

"But if you had your own career, couldn't you still do that?"

"*Non*. The business gives us all jobs and a sense of purpose. I may not be as religious as my family, but I still thank God every day for blessing me with the family he gave me."

"You're very lucky," she said, rubbing her cold nose.

"What about your family in Australia?"

"My parents died when I was ten. They'd gone to the movies and I was spending the night with my grandparents." She stopped speaking as her heart grew heavy, as it did every time she thought about that terrible night. "They'd bought an ice-cream, were walking on the side walk holding hands when a drunk driver drove into them."

"They both died? You were left alone?" His voice was filled with despair.

She nodded, hating the driver who'd spent a few years in jail while she had to live with the pain of being an orphan for the rest of her life. "My grandparents took me in and raised me with love."

"Your other grandparents?"

"Were older but still showered me with love. I would spend time with them but it was Gran and Grandpa Ronald who I lived with."

"And they did a superb job. You've grown into a beautiful, caring, responsible woman. They must be very proud of you," he said.

"They are, thank you."

"And if I may ask, why did you come only with Madame Lonsdale? Your grandfather—"

"He passed away one year ago. I still miss him." She sniffed before wiping her cold nose with her gloved hand. "Pop served in the army during the Korean War. Gran said he never spoke about it. Now, we'd call it shell shock but then, there was no emotional support for him." She sighed, thinking of her beloved grandfather. "He hated travelling and would never go on a plane. We accepted it and rarely went on holidays because he preferred to vacation at home."

"Was that difficult?" he asked, his voice filled with concern.

"No, he was a kind man, but that was him." She took a steadying breath. "After he died, Gran talked about travelling but I never expected her to book us a trip to the Holy Land."

"She surprised you?" he asked.

Nodding, she continued, "She certainly did. Gran likes stability and constancy, never one to do something spur of the moment. For as long as I can remember, every year she hosts Christmas at her home, inviting strays—"

She caught the curious lift of his eyebrow. "Strays?"

"Sorry, that's an Australian-ism." She paused thinking about the annual rituals they went through in preparing a memorable Christmas for strangers who were now friends. "It's for people who have nowhere to go on Christmas and are lonely." They stopped walking to face each other. "Every December, we spend the month cooking and freezing food in anticipation of the guests we have on Christmas Eve and Christmas Day. Anyone who is alone is invited and over the years the number of attendees has grown to twenty or so."

Jacques whistled appreciatively through his teeth. "That's a lot of people."

"It is. I used to resent Gran for overdoing it and the amount of work we had to do," she confessed in a low voice, ashamed at her insensitivity for the lonesome people who relied on them to have somewhere to be on Christmas Day.

"They became your friends?" His insights warmed her tummy making it goey soft; it was one of the many qualities she liked about Jacques.

Massaging her heart with her palm she said, "Yes. Over the years, we've had regulars coming and now they're like family." What she didn't want to tell him was that their disappointment on missing the annual event this year had weighed heavily on her shoulders. With her and Gran away, many had nowhere to spend Christmas Day, except in a shelter. Prior to leaving for Israel, Kiara had organised for many to be invited out, however, it'd been a stressful, nerve-wracking experience as colleagues and friends had been reluctant to invite strangers and the homeless into their houses.

She shrugged away the entrenched exasperation, having made a heartfelt commitment to herself that she'd never let down these friends again.

"But you both must love doing it." It was a statement rather than a question.

Nodding, she said, "Having people to celebrate with has helped Gran cope." She swallowed the sadness struck in her throat and continued, "You see, my parents died just before Christmas. Gran lost her daughter and son-in-law and with such a small family, she compensated by filling our home with guests."

They continued walking. "I see." He looked at her. "We're very alike, in that we have a strong affinity to our family."

"I see that too." She grinned.

"Tomorrow is Christmas Day and we'll be sightseeing in Jerusalem, visiting churches, the Western Wall, Temple Mount, and Mount Zion. It's a fantastic day and then the day after we head south. To Jericho and the Dead Sea," he said, rubbing his chin. "It's winter so we usually take our guests to enjoy the hot mineral pools but if you're brave enough" —he paused— "let's coat ourselves in mud then swim in the Dead Sea. You'll love it." His voice was filled with elation and exuberance.

The infection of his excitement made her smile. "It sounds like fun."

He took a step closer and said with a smooth, reassuring voice, "It will be fun. And we'll be doing it together."

Together! The idea of doing something special with him made her heart sing for joy. It wasn't everyday she got to float in the Dead Sea with a bloke whose smile made her tummy flutter.

She couldn't help herself from asking, "Do you have these special tours for all your guests? The light show? The Dead Sea?" Part of her was worried what he would say and the other part was desperate to know. She liked him but perhaps he was simply being courteous since she was the only one his age on the tour? She hoped there was more between them, even if it was going to be only till she returned to Australia.

He stopped walking and took her hand in his. Despite the warm gloves they wore, she could feel his body heat. "Kiara, since you literally knocked into me on the first day we met, I've wanted to spend time with you."

"Really." It was more a statement than a question but the word tumbled from her lips.

"*Bien sur.* You're interesting and fun to be with," he said with certainty.

And you're totally hot and great to be with, she thought. "Wow," she replied. He liked her. The thrill of his words made her want to dance a jig.

"I like being with you."

"And I like being with you," she admitted in a low voice. Jacques was so very different to the blokes she dated in Australia. Not one of them would happily introduce her to grandparents within days of meeting, let alone be upfront with their feelings. On top of that, he was proud to be Israeli, proud to be religious, and proud of his French heritage. There had to be something said about passionate, French men.

"*Magnifique*," he said, interrupting her thoughts before brushing his lips against hers.

Kiara shivered with anticipation, very thankful that circumstances had led her to Jacques. It was probably only going to be a holiday romance. The thought of their togetherness having an end date made her heart grow heavy. They'd barely known each other a few days, not enough time to know each other well. But if this is all she was going to get, she was thankful for it.

Not only handsome, smart, and interesting, but Jacques was making this tiny country come alive with his knowledge and wit. What had started out as a labour of responsibility for her dear Gran was becoming an exciting chapter in her life and having a profound impact on her.

Since it was Christmas Eve, she sent a silent prayer skyward, saying thanks for the inspiring opportunities she'd been blessed with. For not only meeting a wonderful bloke but meeting his family and being included in their lives and stories. Having never had exposure to such compassion and community before, she knew this trip was becoming more and more special as each day passed.

* * *

THE DAY after Christmas Day in Australia was Boxing Day and many Australians spent the long summer day either shopping during the sales or watching the cricket on TV. Being a public holiday, families tended to spend time together or be with friends. Kiara usually spent the day cleaning up or helping out in a homeless shelter with her gran.

It felt truly decadent to have had a leisurely breakfast before driving to Jericho.

"After the last supper, Jesus walked with his disciples from Jericho to Jerusalem and it would've taken them seven hours or so," Jacques advised as they sat side by side in the mini-bus, being expertly driven by the driver.

"It's not that far?" She felt her brow crinkle as she contemplated the long walk.

He pointed out of the window. "About twenty-five kilometres but the terrain is mountainous."

"Much easier being driven," she said, grinning.

"*Bien sur.*" He chuckled.

A few hours later they arrived at the Dead Sea; they were in the desert, surrounded by inhospitable terrain of sand and rock. During the summer, the temperature hit the mid to high forties Celsius. A punishing dry, hot heat. Farther down the road was the proud site of Masada and she hoped to have time to visit it.

Lucie shepherded the travellers to a luxurious day spa. "Ladies and Gentlemen, we'll be here for a couple of hours. Please follow me and I'll show you where the pools are and then where you can change." Everyone followed Lucie except Kiara and Jacques.

"I feel like a school kid skipping school," she said as they walked in the opposite direction of Lucie and the group.

He pointed to the sky. "The sun is shining and you're here with me. It is better than a day skipping school!" They hopped into the mini-bus and the driver took them a few hundred metres away to a private beach.

"I chose this one because it'll be quiet," he whispered in her ear.

At the beach, they took their bags and headed to a large

hut. "Get changed to your bathing suit and I'll meet you here in a few minutes."

The sun was out but the air was cool. Kiara estimated it to be around fifteen degrees Celsius, which wasn't too cold, but not warm enough to be prancing around in bathers. However, she reminded herself that it wasn't every day she got to visit the Dead Sea and headed inside.

After twisting her long, thick hair into a messy knot, she changed into her bathers and then tied her towel around her body so that it was secured by her armpits. Walking out, she almost swallowed her tongue. Jacques stood there in a pair of black bather trunks that showcased his physique to perfection. She'd already admired his long legs and how good they looked in jeans but they looked even better without jeans.

He had the right amount of definition in his arms and abs and had a sprinkling of dark hair across his chest. She breathed a sigh of relief remembering she was wearing sunglasses. Hopefully, he hadn't noticed her ogling at his broad shoulders and flat belly.

He held out a small tub, about the size of his fist, to her. "Mud, for your skin."

She took the plastic container and removed her towel, leaving it on a nearby chair. Feeling a little self conscious in her old bathing suit, she pretended she was comfortable standing near naked in front of him. Despite their time together, they'd only known each other for a few days and to be honest, she wasn't confident about her hourglass physique. Unlike her friends who confidently wore bikinis to the beach, she often used a sarong to hide her large breasts.

"Put the mud all over your skin, you can even rub it in your hair," he instructed, not noticing her discomfort standing in front of him in her navy bathers.

"Really?" she asked, shocked at the idea of putting mud there.

"Your hair is beautiful so it's up to you whether you want to cover it in mud," he said.

Her tummy twisted; he thought her hair was beautiful. Her long thick hair was difficult to manage and she often tied it up in a ponytail or bun for convenience. But since he liked it, she'd try whatever he suggested. Opening the jar, she stuck her fingers into the black mud before smearing it along her arms, legs, and face. It took time to coat her skin. "It's tingling my skin," she said to him.

"Why do you think so many people come here? The properties of the sea are amazing. You can buy some mud and take it home," he added. "There are shops everywhere that sell beauty products with the minerals of the sea in them."

The idea of being at home without him made her heart sink. Pushing aside the sadness, she focussed on the here and now. Besides, she could always buy some mud and take it home. It would be a way to remember this special day and the fun romance between them.

"Here, let me." He drew her close before rubbing mud onto her back. She almost purred with pleasure at the touch of his fingers.

"I must look ridiculous," she muttered.

"No you don't," he reassured her. "Now, come and sit, I'll do your hair."

With unsteady fingers, she removed the elastic from the messy bun and her long, thick hair tumbled down. His hands massaged the black mud through her hair and she almost cried out with the pure pleasure of it. The man certainly knew how to expertly touch and what he was doing was G-rated. A shudder of need ripped through her as she thought of him and his X-rated touches.

Once he'd finished, he walked around and took her plastic container, handing it to her. "Would you help me?"

She stood and he sat where she'd been. Dipping her

fingers into the mud, she then smeared it over his strong shoulders and down the V of his back. He had the physique she loved in a man, not overly built up but muscles and strength all in the right places from physical exercise like chopping wood rather than hanging out in a gym.

Jacques called over a tourist who was yet to get covered in mud and asked her to take a picture. Using his phone, she snapped a photo of them covered in black mud wearing cheesy grins.

With flip flops to protect their feet, they walked to the water's edge and Kiara was pleasantly surprised at the warmth of the water. "I thought it would be colder but it's still cold." She shivered at the idea of immersing herself in the water.

"You travelled for two days to get here." He pointed to the ground. "To Israel. Who knows when you'll be back. Just enjoy the experience." His reminder was sincere, not mocking, and she placed her muddied hand in his as they walked into the water. With his spare hand he indicated large clusters of crystals. "There are salt build ups and they're sharp. Make sure you avoid them, you don't want to scratch your skin in salty water."

She shivered at the idea and carefully avoided them as they walked into the sea. An odd sensation due to the water's buoyancy gripped Kiara's legs, making her feel she was about to fall. Lowering herself in the shallow water, her legs popped up so she ended up with a small splash lying on her back. "Goodness," she cried as her body remained suspended on top of the water.

"The water is very salty, don't splash your eyes," he warned.

"I'm being careful," she reassured him. "But I think I just lost a flip-flop. I can't see as I'm lying down."

Using her hands as paddles, she moved around and saw

Jacques retrieve it. "Got it," he said, walking over and placing the mischievous flip-flop back on her foot.

"Thanks," she said before she stretched out, floating on her back staring at the blue sky. Here, at the lowest place on the earth, the tension seeped out of her while she enjoyed the incredible sensation of being weightless.

For a few minutes, she allowed herself to forget about the weight of her workload, the disappointments of dating, and the fuss of family.

For that time she was at peace and felt truly happy. Something she hadn't experienced for a while.

CHAPTER 4

"*How* are you feeling?" Jacques asked, helping her walk out of the sea.

"Amazing," Kiara said, unable to help the silly grin tugging at her lips. "Thanks for bringing me to the beach. As much as I would've liked the warmer indoor, thermal pools, floating in the sea was an unbelievable experience."

She shivered. "I've still got mud on me," she said, raising her arm up. "It didn't all wash off."

"See those showers there" —he pointed to a row of outdoor showers— "we wash off there. The water is hot, thermal hot."

Under the warm water, they helped each other clean the mud off their skin and Kiara found herself tracing her hands up and down his back. "There's still some mud," she lied, enjoying the feel of his skin under the run of her fingertips.

Finally clean, they walked up to the hut and retrieved their towels and Kiara happily wrapped hers around her body to protect it against the cool air.

"Get dressed and dry your hair, I'll meet you out here. Don't rush," he said, brushing his lips across hers. A zip of excitement ran up and down her spine and she nodded in reply because her tongue seemed to be embarrassingly stuck to the roof of her mouth.

Much later, back in her clothes, her almost dried hair tucked into a warm beanie, she met Jacques, also dressed. He handed her a paper takeaway cup and said, "I bought you a coffee."

Her heart melted at his kind gesture. "Thank you," she said, taking the cup and inhaling the fragrant aroma of fresh coffee.

From his other hand he held out two packets of sugar. "I couldn't remember how many you took."

She took both and walked to the table to add them to her coffee. Looking at her watch she said, "Shouldn't we get going? We need to meet the others."

He stood close to her. "I've organised a surprise visit for you."

Turning to look at him she felt excitement bubble in her belly. "Another?"

"I'm taking you for dinner." His evasiveness and lack of explanation made her want to know more.

"Where are we going? What about the others?" A buzz of vivacity made her words jumble.

If he noticed her enthusiasm, he didn't comment. Instead he took her hand in his. "The others are returning to Jerusalem and we can too but if you want" —he lowered his voice— "we'll go out for dinner, just the two of us."

"Here?" She looked around, which was silly really, because they were still at the beach. She hadn't noticed any restaurants on the drive down but perhaps they weren't on the main road.

"No," he said. "This area is full of resorts and hotels. I want to take you somewhere special, it's between here and Jerusalem."

She wanted to go, desperately, but a niggle made her ask, "Why isn't Gran and the others joining us?"

His thumb drew comforting circles on her wrist, which eased the rigidity in her muscles.

"We usually find our guests are tired after the treatments and prefer to rest en route to Jerusalem." His voice soothed away her concerns as he explained. "We then have dinner at the hotel and they have an early night, especially since we have a big day tomorrow, driving north."

"Well, I can understand that. I'm actually pretty tired after the swim and mud," she admitted.

"Our itinerary is really full, there's so much to see that can't be condensed into six days." He paused. "We did consider changing the tour but feedback has recommended we keep it as is. We like to keep a steady, not an exhausting, pace."

"Fair enough." She took a savouring sip of coffee. "Then yes, I'd love to go out to dinner with you." Only a medical emergency with her gran would keep her away and then, it would have to be life threatening. Looking down at her jeans, boots, and woollen sweater she said, "But I'm not really dressed for it.

"It's perfect," he said, brushing his lips across her cheek. "Let's go, the rental car is parked close by."

* * *

TWO HOURS LATER, she and Jacques were sitting on a camel as the guide steered the animal along the rocky path in the Judean desert.

Kiara turned her head to look at Jacques, gripping the handles with an intensity that would've impressed Superman. "If you'd told me this morning that we would be in the middle of nowhere on a camel ride at dusk, I would've never believed you."

His cocky smile showcased his beautiful white, straight teeth and she took a steadying breath as she took in his gorgeously handsome face.

The camel gave a loud snort as it meandered along its designated path in apparent total boredom. It appeared uninterested in the people on its back especially the female one who was stunned, terrified, and exhilarated all at the same time. Clutching on, Kiara looked around at the spectacular desert scene stretched out in front of her made up of hills and valleys.

Glorious fingers of colour stretched across the sky reminding her that biblical people had travelled in this area thousands of years before her and would've seen the same stunning setting. Goose bumps broke up across her arms and again she said a silent prayer of thanks to be experiencing something so inspiring and wonderful.

The ride ended and once the camel was seated on the ground, they hopped off. Jacques held her hand as he spoke. "This is Genesis Land and is where the Jewish Patriachs lived. Our tours focus on Christ and his life but I love this place, it's magical. It gives you a chance to experience life as it was when Christ lived."

They entered a large tent and she noticed all the staff were dressed in clothing from biblical times. A man with a kind look in his eyes and a snowy white beard approached them. "Welcome to my home, I'm Abraham."

Kiara gasped. "You're Australian."

The man gave her a wink before returning to character and explaining about Genesis. "This was where Abraham welcomed travellers and where I welcome you today."

Refreshments were served and "Abraham" continued to greet and talk with the other guests.

Jacques took her hand. "Come."

"We're not staying for dinner?" A tad of disappointment inched along her spine that they couldn't stay longer. She was intrigued and interested in the surroundings and wanted to know more.

"We're eating separately," he said before they made their way to a smaller tent, separated from the main one by at least fifty metres.

Kiara stopped and looked at where Jacques had brought her. She sighed with contentment and also with delight at the smaller tent designed for intimacy. The open side faced the wide space of the desert but the sides protected from the cold while hurricane lamps provided them with light.

"Jacques, this is amazing, thank you for bringing me here." She turned and pressed her mouth against his. It was supposed to be a friendly kiss of thanks. But as their lips met, his arm came around her waist and he tugged her close.

Her eyes fluttered closed at the gentle touch of his lips and she sighed with the perfect feel of them coming together. Sure, he'd lightly kissed her but nothing could prepare her for the gentle teasing of his mouth against hers now.

Despite the warm layers of their clothes, she snuggled up to him, loving the warmth of his hard body. The citrus tang of his aftershave teased her nostrils and she wrapped her hands around his neck, pulling him to her. The kiss started tentative and gentle while they got to know each other. But before long, she opened her lips, welcoming and inviting more. Within seconds the gentle kiss became more exploratory and deeper. His tongue swept her mouth and she moaned at the delicious feel of him.

One of her hands moved and her fingers threaded themselves through his hair and he groaned in reply.

His mouth left hers and pressed tiny kisses along her jaw line. "*Cherie.*"

Her heart leapt to her throat at the sound of his deep voice whispering to her. Forgetting the cold night air, she snuggled into him before his hands cupped her cheeks and he kissed her again, this time with precious slowness and beauty that made her want to cry.

The clearing of someone's throat made them pause. "I think someone wants us," she said in a subdued voice, unable to mask her disappointment at the interruption.

They turned around, still holding each other close to see a youth holding a tray of food. "Er, um, sorry—"

Jacques took a reassuring step toward him. "Don't worry about it." He took the tray from the young man and said, "I'll take it from here."

Worry lines creased his forehead. "Are you sure?"

"It's fine," he replied in a convincing tone.

The youth shrugged and left them.

Jacques's head tilted toward the tent. "Let's go."

He placed the tray on the low table before they settled themselves on cushions around it. Tiny flickering tea lights in the tent gave the space a comforting yet romantic feel. Despite it, it was still cold and Kiara was grateful for the warm parka she was wearing although if she was honest, she'd rather be cuddled up to Jacques and his warmth.

"*Bon appetite* and *betavon*." He pointed to the array of tiny dishes he'd strategically placed before them.

"*Betavon*." Happy eating, she replied in Hebrew.

Watching him serve her some marinated olives, she asked, "Should we talk about our kiss?"

He looked up and she almost laughed at the angst look on his face. "Why?"

Clearing her throat, she took a small sip of water. "I don't know. I um, I was thinking—"

"Don't think. We're here together. Being with you is special."

Sucking in a sharp breath, she couldn't believe the honesty in his reply. When had a bloke been so upfront and outright with her before? She couldn't remember.

"Eat up and we'll talk," he said, handing her a piece of warm pita.

"I can't believe how hungry I am. Just being outdoors has built up my appetite," she enthused before dipping her bread in the hummus.

They chatted about inconsequential things before he said, "Kiara, I know we've only met but I feel a connection to you." His hand pointed to himself then her. "You're only here for a couple more days but let's enjoy it together."

Her heart sped up and thumped away. "What about the tour?" To be honest, she just wanted to be with him. A guilty thought spiked her in her tummy that she hadn't thought about her gran for the past two hours. Selfishly, she wanted to be with him, kiss him, and talk with him. Besides, she was supposed to be caring for and accompanying June, not gallivanting with the handsome Jacques.

"We'll do things alone and with the others," he said, placing a comforting hand on hers.

She lifted her eyebrow, surprised he had time to be with her. "Really? I know you have a tour to run and we can't impose on Lucie."

"Lucie owes me," he added, chuckling, but didn't elaborate. "Besides, she's very competent and can manage without me."

"Okay," she said, smiling. "I'd like that."

"Me too," he said before giving her a soft kiss on her lips. "Let's eat, they'll be bringing out more food soon."

Jacques was correct and soon the nervous youth approached the tent with plates of roasted chicken, vegetables, and spiced rice.

"This smells heavenly," she said while the young man cleared their appetiser plates away.

They served themselves and ate before Jacques asked, "Tell me about yourself. What do you do in Australia?"

She lowered her cutlery and replied, "I work for a large IT firm as a project manager. I'm currently managing the roll out of a new system software, which is a two-year-long plan."

He looked impressed. "And do you like what you do?"

"I do, but it can be stressful work managing so many people." She breathed out a sigh of frustration thinking about an incident that had happened just before she left Australia. "Things happen and I feel that I'm constantly juggling. I like what I do but I honestly can't say that I love it."

"And what do you love?" He stressed the word love.

She shrugged, surprised at the question because no one had ever asked her that before. "I don't know," she admitted. "I love being with my grandparents and love walking along the beach and having catch-ups with my friends. But as far as work goes, I don't know." She took a sip of water before continuing, "I did a business degree at University and had no idea what to do with it. A graduate opportunity came up at the company I work for and I took it. For two years I moved and worked in different departments. I like the managing aspect of my job and chose to stay there. But it's not a dream job. It's a good job and pays well."

"The money is important to you?"

His question was gentle, not accusing, so she answered with honesty. "Having a good income means I can provide for myself and Gran. I'm proud of what I've achieved."

"You should be." His eyes were filled with compassion and sensitivity. "After losing your parents, you've grown into a stunning woman who cares for her family. You could've wrapped yourself in anger and hate but all I see is your beauty, a caring nature, and kindness for others."

Her jaw dropped open and she stared at him. Her? Stunning? With her difficult hair to manage, hazel-coloured eyes, and overly curvy body, she'd never thought of herself as stunning. Stunning were her friends who effortlessly wore skinny jeans, tiny bikinis, and singlet tops without a bra. She savoured his compliment like you'd enjoy a piece of soft Turkish delight. A warm glow of acceptance of who she was warmed her skin. "That's one of the nicest things anyone has said to me."

"It's true," he said. "You've suffered adversity and yet you worked hard, studied, and cared for your grandparents. You even came on the tour to look after your *grand-mère—*"

"But of course, I couldn't let her come all the way here on her own," she said in an indignant tone. Not that there was any need but it came out of her lips like an automatic reflex.

His finger trailed gently along her cheek. "And that's what makes you so lovely, your caring nature."

She pressed her lips together to stifle a sob. Never had a man shown such kindness and insight. A past boyfriend had made disparaging remarks about her devotion to her grandparents, making her ashamed. But in light of Jacques's admission, the ex-boyfriend now seemed shallow and inconsiderate.

Silence filled the tent before he said, "Come, let's enjoy the rest of our dinner."

Kiara fell asleep on the hour's drive to Jerusalem and apologised when Jacques woke her. "I'm so sorry that I slept."

They were parked outside her hotel and even though it wasn't late, there were few people around.

"You were tired." He traced his finger gently along her jaw. "Go sleep, we have a big day tomorrow." He pressed his lips against hers. "*Lila Tov*, sleep well, my beautiful Kiara, I'll see you in the morning."

"Good night, Jacques, thank you for the most amazing

day…and night. It was so special and I love what you organised." She kissed him firmly on the lips. The sound of a wolf whistle made her look up and a young man walked past, laughing, before waving at them.

Blushing, she said, "I'd better go inside. I'll see you tomorrow."

He kissed her back and this time, she didn't care if all the hotel employees came out to watch. Jacques's kiss made her feel special, wanted, and desired.

* * *

THE FOLLOWING day they travelled two hours to Galilee where they stopped at sights where Jesus performed His miracle of the fish and loaves as well as where He preached His Sermon on the Mount. Due to the age of the travellers, the pace was slow allowing Jacques and Kiara to talk and steal kisses when they thought no one was looking.

After a leisurely lunch, they were taken on a boat ride on the Sea of Galilee and while Lucie talked to her charges, Jacques and Kiara snuck out quietly to the back of the boat to be alone.

"I'm starting to feel naughty, leaving the group like this," Kiara confessed, giggling.

"Lucie has a lot to say and then she allows time for prayer and reflection," Jacques said. "Can you feel how special this place is?"

"I do, there's a mystical energy that I can't quite work out."

His arm swung around. "This area is special for us and for the Jews. It's where their laws were first written down hundreds of years ago." He pointed in the direction of the shore. "Over there, are their graves and many Jews visit to pray."

She turned to look over at the shore, placing her elbows on the boat to steady herself. "It's so beautiful here."

"It is," he agreed. "Kiara."

The way he said her name made her look up and she could see some strain around his eyes. "Are you okay?" she asked.

He brushed her concerns away with a wave of his hand. "Fine." He paused. "I want to talk to you, privately."

"Should I be worried?" she joked but stopped saying anything further seeing the tightness around his jaw.

"Kiara, we've only known each other a few days but you're leaving tomorrow night. Tomorrow we go to Nazareth, Mount Carmel, and then to the airport." He faced her and held her hand. "We have little time and I need to know how you feel about me?"

"What do you mean how I feel about you? Surely you know I like you," she said in a shaky voice. Of course she knew they were leaving soon, her packed suitcase was in the mini-bus together with Gran's.

A small smile touched his lips. "I know you do, but I need to know how you truly feel about me. Whether you would stay here after the tour?" His arms hung loosely by his side. "I can't bear the thought of you returning to Australia. It's so far away."

Shock stunned her and she didn't know what to say. Stay here? What about her life, her job, her gran?

She'd wrongly assumed theirs was a holiday romance, something to savour now and let go when they returned home. The notion of him wanting to make things more serious, startled and surprised her. "Y-you w-want me to stay here? What about my job?"

He nodded and took her gloved hand. "*Cherie*, I'm in love with you, I don't want to lose you."

What? "Love?" Her eyes narrowed with scepticism. "You

can't fall in love in a few days." It wasn't possible to love someone after such a short period. She was on holidays, away from her daily life. She wasn't supposed to find the man of her dreams in a country halfway across the world from her.

"How can you love me when we've barely known each other a week?" Her voice lifted and came out as a squeak.

"Kiara, I'm thirty years old, not a teen. I know how I feel." He took her hand and placed it over his heart. "Since I met you the day you arrived in Jerusalem with your contagious smile, your *joi de vivre*, your intelligence, and your love of family, I've known since then that you're the woman for me." He lifted her hand and kissed her knuckles. "Please stay and give me time to show you that I'm the man for you?"

Her breath hitched. "I can't, my gran. I have to take her home."

"You won't consider it?" His body sagged against the side of the boat.

For a moment, she didn't know what to say. Love? Stay in Israel? The beauty of their surroundings contrasted sharply with the riotous emotions jabbing at her belly. She fiddled with her hair, desperately trying to find the right words.

"Jacques, being with you has been incredible and I have loved every minute but I never expected this." She drew in a steadying breath. "I have responsibilities. I can't just pack up and come and live here. What would I do? Where would I live? And what about Gran?" A wave of dizziness had her clutching the side rail.

"My life is in Australia, not here," she said in a defiant tone. "Your life, work, and family are here but mine are over there." She flung her arms in the air as exasperation gripped her making her muscles stiff and strained.

"I know it's a lot to ask," he said in a low voice filled with compassion. "But I hoped if you felt strongly about me—"

"I do, I really do," she said, clutching his arm. "But it's too much. My life is not here." She gulped down some air. "But I wouldn't expect you to move either. You belong here with your family," she said in a reassuring voice. "I love your big family and would love to be a part of them, but it's too soon. We don't know—"

His spine straightened and he crossed his arms. "You're almost thirty, like me. We're at an age when we know what we want. I don't need to date you any more to know that you're the woman I want."

She was almost thirty, but unlike him, she wasn't sure what she wanted. Her love life had been pretty uneventful and despite some boyfriends, she didn't trust her heart. With her last boyfriend, she'd ended up liking his family more than him. It'd taken *him* to point it out to her, she hadn't seen it. How could she make such a momentous decision, in such a short time?

Pinching her nose she said, "I came on a tour accompanying my gran, I never expected to meet someone special or fall in love—"

He pulled her to him, crushing his mouth to hers. "I knew there was love."

Wrenching her mouth from his, she placed her hands against his chest and pushed him back. Taking a step away from him she admitted with honesty, "I don't know, I've never been in love. I don't know if what I feel for you is love or affection."

A pained look crossed his eyes. "My family will welcome you, care for you, love you—"

She raised her hand to prevent him from saying something else. "Stop. It's too soon."

He gathered her close. "You're here in the country where our Lord was born at the time we celebrate and honour His birth. Something very special happened last week and I believe it to be a sign that we're to be together."

She felt her brow crease with questions. "What do you mean, a sign?"

Pressing his lips to her forehead he said, "Please listen to my story. All Israeli men are conscripted into the army for three years and then, till we're fifty or so, we're part of the reserves."

"You were in the army?"

"Of course," he said. "Every year I have to participate in training. There's a new operating system we have to learn. This year I was called up for three days over Christmas."

She gasped. "You were going to miss Christmas because of some…training?"

He shrugged away her concerns. "It's what we do here," he said in a heartfelt tone. "I was disappointed but had accepted it. It's the first year it's happened. A couple of weeks ago I had dinner with friends including one who I met on my first day in the army. I mentioned, in passing, about it. Since he's Jewish and didn't want me to miss out being with my family on Christmas, he swapped training with me. I attended the week before you arrived and he took my place over Christmas."

"That's so nice of him," she said.

He took a small step back and held her shoulders, looking at her intently. "But don't you see? If I'd attended the training when I was supposed to, I wouldn't have met you. Gabrielle would've taken my place and I would've worked in the office rather than on the tour." His eyes sparkled with excitement, matching the blue sea around them. "It was meant to be, we were supposed to have met."

She blinked rapidly, trying to digest everything she said. "It's very special but I can't allow the kindness of your friend to persuade me to do something that I don't know if I want to." Her voice babbled and the words tumbled out. "We live so far away from each other without an ability to spend more time together. I can't just turn my life and Gran's over a holiday romance."

A despondent look crossed his eyes and his shoulders slumped. The joy and excitement in his smile was now gone and his skin had an ashen tone. "I'm sorry, Kiara, I thought this was more than a holiday romance for you." He leaned against the railing and pushed his hands into the pockets of his jeans. An uncomfortable silence hung between them.

"I'll respect your decision," he said, the skin stretched tight along his jaw. "I don't want you to feel uncomfortable on the tour, after all, this is your vacation." He cleared his throat. "I'll ask Gabrielle to fill in for me and I'll return to Jerusalem."

Shaking her head she said, "You don't have to do—"

"Kiara, I don't want there to be any uncomfortable moments between us. I want you to enjoy the rest of your tour with us." He took a deep breath. "You've come a long way to be here and I don't want to spoil it. I'm sorry if I upset you."

She wanted to tell him he hadn't upset her but the words were stuck in her throat. She'd messed things up between them. She'd hurt him with her inability to confess love. But she also didn't want to lie to him. Falling in love so quickly was the stuff from her romances that she loved so much. Realistically, she struggled to believe it could happen to her.

Taking a step toward her, he brushed his lips against her forehead. "Thank you for being honest." Stepping away, he pulled his mobile phone from his pocket, turned it on and looked at it. Switching it off he muttered something in Hebrew before stuffing the offending item back to where it came from and walked away.

Self-doubt and uncertainty zipped along her spine. But it

was too late now, she'd made her decision. Perhaps the magic she'd been looking for was them being here and her experiencing something wonderful. The swim, the dinner, the sightseeing, everything had been so very special and she was grateful to have experienced it. Asking to find love, on top of that, made her feel selfish and not appreciative of what she had. Best to accept him leaving her and enjoy the rest of the trip. With her shoulders bowed with failure and loss, she returned to the others.

*T*he rest of the day passed in a haze of more sightseeing, afternoon tea, and time for personal reflection.

Seated at dinner, the group except Kiara, was surprised to see Gabrielle arrive with her pretty smile and infectious gaiety.

"Shalom, friends, unfortunately, we had an incident with the computer systems and since Jacques is so much better at it than me, he's dealing with it and I'm here to look after you till the end of the tour." Her voice was lightly pitched and vivacious. Unlike the others, Kiara knew that Gabrielle no longer ran tours as she and her husband lived in Tsfat so she could focus on her art.

Biting her lip to supress the sadness in her heart, Kiara fiddled with her serviette.

"I love this restaurant and the food is amazing." Gabrielle pointed to the appetizers already on the table. "*Betavon*. I'm going to come around and ask you individually about your reflections of today and what inspired you. After dinner, Lucie and I are going to talk about taking the love and experiences you've had here and taking them home. You've come a long way to be here and this is not just a tour, it's an opportunity for self growth and reflection."

While the others nodded enthusiastically before serving themselves from the array of delicious foods, Kiara nibbled a piece of pita; her appetite had suddenly vanished.

A jab in her ribs made her look at her grandmother. "What's the matter with you?" June asked, her voice filled with concern.

"I'm fine." She brushed June's question away with a flick of her hand. "I'm just a little tired, it's been a long day."

"If you think I'm going to believe your made-up rubbish…" June wagged her finger and spoke in a strict voice. The strict voice she'd used on her when she'd rebelled as a teen by dying her hair black and piercing her ears and nose.

The hair colour and piercings may have gone but Kiara was suddenly that girl again, who needed and wanted her parents but had found comfort with her grandparents.

Kiara's eyes filled with tears of regret. "Jacques left because of me, not because of some…computer issue."

June placed a warm, reassuring hand over hers. "You think I didn't know that? I may be old but I'm not blind or senile. I saw the way he looks at you and you at him. You think I didn't see you kiss? The others may have been interested in Lucie's talk but I didn't miss a thing."

"Oh, Gran." Her chest heaved with painful emotion.

June took her hand. "Let's go over there." She guided them to a quiet corner away from the families and groups of people enjoying the barbequed meats and vegetables.

"What happened between the two of you?" June's eyes were filled with apprehension.

"He loves me," she said in a soft voice.

June's eyes widened with curiosity. "And what's the matter with that?"

"I've known him less than a week." She waved her hand in the air. "He wants me to stay here. But how can I? I need to be there *for you* and the others, plus, I have a job to return to and a home."

"Oh, my dear." June sighed, her head bowed.

"I know," Kiara said, her lip trembling. "Why did I have to meet him *here* of all places?"

June took her hand and said, "Sometimes we find love when we're not looking. I met Ronald and fell in love with him. When he kissed me for the first time I knew he was the man for me."

"B-but, you met him in Australia, you didn't have to relocate to be with him," Kiara insisted, feeling frustrated at her gran comparing her situation to hers!

"Kiara, listen. Do you think it was easy when Grandad came back from war? He had nightmares and spent days in bed, unable to eat properly. I took responsibility for us, found a job, and earned money till he was ready to return to work."

Kiara felt her throat clog with unease and trepidation as to where the conversation was heading. "But you were already married, you knew you loved him."

"Dear Kiara, my precious granddaughter, things happen. You need to believe in yourself and make a decision."

"I made my decision, Gran, and said no."

June nodded slowly. "Listen, if you take me out of the equation, just pretend that it's just you and him, would you stay?"

Kiara looked at her grandmother, the wise, kind woman who'd raised her with such love. "Honestly, I don't know."

June nodded. "Today when you two left us, we had time to reflect and pray. Being where Jesus walked on water was very special and it's a shame you missed it." She looked up at her. "Why don't you go outside? The balcony is right on the water. Rug up and go outside, think, ask for some guidance."

"What do you think I should do?" Kiara asked June.

"Only you can make that decision but what I want to say is that I've never seen you look at a man the way you look at him. Your face brightens when you see him. And you've been on your own for so long." June paused as if looking for the right words. "If he's offering you the chance of love and family, maybe you should take it," she said in a low voice.

"It's such a big decision," Kiara said, sighing dramatically, frustrated June couldn't see the ramifications of such a momentous decision. The alternative wasn't as simple as dinner on the plane, chicken or beef.

June clutched her arm. "No, it's not. I will always be here for you. Your job is a job, that's it. It pays well but you've never had your heart in it. If there is a chance for you to find love here, why won't you take it?"

Cold fingers wrapped themselves around her heart making her shudder. "But what if it doesn't work out?"

"Then you come back to Australia," June said in a flippant tone. "But just think" —she stopped and the skin between her eye brows crinkled with excitement— "what if he's the one for you?"

"It's a big risk." Exhaustion from overthinking weighed heavily on her shoulders making her feel tired and in desperate need to lie down. "I'd have to get a visa, a place to live, learn the language, find a job." She threw her hands up in the air in exasperation. "Do all of this for someone I just met?"

June lifted her chin and Kiara could see a tightness around her mouth. "You're a planner and an achiever. While some of your friends backpacked around Europe after school, you started working and studying at University.

Vacations have been short trips to Queensland or Asia but you never travelled for months."

"But—" Kiara started to talk but was silenced by her grandmother's hand in the air.

"You've been conscientious in your work, buying a house, saving money, and investing wisely. I couldn't be more proud of you, but you've never taken a chance."

"Neither have you," Kiara pointed out.

June sighed. "I got married in the 1940s when things were different to how they are now." She waggled her finger at her granddaughter. "Don't be impudent with me."

"I'm sorry," she said in a low but sincere voice. "I've told him no and now he's gone."

"Details." June rolled her eyes.

The air in her lungs expelled with the exhaustion of introspection. "I don't know what to do, I never expected something like this to happen."

June's hand clutched her arm. "Didn't I tell you something wonderful was going to happen? At the airport?"

Kiara nodded but didn't want to confess to her gran that she had dismissed her speculation at the time. "What do you think I should do?"

June looked at her through narrowed eyes. "Do you really want to know?"

"Yes." She trusted her grandmother implicitly.

"You call your manager and ask for a three-month leave of absence, apply for a visa, and find somewhere to live in Jerusalem."

Kiara's muscles tensed and her neck ached. "I can't do that."

"Then take one month's leave. Stay here and see how you go. But don't return home and deal with 'what-ifs' when you're alone in bed. They won't comfort you like the feel of a man's arms around you."

"Gran, you cheeky girl." Kiara gave her a mock look of disbelief, pretending to be offended at what she'd just said.

Promise of something good happening made June's eyes sparkle with wonderment. "You're old enough to know what you want. If you want to be with him, don't toss it away over a job and an old woman. You have your life ahead. I know his family will care for you."

Her breath got caught in her throat at the daunting thought of leaving her gran and the excitement of a new life with Jacques. "What about you?"

June reprimanded her with a click of her tongue against the roof of her mouth. "Don't make a decision based on me, you do what you want for *you*."

Kiara gave her a mock salute before wrapping her arms around the older woman. "I love you, Gran, I don't know what I'd do without you."

June's bony but strong arms held her granddaughter tight. "When your parents died I made a pledge at their graves to love and protect you always. I only want what's best for you."

"Thanks, Gran." Kiara tightened her arms around her beloved grandmother.

* * *

DURING DESSERT, Gabrielle pulled up a chair and sat next to Kiara. "Kiara, it's your turn. There is no right or wrong answer but I want to know what you've learnt while you've been on tour."

Kiara looked at Jacques's older sister and saw a family resemblance between the siblings. Kiara scratched her chin. "What have I learnt? Umm…I've learnt that there is inherent good in the world and that things are not always what they seem. I've learnt so much history and want to spend time in the future doing more learning in both history and religion."

Gabrielle nodded in appreciation. "Good."

Giving her a silly smile Kiara added, "And I believe that Israelis make the best breakfast buffets."

Gabrielle returned the grin and said, "All true." She paused then said, "And what of love?"

Kiara crossed her arms protectively against her chest before sitting back in her seat. "I think that's a little personal," she answered, unsure of what to say or not say to Jacques's older sister.

She shrugged in reply. "Perhaps?" Leaning forward she said, "I feel entitled to ask since I had to suddenly leave my work and my husband at home caring for our twin five-year-old boys, just so I could take over and help Jacques out."

Kiara's body sagged into her seat at the reality of what he and Gabrielle had done. "I'm sorry," she said with sincerity.

She dismissed her concerns away with a wave of her hand. "I know you are." She paused. "I have to say I was surprised when Jacques insisted I take over. He's never done that before."

A long silence stretched between them before Kiara broke it. In a low voice, not wanting the others to hear, she confessed to Gabrielle. "I came here to accompany my grandmother. I never expected to meet someone as wonderful as your brother. He swept me off my feet. I know it sounds trite, but it's true." A sob got caught in her throat. "Instead of embracing this amazing revelation, I turned him away." She rubbed her tired eyes, still unsure if she'd made the right decision. "And he was worried about me. Me." She repeated the word for emphasis. "Not wanting me to feel uncomfortable, he organised for you to be here." Her heart skipped a beat. "It was really thoughtful and kind, of you both."

Gabrielle placed her hands over hers. "Go after him," she whispered. "Go tell him how you feel."

Kiara felt her brow crease with incredulity. "Really?"

"*Ken*, yes. Besides, it's Christmas time, it's the right time for something wonderful to happen," she added, giving her a knowing wink. "I can organise for you to be on a bus to Jerusalem in the morning. I'll get Papa to meet you at the bus station and take you to him."

Kiara pressed her lips together. Her head was spinning with the idea of her going after him. Even though both Gabrielle and her grandmother felt this was the right thing to do, she was still undecided. Could she do something so impromptu and audacious? The decision to be with him was unexpected, unplanned, and she was unprepared.

Leaning back in her chair she nibbled her lip, reminiscing on what her gran had suggested. Better to make her choice now than regret it when she returned to Australia. Her heart quickened, reminding her that no man had ever made her feel the way Jacques did. She didn't doubt his or her feelings. What she was worried about was the life changing aspect. Pushing aside her worries for her beloved grandmother, her friends, and those less fortunate that she helped out in Australia, she drew in a steadying breath. "Okay, let's do this."

Gabrielle's eyes widened with excitement as she sat straighter in her seat. "*Ken*. Yes." She stood, turned to her sister, and gave her a thumbs up sign. Lucie grinned in reply.

Pulling her mobile phone from her pocket, Gabrielle then dialled a number and then spoke in rapid French. After disconnecting the call, she opened a new browser page and scrolled through. Turning to Kiara, she said, "I'll take you to the bus tomorrow morning and Papa will meet you. It's all organised."

Kiara's mouth dried. With shaky fingers she took a sip of water. She was going after Jacques and hoped she wasn't too late.

* * *

THE FOLLOWING morning after a quick coffee and a reassuring hug from June, Kiara boarded the bus and waved to her grandmother. June was trying to extend their date of departure, but for the time being, Kiara was focussed on what she was going to say to Jacques. Jittery nerves had kept her awake all night and despite the strong coffee this morning, Kiara dozed for an hour.

Arriving in Jerusalem, she was greeted by the sight of snow, her first time. The sprinkling of white made the city look pretty, reminding her of fairy tales.

Jacques's father met her with a warm smile before taking charge and rolling her suitcase to the car. "*Allons-y*, let's go," he said.

The older man didn't say much during the short drive to their apartment block. There, he got out of the car and pointed to Jacques's apartment. "*Bonne chance.*"

"*Merci beaucoup*," she replied, which made his face light up. Kiara was grateful for the few French phrases she remembered from high school.

A few moments later, she knocked on the wooden door to his apartment. She sucked in a sharp breath when he answered it in jeans, T-shirt, bare feet, and a delectable day's growth darkening his jaw and cheeks.

His eyebrows lifted in astonishment. "Kiara? *Cherie.*"

With her heart hammering at the sight of him and nerves in disarray, she asked, "Can I come in?"

"Of course." He opened the door wider so she could enter before closing it behind her. "Can I get you something? A drink? *Café?*"

She shook her head. "No, thanks. I came to talk to you."

A strained silence grew between them before he gestured toward the sofa and they sat opposite each other.

The sparkle in his blue eyes had become dull and she was surprised to see worry lines etched around his eyes making him look tired. Perhaps she wasn't the only one stressed and feeling anxious?

Creating space between them, lest she give in to her needs and cuddle up in his arms, she took a deep reassuring breath and said, "You surprised me yesterday. I-I, um, I just wasn't expecting to hear—"

Any spark of hope of resolving things between them deflated when she saw the crinkle of his forehead and the strain around his jaw. "Let's leave it as a holiday romance, isn't that what you called it?" His voice was soft and reassuring. "You didn't have to come here today," he said, giving her a decisive nod before crossing his arms.

That got her attention and she sat straighter in her seat. "Of course I did." She filled her lungs with air. "I was a little rude on the boat because I was shocked, surprised at your confession."

He sat back into the sofa as though the weight of misgiving pressed heavily against him. "There wasn't much time with you returning to Australia this afternoon. It's not something I wanted to talk to you about over the phone."

She nodded slowly, understanding the pressing need that had weighed heavily on him yesterday. "I understand. I do. And I need to tell you, you did the right thing."

A startled look crossed this face. "I did?"

"Sure." She searched for the right words as her nerves made her palms sweat. Rubbing them on her jeans she said, "This thing" —she pointed from herself to him— "between us, came unexpectedly. I want to embrace it. I want to give us a chance. I have a life in Australia and I'm scared to leave it behind, but I want to try, try leaving it with you." Her heart quickened and her mouth grew dry like the desert sands. "I'm nervous but I know that with you and your family's love, it's a chance I want to take. I feel as scared as if I was standing on Masada about to jump off."

He reached over and took her hand in his. "*Cherie*, I'm here for you. It's a big commitment. I barely slept last night thinking about how clumsy I'd been with you."

"You weren't—"

He silenced her with a press of his lips against hers. "I was forthright and bold but I spoke from the heart. I'm in love with you."

His confession made her tummy feel all squishy and warm.

"Excuse my words, if they're awkward, but they're due to a lack of sleep and my lack of diplomacy. Just know that I want you to stay. I don't need more time to know how I feel but it's a big step for you." He rubbed his hand over the coarse hair on his chin. "If you love me but are unhappy living here, I'll move to Australia. If that's what we need to be happy."

She sucked in a startled breath. "You'd leave your family?"

A small smile touched his lips. "I love my family, they mean everything to me. But *you* are my future. I want to marry you, have children. I don't want to miss that chance because of my obligations." He kissed her knuckles. "It will take time but I can find a replacement and once they're trained, they can take my place in the company and I can be with you."

"You've never been to Australia," she said in a sceptical tone.

"But I'll be there with you." He sighed. "I can't expect you to give up everything and not be expected to do the same."

She threw herself into his arms and snuggled against his chest, breathing in his masculine scent. "I'm scared."

His fingers stroked her hair. "Me too, *cherie*, me too." His fingers came under her chin so she could look up at him.

"We'll do it together. All I know is that I don't want to lose you. We'll do this together."

"I like the sound of that." She smiled at him. "I'm going to speak to the embassy about extending my stay."

"My beautiful Kiara." He pressed his lips against hers. "I want you to be happy."

"I will be happy with you." She kissed him back. "I have to be honest, I've never been in love. I don't know if I'm in love but what I do know is that I love talking with you, I love spending time with you, and I love kissing you."

"I plan to do more than kiss you." He chuckled, kissing her with much pent- up emotion. "But for now, I want you to know that I will love, protect, and honour you. You came into my life as a whirlwind of excitement, smiles, and effervescent. I have never been as happy as I am when I'm with you."

"I'm scared things will fizzle out when the hum-drum of every day life comes between us," she confessed in a low voice. "Over the past few days, we've had this amazing time together. What will life be like when you're touring and I'm alone?"

He held her tight. "You will never be alone. My family is your family. They will care and look after you."

"But where will I live? What will I do?" She didn't want to sound needy but the practicalities were bothering her so greatly that she couldn't relax and enjoy being with Jacques.

The skin between his eyes creased as he looked up at the wall. After a minute of deliberation he looked at her with a smile. "We'll house-swap. You and Lucie will move into my apartment and I will live with my parents."

"You can't do that!" Shock made her blurt out. He'd move out of *his* apartment and live with his parents?

"*Ken*. Yes. This way you don't have to pay for accommodation and your gran will be reassured that my intentions are honourable."

"You'd do that for me?" Her eyes widened as she took in the ramification of what he'd proposed. "I-I don't know what to say!"

"Just say yes and we'll work it out *together*." He brushed his lips across her earlobe. "You can live here and see if you like it. Who knows, maybe we can get you working for us."

"There's a lot to organise," she said, jittery at the life-changing opportunity she was facing.

"They can be managed. What's more important is that we've found each other. I hope that this love between us will grow and develop into something wonderful. Just like your parents and grandparents had. And mine too."

He shuffled in his seat so he sat across from her. "Kiara, magic like us finding love in the most unexpected way is so wonderful that I won't let it go. I believe we were destined to meet. Whether we live here or Australia is not important. What is important is that we're together." He paused and said, "Your grandmother is always welcome to live with us. I would never want to come between you."

Tears ran in rivets down her cheeks. He was right. Some-thing magical had happened and she'd be a fool to ignore such a wonderful opportunity. She kissed him. "My job was important to me and so is Gran. But the joy of being here has reminded me of what's truly meaningful. A family. I want that. And I want that with you."

"My beautiful Kiara, I promise to make you happy, care for you, and love you."

"I know you will. I was supposed to meet you." She smiled at him. "From you switching training sessions to Gran choosing your tour company. It was meant to be."

"It was, meant to be." He leaned over and kissed her with

a thoroughness she longed for. In his arms she felt treasured, respected, and fulfilled.

Gran had been right. Something magical did happen to her and she couldn't be more excited or amazed about it. She'd found love. Real and true love.

THE END

AFTERWORD

Dear Reader

In July 2014 I was fortunate to be selected by a dynamic women's movement to travel to Israel. During those eight days of learning, friendship, and personal discovery, I fell in love with the culture and history of that amazing country.

The tour guides Patrick, Basha, Ken, and Eitan, with their insights, wisdom, and passion, breathed life into history, making it come alive.

The passion for their jobs helped inspire me to create my hero, Jacques Lenoir, whose family runs tours in Israel.

I have to confess that I included some of the highlights of my trip in *A Magical Christmas in Jerusalem.* Yes! I did swim in the Dead Sea—float actually—after coating my skin and hair with mineral mud. And yes, camel rides and Abraham's Tent do exist (although I made some slight changes to suit the romance between Jacques and Kiara!)

If your faith is important to you, then I highly recommend you consider a tour to Israel. The tour guides will make the cities and religious sites come alive with their insights and history. You will love all the amazing sights the incredible country has to offer.

Wishing you a happy holidays and may this time bring you peace and joy to you and your family.

God bless.

Joanne x

ANOTHER MAGICAL CHRISTMAS IN JERUSALEM

*H*e never wanted a family. She can't live without hers. Can a dash of Christmas magic bring them together?

For Lucie Lenoir, being a tour guide in Jerusalem is part of the family business. And nothing means more to Lucie than family. She craves a child of her own, in spite of her infertility. Lucie has another secret desire: to be a romance novelist. But following that dream would be too disruptive to the family she adores.

Australian Tom Connor has come to Israel to attend a friend's wedding and to pray for the healing of the one person he considers family, a woman who grew up with him in the foster care system. Along with surfing every day, Tom finds peace in helping troubled teens like he used to be.

The attraction between Lucie and Tom is instant and

sizzling. In spite of their warm welcome, Tom finds Lucie's big Christian family overwhelming. And he never wanted a child of his own. Can a man who never had a family and a woman who craves one write their own real-life Christmas romance?

CHAPTER 1

*L*ucie Lenoir was downhearted. She had good reason to be. Over the past eleven months, she'd had to move apartments three times and was now living back with her parents.

She'd been delighted that her adored, older brother, Jacques had found love with Kiara almost a year ago. She wanted to be a supportive friend and sister-in-law-to-be, she really had. Initially she'd been happy to share her apartment with Kiara, but then when she and Jacques announced their engagement, Lucie had to move out so Jacques could move in.

Concentrating on her job and the family business gave her focus and direction so she didn't have to dwell on the frustration of packing and unpacking her things.

And just when she thought she'd found *the one*, he dumped her. Ten days ago her now ex-boyfriend had confessed that her infertility and desire to settle down was too *confrontational*. Whatever that meant. She was twenty-nine, was there anything wrong with being upfront? Besides, they'd been dating for two months. Certainly that was enough time of being together and honest with each other.

Mon dieu.

Life could be unfair.

Lucie plastered a smile on her face and pretended everything was fine, when really her heart was breaking in two.

Stealing a look at the happy, soon-to-be-married couple beaming at each other and snatching a kiss every minute or so, reminded her that she was alone, again, and that the only romantic fairy tales she would enjoy were the ones she wrote.

* * *

Tom Connor ran a finger around the collar of his shirt and stifled a groan. When he'd made the decision to fly to Israel for his friend Kiara's wedding, he had no idea how overwhelming it would be. She hadn't warned him of the large family she was marrying into, nor the sheer number of guests at the pre-wedding party.

Crap. He swallowed hard and looked around for a beer.

He made a mental note to contact the airline tomorrow and see if he could change his flight to leave earlier, perhaps straight after the wedding?

He was a quiet Australian guy with few friends and barely any family. Had his adopted sister, Grace, not encouraged him to be here, he'd be back home enjoying summer and his daily swimming and surfing ritual.

Instead, it was freezing cold here in Jerusalem, with snow in the forecast, a week before Christmas.

Tom stood with his back against the wall wondering how so many people could fit in one apartment. A mixture of Hebrew, French and English were all being spoken at a level that he would classify as too loud.

The volume of food was staggering and the only alcohol served was something that he couldn't pronounce and smelt like liquorice. No thanks. He needed a beer, and was wondering how soon he could leave without anyone noticing.

His gaze skimmed the room and stopped as he caught sight of a brunette whose sullen smile matched his own. With her long hair, dark eyes and perfect skin, she was the most gorgeous woman he'd ever seen.

Kiara's fiancé put his arm around her and her smile went from moody to genuine warmth. Her whole face lit up making her look even more beautiful, if that was possible.

He wondered who she was. Did she have a secret crush on Jacques? Was there something going on between them? His hand fisted and he swore under his breath. No floozy was going to create a disturbance between his friend, Kiara, and Jacques, no matter how stunning she was.

Pushing his way through the crowd, he was determined to find out who she was.

* * *

LUCIE BUSIED herself with the table, shifting plates around, removing the empty ones and replacing them with full ones. Her *maman*, aunties and grandmothers had spent the past week baking, for the party tonight. All the rich, favourite French and Middle Eastern pastries that could be easily bought from the markets had been lovingly hand made by the women in the family.

Of course she'd had to help, and had done so reluctantly in between working in the family business and writing her latest romance novel.

Table done, she spun around and walked into someone. Someone she hadn't seen.

"Sorry," she said before looking at the strong masculine chest she'd knocked into.

A pair of the bluest eyes she'd ever seen focussed on her, and she took a moment to admire the man's sandy blond hair, square chin and hard cheek bones. Despite her height and heels, she had to look up, which made her smile. "Hello."

"Hi," he replied.

The skin between her eyes creased as she tried to remember the name of Kiara's friend, the one who came from Australia. This had to be him. Not only ruggedly handsome, he looked like he'd rather be somewhere else. "You're, um. . ."

He held out his hand. "Tom Connor, Kiara's friend." His large hand engulfed hers and his grip was firm but not strong.

A tingling sensation went up and down her arm at the touch of his warm skin against hers. Pushing the unfamiliar sensation aside, she welcomed him with her brightest voice. "Nice to meet you Tom. It's so nice that you came for the wedding. Kiara was so happy you could attend."

"My sister thought it was a good idea," he clarified, with a deadpan tone.

Her fingers fluttered to her throat, surprised that he didn't seem that excited. "Well, I hope you'll spend time visiting Israel before you go home," she said trying to make conversation and find something that he showed interest in.

"I plan to," he said with a nonchalant nod. His reply didn't say much and his eyes darkened, making her wonder if she'd said something wrong. "And you are?" He leaned against the wall, his hands in his trouser pockets.

She blinked rapidly, remembering her manners. "Lucie Lenoir. Sister of Jacques, sister-in-law-to-be of Kiara and general go-to girl.

Her reply must have amused him because his eyes widened and his lips extended to a smile. "This is quite a set-up," he drawled as his head jerked towards the sea of people in the living room.

His sandy coloured hair, aquamarine eyes and lazy grin made her heart flip flop. With his laid-back stance and casual clothes he looked to be the quintessential Aussie man. And reminded her of the hot, Australian actor brothers in Hollywood.

"This is how we do things." Her hands gestured to the crowd in an animated manner. "Our family is large, and we also include family friends at every happy occasion."

"Will it be like this at Christmas?" His forehead creased as though the idea appalled him.

"Probably," she said. "I take it you don't have a large, *overwhelming* family?"

"Not at all." He shook his head as though horrified at the idea.

He leaned forward and whispered in her ear. "Since you look as happy as I do about being here, would you like to play hooky with me?"

"Hooky?" The unfamiliar word rolled off her tongue.

"Let's get out of here. I'd much rather talk to you," he said in a way that was friendly but forward.

Leave her family's event? Unheard of. She should decline immediately, but she didn't.

Her parents would scold her if they knew she left but Lucie had had enough. Over the past year her world had been turned upside down but she'd been obliging and cheerful, never complaining. Making Kiara feel welcome into their family had been important and she was looking forward to having her as a sister-in-law, but being rejected by her ex had stung.

And being jilted just before the wedding, when her family was busy, had meant she'd dealt with the feelings of hurt and inadequacies on her own.

But now some gorgeous guy wanted to spend time with her, and her heart leapt with excitement and in anticipation.

But her family needed her to clean up and assist with the party. She was twenty-nine and sick of being lonely. They would understand, especially her *grand-mere* who'd always encouraged her to follow her dreams.

Going out on a date wasn't a *dream* but it certainly would be more fun than tidying up.

Decision made, she gave Tom a mischievous smile. "I'll meet you outside in five minutes. I need my coat and to change my shoes." Anticipation made her words tumble from her lips and she ignored the embarrassment over appearing too eager.

His return smile made her insides melt.

Right decision, she reassured herself. Besides, he was here for only a couple of weeks. Why shouldn't she spend time with him? It's not like anything was going to happen. He'd return to Australia and she'd return to being the dutiful daughter who accommodated everyone's demands.

* * *

SIX MINUTES LATER, Tom waited impatiently outside in the bitterly cold night air, thankful for his warm coat and beanie. Sneaking out was probably not the best or most courteous thing to do after being included in the family event, but the need to get out had been overwhelming. He couldn't stand being in a room so full of people and noise. Tomorrow he'd call Kiara and apologise, as well as to the Lenoirs, Jacques' parents.

But for now, he'd made a decision to leave with Lucie. His heart skipped a beat as he saw her walking to him. Despite the thick coat she wore, he took a moment to admire her curves and her long legs. Yep, being with Lucie was so much better.

"You came," he said. Despite knowing he was not doing the right thing by leaving, the joy of spending some alone time with Lucie away from the noise of the party was too tempting.

"Come on, let's go before anyone sees us." Her gloved hand took his and she tugged him down the street.

Perhaps they shouldn't leave. Apprehension weighed heavily on his shoulders. "I don't want to cause problems. Maybe we should go back inside."

"No," she said in a firm voice. "Hurry." She picked up her pace walking steadily away from the apartment block.

Trailing, he caught up with her in a few long strides. "Where's your car?"

"I don't have one." She pointed to her boots. "I had to change my shoes, we're walking."

"Suits me," he said as they walked down the street. "Where are we going?" His breath came in huffs in the cold, winter air.

"You choose," she said with a smile. "Either we go to an American-style bar, which has burgers, fries and beer. Or another that's very Middle Eastern in it's décor, food and cocktails."

His lips pressed together with indecision. They both sounded appealing. "Which do you recommend?"

She shrugged. "They're both good. Up to you."

"As tempting as the American one sounds, let's try the other. Since it's my first time in Israel, I feel I should try something different," he said honestly. He was determined to have new experiences while away, and it was time to start now.

"You'll love it." Her voice was filled with enthusiasm. "It's a cosy piano bar and they play anything from soul to blues to funk. But the food is amazing and you can try a cocktail or have a beer."

He didn't really care where he went, as long as he was with Lucie. She was the first woman to make his *desire* stand up and take notice in a long time. He'd have to be blind not to see how stunning she was, and despite her effervescent personality being opposite to his, he wanted to spend time with her. His night had become so much more interesting now that he was with her.

"How long till we get there?" They were walking down the street, the cold biting into his clothes and reminding him of the distances he'd travelled to be here.

"We're in Jerusalem but this is known as New Jerusalem." Her arm swung around to indicate the area.

Looking around at the low-rise apartment blocks that lined the streets, and the well-maintained gardens, he noticed how clean and neat the suburb was.

"What's Old Jerusalem?" he asked.

"The original walled city."

He felt his forehead crease with interest. "The walls originally built thousands of years ago?"

"Yes. Have you had a chance to see the Old City yet?" She asked with enthusiasm.

"Not yet." He rubbed the jet lag from his eyes. "I arrived this morning and by the time I got to Jerusalem, I had a couple of hours to get ready for the party tonight."

"You must be tired," she said with sympathy.

"I am." He yawned. "I slept on the plane but it's a long flight from Australia."

"Would you rather go back to your hotel and sleep?"

He shook his head. "No. After travelling for a day, I need to get out and walk." The cold air revitalised him and he was now feeling more awake than he had been in the Lenoir's warm apartment.

"How long are you here?" she asked politely.

He was only supposed to come for the wedding but had now extended his stay because of Grace. Looking around at the architecture confirmed he'd made the right decision to spend time sightseeing, not just attend the wedding.

"Till the day after Christmas," he said. "Tell me about yourself," he asked, wanting to talk about her, rather than him. "Kiara tells me you work in the family business running tours."

Lucie prattled on about the tourist business her family managed and her role, but Tom noticed there was forced enthusiasm in her voice, making him wonder if she was happy. "Do you like what you do?" He asked as a test to see if her happiness was genuine or not.

There was a pause before she said, "Of course."

Bingo. It wasn't. Over the years, working with disadvantaged teen boys, he'd developed an uncanny knack of reading people. Probably developed after spending years hiding behind a shield of safety and shelter for self-preservation.

Soon enough, they were walking in the city and Tom took a moment to admire the stonework of the buildings around him. Despite the number of low-rise apartments, the streets didn't seem cluttered, but it was very different from Australia where many people lived in houses.

"Almost there," she said as they walked down yet another narrow street.

Despite the late hour, people filled the street. Families, couples and groups of friends milled around, talking and laughing. It seemed everyone had somewhere to be or someone to be with. A reminder of the starkness and bareness of his own home life. His jaw clenched but he supressed the pain, the constant reminder that he wasn't good enough and that a cosy, warm lifestyle was not for him.

Lucie pointed out the sights and he was drawn to the beauty of the city's buildings, a mix of ancient and modern, which was enhanced by strategically placed lighting. The city was beautiful.

He took a moment to admire her. When she spoke about the local sights, her whole face lit up and she was even more lovely than when he'd first met her. Her smile was genuine and infectious, making him forget, even temporarily, about his own issues and frustrations.

"Here we are," she said ten minutes later. The jazz music and warmth welcomed them and he shrugged out of his warm coat. Looking around, he saw an eclectic group of people seated around small tables. Everyone looked happy, as if they were enjoying themselves, and Tom was glad he'd chosen to come here. It was very different from any bar he'd been inside in Australia. A sign told them they made the best hummus, and a large canister at the bar promoted hot punch. Suddenly the need to break out of his shell and try something different tempted him, and not because Grace had insisted he do so.

He frowned in surprise. After years of instability, being the outsider kid, he craved stability. But here with Lucie, a need drove him to break out of the self erected wall of self-keeping he stayed behind. Till now.

She took his hand and led him through the maze of tables, till they reached a lone empty one. Perfect for two.

Seated, he took a moment to look around again.

"Like what you see?" she asked.

He'd been looking at the musicians but he turned around

to look at her, his smile twitching with appreciation. Their gazes met and his lingered a little too long before he replied in a low voice, "Yes, I like what I'm seeing."

It was probably too forward to say to someone he'd just met but he couldn't help it. He felt connected to her in a way that was refreshing but also daunting. He was here for his friend's wedding, he reminded himself, not to seduce Kiara's sister-in-law to be.

He took in Lucie's eyes widening and her jaw dropping, but she didn't say anything.

Not wanting to make her feel uncomfortable, he gave her a warm smile. She'd left her parents' family event for him and he was grateful to be in her company.

"Shall we order?" Her elbows rested on the table and she was looking at him with interest, seemingly happy to be with him.

He stretched in his seat and pushed away the pain of the past that had held him back for so many years. Used to being the loner, he was suddenly really happy and he ached to grasp onto the joy he was feeling and enjoy it a little more. "I'm feeling adventurous, why don't you order for me?"

"Sure, the grilled camel testicles are a house speciality," she said with sincerity.

The adventurous spirit deflated and he stumbled to find the right words.

She chuckled. "You should see your face. I was kidding," she gave him a cheeky grin. "Their specialty is hummus. You'll love it."

Food and drinks ordered, they spent a few comfortable minutes listening to the talented musicians playing jazz. Although he preferred rock to jazz, the music reached out to him and calmed his anxious heart. It was as though he was meant to come here to find some peace after so many years of turbulence.

Pushing aside such thoughts, he focussed on the stunning woman in front of him. "Tell me more about you," he said, leaning forward to admire the most beautiful brown eyes he'd ever seen. He knew it was trite or corny, but he seriously could drown in them.

CHAPTER 2

*L*ucie wondered why being with Tom was making her stumble over her words. Her heart beat a little erratically. Sure he was handsome, but there was something magnetic in the way that he looked at her that made her cheeks warm. No man had ever looked at her in such a way, even her last boyfriend who she thought, at the time, was *the one*.

How did an Australian man who she'd known for only a couple of hours make her want to reveal things? Share intimacies with him that she was too embarrassed to do with her family?

She was love struck for sure, perhaps it was the affect of the lead-up to the wedding and the love she'd been surrounded with over the past year. Jacques and Kiara had fallen in love within days of meeting and initially she'd scoffed at the idea, unable to believe in love at first sight. Or perhaps, she was fearful that her brother, Jacques, was in lust rather than love, and making hasty decisions that affected not just the whole family but the family-run business.

Leaning back in her chair, she enjoyed the music and

wondered what to say to Tom. Tell him the truth? Perhaps. Perhaps not.

She sipped her wine and then looked at him over the rim of her glass. "I've told you about me, I'm interested in you."

A moment of disappointment flared in his eyes before he relaxed in his seat. "I'm more interested in you," he said with a chuckle.

Her lips twitched with amusement. "Looks like we'll be listening to music all night if neither of us goes first."

"Fine." She made a dramatic sigh. "I'll go first. I'm the youngest in the family and have an older brother and sister. Gabrielle lives in Tsfat, which is a couple of hours drive north, with her husband and twin boys. I just adore my nephews who are now six." She took a breath, "And you know Jacques, who's about to marry your friend. The reason you're here in Israel."

"What's your favourite colour?" he asked.

The question threw her off her prepared speech. Blue, she wanted to say. The colour of his eyes. "Um, green."

"And what's the best thing that has happened to you this year?" His deep voice made her skin prickle with awareness, and she was still unable to believe how strongly she was reacting to a man. A man she hadn't even known for twenty-four hours.

Her head bent at the neck as dread weighed heavily in her chest. "Honestly, it's been a rotten year for me." She paused. "I mean, I'm happy for my brother and Kiara but. . ."

"Your family's solely focussed on Jacques? And there's not attention on you?"

Her eyes widened in surprise but she bit back her retort when she saw the teasing in his grin. Unfortunately, there was truth in his jibe. "Will you keep secret what I'm about to say?"

"Sure," he placed his hand on his heart.

"I love Kiara, she's lovely and been really kind to me, but their whirlwind romance has had a big impact on *me*."

His hand reached out and took hers. "Tell me."

"I've told no one because I don't want to seem mean but. . ." She sighed. "Kiara and Jacques fell in love, but she's from Australia and was worried about the haste of the romance and also moving here."

He nodded, understanding the changes they'd both made for love.

"To provide stability for her, he made arrangements, which was really nice. But it was *for Kiara*." She paused. "I had no say. Before he met Kiara, I was sharing an apartment with Jacques. But then he moved out so Kiara could move in. And then when they got engaged, he moved into the apartment and I had to move out and live with *mes parents*, my parents." She fiddled with her rings. "And now they want me to move out of my parents' house and stay with a friend so her grandmother can stay with my parents." She blew out a breath of frustration. "I've gone along with everyone's plans, being accommodating but now it's a little too much."

"I'm sure they mean well, but that's a bit rough on you," he said thoughtfully.

Her gaze caught his and she reflected on his words, taking a moment to understand his colloquialisms. "Yes, thanks. And two weeks ago, my boyfriend and I broke up and no one noticed."

"That can't have been easy," he added with a soft gaze that made her feel he understood her frustrations.

Their drinks arrived and she stopped talking as the waitress placed them on the table, together with a plate of hummus, pita bread and a plate of olives.

"*To da rabah*," she thanked her.

They lifted their drinks.

"Cheers," he said.

"Cheers," she replied, the unknown word rolled on her tongue. "Thanks for stealing me away tonight."

He took a long sip of his beer before lowering the glass and gazing at her with an intensity that made her blush. "The pleasure is all mine."

She sipped her wine to steady her nerves. How could one guy make her insides go to mush and unable to articulate the thoughts concisely?

"I know you work in the family business. Kiara told me about the tours you run here," he said.

Kiara and her grandmother had travelled to Israel a year ago for a Christmas in the Holy Land tour, when she'd met Jacques. "Kiara told me how knowledgeable you are."

Leaning back in her chair, she crossed her arms protectively over her chest and her heart. "I have to be. Not only did I have to study for two years, I also have ongoing assessments on my knowledge."

"Do you like what you do?" He tore a piece of pita and dipped it into the thick hummus dip before gobbling it.

About to agree, as she always did, because she was dutiful and never said anything against her family, she swallowed the fib and said, "Yes and no. I was pressured into the family business and have no choice but to continue working, supporting my parents and grandparents. The business provides for all of them." She paused. "I wish I could do what I really want to do."

"And what's that?" he prodded gently.

Unease fluttered in her belly. As handsome and as wonderful as he was, she wasn't ready to share that with him now. "Maybe later."

His brow lifted with attentiveness. "I'm thinking of getting you a couple more glasses of wine to relax you so you'll tell me everything."

She liked his cheeky grin and the way he listened to her.

For the first time in a while, she felt valued. That someone was interested in her, and not just because they wanted her to do their bidding.

Her boyfriend had left her and her honesty in a flash, and they'd been dating. It didn't seem right to tell Tom everything. They were on a first date. This was the time to relax and get to know each other, not confess her deepest hopes and dreams or her infertility issues.

"Thirsty?" she pointed to the empty glass.

He smiled at the glass, before fiddling with it. "I ordered a local beer. Best beer I've had since I got here."

She made a show of looking at her watch. "You've been in Israel less than a day."

He shrugged with amusement. "What can I say, it's the best, even if it's the only one." The laugh lines in his face relaxed and she took a moment to look at him as he ate a couple of olives.

They each ate for a couple of minutes in a comfortable silence before he said, "Don't think I've forgotten about your aspirations."

She shrugged away his diligence before tearing a piece of pita into small pieces. "It's not that exciting." How could she tell him, someone she'd known for such a short time about her passion, her true calling? If her family didn't understand, why would he?

If only she could be like Gabrielle and leave the family business to do what she loved. "My sister got out before me. She's an artist and is so talented. They live in Tsfat, which is full of artists. She gets to do what she loves."

"But not you?" His focus remained on her as she babbled, not speaking coherently.

Pressing her lips together, she considered what to say, unable to speak of her family with disrespect. "My parents need me in the business. Gabrielle helps occasionally but she's a mother so. . ."

"It falls on to you," he said softly.

The band had taken a break but the chatter around them faded as she focussed on Tom and his interest in her. "That's what families do."

"I wouldn't know," he added.

Pain and discomfort at those three small words stabbed at her heart, reminding her that not everyone had a loving family like her. "I'm sorry," she said with sincerity.

"Don't be." He added with a nonchalant shrug. "Years ago I gave up the idea of finding love and having a family when I was shifted around the state foster system." He looked away, and caught the gaze of a barman. He lifted his empty glass, indicating another, before returning to look at her. "After my mother abandoned me, when I was ten, I was moved from one family to another."

She sucked in a sharp breath, unable to imagine the pain and tragedy of his past. "That's awful." Her brain was full of questions and they all started with *why*.

"I don't need any sympathy." He looked up and gave the waitress a thanks and thumbs-up as she placed a glass of beer in front of him. Taking a long sip, he placed it down and continued his tale of woe. "For six years, I was a miserable kid who stole, lied and cheated. No one wanted me and in hindsight, I realised I pushed everyone away because I hoped, deep down, my mother would come back for me."

A light headedness of despair made her squint. "That's common for neglected or deserted children, yes?"

He leaned back in his chair, seemingly comfortable to share his past with her. "After being caught shoplifting *again*, I was back in court but the judge was surprisingly under-standing, considering my rap sheet and sent me to a couple who cared for delinquents like me. They lived in the countryside and took in a few kids every few months."

"They sound very kind, if they were willing to take in troubled children," she added, wanting to know more.

His face softened and the lines around his jaw disappeared. "Bruce and Betty changed my life, for the better I should add. They straightened me out, taught me a trade and made me realise that there are good people in this world." He paused, to sip some of his beer.

"They sound incredible," she added, very interested in people who devoted their lives to helping others. "Tell me more," she prodded him.

The music started up again and despite him speaking louder, she leaned forward so she wouldn't miss a word.

He cleared his throat. "They live on a farm and we were expected to help with the running."

She crossed her arms, studying his handsome face. It was hard to imagine that he'd been a troublemaker as a young man. It didn't match the seemingly well-adjusted, confident and well-spoken man seated in front of her. "I'm assuming you didn't at the beginning," she said.

"Too right," he said with a wink. "But if you didn't help, you didn't eat."

She gasped, unsure if that was a good way to treat disobedient adolescents. "How long did you hold out for?"

"Two days. It was torture. The food smelt so good, and I sat there, sullen, pretending I wasn't hungry when the whole time, I just wanted something to ease the pains in my belly." He sipped his beer before continuing. "There was no reprimand or telling off once I started contributing. In fact, they told me I was quite welcome to leave and they'd drive me to the nearest train station. All I had to do was ask."

She nodded slowly, absorbed in his tale. "I'm assuming you didn't."

"It was a working farm that sustained us all. I learned to milk a cow, collect eggs, feed the chickens and grow vegetables. At sixteen, I'd survived eating takeaway food and scraps from bins. Over the months, I grew stronger and healthier than I had ever been. And being outdoors and surrounded by such caring, warm people, I changed, not just physically but mentally too." His blue eyes brightened and she could see how positive the impact of farm life had been on him, and how willing he was to share this with her.

She felt herself nodding again, desperately interested to hear more about Tom's teen years. Her first impressions of him were that he was self-assured, kind and confident. She wouldn't have believed he'd been a wayward child who'd been in trouble with the police. He didn't seem the kind. Obviously, the foster parents had done an amazing job in helping him.

"I loved the horses, mucked their stalls and was happiest when I could ride them. It took me months of hard work to prove to the Connors that I was worthy of them. To them, the horses had to be cared for and it was something to be earned, a reward as such. After months of good behaviour, I was given that chance. One of the happiest days of my life."

Tilting her head to the side, she asked, "How long did you live with them?"

"I was only supposed to stay a few months but ended up staying three years," he confessed with clarity. "But eventually, I helped them with the kids that came to stay. Seeing these moody teens reminded me what I had been like when I arrived. Just like me, many resisted work until the hunger pains cramped their bellies, and they started to help out."

"Did all kids have such a good experience as yours?" she asked, absorbed in the incredible program that transformed the lives of the teens.

He shook his head. "Most, but not all. You had to want to

change, even if you didn't know it at the time. But I can tell you that clean air, good food and hard work made me feel physically and emotionally better. After that, it was easier to clean up my act."

Her nose crinkled at the term, not understanding why he needed to shower.

"Sorry, I meant that I needed to fix myself up, and become a better person. I couldn't do that hanging out with a bad crowd, eating unhealthy food, and being on the wrong side of the law."

Her lips twitched with amusement. "Did you make friends?"

A smile lit up his face and she realised she'd asked the right question. "My sister, Grace." He raised his hands defensively. "She's technically not my sister, but I love her like she is. She was sent to the farm a few months after me and the abuse she'd endured was awful. I guess you could say we helped heal each other."

"Tonight you said that your sister encouraged you to come to Israel for the wedding," she said slowly, remembering his words back at the apartment.

"Yes, but she has her own selfish reasons for me being here," he said in an off-hand manner.

"She wanted to get rid of you for a couple of weeks?" she joked. "I'd do that to my brother in a heartbeat," she said with a grin. "He's been annoying me since I was born."

"Unfortunately, the reason is true but also sad," he continued and she could see real pain in his eyes. "She was recently diagnosed with breast cancer, and since she found religion over the past couple of years, I'm here to say prayers for her." He paused, his shoulders straight and stiff. "Grace is my world, knowing she's sick and on the other side of the world is tearing my guts to pieces. I should be there but she wants to me to pray for her at a few places. She really believes in that stuff."

"You don't?" She lifted her eyebrows with curiosity.

He shrugged away her surprise. "I just told you my background. It's not like I've had a chance to learn about God or anything."

"But Grace did," she said with resolution.

"Despite everything she has been through, she has a devotion to God and truly believes that there is a reason for everything, even if we don't know what that reason is." She could see disregard in his eyes. He clearly did not have faith like she, and obviously Grace, did. Releasing a sigh, she wondered if believing in something would help him let go of the past? Although she could see he'd already done an excellent job of that and had become a worthy man.

He ran his fingers through his hair and took a ragged breath. "Grace is one of those beautiful women who has had everything bad life could throw at her. When I met her, she was a traumatised teen girl ready to kill herself. But after time on the farm, away from her parents and with the Connors, she developed into this amazing woman. She started going to church and helping others."

He blew out a long breath. "If you knew how badly she'd been treated, you would appreciate how incredible she is."

Was he secretly in love with her? Lucie wondered. He seemed very devoted to Grace. Or was it simply the devotion of two young teens who'd bonded due to their unhappy childhoods? That couldn't have been easy. Her disappointments over the past year paled in significance when she compared her warm, caring, family life to Tom and Grace's.

He continued, breaking her thoughts. "Grace went to school and became a social worker, helping others through outreach in her local church." He paused. "A few weeks ago she found a lump in her breast."

"How awful," her belly sank at the sad tale, and she made a note to pray for Grace's full recovery.

He turned the glass around, seemingly absorbed in the fiddling before he looked up. "I've known Grace for fourteen years; I'd give my life for hers. I'm here because it's what she wants."

"I'll help you," she said immediately, her offer genuine and heartfelt. "I'll take you to the sites she wants, and I'll organise my friends and family in prayer group for her." Faith was important to her family, a text message to them would result in lots of prayers.

Shock made his jaw open wide. "You'd do that? You don't even know her."

She blinked rapidly. "Whether you have faith or not, you've come to the right place for prayers. This is the birthplace of Jesus, our Lord." She paused and gave him a small smile. "We're going to do everything we can, spiritually, to help Grace. The rest of it will be done by the doctors."

His face crumpled in a mixture of joy, sadness and disbelief. "You don't have to pity us."

She reached out and took his hand. "I don't. But my family and I believe in the power of prayer. Let's do what we can for her," she added with genuine sincerity.

He nodded and she could see his eyes cloud with bewilderment, before he lifted his glass and took a couple of large swallows.

"Have you got the list of places to visit?"

"Yes. I'd planned to hire a car and drive around but I stupidly didn't take into consideration the difficulty of travelling here. You drive on the other side of the road, and it's very different here from Australia." He paused. "I may need help. Do you have a tour I can go on?"

She shook her head. "Not with the wedding. We're not running any until after Christmas." When the family had made the decision to take a break with work all those months back, she'd been worried whether it was the right decision. It seemed it was, for all the reasons she could never have imagined. She would now have the time to help someone in need. Someone she liked. Someone she wanted to be with.

His face fell, a look of hopelessness crossed his eyes. "Can you recommend someone who can help me?"

"Yes, me," she announced with pride in her voice. "I'll take you."

"Aren't you busy? Won't your family need you?" His forehead was creased with astonishment.

Her eyebrows lifted. "No thanks, I'd rather be with you. Besides, after the story I tell them about you, they'll be begging me to take you," she chuckled at her own cleverness. She knew her family only too well. They'd probably insist she take him, if they heard about Tom's story.

Instead of happiness, worry lines marred his handsome face. "I'm not a charity case, and I don't want you sharing private details about my life with them," he said, his voice frustrated and filled with annoyance.

She reached out and took his hand. "Don't worry, I'll tell them about Grace needing prayers. That's all. Your family secrets are safe with me. I promise."

A smile replaced the frown and his whole face lit up. "Thank you, that means a lot to me."

"You're welcome. Is tomorrow too soon to start?"

"Tomorrow would be perfect," he replied, giving her a dazzling smile that melted her insides.

Tomorrow could not come fast enough.

She. Could. Not. Wait.

*T*he following morning, Lucie hummed one of her favourite Christmas songs to herself as she walked to the YMCA where Tom was staying. Fatigue and jet lag had him yawning and apologising last night. They'd left soon after finishing their meals, sharing a taxi to where he was staying.

He'd fallen asleep on the short ride there, and had been groggy when he'd thanked her and exited the cab.

She hoped he remembered to be ready, and had sent him a reminder text this morning.

Walking into the open reception area of the YCMA, she found Tom leaning against the wall, looking refreshed and fit. His hair was still damp as though he'd only just showered.

"*Boker tov*, good morning," she said, walking up to him.

"*Boker tov*," he replied. "I've been practising a few phrases this morning."

"Good to hear. Are you ready?" A flutter of joy filled her heart as she looked at him; he was as handsome as she remembered.

"I didn't have time for breakfast this morning. I'll need to grab something on the run," he said, rubbing the back of his neck.

Running? That didn't make sense to her.

Her face must have shown him her confusion as he said, "Sorry, I'll get something while we're out." He stretched his arms above his head. "I slept in and was thankful for your message. I don't remember giving you my mobile number, but I'm glad you sent me a reminder text."

Her cheeks warmed at the compliment. "All part of the service," she said. "Have you got Grace's list?"

Extracting his phone from his pocket, he fiddled around and displayed a screen listing the locations he hoped to visit.

"That's a lot of places. Do you know that they're not all in Jerusalem?" Her finger traced along the length of the phone and she felt her forehead crease.

He bit his lip in frustration. "No, I assumed most were, apart from the obvious places like Bethlehem and Sea of Galilee."

"There's a place nearby that has good coffee and pastries. We'll go there and talk about the list, and where you want to go first," she said, tugging gently at his coat, as they made their way to the door.

* * *

A FEW MINUTES LATER, they sat in a tiny café, which smelt of the rich aroma of coffee, butter and sugar.

Seated close, Tom kept apologising for knocking Lucie with his knees. The table was small and there was not much space.

Taking his phone from him, she re-read the list and he took a moment to gaze at her pretty-ness. Last night, before he fell into a deep, coma-like sleep, he wondered if Lucie had been a figment of his jet-lagged imagination. The text this morning told him she wasn't, and seeing her again reminded him of why he'd made an effort to meet her last night.

From the length of her long brown hair, almond shaped eyes and full lips, she was the most beautiful woman he'd met. But he'd also been attracted to her smile, caring nature and witty conversation. If she had a flaw, he had yet to see it.

"Grace has chosen the places that Christians come to when wanting to walk in the footsteps of Our Lord or to connect to their faith." Pointing to the mobile phone, she said, "Depending on the amount of time you want to spend at each spot, we can cover these in two days."

Tom looked at the flush in her cheeks that was not only from the warmth of the café but also the excitement of visiting these holy sites. She may claim not to love her job, but her gushing enthusiasm was saying something else.

"What's Via Dolorosa?" he asked, pointing to the screen.

"You may know it as the Way of Sorrows. It's the path Jesus took from his trial, to his crucifixion, to his tomb," she explained.

"She also wants you to visit the Church of the Holy Sepulchre which is in the Christian Quarter of the Old City, easy for us to get to." She took a quick sip of her coffee. "The Church is considered by many to be very holy as it was built on the site of Jesus' crucifixion. Then we'll see the Garden Tomb, which is considered to be the location where Jesus was buried. We'll be able to see the chamber and then go out to the gardens, giving you some time to reflect or perhaps pray for Grace's recovery.

"And finally, if you want, we can go to Mount Zion, which is also in the Old City, here. It's where Jesus and his disciples had their Last Supper."

She bit her lip as she scrolled up and down the list. "Grace hasn't mentioned the Mount of Olives, but I'll take you there. It's mentioned many times in the bible as a place that Jesus would go and pray. Many believe that's where he ascended to heaven. It also has the most spectacular views of Jerusalem. It's beautiful there."

"Sounds great," he said. "Even for my own selfish purposes, I'd love to see it. The place sounds fascinating. Just remind me to say prayers along the way." He chucked. "I might forget since I'll be a tourist."

"Grace has mentioned Bethlehem, Sea of Galilee, Capernaum, Nazareth and Yardenit," she said before draining the remainder of her coffee.

"I'm assuming that will involve a lot of travelling?"

"*Ken*. Yes. I can take you but we need to work it in with the wedding plans and the wedding itself," she said. "Do you have a particular place you'd like to visit?"

He shrugged, unable to answer because he had no idea. "What do you recommend?"

"They're all great places, but if you have to pick one, may I suggest we visit Capernaum? It's on the Lake of Galilee and it's full of history, both Jewish and Christian. It's also where Jesus performed his miracles. I think Grace would like that."

He nodded in agreement. Not just beautiful, she was smart and interesting, too. "Sounds great. I've got good walking shoes on, so we'll do Jerusalem today and tomorrow, and then go to Capernaum?"

She shook her head with disappointment. "No, we have the wedding. We'll have to go after."

"Do I need to hire a car?" he asked.

"I'll borrow Jacques' car. He owes me," she said with a wink.

"Ready?" He pointed to her empty coffee cup.

"*Ken*, let's go," she said, standing and shrugging on her coat.

* * *

AT THE CHURCH of the Holy Sepulchre, they walked around and Lucie pointed out artefacts of historical interest. Outside they made their way to a steep wall of rock.

"This was unearthed in 1867," she pointed to the rock-cut tomb. "Archaeologists are still divided about whether this is where Jesus was buried and resurrected."

He looked around. "What do you think?"

She shrugged. "I've read both arguments and they each have valid points."

"One argument must have swayed you more, surely?" he probed, keen to know her thoughts.

"I love this place. The energy is so peaceful," she continued. "Most of the tourists I bring here don't seem to care whether it is the actual site. They usually tell me that this place is like an oasis of calm amongst the everyday bustle of modern Jerusalem."

His eyes widened in reply. "That's an apt way of putting it. This place is so tranquil that I can't believe we're in the middle of the city."

They walked through the ancient site before wandering through the beautiful, well maintained gardens.

"Whether this is the site or not, it's a wonderful place for worship and reflection," Lucie said in a quiet voice, as though not to disturb the tranquillity of their surroundings.

The air was cold and Tom was grateful for the warm coat, scarf and beanie he was wearing. There were few tourists around, and after a short stroll, a wave of peace settled on his shoulders, reminding him that this was the perfect place to pray for Grace.

His lungs ached with embarrassment. He had no idea how to pray or what to say. Having never been taught and not having a Bible, he felt the weight of responsibility pressing down on his chest. How could he do the right thing by Grace?

Lucie came up to him and tugged something out of her knapsack. "This will help you," she handed him a small book on the healing power of prayers. Flicking through it, his eyes widened at the number of prayers and the Bible passages that he could read.

"There are so many," he said, flicking through the well-worn pages.

"At the beginning, there are some specific prayers that my tourists like. The Healing Prayer is the most popular," She pointed to a half page prayer in English.

"Do I just read it?" He felt his forehead furrow in confusion and bashfulness.

"Yes," she gave him a genuine smile that pushed aside his feelings of inadequacy. "Go sit over there," she pointed to a wooden bench in the winter sun. "Read the passages that you like and then perhaps a personal prayer will come to you. If it doesn't, don't worry."

"Okay," he said.

"I'm going to sit over there," she pointed to a bench close by, "And do my own prayers.

"Do you need your book?" Worry tightened in his belly that he was inconveniencing her.

"I'll use my cell, I've got electronic copies," she raised her phone with a grin.

He made his way to the area Lucie recommended and started to read her book. The passages were filled with words of kindness and acceptance, and when he'd finished, he recited an extra prayer for himself, asking for inner peace. Despite his scepticism about prayer, he did it anyway as it felt right to do in this serene environment.

His breath caught in his throat when he looked at his watch, he'd been reading and praying for half an hour. How quickly the time had passed. He stood and stretched his legs before walking to Lucie. "Thank you for your prayer book."

He handed it to her. "Being here has been an emotional and meaningful experience," he added with honesty. "I'm surprised how good I'm feeling now. No wonder people come here to worship and reflect."

She stood and looped her arm through his. "I'm glad you enjoyed it. I love this place. As I said before, whether this is the official site or not, it's still a wonderful place to find peace."

The breath hitched in his throat as he took in her gorgeous, genuine smile and the relaxed manner of her speech. As much as he wanted to confess, he wasn't confident enough yet to tell her that this time had had a profound affect on him. He now understood, after so many years, the depth and value of Grace's faith, and the positive impact it had had on her.

* * *

HOURS LATER, they trudged into a café and Tom collapsed in a nearby chair. "My feet are killing me. How much walking did we do?"

"Hours," she said.

"I need food and then to collapse in bed," he said. "I don't care how close we are to the YMCA, I'm getting a taxi."

"Shall I order for you?" she pointed to the board above the food counter. The menu was displayed in both Hebrew and English.

"I'm not that tired," he growled with a playful tone.

After each ordered a sharwama and a plate of fries to share, they sat at a small table and Tom drained a bottle of water. "I needed that." He looked at her and said, "Thanks for today. It was so interesting. I was expecting it to be tedious—no offence. But you made each place come alive with your knowledge."

"*Bevakasha*, you're welcome," she added with a slight blush to her cheeks.

"Seriously, it was so interesting. I can't wait till tomorrow," he said, and he meant it. Being with Lucie was a bonus. Her ability to make history come alive was incredible. He'd been duty-bound in coming to Israel but now was glad he had the opportunity. He'd messaged Grace with many photos of him making prayers, and she'd replied with dozens of heart and kiss emoticons.

"Grace must be thrilled with your progress so far," she said, as if reading his mind. "But tell me, why did you come for the wedding? If you're not a traveller, it must have been a big decision to come here." Her finger pressed on the table.

He expelled a long breath. "You're right. I came because of Kiara and her grandmother June's kindness. Over the years we've been invited to their place countless times." He fiddled with a paper serviette. "At Christmas and Easter, and even for some Sunday lunches, Kiara always made sure to invite both Grace and me."

"What about your foster parents?" Lucie leaned forward with interest.

"Sometimes we spent it with them but other times we stayed in Melbourne. They don't live close to us. Kiara has shown us kindness that I will always be grateful for. How could I not come for her special day? Even if I had to travel twenty-four hours to get here," he said with a mischievous roll of his eyes.

"I loved the work Kiara and June did in Melbourne. It's probably one of the reasons why she fits so well into our family," she said with a twitch of her lips.

"I think it's more because she and your brother are in love," he added with a waggle of his eyebrows.

She chuckled in reply.

He took a moment to look at her. Unlike him, she didn't

look tired from the copious amounts of walking they'd done. "I'm pretty fit, but I found it hard walking on the cobblestones."

"That's Jerusalem," she said. "You get used to it."

"This is a beautiful city but I miss seeing water," he said with sincerity. "I love to surf, even in winter. It's my way of being alone and relaxing."

She lifted her eyebrow. "I know you're not religious, but have you thought that maybe the water is washing away all the difficulties and hardships?"

He was about to deny it, but instead he stopped and considered it. It did make sense, even if he didn't want to believe it.

"I'm a loner and have few friends," he said in a quiet voice. "I'm used to being on my own."

She nodded then looked up as a young man deposited the plates of food in front of them.

The tantalising smell of barbequed chicken, salad and spices teased his nostrils and his mouth literally watered as he looked at the food in front of him. "This looks amazing."

"*Beteavon, bon apetite*," she said before eating a fry.

With each large mouthful of food, the Middle Eastern flavours exploded in his mouth and Tom had to remind himself not to make noises of enjoyment. He'd finished everything before Lucie had even eaten half of her food. "Everything tastes so good here."

"It's fresh," she said. "Israel grows a lot of vegetables and fruit."

"I can tell," he said before stifling a yawn. "Sorry, it's the jet lag not your company."

"I'll take you back soon. Mind if I finish?" She pointed to her plate.

"Of course not." He leaned back in his chair, stretching his calf muscles. He patted his belly. "Remind me, is it Monday today?"

"Yes. And on Thursday, it's the wedding," she clarified, muttering *of the year* under her breath.

"Why Thursday?" he scratched his head. "In Australia, most couples get married on a Saturday."

"Jacques and Kiara were going to marry on Saturday but then our Jewish family friends couldn't make it, as it's their Sabbath, so they're marrying late Thursday afternoon and there is a reception straight after."

"Will there be a lot of guests?"

Her forehead crinkled as if she wasn't sure whether he was joking or not.

He wasn't.

"Of course. There will be hundreds," she clarified.

"Great," he muttered under his breath. It sounded like a form of torture. The only good thing would be that Lucie was also going to be there. The thought made his heart skip a beat in anticipation.

"While I finish eating, why don't you tell me more about you?"

He shrugged off her interest in him. What to tell her? He'd already confessed about his delinquent past. Surprisingly, she was still interested in him. Or rather in helping him. He wasn't sure whether she felt obliged to be with him or simply liked him for him. Probably the former.

"Most people love talking about themselves," she said before taking a long sip of water.

He didn't know what to say, so he said nothing.

"Tell me what you do," she prodded him.

"I'm a handyman. I fix things. When I was at the farm, I helped Bruce fix the fences and other things on the farm, and I found I was good at it. When I moved to Melbourne, I worked with a guy for a while and learnt about running a business. A couple of years later, I left him and started my own."

"That's impressive," she said.

"On the weekends and one week night, I work with teen boys, and teach them the skills of building and fixing. It's a good ability to have. The way I look at it, most of them won't finish school but at least I can make them more employable."

"It's very noble of you," she added with sincerity.

"I got a break fourteen years ago. I just try to help these boys out. Sometimes they listen to me and sometimes they don't. The ones who do, see something of themselves in me. They know I'm not lying and only want them to succeed."

He scratched his chin. "Once the boys turn eighteen, they're adults. If they get sent to jail, they'll be in an adult facility and that's just bad news." With a heavy chest he reflected that he could've been one of those sent to an adult correction facility and not had the opportunities he'd been given. It had motivated him to reach out and help boys who were like him.

"You're really making a difference in the world," she said with genuine warmth, before finishing her dinner.

He shrugged off her compliment even though it warmed his heart that she appreciated the hours he dedicated to helping the teens.

"How different my life would've been if I hadn't ended up on the farm?"

She focussed her gaze on him, nodding slowly.

Sitting straighter in his chair he said, "Even if only a few want to change, I can put them on the right path, so they can grow up and become good men."

She started to eat again. "We need more people like you in this world."

He slumped in his chair. "You're giving me more credit than I deserve. I'm not that special."

She dismissed his reply with a wave of her hand. "You've been through a lot and look at where you are. You have a business, you mentor young men, and you have a sister who obviously loves you. That's pretty good for a boy who grew up on the streets."

His neck warmed and he cleared his throat with acute embarrassment. "Tomorrow we'll go to the Mount of Olives?" he asked changing the subject away from him.

She placed her hand over his. "Sure."

* * *

THE FOLLOWING day was similar to the first. They walked for hours, Lucie explained the historical reasons for their visits, and Tom took countless photos.

"Your insight into the country and history is fascinating," he said, as they sat, drinking a bottle of water.

"It's my job," she said with a you-know-that raise of her eyebrow.

"I came here for Grace but I'm really glad to be here. I've never travelled much before." He paused and gazed at the magnificent sprawl of Jerusalem in front of him. "I always found excuses, not having money or time, but I could've done this."

"You're here now," she said softly.

He gazed into her brown eyes and wondered if she also felt the attraction between them. They'd spent so much time together, and it had grown so quickly. Was it just her being kind to him, a lonely traveller, or did she feel something more?

A need to know burned inside of him. He'd never felt such an intense desire for any woman. He was drawn to her and wanted to spend more time getting to know her. The practicalities of her living on the other side of the world to him paled in significance and his focus was just her, and the smooth skin on her jaw and the almond shape of her eyes.

Magnetised by something he'd never felt, he shifted closer to her and when he saw her eyes widen in anticipation, he leaned forwarded and did what he had wanted to do since he'd seen her at the Lenoir's pre-wedding party. Kiss her.

His hands came up to gently hold her face before he slowly brushed his lips across hers. Not wanting to rush or miss a moment, he savoured every delightful second. She moaned against his lips and he accepted the invitation to do it again and again.

"Lucie," he said softly.

In reply, her arms came up and her hands circled his neck.

Forgetting it was freezing cold and they were in a public place, he kissed her again, this time more deeply and in that moment, the world around them ceased to exist. All his focus and interest were on her soft lips and the tug of desire that whooshed through his veins.

Pulling back reluctantly, he tugged her close and kept his arm around her shoulder. "I don't think we should scandalise the other tourists," he said in a low voice, before pressing his lips against her forehead.

She leaned her head on his shoulder and they sat there for seconds…or minutes, he didn't know. But having her in his arms created heat and extreme joy in his chest. Never had he felt this content or happy in his thirty years. Something magical had happened since he'd arrived in Israel.

He'd come to Israel for Grace, to pray for her recovery as well as to attend Kiara's wedding, but all he could think about was Lucie. Lucie with her sense of humour, beauty and strong family loyalty, had him holding her tight, reluctant to let her go.

For years he'd never got close to any woman, and always

been upfront about his intention of never settling down or having children. The thought of passing his rotten DNA to a helpless baby made his stomach churn.

He wanted to tell Lucie about his reluctance to have a family of his own, but the words wedged in his throat as her body heat radiating towards him provided him comfort and consolation.

Not wanting to ruin this perfect moment, he said nothing.

CHAPTER 4

*L*ucie snuggled in the warmth of Tom's arms and wondered if things could be any more wonderful than they were.

When he looked at her, her insides dissolved with lust and need, and now she understood the haste with her brother wanting to be with Kiara.

She wasn't sure if she and Tom were *in love* but what she did know was that he was the kindest and bravest man she'd met. And she desperately wanted to spend more time with him. Could he be *the one*? Was that why she'd endured so much dating disappointment, because she had to wait for Tom? The thought excited and also terrified her.

He was Australian and lived on the other side of the world. It wasn't as easy as just falling in love. They had a lot of issues to resolve if they were to have any future together.

She mentally slapped herself. They'd only known each other for two days, besides he might just see her as a holiday romance. Someone special for the time he was here.

The realisation deflated the bubble of happiness in her

belly, and she reminded herself that it was a kiss, just one kiss.

Breaking away from his embrace and tantalising warmth, she stood. "It's cold, let's get moving," she said, using her best tour-guide operator voice.

Disappointment crossed his blue eyes. "Sure," he said, standing slowly. "What's next to see?"

Not wanting to ruin their moment or time together, she placed her cold hand in his and smiled. "Come on, I'll show you."

His return smile made her heart melt. He really was that gorgeous and when he looked at her like that, she felt herself flushing like a schoolgirl.

* * *

FOR THE NEXT TWO DAYS, Lucie was obliged to spend time with the family and help with the wedding preparations.

Keeping in contact with Tom via text messages, they chatted endlessly and she was secretly jealous of his ventures to Tel Aviv. Over the space of a day and a half, he'd managed to visit two museums, the old section of the city, do a Segway tour of Jaffa and have a run along the beach. Her favourite photo of him was taken at dusk, with him holding a beer bottle with the beach in the background. He'd signed it, *wish you were with me*.

She wished she could've been there with him and found herself uncharacteristically snapping at her *maman* and *grand-mere*, for the smallest trivialities. Despite apologising after, they gave her a look, which meant they each knew something was going on and she was going to have to tell them later.

Anticipation of seeing Tom that night, at the wedding, bubbled inside of her.

In her bridesmaid dress, styled hair and expertly applied makeup, Lucie felt beautiful, and was looking forward to Tom's reaction.

There wasn't much opportunity at the church, with the hundreds of guests crammed inside before they made their way to the reception, at the hotel.

Caught up with the wedding party and couple, Lucie desperately searched for Tom but couldn't see him.

A tightness in her chest made it hard to breathe when she couldn't see him amongst the hundreds of people attending the wedding.

With his height and blond hair, he would be easy to spot. At the thought her limbs felt heavy and she sighed, wondering if he was having too much fun in Tel Aviv to attend the wedding. She knew how much he hated crowds. Was he staying away from it, or her?

The feelings of worthlessness and hopelessness swamped her as they had in the past, as she obsessed over why he wasn't here.

An hour into the reception, everyone was enjoying the event except her. Despite the fake smile she'd plastered on her face, she was deeply disappointed he wasn't there.

Hands snaked around her waist and tugged her aside. "Miss me," a deep male voice asked, making her heart skip a beat.

She blinked rapidly before spinning around and throwing her arms around Tom. "You're here, finally."

He held her tight. "Sorry I'm late. The bus broke down. I'm sorry I missed the wedding. Did everything go well?"

"Perfect," she said, moving her hands around his neck.

"You look incredible, so beautiful," he said, his gaze roaming her body.

Bouncing on her toes, she said, "I was worried about you."

"I couldn't message you. I was helping the driver and my

phone fell from my pocket onto the road, shattering into pieces. I need a new mobile."

"Always the hero, the fixer. We'll get one tomorrow," she said, with excitement.

"And then we're heading north?"

"*Oui.* Just you and me," she said with a lift of her eyebrow.

"I can't wait," he said before nuzzling her neck.

"Lucie," a voice called out.

Her heart sank, remembering she was at her brother's wedding behaving shamelessly. Breaking away from Tom's arms, her face flushed with the embarrassment of being caught by her grandmother. In rapid French, she was reminded that if she wanted to kiss her boyfriend, she shouldn't be doing it in front of everyone.

Lucie couldn't help but giggle at the older woman and kissed her cheek, promising to behave better. The grandmother whispered to her in French about Tom's handsomeness, which made Lucie blush.

Touching her face with a gentle stroke of her fingers the older lady said, "Now I understand why you've been behaving the way you have, *cherie*. You've been missing him."

She walked off and Lucie caught Tom's face, he was completely baffled about what had just happened.

"Was she upset with you?" he asked.

"She reminded me that if we're going to kiss, we shouldn't be doing it in front of the guests," she replied.

He chuckled. "Shall we dance?" he asked, leading her to the dance floor.

They spent the rest of the wedding together. The casual ambiance meant guests could sit where they liked, and Lucie enjoyed every minute.

With her ex-boyfriend breaking up with her so recently, she was sure she was not going to have a good time at the wedding. But in Tom's arms, with his ability to make her feel special, she was the happiest she'd been in years.

Taking a short break from dancing, they stood at the bar.

"You're a good dancer," he said, handing her a glass of champagne.

"So are you," she replied with a wink. Lifting her glass she toasted, "To having fun."

He replied with a lift of his glass of water, "To having fun, *with you*."

Had the heat been cranked up, because suddenly her skin was burning hot. Draining her glass, she reached over and drank his glass of water.

Giving her a questioning lift of his eyebrow, she shrugged and said, "I'm thirsty."

The party continued late into the night, and when the band played a love song, he held her close. "I've never enjoyed an event like this before."

The fairy lights, and disco ball created a romantic feel in the large room and she sighed. "This is what I love to write about." The words slipped from her lips before she had time to think about telling him her secret. Obviously the happiness and joy of the wedding had loosened her tongue.

"Write?" he asked, before he stopped dancing. "You never told me you write." His eyes held interest, wanting to know more.

Her smile wavered, unsure of his reaction. "Promise you won't laugh?"

Placing his hand over his heart he said, "Promise."

She leaned towards him and whispered in his ear. "I write romance novels but we don't talk about it."

A twinkle of mischief appeared in his blue eyes. "Why the secrecy?"

She consciously pushed away the flutters in her stomach that always appeared on the rare times she confessed her secret occupation. "It's not seen as a good career choice. My family wants me to help out in the business, not be an author." They continued to dance, but her legs were wobbly and she held on tightly to him. "It's not that they're not supportive of me. They are, but they see writing as a hobby."

The palm of his hand pressed against her lower back, bringing her closer to him. "But you want to write instead of being a guide?"

"I do, it's what I love. I've submitted many times and been rejected." She paused. "But I just keep writing."

"You'll get there, I know you will," he said before pressing his lips to her forehead. "What do you write?"

"Contemporary romance."

"Do you have handsome heroes who are good with their hands?" And to prove his point, his fingers trailed along the bare skin of her arms.

Every skin cell tingled in anticipation, wanting more. "Actually, no. My heroes are billionaires, brought to their knees by love."

"I'm assuming you don't have heroines who are hapless and in need of rescuing?"

Her chin lifted in defiance, used to having to defend the genre she not only loved reading but writing for. "Of course not. They are strong and determined. Just like the hero, they don't realise how great love can be until they find it with the right guy."

"Falling for a rich man has its benefits," he said with a tone that had her wondering if he was being conceited or practical.

"It's fantasy. Who wouldn't want to be whisked away to a private island and seduced? But the love and emotions I write are real and intense. They occur between people whether they're rich or not." The words tumbled from her lips as her blood pressure rose. Why did she have to defend herself all the time?

They continued to dance before he said, "Would you let me read one of your books?" His gravelly voice made her shiver in exactly the same reaction as the heroine in her latest story.

Her nose lifted with irritation. "Certainly not."

"Come on, I'm a twenty-first century guy. I'm into stuff like that," he prodded.

Relenting, she said, "We'll see," hoping to deflect the conversation away from her because there was no way she would let him read her tales of love.

Not even her family or best friends were allowed access to her stories.

Apart from a social media presence, under an alias, Lucie Lenoir was a tour guide operator helping in the family business, not an author who wrote sweeping tales of grand love and romantic gestures.

A scuffle broke out in the corner between two young teens. What seemed to be a play fight escalated to punches as the older men tried to keep them apart.

Tom broke away and sprinted across the half empty room to where the young men were throwing curse words at each other.

Walking between the two of them, he grabbed both boys, leading them to a corner. Tom hadn't bothered checking if their parents minded, he'd just intervened and taken over.

Taking a seat nearby, she watched with interest as he got the boys to explain their frustrations to him and to each other. Tom's patience was clearly on display as she watched him nod and pay attention to each. Although she couldn't hear what was being said, his calm disposition had a positive effect on the teens. And after about fifteen minutes, the boys reluctantly shook hands with each other before thanking

Tom. They each left and Lucie wasn't surprised to see the startled looks of the families who'd watched the intervention with interest.

Tom swaggered towards her and she took a moment to admire his height, long, lean legs and sculptured abs under the shirt and tailored pants he wore. He had the charm and looks of a movie star, not an ordinary guy who fixed things and spent time with delinquent young men.

"I'm impressed," she said as he stood before her, lifting her to a standing position.

He shrugged away her compliment. "I've dealt with worse. They've got hormones and they may have snuck a drink or two. It's a bad combination. I just listened to them."

"I watched you. You were so patient with them. You did more than listen to them." She wanted to let him know that what he did was special. It reminded her how wonderful he was and that despite everything he'd been through, he was helping others.

He shrugged away her compliments. "It's what I do. I like kids."

"Your children will be lucky to have a great dad like you." She placed her hand on his arm, complimenting him with a reassuring tone.

The joy in his face slipped off like a mask and she was surprised to see the look of regret in his eyes. "I have no intention of breeding and passing my DNA to some hapless child," he said. She shivered from the coldness in his tone.

Her mouth opened, but words did not come. They remained stuck in her throat. How could someone so kind, generous and forgiving not see themselves as such? She wanted to laugh his comment off. Surely it was a joke? But she saw the skin around his jaw tighten and a muscle tick near his eye and she knew he was serious.

Her mind raced, unable to comprehend the situation and

she rubbed the pain in her temples away. Blinking rapidly she realised that Tom could only ever be a holiday romance. Nothing more could come of their developing romance. Because unlike him, she craved a family and wanted desperately to find a husband. Her stomach sank. Only two weeks ago, her ex-boyfriend had told her she put too much pressure on him. And now she was doing it again with Tom, but this time the pressure was on her.

But she couldn't help it. Thanks to the endometriosis she suffered, the only way for her to have a biological child was with the help of IVF. And she was approaching thirty. Either she found a husband soon or she'd start the process using donor sperm. Her determination to be a mother was too important to her. She wasn't prepared to give up that goal.

The romantic dreams of her and Tom evaporated as quickly as the guests tonight when the music finished. She could see him, fall for him a little more and have her heart broken yet again, or she could stop seeing him, and protect her heart from his gorgeous smile and generous spirit.

She placed a hand over her chest and massaged her heart, as her muscles clenched. Blinking back tears, she apologised to Tom, turned and made her way outside to get away from the guy she had thought might be the one for her.

CHAPTER 5

*T*om watched Lucie sprint away from him as though the building were on fire.

He scratched his head, reflecting on what could've upset her so. Was she upset that he didn't want biological children of his own? Was that so bad that she'd run away? Or was she running from him? Knowing he really wasn't that decent or deserving. Despite everything he'd achieved and the man he'd grown into, there was still a small boy trapped inside wondering why his mother had rejected him and never sought him out.

It was the reason he'd struggled to settle down and find love. Would she leave him like his mother had? The easiest way not to deal with such heartache was to stay emotionally detached.

It had never bothered him…till now.

They'd only known each other a few days, had shared some playful kisses but had made no commitment to each other. He let out a long breath, wondering if dating couples talked about children so early in a relationship.

Before racing after her, he found their coats and then

went looking for her, expecting her to be in the lobby or outside garden.

He found her easily in the cold, shivering, looking forlorn and despondent. Drawing her towards him, he placed her warm coat around her and held her tight.

"Did I say something to upset you?" he asked. "Or am I missing something? I haven't dated anyone for a while." He wanted to keep his tone light but struggled to, seeing the sadness in her eyes.

"It's me, not you," she said, not maintaining eye contact.

"That sounds like a line," he said, concerned. "It's pretty cold out here. Do you want to go inside?" His head nodded towards the door.

Shaking her head slowly, she said, "Not yet, I don't want my family to see me like this."

He took in the look of her eyes, vacant and hollow, and agitation wormed its way into his belly. He hated seeing her so despondent.

Tightening her coat around her, he noticed a tremble in her lip before she spoke. "I'm sorry. I have to confess that I'm a romantic and after my boyfriend recently broke up with me, I was humiliated and upset. And then I met you with your happy-go-lucky attitude and playful smile. I thought you had it all till you confessed about your childhood."

She paused. "But that made me like you even more. That you were able to overcome adversity and do so much good, over the years. The romantic side of me fell for you. But I have to be honest, I want children, I want a husband and I want a family."

Her hand fisted and lightly beat against her heart. "It may seem old-fashioned but it's what I want. And I thought you might be the one. And it may seem silly that I'm twenty-nine and hoping to be swept off my feet by the right guy, but I am."

He kissed her nose, then gathered her in his arms as he reflected on her confession. He should've seen it, he was street smart and knew someone like him was not the right man for her. He had a shady past and an inability to see himself as worthy of being a husband and a father. It was why he preferred to help teens out. He could be there for them but not be emotionally involved.

"Sweetheart, there's nothing wrong with wanting those things. To be honest, I wish my mother had wanted to be there for me. It's a child's dream to have parents who love and want them."

Looking up at him, he saw hurt and confusion in her eyes.

He continued. "I had a rotten childhood and was not a good boy. I stole, I cheated, I lied."

She clutched his arm. "But you've overcome that and become an honourable man."

"No," he said defiantly. "I don't know how to love. I'm incapable of it."

"That's just what you've been told," she said with a toss of her hair. "Look at what you did in there." She pointed to the hotel reception area.

He snorted. "That's not love. That's me understanding the pull of hormones and recklessness of youth." He blew out a long breath. "I just think it's better that I spend time helping kids I can't mess up. There are plenty of babies being born every year. A couple less won't make a difference." He paused to look at her. "Does it matter to you?"

She sagged into his arms and held on to his waist. "I have a condition that means that I need medical assistance to have children. I just wanted to find the right man and start the process. I'm not getting any younger and I just want the best chance of having a child. Is that so bad?"

"It's not. It's honest and I thank you for sharing it with me, I'm sure it wasn't easy," he said in a low voice.

"No, it's not. It's actually embarrassing." She shuffled backwards, away from him.

He could see she was retreating from him, both physically and emotionally. And he understood. At this age, many women wanted to find a husband and settle down. "I'm sorry I'm not the man for you," he said honestly.

"It's a shame, because I really like you," she said.

"I really like you," he said with honesty. She was the first woman he could see himself having a long-term relationship with.

"I need to go." She gave him a pained look that made his heart ache in response. "Let me think about our trip and I'll call you tomorrow. Bye." She gave him a look of sorrow, before she turned around and headed to the warmth of her family, away from him. He remained where he was and where he belonged. On the outside.

* * *

THE FOLLOWING MORNING, Lucie collected Tom from the YMCA, having borrowed her brother's car for the drive north.

He handed her a coffee in a take-away cup before throwing his bag in the trunk and getting into the front passenger seat. Looking at her, he said, "I'm surprised you called me this morning."

"Thanks for the coffee." She took a grateful sip, before swinging the car out into the chaotic Friday traffic.

She drove, not speaking, till they reached a red light and the car stopped. "I didn't sleep much and thought about our conversation. The problem is with me, not you. I have high expectations for myself and knowing I need IVF to be a mother has made me look at my relationships in a different way." She paused. "Plus I'm too honest, which scared my ex-boyfriend."

The traffic lights turned green and she started to drive, her focus on the road.

"Is that why you and your ex broke up?" He liked that she'd been so truthful with him and he knew where he stood with her. Not all women were like that. It made him like her even more.

She nodded. "He didn't like the pressure. At this stage in our lives, I thought being honest and upfront was best."

"You did the right thing telling him. It's his problem if he can't accept it," he said.

"You can't accept it either," she said in a low voice.

"But I've also been honest with you, too. Besides, I like being in your company. You're one of the smartest and most interesting women I've met. I'm surprised no one has snapped you up." He paused. "Why did you call me this morning?"

"I'm not sure. I barely slept last night and I blame myself for being so confrontational. You're here on holidays and I'm putting pressure on you, which was unfair." She gave him a weak smile before returning her focus to the road. A long stretch came up and he noticed she relaxed into the seat as the city melted and they made their way up north.

"You're here for Kiara, and for Grace. After I reminded myself of that, I knew the right thing was for us to remain as friends and for me to take you to Capernaum."

"You're very brave and I admire your spirit," he said, looking at her profile. Despite everything, he was delighted to spend time with her. Even knowing that she was looking for a husband to make her a mother didn't worry him as much as he expected.

He noticed a faint blush highlight her cheeks and bit his lips to keep from smiling.

"How long is the drive?" he asked, looking at the road.

"Around two hours."

"You look tired," he said, resisting the urge to trail his fingers down the side of her face.

"I'm fine. I'm still bubbling inside with the excitement of the wedding," she confessed. "I still can't believe my brother is married."

"Isn't your family going to miss you?" he asked, genuinely surprised that she was with him instead of them. "I'm surprised they didn't want you to stay in Jerusalem."

"I know how to talk to my parents and how to manage them," she said with a sneaky look at him. "Besides we're only away for two nights, and back on Sunday." She threw her hands up in the air before settling them on the steering wheel.

Deciding it was a good idea to change the subject, he said, "I read up on the city and area and the history sounds so interesting."

"It is. You'll love it."

The rest of the trip passed amicably as they drove north and Tom was surprised to see snow. "I didn't realise how cold it is, I always assumed it was hot here."

"It's very hot here in summer, but the winter can be cold and bitter. In the south and Tel Aviv, it's milder." She paused. "You would've noticed when you were there."

"I did. It was sunny but cool. I went swimming in the sea, the locals laughed at me. But I'm used to cold water."

She smiled and her face lit up in reply to his audaciousness. He loved that she wore her emotions and didn't hide behind them, unlike many women he'd previously dated. It was refreshing to be with someone so open and straightforward.

He admired the beautiful scenery through the window and she expertly managed the roads and pointed out areas of significance to him.

The rest of the day passed in a blur of visiting historical sites with Lucie explaining it all to him.

In the early evening, he could see the tiredness in her eyes and lines of strain marred her pretty mouth. She didn't argue when he suggested a quick meal and an early to bed. After yet another delicious meal of grilled chicken, pita and dips, he bade her good night.

They were staying in a budget hotel, run by friendly staff, and after she retired, he was reluctant to sit in his room. Restlessness made him walk around the cool night. On impulse, he rang Grace and was happy when she answered the phone.

"You sound tired," he said, concerned at her less than vivacious chatter.

"Tom, it's three in the morning," a sleepy voice replied.

His heart shot to his throat. "I'm so sorry. I totally forgot about the time difference. I'll call you back."

"Don't worry," she reassured him. "You've woken me up, so tell me everything."

He told Grace all about the wedding, and how beautiful Kiara looked, avoiding too much detail about Lucie.

"How's your treatment going?" He'd helped her financially to get the best treatment, and was determined that he would not lose her. They may not be related by blood, but he loved her like a sister and would do anything for her.

"The good news is that it seems the cancer hasn't spread," she announced. "They've removed it, with part of my breast. I'll need reconstruction at a later stage but it looks like I won't have to endure chemo."

He whooped for joy and brushed away tears of relief. His

baby sister was going to make it. "I'm so relieved. Thanks for making my night."

"I have more news," she said in a way that made him stop and pay attention.

"Tell me," he said as a spike of concern hit him in the plexus. Was she okay?

"I met someone special. He's a radiation therapist. He's amazing and I'm totally in love. I sound like a teenager but I'm already thinking about us getting married and," she paused, "I can see us having a family one day."

He heard her expel a long breath.

"If I can have children," she clarified in a tight voice.

His heart ached, knowing what she'd been through and the impacts of radiation therapy and cancer treatment may have had on her body. "There are options."

"I know." She cleared her throat. "Matteo is amazing and I see him as my life partner. We'll be able to deal with this together."

Shock radiated through him, making him stop and process what she'd just said. "Th-that's sudden," was all he managed to say.

Whether it was early morning or that Grace didn't care, she chatted on. "I can't wait for you to meet Matteo."

His mouth was as dry as the desert sands and his tongue seemed to have tripled in size, making it hard for him to talk. "Tell me more."

She chatted about how they met at the hospital, how handsome he was, and how wonderful he made her feel. "He's even met mum and dad," she admitted with a canny tone.

Surprise hit him with the force of a tidal wave. "You've introduced him to Bruce and Betty? Already?" He sucked in a sharp breath. "I've only been gone a week."

There was a pause. "I-um, ah, met Matteo before you left."

"You didn't tell me." His voice was accusatory, even though he didn't mean it to be. Why hadn't she told him about her boyfriend?

"It all happened so fast." Her words tumbled out. "I was going to tell you. Don't get all big brother on me. Mum and Dad love him, and they think we're a perfect match."

His chest ached as though he'd been punched. "In a week, you've gone through cancer treatment and met the love of your life?"

"Well, yes," she said. "Aren't you happy for me? It's like your prayers for me came true."

He ran his fingers through his hair. He'd come to Israel and prayed for her to be healthy, and she was. The treatment had been successful, so far. Why couldn't he be happy for her? It was ridiculous. He should be thrilled that she'd also found love. So why wasn't he punching the air in excitement. He felt like punching himself for being so mean.

"I am happy for you," he said forcing joy into his voice. "You deserve it."

"I know. For years, I didn't think I'd ever find love. But I look at Mum and Dad, and everything they did. And after I found my faith, I prayed I would find someone special." Her voice was filled with happiness and excitement. "Once I'm better I'm going to do some charity work, support other women with breast cancer."

"You have everything planned out." It was a statement not a question, and he said it warmly and with conviction.

"Yes, I've found my way. After all these years of being alone, I've found a man who loves me despite my unhappy past and questionable decisions. He's looked beyond that and sees the *me* that you see."

"You're very lucky to have found someone special like that." He chuckled. "Does he know you have an older brother who's overprotective of you?"

She gave him a shriek of laughter. "He's Italian and comes from a large family. He's got younger sisters, so you and he will get on fine." She paused. "I thought I was going to be overwhelmed by his family, but they have been so welcoming and I can't wait to spend Christmas with them. It sounds silly, but I really feel like all my Christmases have come together now. I've never been so happy," she gushed.

His heart softened with gratitude and appreciation. "If Mum and Dad like him, then I'm sure I will too. You deserve happiness."

"Thanks, you're the best brother and friend I ever had. Just because I'm with Matteo now doesn't mean I won't see you. You'll be invited to spend time here with us. You're my family," she said with sincerity.

But things were going to change. Grace had found someone special and he'd been invited, but he'd be the *outsider* again. Invited because it was the polite thing to do.

But this was the path he'd chosen for himself. This was what he wanted. Right?

Grace yawned and he apologised again for waking her. This time she didn't insist on talking, and blew him a kiss over the phone before disconnecting the call.

He was happy that Grace had found love and her treatment had been successful. He'd still visit the biblical sites tomorrow with Lucie, and make further prayers that Grace would remain cancer free and be able to have children.

Lucie. Her name made him breathless and for a moment, the impact of her candid words at the wedding, whizzed past him. Like Grace, she had issues that would impact her ability to be a mother. And now it didn't seem so confrontational that she'd been honest. Even though they had only known each other just under one week. A sense of understanding settled on his shoulders and he walked around the ancient town, watching as his warm breath puffed into the cold air.

When his feet grew cold and his body felt weary from the long days of walking, he headed back to the small hotel they were staying at. It didn't take long before he'd showered and collapsed in bed, deep in sleep.

* * *

THE FOLLOWING MORNING, they met in the lobby as planned. "*Boker tov*, good morning," she greeted him with a warm smile. "Did you sleep well?"

"I did. Thanks," he said. Being honest with himself, he'd been up early this morning thinking about Lucie and Grace. Two different women in their backgrounds and personalities, but they were linked through him and by their strong determination to achieve what they wanted in life.

"It's the Jewish Sabbath today so many places will be closed, however, I've made reservations for us to have lunch at a local fish restaurant. It's for tourists but the food is excellent and the views are stunning. You'll love it."

They drove to a small bakery and each enjoyed a pastry and coffee for breakfast.

"I have to confess, I really like the flavours of the Israeli foods."

Lucie chuckled. "It's a blend of so many cultures. Israelis have come from all over the Middle East and Europe, and they each bring their own distinct spices and seasonings to their cooking."

He patted his flat belly. "I know there are some differences, but I've enjoyed everything."

She looped her arm through his. "Ready to play tourist?"

"Sure," he said, as they made their way to the car.

Over the next few hours they drove around the Sea of Galilee, where Lucie spun the story of Jesus and his ministry work in to the sites they visited. At ancient archaeological remnants she brought his teachings to life against a backdrop of magnificent scenery.

Despite rarely going to church or having much faith, he was captivated by the incredible desert scenery, and the stories she told.

Even he knew about the miracles of the fishes and loaves, but to be there and to see where it happened, made goose bumps run up and down his arm. For the first time, he understood why Grace had found faith and attended Church on a regular basis.

He forgot to make the prayers he said he would, as he walked around the beautiful remains of a fourth-century synagogue.

"We believe this is where Jesus preached and gathered his first disciples," Lucie said, as they walked around.

But he barely heard, totally captivated by the ancient ruins and the beauty of them.

"Tom?" she gave him a gentle nudge.

"Huh?" he turned to look at her.

"Time to eat," she looked at her watch. "I booked a late lunch, but we should go now. We can see more after," she added.

At the restaurant, he gazed at the blue lake while leaning back in his seat. The place was definitely geared towards tourists, but he understood why. The view from the large windows was incredible and if the food tasted as good as it smelt, he knew he'd need another long walk this afternoon.

"You can either have the whole baked fish or fillets," she said. "Depends on how hungry you are." She added with a grin.

He'd seen the portion size and went with the larger one, determined to try the whole baked fish, and he was able to enjoy a variety of salads from the salad bar.

After ordering their meals, they sat across from each

other and instead of gazing at the view, he looked at Lucie. With her hair bundled in a ponytail and her face scrubbed of makeup, she looked so much younger. The exertion of their walking and sightseeing for the day had resulted in her skin looking healthy and pink.

"Thank you for bringing me here. As beautiful as Jerusalem is, I have enjoyed our time here and would like to stay another day. Do you think your parents would mind? Otherwise, perhaps you could travel home and I'll get a bus back tomorrow or Monday. There's something about the lake, and the surrounding beauty that's drawing me to it."

"You love the water and surfing. You didn't have that in Jerusalem, perhaps that's why?" she suggested with a smile.

"Perhaps?" He nodded slowly.

"I don't want to cause friction between you and your family, so I'll understand if you want to drive back after lunch."

"I can't just leave you here," she said, her forehead creasing with surprise.

"Of course you can. Just show me where to get the bus and I'll work it out," he said with sincerity. "Everything I've seen so far has been incredible but I did it for Grace. I want to hike and also try out the thermal springs. That's for me to do, nothing to do with her."

The waiter arrived at that moment to place their plates of fish in front of them, before reminding them about the self-serve salad bar.

When he left, Tom said, "This looks delicious. Thanks for bringing me here."

"*Bevakasha*, you're welcome," she said before placing a hand over her heart. "It's been wonderful showing you my country. Let me speak to my parents after lunch."

"Of course." Cutting a small piece of fish, using his cutlery, he savoured every mouthful. What was it about this country that had him enjoying the rich flavours of his meals? Back in Australia, he just ate, but here he really allowed his tastebuds to relish his meals.

Over cardamom spiced coffee and a plate of fresh dates, his belly full, he leaned back in his chair. "Last night after you went to bed, I spoke to Grace"

"How is she? How's her treatment?" she interrupted, sitting straight, her gaze focused on him.

"Going well. They've removed the cancer and it doesn't seem to have spread. She's still got a long way to go but it's looking positive," he said before expelling a long breath of gratitude.

"Thank God," she said clasping her hands together in a prayer position. "That's good news."

He leaned across, knowing it was forward and took her hand in his. Ignoring her gasp of surprise, he used his thumb to draw gentle circles over the pulse point on her wrist. "I, um, she has a boyfriend, someone serious. I thought she was like me, avoiding a family because of the past but she's embracing it, already diarising when she will be cancer free and able to try for children."

He paused, his heart hammering hard against his ribs as he confessed what had been playing on his mind all day.

"I know it's only been a few days, but I'm thirty and know an amazing woman when I meet one. I don't want to let you go. You're smart and beautiful, and you're the first woman to make me question my decisions about fatherhood."

He watched her eyes widen to the size of saucers and her mouth open.

"Let me finish. This isn't easy for me to say." He raised his hand in the air like a traffic policeman. "Unlike you, I didn't grow up in a warm family, surrounded by cousins, aunts, uncles and family friends. If I hadn't been sent to the farm, I would've ended up in jail, on drugs or both." He straightened his shoulders and inhaled deeply through his nose before exhaling through his mouth, as he found the confidence to continue. "I'm jealous of what you have and would love to have a family like yours, but I don't know how to be a good father or husband."

She grasped his hand, holding him tight. "I can help you."

"I know," he said feeling his muscles tighten in response to what he was about to say. "But I don't know if I will ever change my mind about children. I know it's important to you, but I don't want to disappoint you."

"You're not. You've been incredibly honest," she said, her cheeks flushed pink. "I want to be with you. I don't want to hurt or upset my family but I want to be here, with you." She stood, leaned across the table and brushed her lips against his. "I've never met a man who makes me so happy. I know it's only been a few days but my heart is filled with joy and, like you, I'm old enough to recognise this special bond," she pointed from herself to him, "between us."

He took her hand, and lifted it to his mouth, kissing each knuckle. "I'm the luckiest guy, to have met you." His heart tingled with warmth and for the first time he understood the expression having a *full heart* because this was what he was feeling for the first time. He couldn't stop grinning and lifted the tiny cup to sip the strong coffee in an attempt to hide his eagerness behind it.

After settling the check, he took her hand and led her to the private beach next to the restaurant. Walking hand in hand, Tom had to restrain himself from punching the air and running up and down beating his chest. He was here with a woman he admired, liked, wanted to be with. Was this love? He wasn't sure but if someone told him it was, he would believe it.

"Thank you for your trust. I'm sorry that I'm not the exact man you wanted, but I promise to always respect and honour you." He stopped walking so he could hold her tight. "I've never felt like this before, it's very new for me. I need a bit of help," he confessed in a low voice.

Her hands reached up to clasp his neck. "I'm here for you. We can do this together."

* * *

TWO HOURS LATER, they settled into their private wood cabin at a hotel that offered spa facilities. Walking onto the deck, Tom looked around at the magical tropical view, the palm trees, lush vegetation and the sounds of running water in streams. Tranquillity and peace settled on his shoulders.

Lucie came out and put her arms around his waist. "It's cold and you're outside."

He spun her around to kiss her forehead. "It's colder in Melbourne in winter. I'd go swimming in the outside pools." He pointed in the direction that they were.

"Well, we'll be in the inside ones, thank you," she said. "You can always have a spa out here," she pointed to the jacuzzi. "They run water from the thermo-mineral springs into it."

"Sounds perfect. Any place to see you half naked will be my pleasure." He waggled his eyebrows playfully.

She gave him a playful punch to his arm. "Ready?"

"Of course," he said, wearing the newly acquired swimmers he'd bought at the boutique shop.

In the internal pools there were plenty of others enjoying the mineral-rich waters. He'd been tempted to book a private pool for them but didn't want to make Lucie feel pressured. The suite he'd booked had two bedrooms and he'd leave it up to her where she wanted to sleep tonight.

They spent time in the warm waters chatting with the

other guests, while holding hands under the water, away from curious eyes.

Drawing her aside, he said, "I'm embarrassed to say this, but I feel like both my physical and emotional side have been nourished."

"It's not silly. You've discovered prayer and how wonderful it can be to be spiritually aware. And well"—she nodded towards the pools—"this place is amazing, I feel totally pampered. How could you not feel amazing in an amazing place like this." She paused. "I have to confess, I've never been here before."

"Really?" His eyebrow lifted. "And you're a tour guide," he mocked her with a playful tone. "Did you want to have a treatment like a massage or something?"

She pushed herself closer to him so he could feel her skin despite the whoosh of water between them. "Only if you're doing the massage." Her low, sexy tone made him swallow his tongue.

Despite the family friendly atmosphere, and the inappropriateness of him admiring her curves in the black bikini she wore, he whispered, "It will be my pleasure." He ran his hand, along her thigh, then up along to caress her bottom. "I can't believe how lucky I am to have met you. I don't want you to feel pressured but..."

She turned to face him, brushing her lips against his. "I want to be with you." She paused. "All night," she added in a low voice.

His limbs tingled with delight and expectation, knowing he'd soon be able to pleasure her and show her with his fingers and lips how much she meant to him. He may not be able to say the words—it was too soon for him. He was carrying too much hurt and angst from the past, but he'd show her. Show her that he was willing to make compromises for her, because she was worth it to him.

CHAPTER 6

*L*ucie woke the following morning, fluttering her eyelashes open while taking a moment to recognise where she was. Naked and in Tom's bed. Turning over, she was surprised to see it was empty, only an indentation on his side to remind her of the amazing night they'd spent together.

Their lovemaking had been incredible and she was totally smitten with Tom. What they'd shared last night had been very special, and she felt totally loved as they'd expressed themselves using their lips and fingertips rather than words.

Any doubt of him being the man for her was obliterated. Not only kind and generous, he was loving and patient. Now that she'd found someone extraordinary and unique, they had all the practicalities of them living in different countries and visas to sort out.

"Tom," she called out, surprised he wasn't still in bed with her. Grabbing a hotel-provided robe, she slipped it on to walk around the suite and discovered she was alone. Not only alone but he'd also removed every trace of himself from her. The wet towel in the bath tub told her he'd had a shower but his toiletries and clothes were missing.

Slumping in the chair, she felt her heart race with anxiety. Surely there was a good reason why he'd left but she couldn't think of one. Grabbing her cell phone, she sent him a message but there was no reply.

Looking out the window, she noticed their car was missing. Where was Tom? He wouldn't have left her here, would he?

An hour later and Lucie's belly was hollow inside. After a check with reception, there were no messages for her, and Tom was still missing. Had something happened or had she scared him off?

She knew commitment was not easy for him, and he was trying. Had it become all too difficult and he'd left. Had the pressure of her maternal instincts and making love scared him off?

Had he needed to get away?

She swatted away a niggle of shame that he'd said the right words just to get her into bed. No. She knew he wasn't like that. He was honourable.

Where was he? And why was everything missing?

After showering and changing into jeans and a warm shirt, she messaged him again. No answer. Now her stress levels were at an all-time high. The glow of their night together had disappeared and she scrolled through the Internet, seeing if there were any major delays or accidents on the road. There were none.

Closing her eyes, she said a short prayer. If he returned to her, she'd find a way for them to be together.

Thinking about her grandparents and how they'd raised other people's children after the war, she considered her own determination to have a biological child. Her grandparents had loved and nurtured children who were not biologically theirs but had loved them as much as their own. Could she do the same? With Tom's love and support, could she take the brave step of being a mother to teens and loving them? Guiding them? Giving them hope?

When the thought didn't scare or worry her, she knew that with Tom by her side, they could be amazing parents. As much as she wanted her own child, she didn't want to be a single parent. After an incredible night with Tom, she knew he was her love, the other half of her.

An hour later, in a rush and fluster, Tom walked into their cabin and she jumped into his arms, grateful for his return.

"Where have you been? I've been so worried," she cried out, pressing kisses to his face.

"I'm so sorry," he said, his face filled with stress and angst. "I went out to surprise you with a coffee and pastry, got lost and ended up in Tsfat."

"What?" Tsfat was more than a thirty-minute drive away.

"I'm not used to the left hand drive, and made a couple of wrong turns and couldn't get off the highway." Embarrassment made his cheeks flush.

She could see the worry and strain around his jaw and knew this wasn't a story he'd made up.

"I thought you'd left me," she said in a quiet voice.

Gathering her in his arms, he said, "Never. And after last night, how could you think I'd ever leave you." He pressed kisses along her forehead and jawline before kissing her mouth with an intensity that made her breathless.

"I tried to find the bakery from yesterday, and I got lost. You don't have GPS in the car. I used my phone but somehow I ended up going the wrong way." He ran his fingers through his hair. "I'm driving on the opposite side of the road which was confusing plus there are no breakdown lanes on the highway, so I couldn't pull over and call you. I was going to text you in Tsfat but then my phone died. I forgot to charge my mobile last night." He paused. "I was a little preoccupied with you," he said in a low husky voice that made her toes curl.

"I'm glad you're back," she confessed, holding him tight.

"I barely slept last night. While you slept, I packed my bag, got ready for our hike, and then went outside to watch the sunrise."

The stress of his disappearance and subsequent return made her cry. "Sorry, I've been agitated all morning, concerned about you."

"I didn't mean to worry you," he said, leading her to the couch. "I was so frustrated with being lost. But I'm here now."

They sat opposite each other. Lifting her hand to press a kiss on her wrist, he said. "It will soon be Christmas and I want to spend every minute with you, and also your family. You are a jewel and I'm so lucky to have you. I know it's soon but I want to be with you, spend time with you. You're the woman for me. I apologise if I'm being too forward but…"

Throwing her arms around him, she cried, "I'm crazy for you. I want to be with you always. And I'm so lucky to have you in my life."

They held on to each other for a few minutes. "I'm going to extend my stay so we can work things out between the two of us."

Her heart lifted. "Really? I'm so happy."

"We belong together, but I need to ask you, we have issues between us. Is our love enough?" His voice was low but filled with nervousness and apprehensive honesty.

"You haven't told me you love me yet," she said, trailing her fingers down the side of his face.

"You haven't told me either," he replied with a grin. "But if you didn't know after last night…"

"I love you," she said, throwing her arms around him. "I waited years and can't believe I've found you when I least expected it."

"From the moment I saw you at your parents' place, I knew you were special. I can't believe how lucky I am to have found you. You've accepted me with all my faults and rotten background." He lifted her hand and pressed a kiss to the pulse point on her wrist.

"But you're not that teen anymore. You've become a loving son and brother. You mentor young men, making a difference to the world."

"But will you be happy with a man like me?" he asked with genuine concern.

"How can you ask that?" she asked with surprise. "You are generous and kind. Your past doesn't define you. Look at who you are."

"You see the good in me, that I don't always see," he confessed, before brushing his lips against hers.

He lifted her so she sat on his lap, his arms around her. "I have a proposal for you."

She snuggled against the warmth and strength of his chest. "Tell me."

"I'll move here because I'm not taking you away from your family, but I can't live in Jerusalem. I'm sorry. I need to be able to surf. Will you live with me in Tel Aviv?" He paused. "You can write and not be a tour guide, but I will need your help for me to work here. But I will support your writing career."

He drew in a long breath. "I would like to continue looking after teens and helping them like I did in Melbourne. But we do it together. It's who I am. I can't just be a husband to you. Is that okay? I'll be taking you away from your family and your career."

With her arms around his neck, she breathed in the lemony scent of his aftershave. They'd both be making changes for each other. Could she do it? "I'm scared," she said in a low voice.

"Me too," he replied, nuzzling her neck. "Can we be scared together and work things through? If it's too much, we can relocate but I need to swim and surf each day. You know that it's the only way for me to stay calm and focused, especially when dealing with the teens."

"You're leaving Australia to be with me. I think I can live an hour's drive from my family," she said pressing kisses along his jaw.

"And what about children?" He looked at her and she could see real pain in his eyes. "I don't want you to think that I will magically change my mind because we're together," he said.

" I know. It's something I've always wanted, but while I was waiting for you this morning, I realised that I wanted you more. I don't want to be a single mother. I want you, and to be with you always. I know you'll make me happy, and perhaps, we'll adopt or we can raise these boys together."

He crushed her to him. "I don't deserve you."

She held him close and could feel the anguish of emotions he was battling. "We'll do it together."

"This is going to be the happiest Christmas ever. My first with you, surrounded by family," he said with sincerity. "I can't wait to spend my life with you. The next year will be hard, I have to relocate. . ."

"I trust you," she said.

"I love you, more than I ever thought was possible. I'm going to make you happy and be your biggest fan." He kissed her again.

She trailed her fingers down his face, her heart bursting with love. "I believe the magic of Christmas has brought us together, from different sides of the globe."

"And that magic will keep us together, forever," he said before kissing her again.

EPILOGUE

One year later.

Tom snaked his arms around his wife, kissing her neck. "Happy Christmas, my beautiful," he said.

"Happy Christmas, darling," Lucie said, turning around to kiss his mouth. She'd just finished decorating their home with tinsel.

"Thank you for finishing off the decorations," he said, looking around the room at the festive trimmings and ornaments.

"We got a little distracted when we were supposed to be decorating together," she lifted her eyebrow in a knowing way.

"What can I say? You were leaning over and I couldn't help but admire your bottom." Even a year later, he was still wildly attracted to Lucie. Every time they made love, he realised how lucky he was to have found her.

"How was your swim?" she asked, pointing to his still damp hair.

"Perfect," he replied. "I'm feeling great."

"I can't believe you're swimming when it's so cold," she shivered. "It's winter."

"It's not that cold," he said before placing his cool hands on her lower back.

She shrieked in surprise.

"When do we have to leave?" He nuzzled her neck, giving the smooth skin a tiny nip with his teeth.

They were due to visit her parents to spend Christmas with them. "We've got plenty of time," she said, placing her arms around his neck and kissing his mouth.

"Can we stay here instead?" He lifted her, before carrying her towards the bedroom in their small apartment.

"No." She pretended to reprimand him. The family affair was something they could not miss. "Stop, what's that?" She wiggled out of his arms, after seeing the present he'd just bought.

"It's a gift for you," he said with a frankness that didn't match the twinkle in his eye. "What does it look like?"

She ignored his silliness. "Can I open it now?"

"No, you can open it on Christmas Day," he said using a stern voice. "It's to go under the tree."

Ignoring him, she raced to the bench and tore open the wrapping. "I thought we said no presents."

"You said no presents. I didn't agree," he said. "Besides, now that you're going to be a famous author, I'm looking forward to being a *kept man*."

She grinned. "Apart from our wedding day, being accepted to write for my favourite romance publisher was a dream come true."

"You're sure, you don't want to move back to Jerusalem and do tours? You're very good at it," he added with a caress of her bottom.

"Forget it." She playfully punched his arm. "I love supporting your business and being able to write."

"You're the best marketer, getting me jobs so I'm busy all day. Is that so I'm not here and you can write?"

"Of course." She grinned at him. "Now let me finish opening my present."

Tearing off the paper, she opened her mouth, no words coming out as she looked at the box.

"Do you like it?" His voice sounded anxious as though he wasn't sure if he'd made the right decision to buy it for her.

"I don't know what to say," she said, her eyes filled with tears.

"Darling," he gathered her in his arms. "You've made me so happy. I bought the pregnancy kit to tell you that I'm prepared to support you in us having a child together. I've let go of the anger and disappointment of my past, all thanks to you. You're absolutely precious to me and I just want to make you happy."

"You do," she said, dabbing her eyes with a tissue. "I just never expected this."

"There is a caveat with the gift," he said with a serious tone, moving her to the couch. "I uprooted myself from my small family in Australia, and left behind the boys I was looking out for. We start IVF, but if it becomes too hard or it places too much pressure on our marriage, we're stopping. I've read so many stories of the stresses that can kill a relationship. I didn't move to Israel to lose you. If you agree to my conditions, then I will do everything I can to help you with your secret wish.

"We made sacrifices for each other, and I know you never expected this. I'm doing it because I love you. I want to make you happy. But I don't want the stress of hormones and medical appointments to destroy what we have. Can you promise me that?"

She flung her arms around him, holding him close. "I promise, a million times I promise. I love you more than anything. I would love for us to have a child, but I don't want to lose you."

"You won't. We're in this together, my talented, beautiful wife." He kissed her nose before his hands cupped her bottom and he shifted her so that she sat astride him. "And now, I want to make love and show you how much I love you."

"We've got plenty of time before the family Christmas gathering," she said, unbuttoning his shirt.

"Christmas with your family may just have to wait. As much as I love them, I love you more." He whipped off her T-shirt, throwing it to the floor. "Happy Christmas, my darling. I love you more and more each day. You've made me the happiest man." He kissed her mouth before pressing kisses along her bare shoulder.

"I love you, so much," she said running her fingers up and down the contours of his chest. "And now, I want to show you how much," she said before kissing his reply away.

THE END

CHRISTMAS KISS, NEW YEAR'S WISH

"*Bad enough to be caught kissing your best friend, but to be caught by your sister who would have no compunction about keeping it a secret was truly unfair.*"

TAYLOR WILLIAMSON MAY HAVE a massive crush on her best friend, Luca Bianchi, but their twenty-year friendship is too important to lose over one kiss, make that two kisses, on Christmas.

Luca only sees her as a friend, and he's about to return overseas for a two-year contract, so no more kissing. Right?

Taylor may wish for their Christmas kiss to lead to more. But how can she hold on to him when he was never hers to begin with?

To my 10K Angel gals – thanks for the support, advice and friendship xxx

CHAPTER 1

"*Y*ou two should be kissing not talking," Danny said, clapping his hand on Luca's shoulder, poking his face between the two friends dancing. Danny was a friend of both of their families, having known them since they'd both been babies. "If I was younger and not happily married, I'd be kissing Taylor, not just dancing with her." He waggled his eyebrows at the friends. "Just saying," he said before melting back into the crowd of dancers, leaving them alone.

Taylor Williamson squirmed in her Mary Jane heels whilst her best friend, Luca Bianchi's lips twitched with amusement.

"It's really not funny, and it's getting tiresome," she said.

"Our families have accepted us, but it seems *their* friends can't get used to the idea of a man and a woman being friends." He lifted his brow and gave her one of his bone-melting grins. "Don't worry about it."

Taylor wouldn't have worried about it if she didn't have a crush the size of a small planet on Luca. With his dark brown eyes, high cheek bones and chiselled chin, he was the quintessential handsome Italian bloke that women fell for. Including her. Except, he was an unassuming, intelligent quiet self-confessed geek like her. They were the same except for the intelligent part.

Luca was smart, really smart, and she often felt stupid when he expounded his excitement over electrochemistry.

"I bet your parents are happy to have you home for the next two weeks?" she said with a smile.

"I think I'll stay at a hotel," he drawled with a roll of his eyes.

"Your parents will kill you, and then me. They'll blame me for your bad behaviour," she said with a sigh.

"I could always stay with you," he whispered in her ear.

"Oh, the scandal," she said with a dramatic voice. "Our parents would have us married off in a heartbeat." Her heart quickened at the thought. As much as she loved Luca as a friend, she needed to keep those self-imposed boundaries between them because if she didn't, she'd toss her good-girl principles to the side and kiss him. Really kiss him. Like a lover, not a brother.

The music from a by-gone era played in the Bergman's living room, and they continued to dance. Not only was he hot, but he was an excellent dancer. Could the guy be any more perfect? Nope.

He held her close, moving her around the carpeted living room under strings of festive, fetching, fairy lights.

His breath warmed her cheek. "I can't remember the last time we danced together at the annual Clarendon Close family Christmas gathering?"

"That's because for the first time, you didn't bring a date with you," she replied.

"Ouch." He pretended to look upset.

"None of who liked the intrusion of your *female* friend," she added. Taylor's heart twisted with hurt as she remembered the past few Christmas catch-ups where she'd been on her own and Luca's dates had made it known that they didn't see her as a threat. Because she wasn't pretty enough, slim enough, sexy enough. Since high school, Taylor had known she wasn't "enough" when it came to Luca.

Luca dated gorgeous, slim women, not ones who looked like her. It wasn't that she was fat, but it seemed that Luca didn't fancy his dates with generous curves and large breasts. He preferred stick-slim women, like her sister. It had been years since they'd dated and despite Jenna saying she found Luca boring, Taylor had still not recovered from the betrayal of her friend dating her sister.

Lost in her thoughts, she didn't realise that he was talking to her.

"Taylor?" He gave her a nudge.

"S-s-orry, what did you say?" Her cheeks warmed at having being caught day dreaming about him, yet again.

"I wanted to know how your shop was coming along?"

"Thanks for asking. Even with the lead-up to Christmas, I'm still running at a loss. But only a small one," she added. She loved what she did.

"I'm proud of you," he said. "*To follow your dream*."

She gave him a playful punch, chuckling that he would use an Elvis Presley movie title to congratulate her. Typical Luca. "Of course, you'd find a way to link Elvis to my vintage clothes shop." She rolled her eyes. "*Follow Your Dream*, one of his earlier movies?"

He pulled her closer to him and asked, "What year did the movie come out?"

"I have no idea but I'm sure you do," she said with a grin.

"1962," he whispered.

The light breath against her ear made tiny goose bumps scatter along her arms, and she wanted to groan because of it. How come the guy who had the biggest affect on her could never be hers? Life was unfair.

He twirled her around, and her classic 50s style swing dancing petticoat and skirt swished around her calves.

They continued dancing and he held her close.

"Your super brain is starting to bug me." She pretended to be annoyed. "Perhaps everyone here would love to know about your fascination with Elvis." She paused for dramatic affect. "Or should I say, your obsession."

His eyes darkened. "You wouldn't dare," he said in a low, faux-menacing voice.

She bit her lip, trying not to laugh. Who would believe Luca, with his seriously hot looks and NASA-worthy intelligence, would be so worried about everyone knowing his love of Elvis Presley's music?

Unlike him, she was out and proud of her love of all things vintage. Whereas he hid behind a wall of secrecy. She never understood his reluctance to share and had often poked fun at him, when they were alone.

"I don't think anyone would mind," she said. "Elvis is awesome. Why are you so worried what others think?"

"You're treading on dangerous ground, Taylor, and you know it," he said with a playful tone, but his dark eyes conveyed the depths of his true feelings. He was embarrassed about his obsession with music from a by-gone era. Obviously, it didn't fit with his professional image.

"Fine," she said. "But if you ever want to dress up in leather..." Her skin warmed at the accidental suggestion. "I meant, if you ever dress up like him, I'd love to see it."

"There's more chance of you selling your shop to your assistant than me doing that," he said in a low voice.

"In other words, it's never gonna happen." She gave him a grin.

The song ended and their host, Sue Bergman, announced that they were serving dinner.

"Thanks for the dance," Taylor said before doing a twirl. "I'm so happy to have you here." And she was. Despite her long-time crush on her best friend, she just adored him and had missed spending time with him whilst he'd been living in the USA, working for NASA. "You've been gone two years already," she said. "I've missed you."

He lifted her hand and kissed her knuckles. "I've missed you, too."

They walked to the dining room where a large buffet had been spread out with an array of foods, predominantly prepared by their hosts, Sue and Saul Bergman, and the families of Clarendon Close.

"I've missed these family get-togethers. I've got friends and work colleagues, but nothing like this," he pointed to the room full of families, who'd known each other for years.

It had all started years ago when all the children in the court, in suburban Melbourne, used to gravitate to the Bergman house on the evening of Christmas Day. Being the only Jewish family in the small group, they were happy to have all the children come over whilst the adults were recovering from Christmas eating and cleaning up. It became a tradition that if you wanted to have fun, you went to the Bergmans'. It started with games, movie nights and over the years, it grew bigger to an event that the parents wanted to be a part of.

The families who lived side by side, in the small court became a community and even when the children grew up and moved on with their lives, the parents still met on the evening of Christmas Day and on New Year's Eve.

Most of the time Taylor was there. She loved the vibrancy of the families, and catching up with her friends. And as much as she didn't want to admit it, it connected her to Luca.

They'd met as cheeky seven-year-old neighbours, who rode their bikes together, did homework together and became the closest of friends.

Taylor filled her plate with the delicious Moroccan chicken stew Sue had made and an array of salads, before they sat at a nearby table.

"How's work going?" she asked between mouthfuls of the delicious dinner.

"Good. Really good." He sipped his wine. "I've been offered a contract to stay on for another two years," he announced.

Her heart skipped with joy and then plummeted to the carpeted floor. It was a difficult balance of being happy for someone you cared about, but missing them as well. "Congrats, that's fantastic news, Luca. Your parents must be so proud of you," she said with sincerity.

"Having my work being bought by NASA has brought me financial gain, but as you know, I did it more for the prestige."

She punched his arm. "You scientists, always after fame. But if you don't earn money, you can't continue to do the amazing work you do."

He lifted his brow. "Exactly. Mum and Dad now understand my years of studying, even though they've begged me to get a 'real' job for years."

She placed her cutlery on her plate and looked at him. "You are so smart and so gifted. Of course you should continue to work on your dollpants."

"It's *dopants*, and I work on making their reactions more rapid." He paused and gave her a genuine smile. "But you're my biggest fan. Thank you." He raised his glass to her. "Thank you for believing in me, even when others didn't."

She felt herself blush. "You're welcome and you deserve every bit of success. You've worked hard."

They finished their dinner, drank a glass of champagne and even though they chatted with family friends, they stayed close.

In the living room, with the music being played on the jukebox, Taylor danced with Luca again. They laughed, they talked and drank more champagne till Taylor was a little tipsy. She didn't care. She hadn't had so much fun in ages, and she loved being with Luca. Despite him not seeing her as girlfriend-material, he was her friend and had been for over twenty years.

Girlfriends may come and go, but their friendship was rock solid.

"It's Mum and Dad's turn to host the New Year's Eve party this year. Tell me you'll be there," he said.

"Of course I'll be there," she said.

"Are you bringing a date?" he asked bluntly.

"No, are you?" she replied, holding her breath. She certainly hoped he wasn't. Having been so busy with her shop and work, she'd barely been out socially.

And knowing Luca was going to be back in Melbourne, she'd hedged her bets and hoped he was still single so she could spend time with him. . .as his friend. She *knew* he didn't see her as anything more. Besides, she'd rather have him in her life as a friend than not at all. It was why she'd never confessed her feelings for him. It would spoil their friendship.

The music swirled around them as they continued to dance, and it felt like minutes rather than seconds before Luca replied. "No."

His reply made her giddy with joy. "We can go together." It was a statement not a question, and her heart warmed at the tug of a smile at his lips.

"I would like that very much," he said, before giving her a twirl.

Luca was a great guy and she was glad to have him in her life. It didn't matter that they weren't romantically involved, she reminded herself yet again.

An hour later the music stopped so the families could enjoy dessert, and the friends walked outside in to the balmy, summer's eve. "I've missed this," he confessed as they strolled to the back garden.

Chairs had been set up but they were alone since everyone was clambering to fill up their plates with the amazing array of desserts offered.

"I've missed you," she confessed in a low voice. "I know we message each other all the time, but it's been fun having you here."

He nodded but didn't say anything. Leading her to a small table with two chairs, they sat. She took a moment to remove her heels and rub her sore feet.

"These shoes are comfortable but my feet are killing me after all that dancing," she confessed.

"You look lovely, as always," he said, his eyes travelling from the tips of her toes up along the red gingham material of her hourglass dress, to her lips, which were probably no longer coated in lipstick.

"Thank you," she said, continuing to massage the balls of her feet.

She looked up and caught him staring back at her. "Do I have something on my nose?" She felt the skin crinkle between her eyebrows.

"No," he said simply.

She sat up in her chair wondering if there was something wrong. "Are you okay?"

"I'm fine." He dismissed her concern with a flick of his wrist.

She caught his gaze, her eyes locking with his. Her breathing became rapid and it had nothing to do with dopants or the warm summer evening. He was looking at her, really looking at her and she felt her belly twist in knots.

He was not only handsome but seriously sexy, and tonight was no exception. Unlike most of the Australian men she knew, who'd wear shorts and T-shirts to an event. Luca, thanks to his strict Italian parents, wore tailored pants and a shirt. The shirt highlighted his broad shoulders and his slim hips. He knew how to dance, appreciated good food and had impeccable manners. But it wasn't just his charm, she adored him. He always made her feel special and important. He'd protected her at school when kids laughed at her early-development. With an hour-glass figure and generous breasts at twelve years old, she'd been the bastion of ridicule at school. Especially with her older, extroverted sister, who was tall and slim with dead straight hair. Was it any wonder Jenna modelled lingerie and swimwear?

Besides, she'd found a way to hide her figure through her love of vintage, hourglass dresses and large skirt prom dresses. Even if someone gawked at her style, she was comfortable in what she wore.

Looking up, she saw Luca staring at her with those dark eyes, she felt herself grow flustered.

She rubbed her nose. "Have a smudge?"

He gave her a lazy smile and took a moment to reply. "No, you don't." He stood and held out his hand to her. "Come on, let's get some dessert before it's all gone."

She stifled a giggle, because knowing how much food there was, there would be plenty of leftovers. "Sure." She took his hand and they walked back inside the house.

CHAPTER 2

*T*hose with young children left the party soon after dessert was served. They were tired and so were their parents.

Taylor looked on as children were lifted and carried, rubbing their eyes. A small jab of jealousy hit her in the belly. She hoped one day she'd find a man who loved her for who she was, curves and all, and not because of her famous sister.

Another hour passed as they chatted with friends they'd know since they were at school. Taylor and Luca stayed close to each other, sharing news and enjoying the social aspect of the evening.

For the first time in many years Chanukah and Christmas fell on the same day, and the Bergmans had spent considerable time decorating their home and making it festive. Games and crafts had been organised for the little ones, Chanukah candles lit and songs sung.

A group of friends in their early twenties commenced a drinking game using the dreidels that the children had previously been playing with.

Seated in a circle, they encouraged everyone to join in.

With trepidation Taylor sat next to Luca, worried about the game. A couple of years back, they'd played "tell us something you don't know" and someone had written down "I secretly am in love with Luca." It had been one of the most embarrassing moments of her life. She'd later found out her sister had written it and was still laughing about it.

She sat away from Jenna and close to Luca, ready to leave if necessary.

Gabe Bergman spoke out. "You all know what a dreidel is." He lifted the plastic top for all to see. "Each side has a Hebrew letter, nun, hey, gimmel and shin. If it lands on G, you have to gulp your drink, H means you drink half your drink."

Everyone around the table cheered.

"If it lands on S you have to say something revealing about yourself." There was a mix of chuckles and gasps from the group.

"And if it lands on N you have to kiss someone."

Jenna interrupted. "Kiss starts with a K not an N."

"It's my game but just so you know, kiss in Hebrew is *neshika*. I've even brought some mistletoe," Gabe pulled the mistletoe from behind his back, displaying it with a grin. "Since we're having a Christmas/Chanukah party. But you do have the option of a cheek or lip kiss." He pointed to his sister, Ruby, sitting opposite him.

The group laughed as Ruby gave her brother a rude finger gesture.

"Who wants to go first?" Gabe asked.

"I will," Jenna said.

Taylor wasn't surprised. Jenna had an outrageous personality, a different boyfriend each week, the uncanny ability to make people laugh and was stunningly beautiful. She should be jealous of her sister but she wasn't. Except, that she didn't like that her sister had briefly dated Luca and then ended it because he was "too boring"—her words!

Really? Taylor hadn't thought so.

Gabe handed the dreidel to Jenna who spun it across the table. Of course, it spun well before landing on G. "Cheers," she said before draining the alcohol in her shot glass.

Everyone was in a party mood, and the answers had everyone laughing and cheering as they played. After a couple of rounds, Luca spun S and he had to tell something about himself.

"I've just sold my work to NASA," he announced with pride. The fifteen game participants, seated around the table, clapped with vigour before toasting and drinking to his success.

Then it was her turn. Taylor spun the dreidel, her heart thumped against her ribs. So far she'd spun G each time and was feeling a tad tipsy from the chocolate flavoured vodka she was enjoying.

It spun and her eyes opened wide as it landed on N.

Jenna clapped her hands in delight. "Time to pucker up, sis," she said in a sing-song voice.

Turning to Luca, she intended to kiss his cheek but at the same time he turned to look at her, so her lips landed on his.

She gasped and she pulled back as though she'd kissed a burning torch. "S-sorry," she said, her underarms became suddenly warm and sticky, despite the air conditioning in the room. "I meant to kiss your cheek."

He leaned towards her and whispered in her ear. "Don't worry. I enjoyed it."

She didn't know what to make of it, and her cheeks warmed as the friends around the table started to chant, "Kiss, kiss, kiss, kiss, kiss."

Despite her protestations, they continued to bang the table with their hands, insisting she kiss Luca again.

Her gaze caught her sister's smile—Jenna was obviously the inciter. Darn her. If she could cause trouble for the sake of causing trouble, Jenna would do it.

The noise grew louder and she was sure the whole suburb could hear the screams for her and Luca to kiss. What the heck? She needed to shut them up, so she turned to her friend of twenty-plus years and pressed her lips against his.

His hands came up and anchored her face to his.

Darts of need and want exploded in her belly and she had to resist climbing onto his lap and kissing him more.

His lips were soft and despite the raucous noise, she caught a waft of his aftershave. Tangy and spicy.

It was only seconds, but it felt longer. Finally, she sat back on her seat, feeling dazed. Her head swam and her lips tingled. She wasn't sure if it was the alcohol or her own stupidity that had made her kiss him so blatantly.

Later, she intended to apologise to him and blame the kiss on drinking too much sweetened vodka. But for now, she smiled at everyone, avoided Luca's gaze and pretended that kissing her friend was all part of the dreidel drinking game.

The game continued and answers became more outrageous as more alcohol was consumed.

"I can't drink this much, I need a coffee," she said to Luca.

She wasn't drunk, but it was an excuse to get away from the game. Besides, she was soon due to spin the dreidel and she was worried about getting N again.

Had she the confidence, like her sister, she would've grabbed the mistletoe and kissed whoever she wanted. But she wasn't her sister, in more ways than one.

"I'll come with you," he said, standing.

"You don't have to," she replied.

"Thanks Gabe, good game," he said, before taking Taylor's elbow and leading her to the kitchen.

She said nothing.

"It's almost midnight. You sure you want to drink coffee? You never drink caffeine before you go to bed," he said.

Trust him to be so thoughtful, she thought.

"You're right. I'll have a tea instead," she said before making her way to the urn.

He left her and returned a minute later with her shoes, dangling from a finger. "You forgot these and apparently your sister is not wearing underwear tonight."

Taylor gasped at her sister's audacity, concerned about what Luca would think. Would he leave her and trail after Jenna? He wouldn't be the first.

"Jenna is too cheeky for her own good. She loves the shock value. I wouldn't be surprised if she just said that," she said with a roll of her eyes.

"Nothing about Jenna surprises me," he drawled, fiddling with a plastic spoon.

"And here you are, with the sister," she said flattening her back against the wall.

"I like you better," he said in a low voice. "You're clever, creative and funny." He looked over his shoulder as if checking to make sure they were alone. They were. "You love Elvis's music as much as I do and—"

"I'm a vintage lover," she interrupted.

"Actually, I was going to say that you are a good kisser," he clarified with a lift of his eyebrow.

The laughter from her lips was forced and fake. But she couldn't control the thump of her heart after hearing his confession. "Y-you think I'm a good kisser?"

"For sure," he said with a twinkle in his eye. "Want me to prove it?"

Taking a step back, she felt her back pressed against the wall.

His palm rested against the wall, near her face and his

stance was casual, as though talking about kissing with your friend was perfectly normal.

"Um, I don't think so," she said, her throat dry and parched despite the coolness of the room. "It's getting late. I think it's time for me to go home." Her words tumbled from her lips as his closeness warmed her.

"Okay. Good night, Taylor, Merry Christmas," he said before brushing his lips across hers.

She shivered with need.

How could such a brief touch of his lips create such fire in her belly? For years she'd been able to keep her attraction for him at bay. By why now? Why the inner turmoil and the desire to taste his lips another time?

Perhaps it was too many champagnes? Or the way he'd held her as they'd spent most of the evening together.

Despite their friendship, they hadn't spent so much time one-on-one for a while, thanks to a succession of girlfriends and him working overseas for the past two years.

He was leaving soon. Surely they could put the madness between them aside and go back to being friends again? It was only a kiss. Did friends kiss? She had no idea about that, but she did know that the urge to taste him again was so strong that she was struggling to fight it and finding reasons why she shouldn't.

What if he laughed at her? She wasn't glamorous and she wasn't sexy. Could she do it?

The spicy scent of him invaded her nostrils. The noise of the party faded, until it was just the two of them. Lifting herself off the wall, she inched slowly towards him. She could do this.

She was a strong, sensible, capable woman. Giving Luca a kiss...piece of cake, right?

Wrong.

"So that's why you left the game?" Gabe strutted in to the kitchen, a silly grin on his lips.

"Who are you? My mother?" Luca insisted with a playful tone.

"Just came for some more beers," he said opening the fridge. "Oh, you may want this," Gabe said, handing him the mistletoe before loading up with half a dozen long-necked bottles. "Later," he chuckled before returning to the table of friends in the other room.

Luca tickled her nose with the leaves. "They do enjoy having fun at our expense," he said.

"They most certainly do," she breathed out. Had the moment passed along with her confidence? Maybe she'd find another time to follow through? Unlikely.

Lovers came and went but friendship was stronger. She needed to remind herself of that next time she had the unexpected urge to kiss him.

"Happy Christmas, Taylor," he said placing the mistletoe above her head.

He brushed his lips against hers and this time she didn't push back but rather cupped his face with her hands and kissed him back. Kissed him the way she'd only dreamt about. Kissed him in a way that she knew she shouldn't... but was doing anyway.

She closed her eyes and she took a moment to feel the hardness of his arms around her. How strong he was and how wonderful it felt to be pressed against him.

His hands settled on her hips, anchoring her to him.

He opened his mouth wider and she followed his lead, loving the delicious taste of him.

They kissed and kissed, and soon enough she welcomed his tongue.

Her hands cupped his neck and they kissed more before his lips trailed along her cheek and to her ear.

She wanted to say something funny, witty or sexy but was too worried about breaking the spell between them. He nibbled her ear before running his tongue along the length of it.

Her nipples tingled and she longed for him to touch her. . .all over. His mouth returned to hers and one minute the kisses were sweet and the next minute they were hot and heavy. He pushed her against the wall, his mouth making tiny bites along her neck, then on to her shoulder.

She was ready to pull his shirt from his pants when she heard, "Ooops, sorry!"

They'd been caught making out in the Bergman's kitchen and Taylor was mortified.

The kiss couldn't be kept between the two of them and forgotten; it was out there, and everyone would know.

Taylor opened her eyes to find her sister standing near them, her arms crossed against her chest, her forefinger wagging at her as a chuckle escaped her lips.

"Enjoying ourselves, are we?" she said with a tilt of her head and a look that said, "Gotcha."

CHAPTER 3

*B*ad enough to be caught kissing your best friend, but to be caught by your sister who would have no compunction about keeping it a secret was truly unfair.

The blissfulness of their shared kiss disappeared as Taylor turned to face her sister.

"It was a kiss, friends do that," she tried to argue with her older, more street-savvy sister.

"Yes, I kiss my friends like that all the time," Jenna said. "And if you think I'm going to keep this quiet and between us," she placed her hands on her heart, and paused for dramatic affect, "you've got another think coming. Toodles," she said with a wave.

Taylor watched her sister saunter out of the kitchen in sky-high heels and felt her body burn in anger and annoyance. Typical of Jenna to find a way to make her look bad, again. Wasn't it enough that she'd been blessed with all the awesome family DNA?

"Guess what I just saw," Taylor heard her sister cry out. "Taylor and Luca kissing."

Taylor buried her face in her hands. "What a mess," she said.

He grabbed her hands and brought his face to hers. "Listen, Jenna loves the attention. Let's pretend we don't care what she's saying and hopefully it will be forgotten."

She nodded as her belly fell and splattered over the white tiles on the floor. Yep. He wasn't interested in her at all, and the kiss had been a mistake. Best to blame the kiss on something and go back to being friends.

"You're right." She took a step away from him, turning her face so he couldn't see her disappointment. Her breathing was rapid and she could feel her heart pattering away. It was pathetic of her but instead of being strong, she chose to escape. "I've got to go to the toilet. Back in a minute." She rushed past him and headed towards a nearby bathroom.

With the door locked, she pressed her back against it and took a number of long breaths, in an effort to slow her heart rate.

You can do this, she reassured herself. *It's not as bad as it seems.* Oh yes it was, she thought with despair. Who was she trying to kid?

* * *

LUCA WATCHED Taylor scamper away as if she were being chased by a pack of zombies, keen on her being their next dinner.

If he wasn't confused, he'd find the situation amusing. But he was confused about what to think of their kiss. Despite her not being close to him, he could still smell the subtle flowery perfume she favoured and his lips longed to taste her again.

The kiss was wrong and totally unexpected. He touched

his lips and could still feel them tingling from the mind-blowing kiss they'd just shared.

What was supposed to be a fun, friendly, platonic kiss had turned into something more. It hadn't been planned. The idea of kissing her struck him suddenly, he had no idea why. He'd acted without thinking, but then things had gotten out of hand once their lips had touched and he'd forgotten all the reasons why he should stop. Her scent had driven him crazy, and that little moan of hers in the back of her throat as he plunged his tongue into her mouth had him wanting more.

Why now? For years he'd spent time with her and never once thought about taking their friendship to a different level. He valued her too much and he knew that if things didn't work out, he'd lose her. She was too important to lose over sex.

She'd never hinted at them dating, and seemed content with being friends. It had suited them both…until now.

He was torn between wanting to kiss her again and apologising. He was sure that kissing your friend on Christmas was a bad idea.

Taking a deep breath, he sauntered into the room where the twenty-somethings were still playing their dreidel drinking game. Time to "face the music" and fix things, because he couldn't bear the thought of his closest friend feeling embarrassed or ashamed of what had just happened.

"How's the game coming along," he asked with a smile, before grabbing an unopened beer. He raised the beer and toasted them, "Merry Christmas, Happy Chanukah."

Leo sniggered, "Merry Christmas, lover-boy."

He clicked his tongue but the reality was, he wasn't as *laissez-faire* as he pretended to be. Time for some deflection. "I heard you've got women *falling* over themselves to be with you, Leo" Luca said with a wink.

The group, having had a number of drinks, hooted and

cheered Luca on. Leo had a new job at a plush retirement village, in charge of events and outings, and most of the female residents were trying to match him with their grand-daughters. Every day he was "introduced" to a young lady who just happened to be visiting her grandparents.

Leo was now being ribbed by his friends who thought the match-making situation was hilarious. Great, he'd deflected well.

When Jenna tried to bring the conversation back to him, he complimented her on her ability to keep cool in the hot weather by not wearing underwear.

Again, the inebriated group started clapping and cheer-ing, more interested in Jenna and Leo, than in Luca, who most of them considered pretty boring and ho-hum. So what if he'd kissed Taylor?

One of the young men then outrageously concocted a story about one resident, in the aged care, wanting to date Leo, herself. Everyone banged their hands on the table, laughing at the idea of Leo's date at the New Year's party attending with her walking stick.

Mission accomplished, he silently congratulated himself.

Luca left his beer and slipped out to look for Taylor. After a few minutes, he found her in the garden in a darkened corner, barefoot, legs outstretched and lying on a chaise lounge.

"You okay?" he asked, before grabbing a chair so he could sit next to her.

"Sure. Jenna is very good at embarrassing me. She's got it down to a fine art," she said.

The day's summer heat had subsided and the evening's air was now comfortably cool.

"I brought you something," he said, handing her a wrapped ice-cream.

"My favourite," she cooed, holding the individual strawberry ice-cream covered in chocolate and looking at it with love. "Where did you find it?"

"I checked the freezer, seems the Bergmans also love your favourite ice cream as there were two boxes of these." His elbows rested on his knees.

"Thank you. You know me too well," she said, unwrapping it and then taking a large bite. "Yum," she murmured.

For the first time ever, Luca felt uncomfortable watching her enjoy the dessert. Stupid, he knew. It was almost as though he were in a parallel universe where the rules were different. He didn't like it. He wanted things to go back to the way they were. Precise, systematic and orderly.

Feeling awkward simply from watching her eat made him squirm in his seat and wish he had a beer or three in his hand. He cleared his throat. "I-um, spoke to the group. Good thing I keep up to date with their lives on social media." He chuckled. "All I had to do was mention Leo…."

"About the ladies wanting to marry him off?" She squealed in delight.

He lifted his eyebrow. "Of course."

"Thank you, Luca. I like how you think," she said before taking another bite of her treat. Within a minute it was all gone and she ran her tongue up and down the wooden stick to extract every last bit of chocolate.

Inappropriate thoughts exploded in his brain and he had to look away, pretending to focus on how neatly the lawn had been cut. He took a deep breath, wondering if the sun had suddenly appeared at 1 a.m. as he was feeling hot and bothered.

He turned to her and his gaze clashed with hers. "Look," they both spoke at once.

"Sorry, you go first," she waved at him.

He cleared his throat again, wishing she'd offered to go first. "I'm sorry to have put you in a compromising situation with the kiss. It was stupid of me. I was just mucking around." He paused to take a deep breath and control the nerves that were threatening to squeeze the life out of him. "I'm sorry. It was a mistake and I don't want to lose you as a friend."

She wiggled her bottom so she could sit closer to him and grabbed his hands in hers. "You won't lose me. It was just a kiss, don't worry about it." There was an intensity in her blue eyes that reassured him that she'd accepted his apology and everything would go back to how it was.

"Thank you for the apology, and for dealing with my sister. My hero," she sang out. She stood and brushed her lips against his cheek. "You're too important to me to lose over something as silly as a kiss," she said. "Come on. Let's go back inside."

She held out her hand. He took it and stood. Something about what she said made him uneasy, but he had no idea what or why. Everything seemed fine so he was probably worried for nothing. Enjoying the soft press of her hand against his, they walked back inside the house.

* * *

A COUPLE OF HOURS LATER, Luca was lying in bed alone in the bedroom of his parents' home. Science awards, trophies and photos still adorned the shelves of his boyhood room.

He'd been tossing and turning, unable to fall asleep. Pushing off the sheets, he stood in his boxers, his skin burning and on fire with need and want. An erection tented his shorts and he looked down and shook his head. Wrong, wrong, wrong.

He scratched his head and made his way into the bathroom to wash his face. How had this happened? How had a kiss turned his world not just upside down but inside out?

He could blame his inability to sleep on jet-lag but the truth was that desire was coursing through his veins at high speed, and all he could think about was Taylor and her curves. He itched to cradle her breasts in his hands and taste the sweetness of her skin. What the hell? He put the brakes on his inappropriate thoughts.

She was his friend. She trusted him. She'd always been there for him.

Wanting to suckle her nipples was ridiculous and he banished the thoughts.

They'd been friends for a long time and even though she didn't flaunt her body, she couldn't hide her hourglass figure and gentle curves. He'd seen her in a bathing suit and had admired her, but that had been it. Never once had he thought about peeling it off to see if her nipples were dusty pink, like her lips.

A plethora of Italian curse words tumbled from his mouth. He had to stop thinking about her like that. He was determined not to break that trust and special bond between them.

Despite the cold water he splashed on his face, he was still fretful and unable to focus. Grabbing his exercise clothes, he decided he'd run off his frustration, and hoped he'd be able to sleep when he returned.

* * *

THE FOLLOWING day was Boxing Day, the day after Christmas Day when most Melbournians headed to the malls for the sales or relaxed watching the cricket.

Taylor had barely slept all night and had been grateful that her early rising friend, Amber, was happy to walk along the beach-front from Elwood to St Kilda at 7 a.m.

"After all that eating yesterday, I could use a walk," Amber said as they made their way briskly along the three-kilo-metre coastal route. "Great idea of yours," she added with sincerity.

Taylor yawned. "Only *you* would be happy to be up so early."

Amber took a swig of her water bottle. "It's going to be a scorching hot day today, so an early walk is perfect. Are you opening your shop today?"

"No. The shop owners in the street talked about it and we felt it wasn't worth it. It's a public holiday. People are enjoying summer, so we made a collective decision not to open."

"You deserve a day off."

"Last night Luca kissed me and I kissed him and it was great, I pretended it didn't mean anything to me, but it did and I want to kiss him again." The words tumbled from Taylor's lips before she could stop them.

"What?" Amber skidded to a halt and grabbed her friend's elbow. "How did you two just start kissing? We've talked about this for years and you've always said you couldn't pursue a relationship because he meant too much to you?"

"It was at the Christmas party last night at the Bergmans."

"Am I the only one that thinks it's weird that the only Jewish family on your street is the one hosting the Christmas party?"

"Amber," she said through gritted teeth.

"Sorry. Every time I hear that, I laugh. Let's go back to you and Luca making out," she said, her voice full of curiosity.

Taylor cupped her burning hot cheeks with her hands. "He's such a good kisser. I wish I didn't know that."

"He's hot! Of course he'd be a good kisser," Amber said with a roll of her eyes.

"You're not helping," she hissed at her friend.

"So you two kissed. Just pretend it didn't happen," Amber suggested.

They recommenced their walk to St Kilda beach. "I would, except my dear sister Jenna saw us."

Amber muttered an expletive under her breath. "I'm assuming she broadcasted the news."

"Would you expect anything else from her?" Taylor asked followed by a frustrated pfft.

"What did Luca say?"

"After he distracted everyone about the incident, he brought me my favourite ice cream and apologised," Taylor said with a sigh.

"The guy is so perfect, I want to marry him," Amber said. Seeing the fury in her friend's eyes, she rebutted, "I'm just saying okay, I'd never date him." She paused. "Although, if you don't say something soon, he will marry someone else and you'll lose your chance at love and your friendship."

"No, I won't," she said with fierce determination.

Amber rolled her eyes again. "Do you really think his fiancée and then wife will want you anywhere near her husband? Look at you! You're gorgeous. You two have chemistry that will make her burn with jealousy." She waved her finger at her friend. "Mark my words, once he's engaged, your friendship will dissolve. She will see you as a threat and will pull him away from you. And don't forget when she's on her knees—"

"Amber!" Taylor cried out. "Really?"

"If you don't like honesty, then we can talk about our Christmas presents instead. Trust me when I say that if he marries someone that you don't know, you will lose him because she will be resentful of your relationship."

"You're not being very positive."

Amber shrugged. "Perhaps his wife won't mind but if you look at couples, you'll see the same pattern repeating itself. If the wife doesn't like the friend, the husband will only see him, or in your case, her, on his own. And eventually, once there are kids and they are doing *couple* things and family things, you'll see him less and less."

"That's something to look forward to," Taylor said, sarcasm dripping from every word.

"I'm a realist, it's my job," she added with a shrug.

"Working with couples struggling with IVF did not give you that insight," Taylor insisted, surprised by her friend's insights.

"Of course it did," she waved her friend's belief away with a flick of her wrist. "In our sessions, all sorts of things come up and I'm telling you to listen and trust me." She took a quick sip of water. "You'll be seen as a threat. You two are too cute together. You can finish each other's sentences because you've been tight with each other for so many years."

"Why are you telling me this now?" Taylor felt the skin between her eyes crease with interest.

"Because you kissed and you've crossed a line."

"But we've agreed to going back."

"You two can agree to whatever you want," her friend said at her, "but I'm telling you, you're both going to see things differently." She paused. "When are you next seeing him?"

She expelled a large breath. "Today, we're all going to his parents' house to watch cricket and then swim."

"I assume you'll be swimming in a bikini, not clothes?" She added with a lift of one brow.

"Well, yes. . ." Taylor stopped and thought about what her friend had said. "He'll be seeing me differently?"

"Yes. You both may agree to be friends, but you've kissed now. Pretend all you want, but it aint gonna happen. Besides, you've had a crush on him for so long that you're going to find it hard to keep those platonic feelings in tow now." She pointed to her friend's heart.

"Crap," Taylor said. They walked in silence as she pondered what her friend had said. She gazed at the bluer than blue water of Port Philip Bay as a gentle breeze with the promise of a long, hot day, caressed her skin. Turning to her friend she asked, "What do I do?" Her legs felt as steady as though she were standing on quick sand, and she was sinking fast.

"You have two options." She ticked off the options using her fingers. "The first is that *I* marry Luca so you two can be friends, because I love you and don't see you as a threat."

"Really, that's not an option." Taylor said, her voice dripping with sarcasm, unable to believe they were having this discussion.

Amber ignored her theatrics. "The second option is that you tell Luca how you feel and go for it."

"What?" she almost yelled back. "Are you sure you didn't have champagne with your cereal this morning?" *Go for it?* Her friend's comments were too outrageous and too ridiculous for consideration. "How about option three? We do nothing and go back to how things were?"

Amber looked at her, annoyance stretched along her jaw. "If that's what you want, do that." She turned and started to walk slowly away from her friend.

Taylor could see the unease in the slump of her friend's shoulders, and she raced to catch up to her. "Don't worry about it, everything will be fine. Luca and I will be fine."

"Fine," Amber said with a concerned sigh. "Just keep telling yourself that."

CHAPTER 4

*G*o *for it*? With Luca?

The idea thrilled her and freaked her out, all at the same time. After her friend's outrageous suggestions, they'd agreed to not talk about Luca anymore. After hours of chatting, an icy cold coffee on the beach and a playful swim in the bay, Taylor drove back to her parents' home.

Since opening her own business eighteen months ago, she'd reluctantly moved back into the family home so she could focus on building her business. She could no longer afford to rent an apartment as well as the shop, and her parents had generously allowed her to live at home while she established her vintage clothing and home-wares business.

After a quick shower, she sat on the back porch sipping a coffee as she reflected on Amber's words. It made sense. But she was far too sensible to allow a jealous wife to come between them.

It was time to move on and banish any such ideas. She was twenty-eight, and he was a year older. They could always

178

be friends but Amber was right. Once either of them married, their friendship would change. It would be there still, but it would have to be different.

Her mobile pinged and she looked at the screen. *You okay?* Amber texted followed by purple and red hearts. *Yes*, she replied. *You're an awesome friend, thanks for the advice and walk.* She added some red hearts before sending the message.

All the friends were meeting at Luca's parents' home for lunch, a swim and to watch the Boxing Day test cricket match, and she knew they'd be there all afternoon and evening.

The day was already hot with a promise of even more warmth. Luca was only here for ten days and then would be returning to his career in the US. If she was going to do or say something to him, she needed to do it before he left in the New Year. She couldn't do it over the phone. Cripes!

Despite fatigue, her blood whizzed through her veins in anticipation, and her fingers touched her lips. Why had they crossed that line? As much as she wished they hadn't, they had. Now she knew how good his lips felt against hers and she longed for more.

Clutching her coffee mug, she looked at her parents' well-maintained garden as she reflected on her options.

DESPITE THE TIREDNESS and long run, Luca slept fitfully. At ten o'clock, he sauntered in to the kitchen to find his mother busily making her fresh pasta.

"Good morning, Mama," he said, giving her cheek a kiss. "Busy as always."

She gave her son a warm smile. "We do have everyone coming over for lunch today."

"I'm sure you'll have plenty," he said, his head nodding at the multiple saucepans on the stovetop. "Everything smells amazing."

"I've made your favourites," his mother said.

"Thank you, Mama, you're the best cook." He rubbed his eyes. "But now I need an espresso." He shook his head, "You don't have to make it, I'll do it."

He made two, one for him and another for his mother who had probably been up since early morning and likely hadn't had breakfast. He added three of her homemade biscotti to his saucer and one to hers.

He didn't bother offering to help; he knew she wouldn't accept. As the only son and especially now that he lived overseas, his mother pampered him.

He was a grown man and happy to help her but she was insistent. Instead, he went to the family room and started arranging the furniture so everyone could sit in the air conditioned room and watch the cricket.

He then set up the table in the dining room, organising the trestle tables his parents stored in the garage for when they had large gatherings. All the while he thought about Taylor.

They were friends. He wanted them to stay that way. Hopefully they'd have time to talk and he could reassure her of that.

* * *

At lunchtime, his childhood friends from Clarendon Close, all started arriving. They'd known each other for years and despite some of them now only interacting on social media because of different interests or moving to different parts of Melbourne, they still had a strong bond of friendship.

Their parents still lived here, in Clarendon Close, none wanting to move away from the quietness of the suburban area that so far had avoided densely populated housing development.

Many of the twenty and thirty-somethings often stayed the night at their parents' over Christmas, so as not to miss out on any fun or catch ups. Over the years, the momentum had built with more fun and family activities created.

Luca missed his friends and the neighbourhood hub of gatherings, and it reminded him how isolated he was in the US, away from his family.

Minutes later when Taylor walked in, his breathing increased and his ribs tightened around his chest. Despite the air conditioning, his skin was warm and clammy. His emotions were as tangled as a knot and he had to make an effort to supress any feelings that were not platonic. Taylor was his friend and he needed to respect that. Not jump her just because his body was on high alert, wanting to touch her creamy skin.

He ran his fingers through his hair. Obviously having been single for too long was messing with his hormones.

"Hi," he said, brushing his lips against her cheek. "You look great." He took a step away from her lest he do something stupid like breathe in the warm, summer scent of her skin.

"Not bad yourself," she added, giving his tailored shorts and casual shirt an appreciative eye. Like him, she dressed well.

He took the large glass bowl from her arms and looked though the plastic film covering it.

"It's a tossed salad," she added with a dramatic sigh. "Not very exciting, but it was the only thing your mum would let me bring."

"I love salad," he said, carrying it to the table and placing it in the middle.

She walked up to him. "Your mum is such an amazing cook. I'm a little intimidated bringing anything, even salad, to her table," she confessed in a low voice.

He nodded. "I know what you mean," he said with a chuckle. "She guards her recipes like they're the combination to a bank's vault. I hope she'll share them with me one day."

"You're her son, of course she will," she said with a roll of her eyes.

"Mum's old fashioned and says she'll only give them to my wife," he paused. "I don't know if that means she doesn't trust me in the kitchen or she's trying to marry me off." His chest tightened at the frustration that his mother fussed over him still, and defined success as a good marriage. Almost thirty years old, he'd learnt to not focus on his mother's request that he marry a nice Italian woman. He wanted to marry someone who liked him, not his success with NASA nor his ability to make fresh pasta from scratch. He wanted a woman who liked his quiet disposition and made him laugh.

Her eyes darkened but she didn't say anything, making Luca wonder if he'd inadvertently said something to upset her. He brushed the concern away; she wasn't over sensitive and didn't allow throwaway lines to annoy her.

"Mama made gnocchi for you," he said.

Placing her hands over her heart she said with a sigh, "My favourite. I'll have to thank her for it."

"She loves you," he said.

"Of course she does," she said. "I made sure you studied. In fact, you owe your brilliant career success to me."

He casually put his hands in his pockets. "How so?"

"Every Saturday night when your friends were out and you had to stay home, who kept you company?" she said with a knowing lift of her eyebrow.

"You did," he said with a nod of his head towards her. Taylor had been a permanent fixture in his life, someone who'd made him laugh and made school days tolerable when his strict parents hadn't allowed him the freedoms that other parents gave their teens.

Her forefinger poked at his chest. "While you had your head in the books—"

"I seem to recall you did, too," he interrupted with a chuckle.

"Yes, you're right. Your books were on things I didn't understand like maths, chemistry and physics. Whilst I," she said with a flourish and a wave in the air, "spent time reading Jane Austen and Rebecca Du Maurier."

"Not for me, thanks," he added. His last two years of high school had only been tolerable because of her friendship. He hadn't been allowed to date or do anything that was not related to studying until he'd finished school.

"You stayed with me every Saturday night when everyone else was out having fun," he said in a low voice.

"But when your parents weren't here, we'd sneak watch an old Elvis movie," she added with a theatrical tone.

"You missed out on being with your friends because of me," he said. Her parents hadn't been strict at all, allowing Taylor and her sister to date and go out from age fifteen.

"I liked being with you, besides it made everyone jealous when you asked me to your school prom."

His lips twitched with the memory of the night of fun they'd had dancing at the event. "You stood out—"

She groaned dramatically. "Don't remind me." She covered her face with her hands. "I stood out for all the wrong reasons."

"Just because everyone was in black and you chose pink, it doesn't matter. You wore what you wanted and didn't care what others thought," he said with pride.

She cleared her throat. "I have to confess that I did care, then. Not now, but at the time, I was embarrassed about my love of vintage."

"But I liked you because you didn't fit in," he drawled, remembering how pretty she'd looked in her prom dress and the flare of the wide skirt under masses of petticoats.

She lifted her eyebrow. "But no one wanted to date me because I was too weird."

"Not conforming is not weird."

"It is when you have a sister like mine," she said with a shrug. "Overhearing that guys wanted to date me only to get close to my sister didn't do much for my self-esteem."

"I get that. Your sister is beautiful but you are far more beautiful than her," he said.

Friends were walking in the door and the house was becoming loud with the chatter of the guests. His brow crinkled, wanting to remind her that she didn't have to live in her sister's shadow. He was surprised that she still felt that way now, even after finding her calling and making it a success.

Drawing her away, he led her to his bedroom and closed the door, keeping the noise at bay and giving them privacy.

"Why are we here?" she asked through narrowed eyes.

"I thought you'd moved on, and didn't have hang-ups about your sister anymore," he said leaning against the door.

Standing in the middle of the room, she crossed her arms.

"You guessed wrong. I obviously still do," she snapped at him. "You'd think at twenty-eight, I'd be comfortable being who I am. And for most of the time, I am. But here I am in a caftan and she's wearing a pair of shorts that are the size of my undies." Her breathing grew rapid. "I'm not her and that's fine. But I don't need you to psychoanalyse me."

"I'm not," he said lifting his palms towards her defensively.

She took a couple of steps towards him and poked his

chest a few times with her finger. "Yes you are. I don't need you telling me what I already know." She drew in a deep breath. "Jenna is gorgeous, she's got a vivacious personality and everyone likes her. I've spent all my life in her shadow. But I don't care. I've learnt to love who I am and what I do. She calls me a nerd and perhaps I am." She shrugged off the jibe. "But I don't need you telling me how to feel." She paused. "Besides, like heaps of other guys, you dated *her* and not me."

The last few words tumbled from her lips in a low voice and punched him hard in the gut, as if she'd speared him. They'd never spoken about the few weeks he'd dated her sister. He'd stupidly allowed his need to break away from his parents' control to push away sensibilities. After years of restrictions, he'd gone wild in his first year of University, drinking too much and trying to have lots of sex, as though making up for all the years of studying forced on him by his parents. Coupled with hormones, he'd made some stupid decisions when he was nineteen, regretting them, before focussing back on his studies. After, he'd still gone to parties but his behaviour no longer interfered with him achieving high distinctions in each subject.

He ran his fingers through his hair. "You were my friend."

She raised her hand and placed it on his chest. He could feel the warmth of her skin through the shirt material and he sucked in a sharp breath, not liking the affect she was having on him. Especially after last night.

"I know. But you and every guy seem to overlook me for her. Even my best friend," she admitted in a quiet voice.

"I'm sorry," he started to apologise.

"You don't have to say sorry. I get it. If I was a guy, I'd date her instead of me, too." She shook her head. "Look at her, she models lingerie," she almost shouted at him.

"Why is this coming out now?" he took her hand and led her to his bed where they sat side by side.

She buried her face in her hands. "I don't know. I think it was the kiss and Amber's suggestion that we have an affair?"

His heart spiked with alarm. "What did you just say?" He pushed her hair out of the way to force her to look at him.

"I can't believe I just said that," she said before turning her head, and breaking his gaze.

"Look at me," he said cupping her shoulders. "Why did Amber say we should have an affair?"

"I don't want to talk about it," she said.

"I do. If you're talking about me, I want to know."

Her lips trembled and his stomach tumbled in recognition that he was pushing her and making her feel uncomfortable but a need to know more pushed that aside and all he could focus on was what she and Amber had been talking about.

"I told her about our kiss and she thinks that I might as well have an affair with you because once one of us marries, our friendship will dissolve. She said us being friends will be difficult when you're married because your wife may be jealous of us."

He took a moment to process what she'd just said. Perhaps it was the lack of sleep or not enough espressos but he was still trying to piece it together.

"Don't worry about it, I shouldn't have said anything." She smacked her hands on her knees. "Let's go." She stood. "I shouldn't have said anything. I have a tendency to speak first, think second. My mouth gets me into trouble all the time."

He stood next to her and took in the flush of her cheeks. She wasn't as cool with this conversation as she was making out she was. There was something going on and he had every intention of finding out what.

Starting to walk towards the door, he took her hand in

his and tugged her towards him. "I can see what Amber is saying. A wife may be jealous of our friendship but what I don't understand is why she would think we should have an affair. Why would friends have an affair?" He paused and looked at her intently. "What's going on Taylor?"

CHAPTER 5

*I*f there was a time that Taylor wished for an earthquake to take place, open up the floor and drag her in, she wished for it now. Her explanations, to him, were ridiculous, they didn't make sense. Plus how stupid had she been? Speaking without thought, saying things she shouldn't have.

Not only had she told him about her deepest feelings of betrayal when he'd dated Jenna, but now she had to explain to him why she'd want an affair with him. He was right. Friends didn't have sex...but friends who had secret crushes did.

Telling him *that* wasn't going to happen.

"I think we should get going. People are going to wonder where we are," she insisted, before tugging her hand free from his.

Escape. That's all she could think about. Escape. Before she did something else stupid and confessed more truths.

Tugging her back towards him, they walked to the bed and sat down again. Her heart was racing and she was sure he could hear the *thump, thump, thump,* against her ribs. The sound filled her eardrums. "I don't want to talk anymore."

"But I do, and we're not leaving here till you tell me what's going on," he said with a firm voice. "Don't we tell each other everything?" There was strong determination in the dark recesses of his eyes and the tightness around his jaw.

She decided to go with a flippant attitude to steer the conversation away. "Not everything. I'm sure you're not interested in the latest historical romance I'm reading."

"You're pushing my patience," he said with a growl. "Your answers don't make sense. Why would Amber put *us* and the word *affair* together?" He paused. "Start talking."

She was sure nerves were going to make her vomit on the carpet. Stress and anxiety tore at her guts making her squirm with embarrassment. "You know what Amber is like? She's a romantic. It was a fly-away comment," she said with a shrug, pretending *being* with him was of the same importance as eating lunch. Not so much.

"You're lying," he said, his eyes dark with frustration and anger. "She's not romantic at all, that's why she's so good as a psychologist. She doesn't allow her emotions to become involved." He paused. "But you do."

"Me?" her voice was high pitched, and she inched her bottom, creating space between them.

"Yes, *you*," he said with fierce fortitude. "You're emotional in everything you do, a complete opposite to her and me. I'm methodical and analytical, but you're not."

"Should I be flattered?" She fluttered her eyelashes in an effort to deter him.

His fingers circled her arm. "Stop playing games with me. I need to know."

She stood suddenly, freeing herself from his grip. "They're

calling us. I don't want us to be in here anymore. Last night was bad enough." She walked to the door, and without turning around said, "We'll talk later." She opened the door and walked out as quickly as she could, creating distance between them. She had no intention of talking to him alone again, especially after telling him way too much already.

The room full of people engulfed her and she spent time chatting with friends, before helping herself to a glass of Proseco wine. Draining the glass in a few mouthfuls, she re-filled it, needing a second glass of wine to settle her knotted nerves.

* * *

HALF AN HOUR LATER, thirty guests including children were seated in the dining room enjoying the food Sofia Bianchi had spent days preparing. Despite the warm smile on her face, Taylor could see the tiredness in Sofia's eyes. She could see the toll it had taken on the older woman to prepare such a magnificent meal of homemade pastas, pizzas, stuffed vegetables and roasted vegetables. Yet Taylor knew Sofia's stubbornness and love of family and cooking would not allow her to take shortcuts or ask for help.

The aroma of the herbs, spices and slow-cooked meat made her tummy rumble and she couldn't wait to try every-thing. Despite the fact that Taylor had sat far away from Luca, their gazes met and he gave her a smile that made her tummy dissolve with lust and need. Until today, she'd been able to control her desires but now she wanted to let go of that resolve and have his lips on hers again.

But that would mean an end to their friendship. He lived on the other side of the world where he had an amazing career and so many opportunities. Whilst her life was based here in Melbourne. But the main issue between them was twenty years of friendship, of long chats, enjoying movies together and plenty of laughs.

An affair would be fun and she'd love to, but what would happen after? She'd lose the one guy who'd always been there for her. She trusted his advice over the years and now he'd helped her when she had questions about business.

Before long, everyone had eaten and the empty plates were carried to the kitchen. Parents took their young children outside to swim in the pool, and once the table was cleared the friends sat in the lounge area in front of the TV with full bellies.

"I'm so glad not to have a brat to manage. It's so hot outside. Who wants to be looking after them when you can sit in here?" Jenna said, crossing her giraffe-long legs. In tiny shorts and a singlet top, that would barely cover one of Taylor's breasts, Taylor gritted her teeth and said nothing. Unlike her sister, Taylor couldn't wait to have children and be one of those parents who was always looking tired but happy. She loved children, unlike her model sister.

"Well, it's lucky you don't have a boyfriend then, huh?" Luca said with a wink. Everyone laughed, including Jenna.

Taylor leaned back into the comfort of the couch. She had purposely sat out on a single couch so Luca couldn't sit next to her. Silly, she knew, but she just didn't know what to say to him.

Unfortunately he was too clever for her and carried a dining chair, placing it next to her. No one saw it as anything but ordinary since they usually sat together.

Taylor shivered in anticipation, with him in such a close proximity. His presence meant one thing. He was going to want to speak to her soon.

The only way to not talk was to escape, yet again. Standing, she announced, "I'm going for a swim."

Everyone groaned. "I'm too full," many of them said.

"Looks like I'm on my own," she said before grabbing her beach bag and heading outside. She needed to get away from Luca and the spicy scent of him.

The noise around the pool was loud and full of squeals and children dive-bombing. The parents were relaxing and enjoying time out chatting with friends.

Removing her caftan and high-heeled wedges, she tied her long hair in a messy bun, slathered some extra sunscreen on her face and walked to the gate of the pool.

"Taylor, come join us," Amy said, waving her over. "I love your bathing suit."

Taylor did, too. Recently she'd found an Australian company that designed bathing suits for large busted women. The high waisted pants and bikini top suited her shapely figure, and made her comfortable enough to walk around in it rather than covering herself with a towel.

Lowering herself into the water, she sat with the other women in the shallow end. Despite being constantly splashed by the children, she spent the next hour there catching up on news, while they asked her lots of questions about her business.

Luca came out into the garden. "Ice cream," he yelled out.

The children jumped from the pool and ran with excitement to him to get some dessert.

"You wouldn't believe that they ate only recently, would you?" Taylor chuckled.

Single handed, Luca dealt with the demands for treats from toddlers and older children.

"He'll be a great dad," Judy said, pointing to Luca. "Handsome and loves kids. I'd snap him up in a minute if I wasn't already married."

The women laughed.

"I heard you and he got some tongue action last night." Amy nudged Taylor.

Her belly rolled, still struggling with her feelings. "It was nothing like that," she said. "It was a dreidel drinking game and I spun N for kissing. So I had to kiss Luca." She paused. "It was like kissing my brother." The women chuckled and she felt pleased with herself for deflecting attention from her but when she looked up, she discovered Luca was staring at her. His gaze made her feel hot and cold at the same time.

"Ladies, if you want ice cream, you'll need to get out," he said in a curt voice. "Mama's rules, no eating in the pool."

His cool tone made her shiver despite the afternoon sun, and her skin tingled in response to him overhearing her outright lie. Kissing her brother? No way. She'd enjoyed their kiss more than she should have.

"No thanks, it's so hot that we're staying in the water," they chimed in reply. With the umbrella shading them, the pool was a wonderful place to sit on the lazy summer's day.

Taylor pressed her lips together and looked away, not wanting to catch Luca's gaze again. An urgent need had her wanting to apologise and tell him that his kissing had been amazing, but she was not going to do that, especially in front of her friends.

Exhaustion overcame her, thanks to too much wine, the sunny day and lack of sleep. Stepping out of the pool she told everyone she needed the toilet and would be back soon. She lied. She wanted to escape and pretend everything was how it should be, not how it was.

After changing back into her clothes, she ran into Sofia. Her finger touched her cheek. "You're looking pale, why don't you lie down?"

"I'll just go home, I think," she said, needing to get away from Luca and his demands to talk more about their kiss. It was childish but she thought it best to leave gracefully.

Sofia's face fell with disappointment. "But I made tiramisu for you. It's your favourite," she said with conviction, reminding her where Luca got his strong, Italian determination.

Taylor sighed, not wanting to hurt the older woman's feelings. "I c-can come back," she said, not even convincing herself.

A scowl marred her face. "Go lie down in Luca's room," she pointed in its direction. "I don't want you to miss out."

Taylor leaned over and kissed the older woman's cheek. "Thank you, I will. And thanks for lunch, it was delicious," she added hoping to appease her.

The warm smile told her she'd got it right. And it also made her temporarily forget her issues with Luca. She headed to his room, closed the door, lay on his bed and closed her eyes, blocking out the noise and stresses of the past twenty-four hours, and fell into a deep sleep.

* * *

HER NAME WAS BEING CALLED but she was so caught up in her dream that she blocked it away. She was kissing Luca in the pool, under a blanket of stars and a full moon. It was just the two of them, alone. Her fingers stroked his strong arms, loving the feel of his muscles beneath her touch.

"Taylor," she heard him say her name.

"Oh Luca," she sighed as she welcomed another steamy kiss.

"Wake up," she heard before feeling the brush of fingers along her arm.

The rich aroma of coffee teased her nostrils and her eyes fluttered open.

"Time to wake up," Luca said.

He was seated next to her, an espresso cup in one hand. "You've slept for an hour."

Her heart jack-knifed and so did she, to a seated position. "I-I'm so s-sorry."

"Don't be. We're having dessert," he paused. "I was looking for you and Mama said you were here." He placed the cup on the bedside table. "Come out when you're ready."

Now wearing board shorts and his wet hair all mussed, she said, "You've been in the pool."

"Well done, Sherlock, on your observations," he said. "Everyone has nodded off in front of the TV. Wanna watch a movie together?"

"What about the cricket?" she asked, surprised he didn't want to be with the others.

"I'd rather watch a movie, to be honest," he said. "If I say you can pick, will you join me?"

"Sure but dessert beckons," she said.

The families came inside, the sleeping friends were woken and everyone returned to the dining room where a magnificent array of cakes, biscuits and fruit had been laid out.

Everyone enjoyed the amazing buffet Sofia and others had made, and the room was filled with chatter and laughter. Soon enough, everyone was full again and after the table was cleared, they either retired to watch TV or headed outside to the pool.

No one noticed or seemed to care that Taylor and Luca disappeared together, back into his room. She chose an Elvis movie, knowing how much Luca loved his music but would rather die a death of a thousand cuts than confess to everyone about it.

Unlike him, she was out and proud about her love of all things vintage, even Tupperware. Luca hid behind his reading glasses and complex mathematical problems. Taylor didn't think anyone would care, but Luca did. Being an Elvis fan just didn't suit his image of a sensible, hard working scientist.

On his bed, they stretched back next to each other resting on pillows watching the movie.

"He was so good looking," she cooed, admiring Elvis's handsome face. "It's been a while since we did this," she said. "I'm feeling very nostalgic being here with you."

"I've been away for two years," he said in a sleepy voice.

"Yes, but before then, when you were dating someone, it didn't seem right either."

"I didn't care what they thought. It didn't matter…," he said, lifting himself on his elbow to look at her, rather than the movie. He shifted his body so he was on his side rather than his back.

"Yes, it did. Your girlfriends wouldn't have liked us being alone in your room, in your apartment or mine." She paused. "Same if I had a boyfriend."

"Perhaps," he said, with a wistful tone. "Now tell me why Amber wants us to have an affair?"

She gasped, quite unprepared for the sudden direct question from him. "You got me comfortable, so you could badger me, didn't you?" She said with a pout.

"It's what I do best," he said with a shrug, a sparkle lighting up his brown eyes.

Two could play this game, she thought to herself. Biting her lip to stop herself from smiling and revealing to him her intentions, she said, "Come here and I'll whisper the answer in your ear."

Suspecting nothing, he leaned forward, letting his guard down which gave her plenty of opportunity to go into an attack mode. Taking advantage, she walloped him with a pillow.

"Gah," he said, before reaching for a nearby pillow, and retaliating with a whack to her head.

They belted each other, the play-fight became more rough. Jumping up, she tossed a pillow at his head, before hiding behind the desk.

"I'm going to get you," he said.

"You may be smart, but I'm better at this than you," she shrieked as he snuck around the desk and took aim, hitting her on the back of her neck.

They playfully hit each other till they were breathless and both collapsed onto his bed in a fit of giggles. He delivered a final blow to her head before lying back, and punching the air victoriously.

No way was she going to allow him to win. She was the better fighter than he. Determined to be triumphant she rolled up, sat across his thighs and punched him with two pillows. "I'm the champion, not you," she cried out.

"Never," he cried. Using the strength in his legs, he was able to lift and roll her off, giving him full access to fight.

Laughing she continued to whack with the pillows till he grabbed both her wrists and held on to her with determination.

Tickling her wrist, with his pinkie fingers, she giggled and dropped her "weapons." "You cheated," she cried.

"All's fair in love and war," he said, before flipping her so she was lying down on the bed, her back pressed on the comforter.

Pinned to the bed, her arms above her head, his hand possessively holding them in place and his body over hers so she couldn't wiggle away.

"Looks like I'm the winner. . .again," he said with a jubilant lift of his eyebrow.

She struggled to break free but his strength was too much for her, and as much as she would never admit it, she was enjoying being held down by him. Their ragged breathing filled their ears and her gaze remained on him.

"You're a wild cat," he said. "You need to be tamed."

Their gazes clashed and she stared into his dark brown eyes with such longing that she wanted her arms free so she could grab his neck and bring his face towards hers. "So tame me then," she whispered.

"Taylor, you're looking at me. . ." His low voice was husky. "I don't think this is a good idea."

"It's not," she said but her words didn't match the signals she knew she was sending him. Her gaze locked with his and her rapid breathing and the lifting of her chest was in direct contrast to her words.

Her eyes pleaded for him not to get off the bed and leave. It wasn't right that she wanted them to cross the friendship line again, but she didn't care. She knew how good his lips felt pressed against hers and she wanted to experience it again. . .and again.

It felt likes minutes but was probably only seconds before he made the first move, leaned forward and pressed a soft kiss to her mouth. He leaned back, looking at her reaction, searching for direction. "Tell me to stop and I will."

He paused and when she said nothing, his mouth made its way to her neck, his afternoon shadow lightly scratching her skin and his lips tracing along her skin so softly that it was like a gentle breeze. He released her hands but her arms remained above her head, frozen and unable or rather unwilling to move.

"Something has happened between us, and I need to stop it but I can't." His deep voice breathed in to her ear. "We shouldn't be doing this. You need to tell me to stop." His tongue ran up and down the length of her ear.

Every nerve in her body went on high alert with her skin tingling and begging for the touch of his fingers. The warmth of his breath caressed her ear and she melted with desire. He'd barely touched her and her body was aching for more.

They'd already crossed the line with their friendship last night. Would it matter if they did it again? Yes. No.

She didn't care. All rational thoughts dissipated as quickly as ice under the flood of hot water. She wanted him. Had wanted him for years and now he was hers. It may be one afternoon or one night. She no longer cared. All she now cared about was him quelling this burning need in her.

"Kiss me," she said. "I want you to kiss me."

"Should we talk about it?" His voice was serious despite the heat burning in his eyes.

"No," she said with perseverance. "No more talking." She reached up and with her hands, brought them to his neck and tugged him to her. Their lips met, tentative at first. The kisses were soft, sweet to start with before they explored each other, in a way that was new and tentative.

Her fingers went in his hair while he used his elbows to steady himself and not squash her.

"Do you think. . ."

"Don't talk," she insisted.

He shifted their bodies so they lay side by side. His fingers ran down her face, along her arm to her hip, where it rested there.

"I don't want to hurt you," he said, as though in a final check to ensure she was okay with them kissing even though she'd repeatedly told him so.

"Stop talking and kiss me," she said, inching her face towards his.

For now, she didn't want to think about what was right and wrong. She ached for his touch and sighed as his lips met hers. God, he was such a good kisser. They kissed and kissed.

He pushed the caftan to the side and he pressed kisses along her neck towards her shoulder. Her nipples tingled and her breasts grew heavy.

His mouth went north as he licked and nibbled his way

back to her mouth before they spent minutes, or it could've been hours, kissing.

She closed her eyes and forgot that the house was full of people and anyone could walk in. All she could think about was the amazing kiss and the touch of his hands on her skin. She wanted more and tugged his shirt off so she could run her hands over his abs.

She knew what his chest looked like; they'd swum together many times over the years. But now it was different. She pushed him so he was on his back and she lay next to him, her fingers tracing over the belly muscles and touching the smattering of chest hair that darkened his skin. He was magnificent.

His hands came up to cup her breasts and his fingers teased her through the material of her bra and dress. "You're beautiful, every bit of you," he said through gritted teeth.

She leaned over him to suckle his ear lobe and breathed in his ear. "I want you."

He groaned in reply. "Taylor."

"Luca, where are you?" They heard his mother calling out.

He muttered a number of obscenities as she recoiled away from him like he was physically on fire and retreated to the safety of his en-suite bathroom. In the mirror, she caught a glance of herself, with her hair mussed, her eyes sparkling, and her lips looking thoroughly kissed.

"What a mess," she said to herself as all the reasons why she shouldn't be kissing Luca came crashing down on her. They were friends and if they did take their friendship to another level, how would it work out? He lived in another country. And she had a business and staff to worry about.

Splashing cold water on her face, she reminded herself why she'd kept their relationship platonic. But then she remembered how good he'd felt and tasted just a few minutes before. The bones in her legs dissolved and she sat on the closed toilet seat, unable to stand. Not only gorgeous and funny, he certainly knew how to kiss.

She couldn't hide in the bathroom forever and would have to leave. But for now, she sat and weighed her options. What was she going to do?

CHAPTER 6

*L*uca knocked on the bathroom door. "Taylor, are you okay?"

"Yes," he heard her say.

He strode in circles around his room, wearing down the carpet as he wondered what to do. Had his mother not been calling him, he would've undressed Taylor and made love to her on his bed. And then what?

What did friends do then?

He had no idea. God, what a mess.

He'd seen the look of horror on her face when his mother had been calling him. Somehow they'd got so caught up with the emotions of the day, and it was the third time they'd kissed in twenty-four hours.

He might have been able to talk himself out of last night's kisses, claiming they were part of a game and him being silly. But what about this afternoon? There was nothing playful in the way they'd kissed. Heck, she'd started undressing him and had they not been interrupted, he had been about to rip her dress off.

Lust didn't just burn in his belly, it steamed in his

veins, pulsating through his body. Last night, he'd had a hard-on the size of the Empire State building. Tonight he was not going to be able to sleep. He'd either have to drink a bottle of whiskey and pass out or work out for hours on end and collapse in exhaustion. Neither option appealed.

What did appeal to him was getting Taylor back into bed and finishing what they'd started.

The door opened and he spun around to see her come out, fully clothed, her hair in place but the visible whiteness of her skin told him they'd just shared their last kiss. She'd made the decision to remain friends, nothing more.

All thoughts of tearing off her dress dissipated and he remembered how important she was to him. More important than some great sex.

He strode to her, taking her hands in his. He kissed her knuckles and said, "I'm sorry, forgive me. We've crossed a line we shouldn't have."

She nodded and he could see genuine remorse in her blue eyes. "There's nothing to apologise for. It was stupid and we both made a mistake."

"I should've walked out of here after our pillow fight," he said, still holding her hands. I don't know how it happened, but it did."

"I feel the same way," she said with a shaky voice. "Can we pretend it never happened?" Her blue eyes darkened, pleading with him to accept what she was saying, and he could never say no to her.

"Of course, I blame myself. I was raised with better manners than that. I've taken advantage of you."

"Don't be ridiculous," she snapped at him. "It's just as much my fault. I should've said stop."

"But you didn't." He paused. "Why didn't you?"

Her hands rested on her hips and she rolled her eyes

before saying. "For the same reason you didn't stop. You didn't want to."

Her words hung in the air and they looked at each other, as though each of them were trying to read the other's minds.

"We should get back," they both started to say at the same time.

"Come on," he said. "Many of the families have left but there are enough still here watching TV. In a couple of hours, we'll have the leftovers for dinner. Will you stay?" The friend in him wanted her there, as she'd been for years. But now he was torn, wondering how he was going to control the unfamiliar feelings he was experiencing.

Taylor nibbled her lip, looking like she too was torn between leaving and staying. "Maybe," she said, which didn't really answer his question nor let him know the true affect of what just happened between them.

She breezed past him and he followed, but whereas she went to the kitchen where his mother was, he retreated to the safety of the group in the lounge room.

* * *

Taylor found Sofia chopping vegetables in the kitchen.

"I forgot to serve the lasagne, so we can have that tonight with the leftover salads," the older woman announced.

"I can't believe you did all of this for us. Lunch was amazing, and I loved the gnocchi. Thank you for remembering how much I like it."

The compliment seemed to be given to the air between them as Sofia ignored it and said through narrowed eyes. "What's going on between you and Luca?"

"W-what do you mean?" Taylor retreated, moving to a cupboard to retrieve a glass, and then to the fridge to pour herself some water. Draining her glass, she pretended she wasn't under an inquisition of some sort. "Nothing," she announced with innocence, despite the quick *thump thump* of her heart.

The older woman stood, wiped her hands on a tea-towel before tossing it aside. "I'm not stupid. I can see the looks you're giving each other." She paused as though searching for the right words. "Taylor, I've known you since you were seven years old. You've been friends with Luca since you moved to this street. You don't think I can't see what's going on."

Taylor crossed her arms defensively over her chest. "I don't know what you mean." And she didn't. At least that wasn't a lie.

Her brow furrowed and she took a step towards her. "You're looking at each other differently. I can see it." She pointed to her eyes.

Taylor shrugged, pretending there was nothing there. "He's been away for two years."

The older woman's eyes widened and she wagged her finger at her. "Don't you dare start being smart with me. I was young once, I know what it is to fall in love."

Taylor gasped, then took a step back, leaning against the wall. "You're wrong."

"If you want to be with him, you need to go to America. His work is too important. He didn't do all those degrees to be here, unemployed."

Her breath hitched in her throat. "I know. Luca is so smart, he needs to be there, doing what he does." For the life of her, she couldn't remember what he did. Being accosted by his mum was terrifying enough but to have her put pressure on her was making her nerves form into a messy, knitted ball. "I love what I do, I love my shop. It is who I am."

His mum smiled at her. "I know, I've never seen you as

happy and determined as when you started your business. It's different and unique."

"I don't know why we're having this discussion. Luca and I are just friends. We haven't seen each other for two years and I think the separation has meant we're acting silly around each other. I'm sure we'll be back to normal soon." *As if.* She thought to herself. She'd touched his chest, run her fingertips over the flat discs of his nipples and kissed him with such passion that she blushed recalling every intimate detail. She'd begged for him to kiss her. That's not what friends did.

Because from now on, there would be no more kissing. None.

"Okay," the older woman said in a way that made Taylor think she was not okay with it at all.

* * *

The following morning, Taylor drove to the small strip of shops where hers was. Flanked by a couple of trendy cafes, an organic produce shop and some clothing shops, her vintage business was well suited to the area.

The morning's business was slow. It seemed people had a food hangover after Christmas and despite the cafes being busy, she had few customers.

To distract her from thinking too much about Luca and her poor sales, she removed her Christmas decorations and started rearranging the window display for New Year. Adding some sparkle, she stood back and smiled, admiring the festive, fun scene she'd created with items in her shop.

Back in her shop, she dusted all the shelves and rearranged more stock with barely any interruption. Where were the customers?

By lunchtime, she'd barely had any sales and was feeling

disheartened. Despite knowing business was slow around this time with many either at the beach or heading to the malls to take advantage of the sales, she still had her rent and bills to pay.

The door opened, the bell tinkered and she plastered a smile on her lips to welcome a customer, but her eyes widened when she saw it was Luca.

"Good morning, what are you doing here?" she asked, surprised to see him.

"I came to see your shop and then take you for lunch," he announced, walking through. He whistled low, looking around. "This place is smaller than it looks in the photos you sent me but you've done an impressive job."

Her cheeks warmed at his compliment. He'd already been living overseas when she signed the lease agreement for the shop and she'd valued his input when making the final, nail-biting decision.

She pointed to an area at the front of the shop. "This is where I showcase local talent. These dresses have been made by designers who live here in town."

He nodded. "And these?" He pointed to a rack of clothes that held stunning vintage pieces.

"These are finds from either thrift shops or yard sales," she explained. "I spend a lot of time looking for pieces to sell. Sometimes they need alterations and cleaning, which I do." She paused. "They're one-off pieces and I have a number of regulars who come in each week to see what's new."

They ambled around the shop. "I'm now selling some accessories like purses and stylish hats."

"And the back room? Is it still storage?" He pointed to a doorway.

"Come see." She reached for his hand and tugged him towards it. "I'm so excited about this. Ta da," she said with a flourish. A beautiful table and chairs had been set up, with a sideboard filled with old-fashioned glasses and crockery. The high ceiling, wooden floorboards and cream walls made the room warm and spacious.

"I can now host parties for birthdays or other events. I work with a local caterer, and all the food is served on beautiful china wear. We serve high tea and then after that I give them tips and tricks on make-up and styling their hair," she announced with pride. "I've only had one party so far but it was so much fun and I'm hoping that through word-of-mouth, I'll get more."

"This is wonderful, I'm so proud of you," he said, his gaze taking in the soft furnishings and knick-knacks she'd lovingly found in trash-n-treasure markets.

"Thanks, it means a lot to me," she said with honesty. "I love this shop but I need to increase my sales as I'm barely covering my expenses," she said in a low voice.

"All new businesses take time to create a solid customer base," he reassured her, rubbing her shoulder.

Her heart sank as she told him honestly the difficulty of doing what she did. "I know that but I have to employ staff so they can manage the shop while I travel around Melbourne looking for items to sell. It's expensive but what sells best are the vintage pieces that are discarded, which I fix and then sell." She took a steadying breath. "My customers love the pieces I find but it's time consuming. Paying for staff to keep this place open while I do that is not easy," she confessed. "I love this place but I'm struggling to pay my bills."

He leaned against the wall, and nodded in agreement. "Have you thought about YouTube videos? You can share your knowledge on how you find pieces, how to clean them up. What about hair and make-up tutorials? I'm sure you'd have a lot of people interested and you can reach overseas markets. If you have enough views, you can make money."

Her heart lifted at his suggestion. "That's a great idea, I'd love to do it but I just don't have the time," she said with a long sigh.

"Why don't you make short videos? Not longer than like five or six minutes. Everyone is busy and may not have time to sit through a thirty-minute tutorial but five minutes will work and you can share them on social media."

It was a good idea and her mood improved as she pondered the options. "I like that I can reach vintage lovers who are outside of Melbourne. That's a good idea," she said.

He looked around, "It's pretty quiet, not just here but in the street. Why don't I get us some sandwiches and we can eat in here?" He pointed to the large oak, polished table. "That way if someone comes in, you won't miss out on a sale."

"That would be lovely, thank you," she said.

* * *

THE NEXT FEW days passed in a similar fashion. Luca would arrive around eleven in the morning, and they would have coffee and sandwiches in the beautiful room talking about everything, except their kiss or rather kisses.

He shared his loneliness in living away from his family and her heart ached. Over the past two years, he'd glossed over this, never revealing how hard it was for him to be away from his family.

"You never told me," she said.

"I didn't want to say anything." He shook his head as though pushing her words away. "It's not that important. Besides, recently I started making more of an effort to attend local events, talks and fairs. I've met some interesting people."

He then went on to share the breakthroughs he'd made, thanks to his years of study in electrochemistry. Ideas that were forward thinking and unique, that were being heralded in scientific circles.

He drained the last of his coffee, fiddled with his serviette before looking back at her. "I know we're not talking about Boxing Day but I need to. I can't just pretend it didn't happen. Maybe you can, but I can't. We've been friends for so long and nothing like that has ever happened. Why now?"

Her tummy turned inside out as he spoke. She'd been hoping that he'd never raise the subject again. She knew the answer but was reluctant to tell him so. Taking a sip of water, she wondered if telling him the truth would make a difference. He was going back to the US in a few days. What to do?

"Just be honest with me, as I have been with you," he implored. Taking her hand, he said, "I just need to know why you kissed me. For fun? Too much to drink?"

Recognising that he deserved her honesty, her breath caught in her throat. She opened her mouth before a moment of panic set in. "Just a minute." Jumping to her feet she ran through the shop to the front door to ensure they would not be interrupted. Flipping the sign to "closed," she then returned to him, sitting across from him. "I didn't want a customer walking in," she said before placing her hands in her lap. "I'm nervous."

"Really? With me?" His eyebrow lifted as though he didn't believe her.

"The last time I was this nervous was when you picked me up to take me to your school formal," she confessed in a shaky voice.

She could lie and pretend she'd drunk too much and acted stupidly because of it. But he'd never believe her because she didn't drink much and it wasn't in her character. She chose to give him a version of the truth and leave it at that. They were in their late twenties and eventually they would marry, and as Amber so correctly said, their friendship would change and develop. It might not weather the arrival of a wife or husband.

Taking a few deep breaths to steady her galloping heart she said, "I've had a crush on you for so long that I don't remember not having one."

His eyes widened and his jaw dropped, making his lips form into an O. It looked like he wanted to say something but had no idea what to say. She took that to mean that he never suspected that she'd like him.

She raised her hand so that her palm faced him. "It's okay that you didn't reciprocate my feelings and I have valued having you as a true friend. It's why I never said anything… because I wanted you in my life and the only way to do that was to have you as my friend," she said with genuine emotion. Because she did mean it. She'd rather have him in her life as something than not at all. From riding bikes around the neighbourhood, to watching movies, to giving each other honest advice, they'd been there for each other over the past twenty years.

He started to say something and she raised her hand again. "Let me finish before I chicken out."

"Your girlfriends came and went, but we remained tight. You even dated my sister." Her stomach churned with revulsion, recalling seeing them kiss. "But you were always there for me. Remember that time I stupidly drank too much at Sabrina's party all those years ago and passed out on the carpet. You made sure I got home safely and nothing bad happened to me."

He nodded and rubbed his chin.

"When you dated Jenna, I truly believed it was because you would never be attracted to someone like me. You went for the tall blond look, which is definitely not me." A small laugh erupted form her lips. "But even then, you loved me as a friend. I held on to that love because it was real and meaningful."

She took another sip of water and cleared her throat. "Around you, I can be myself. You like me as I am, and that's what I love about you. You get me. You share your secrets with me. You're there for me always." She paused. "You're more important to me than you'll ever know. I adore you, and love our times together. I never wanted to lose that just because I found you attractive."

Her hands twisted in her lap. "I know you don't like me like *that*." She shrugged. "But when you kissed me during the dreidel game and then on your bed, I melted. I wanted to stop but I couldn't help myself. For years I've supressed my feelings for you but when you're kissing me, how do you think I'm going to react?"

"I-I don't know what to say?" he said, his elbows resting on the table, his gaze solely focussed on her.

"Unless you've decided you want to take things further, then don't say anything." She bit her lip. "Even if you liked me, like that, we've got the Pacific Ocean between us and that I don't know how it can be resolved. Your career is over there and mine is here." She shook her head.

"You told me not to say anything but I want you to know that I do love and value you. And honestly, I've only ever thought about you as a friend, not a lover. You've always been there and I always want you there."

He stood and paced the room. "I'm a quiet guy. I love being with friends and family, cooking, hiking and being active." He stopped and turned to her. "I've never found a woman I want to be with more than you," he said in a low voice.

Her heart leapt then fell again. "Yes, but you wanted to be with me as a friend. I want you to love and adore me as a woman, and you're not attracted to me."

"Who says?" he snapped at her, his forehead creased with annoyance.

"You did." She pointed a finger at him. "You've only seen me as a friend. You said so."

"I love you as my friend but," he paused. "I've fought my attraction to you." He slumped against the old-fashioned fridge, his back against it, his eyes filled with confusion. Rubbing his eyes, he started walking around the room again as though in deep thought.

Her heart ached with disbelief, doubt and dilemma. He may have admitted to finding her attractive but there was no declaration of love. In fact, he was fighting his interest to her.

She stood, took a deep breath of bravery and walked on wobbly legs over to him and took his hands in hers. "You can't force love. The spark is either there or it's not. It's there for me but not for you." She shrugged as a heaviness settled on her shoulders. "It's just how it is," she added in a sad voice.

"I'm sorry." He gathered her in his arms before pressing a kiss to her forehead.

"I know you are." Her arms came around his waist and she held on to him loving the strength and feel of his firm muscles.

He finally pulled back. "Would you prefer I didn't attend tomorrow night's party?"

"No, don't miss it because of me," she said with sincerity. "But I can't go as your date." She cleared her throat. "I need to be on my own." He gaze lingered on the door-way.

"I think I should stay and we talk more," he said at the same time as she told him she wanted to be alone.

She shook her head. "I've embarrassed myself. . ."

"Why don't you call Amber or another friend? I'll wait here till they get here?" He suggested.

"I have a business to run." She sniffed before blowing her

nose. "I wish we could pretend the last half-hour never existed."

"But it has," he said in a quiet voice.

"It has and now you know everything."

"It doesn't have to change things between us," he said with hope.

She laughed but it wasn't filled with happiness or gaiety. "You know that's not true. From now on when you see me, you'll know what's going on here." She pointed to her head and then to her heart.

"We can work through it," he said, before giving her an encouraging smile.

"For now, I don't know how we can, I can't even tell you how humiliated I am feeling right now."

He pressed his lips against her forehead. "We'll get through it."

"I'll see you tomorrow night," she said, hoping he'd take the hint and leave. She wanted privacy to reflect on what had just happened. Mortification ate at every pore of her skin and her jaw clenched with tightness.

"I'm only leaving because you want me to," he said.

Her heart sank on reflection of how badly she'd spoken to him.

"See you tomorrow," he said, before exiting the shop.

"Goodbye Luca," she said.

She was relieved when he left so the tears she'd held at bay could run in rivers down her cheeks. She'd really messed up with him and ruined their friendship because she'd allowed her hormones to mess with her head. Stupid, stupid, stupid.

*T*aylor wanted to work, continue with her day but couldn't. The pain of humiliating herself and knowing she may lose Luca as a friend was so great that she closed the shop early, something she never did, and left.

Agitated and unable to think straight, she headed to the one place that was calming and would be the perfect distraction for her, the beach.

Driving there, she rang Amber. "Any chance you're free to listen to me mope about Luca and watch me drown my pity in ice cream?"

Her friend chuckled. "You wouldn't believe it but I just had a cancellation. I'll see you soon," Amber said before disconnecting the phone.

Taylor arrived at Elwood beach and bought an ice cream from the food truck before sitting down on a bench to stare at the water. The day was warm but not unbearably so, yet the beach was filled with families enjoying time together on the glorious summer's afternoon. Still dressed in her favourite hourglass dress and heels, she stood out amongst the beach crowd, who were all dressed in comfortable, casual wear. She ignored any quizzical looks and simply enjoyed her ice cream. A few minutes later, the salty breeze and holiday atmosphere settled her nerves and her muscles relaxed so her head and shoulders no longer ached.

"Hey stranger," Amber said, sitting down next to her, holding a double cone of rich chocolate ice cream. "This was a good idea, coming here dressed in work gear," she said before eating a large mouthful of deliciousness. "So goooooood," she said looking directly at her ice cream. "We're walking along the water, so you'd better ditch those lovely shoes of yours…and stockings?" Creases lined her forehead. "Why are you wearing stockings, it's summer?"

"You know me, I love stockings," she said with a sigh.

"Does Luca know you wear stockings, as in, wearing a garter belt? If he did, he'd probably swallow his tongue?" Amber nudged her friend with her elbow. She looked at her friend's frown. "Not even a smile? Come on babe, it can't be that bad, can it?" Amber's voice was filled with empathy, having known Taylor for many years.

Taylor stood, her eyes were filled with unshed tears "It is. I'm going to the car to remove my *stockings* and shoes. Back in a minute."

A few minutes later, barefoot, she tapped her friend on the shoulder. "I'm ready." Despite the soothing view, her body ached with the loss of Luca. Stupid. This was why she'd never wanted to cross the line. It reaffirmed that she'd made the right decision all those years ago. But now? She'd allowed her hormones and the joy of Christmas to wreck her carefully grounded plans. And look at what had happened?

Amber removed her shoes and held them as they made their way to the sand. "What a day. Not only do I get to see you, but I get a walk on the beach."

Despite the busyness of the beach, they were able to meander at leisure. The cool water splashed her feet and had a calming effect on her. "Thanks for meeting me," Taylor said.

"The pleasure is all mine, trust me. It doesn't get much better than that." She took another large bite of ice cream before saying. "I should do counselling sessions here, much nicer than my office." She stopped, "Sorry, I'm blabbing. Tell me what happened with Luca."

Taylor took a deep breath and let the words tumble from her lips. "I told him that I've had a crush on him, he told me he likes me as a friend. That's about it," she added with a shrug.

"Rubbish. I think there's more to it, but that's enough for the time being," Amber said. "You can't make him love you."

Her heart grew heavy because her friend's words echoed her own. "I said that to him. You can't force love, that's not how it works."

Amber nodded. "Sorry to pry but please tell me what he said when he found out about your true feelings?"

Because Amber was her bestie and had listened to Taylor talking on/off about Luca for so long, she'd didn't hesitate to tell her the truth. "He was shocked, truly shocked. His mouth opened but no words came out. He loves me as a friend, and if that's all I'm going to get, then I have to accept it. I just hope he still wants me in his life." She gave a dramatic sigh.

"Of course he will," Amber reassured her before finishing her ice cream, then bent down to wash her hands in the sea water. "Things are going to be different, they can never go back to how they were."

She waved away her friend's insights. "I wish he wasn't such a good kisser. At least if it had been bad, I would be less upset."

Amber rolled her eyes at her friend. "Luca's too hot to be a bad kisser. So what are you going to do now?"

"I'm going to avoid him as much as I can, till he returns to

America. Then I plan on dating in the New Year. It's time to get over him and find a man." Her words didn't match her conviction because in the near future she knew she'd be comparing all her dates with Luca. She needed to move on first.

Amber touched her arm, reassuring her she was doing the right thing. "You've been so hung up on him for so many years that you've compared all your boyfriends to him. Is it any wonder you haven't found the right guy for you? You need to stop wishing they were him."

Taylor nibbled her lip and reflected on her friend's accusations. Unfortunately they were true. Despite denials, she'd secretly been hoping that something was going to happen between her and Luca. But that was a fantasy. "It's time for me to move on."

"It is," her friend said.

"I just need time," she admitted in a soft voice.

"I know and I'm here for you," Amber said, giving her friend a warm hug.

They walked along the wet sand and the playful mood of the children calmed her down and the coolness revitalised her.

Amber broke their companionable silence. "Do you mind if I come to your parents' party tomorrow night?"

"I can't believe you're on your own," she said, surprised. "Of course you can. You'll be my date." She linked her arm with her friend's elbow.

"You'll be the best date I've had in ages," her friend confessed.

They giggled before spending the rest of the afternoon walking up and down the wet sand, talking about everything but Luca.

* * *

MUCH LATER, they each got a noodle box and sat watching the waves from one of the many food trucks. The sun set, yet families and friends remained on the beach, as the warmth had not yet dissipated. "I'll see you tomorrow night. Thanks for the best afternoon, I'm feeling so much better."

"You're welcome. I know we're not talking about you-know-who, but something to think about. If he decided he wanted you in his life, as a lover not a friend, would you give up your shop for him?" Her friend raised her eyebrow in a did-you-think-about-that motion?

Taylor went to open her mouth and say *no way*. But then she snapped it shut. Maybe she would? She shook her head. "I don't know." Because, she didn't.

"If by chance Luca decides he's madly in love with you, you should know if you'd be willing to move to America for him," her friend probed.

Her heart spiked at both the ideas of him liking her like that and the viability of her business. "What would I do? My shop?" She scratched her head. "My life is here, not there."

"You need to think about it because if he decides he wants you in his life, you can't say yes and then say no. What's more important to you, him or your business?"

"This is hypothetically speaking of course?" Taylor looked to her friend for reassurance.

"I could say yes, but you know me." She shrugged. "I think it's a good idea to be well prepared." She gave Taylor a reassuring rub on her shoulder. "Just have a think about it."

"Unlikely, but I will," she said to her friend. But she wasn't planning on it. She'd seen the shock on Luca's face this afternoon. There was no way he was going to suddenly realise he wanted her as more than a friend.

"See you tomorrow night," Amber said, giving her friend a warm hug. "Love you."

"Love you more," she said. She may not have a man in her

life, but Taylor was grateful for her friends and her parents in her life.

* * *

TAYLOR DROVE HOME THINKING about Luca, Amber and everything they'd discussed. She was now able to admit to herself that she'd held herself back because of her crush and that it was time to move on.

Tick for Taylor.

Now she had to do it.

But Amber was right, things couldn't go back to how they were because she knew how good his lips felt on hers and for now, she couldn't stop thinking about that.

Berating herself for reliving those heated moments, she turned off her car, exited and slammed the door way too hard. Her car didn't deserve her frustration. Grabbing her purse and shoes, she made her way in to her family home and was surprised to hear voices. In the living room, Luca and her dad were talking.

"Um-m, hi," she said, standing in the doorway, reluctant to go in. Her father was relaxing in his favourite chair and Luca was seated opposite him, a couple of long necked beers adorned the coffee table.

"Darling," her father greeted her, surprise etched on his face. "You're home? Do you want to join us?" He pointed to the sofa.

"Err, no thanks. I want to change."

"Luca's telling me about his work."

Luca flashed her a genuine smile. "You're more than welcome." He stood and walked towards her, brushing his lips against her cheek.

Unable to help herself, she took a step back, scared to be

so close to him. "I'll see you later," she said before turning around and heading to her room.

She heard her father and Luca finish talking and then he left.

The shock of seeing him had meant she'd behaved rudely. How long before she could be in the same room as him and not act like she was on fire and needed to escape? Stupid kiss had ruined everything. She thought that was what she had wanted. She shouldn't have wished for it, because her Christmas wish may have come true but it wasn't what she thought it would be. Perhaps her New Year's wish would be for her and Luca to be friends again? Real friends, like they used to be.

She sighed dramatically before peeling off her dress and heading to the bathroom. She needed a shower, a cup of tea and a hug.

* * *

THE FOLLOWING DAY, Taylor helped her parents, Anne and Jason, prepare for the New Year's Eve party that night, and surprisingly Luca came over. He strung the fairy lights around the garden, and set up the rotating mirror ball in the living room. A jukebox had been delivered, so the guests could choose the music they wanted to listen and dance to.

Usually, she'd make silly jokes to Luca about the music and whether he'd choose his favourite Elvis songs. But today, she said nothing. Instead, she chose a couple of ballads by the Beatles which suited her sombre mood.

She caught Luca looking at her, but they each said nothing.

All the families in Clarendon Close had been invited and the start time was early, so the families could bring their children.

Her mum came into the room, wiping her hands on a tea towel. "I'm keeping the menu simple as it's a hot day. There are plenty of salads, and I'll get your dad to grill the chicken kebabs and the steaks on the BBQ. I've also got sausages for the children."

"Sounds perfect, Mum," she added. "And dessert?"

"I've got ice cream, cake and fruit," she said, ticking each off on her fingers.

Looking at her watch, she couldn't help but think about her sister, Jenna, who was still not here and would turn up when everything was ready.

"Thanks for helping us move the furniture," Anne said to Luca.

"You're welcome," he said with a smile before turning to look at Taylor. "I said I'd pick up some beer and ice for your dad," Luca said, but didn't invite her to join him.

Obviously, he didn't want her there. Taylor's heart sank with sadness. Usually, she'd join him and they'd sneak in an ice cream at the beach. No such luck today. He wanted to be on his own and away from her.

"I'll see you tonight?" he asked.

"Sure," she nodded. "See you then."

The afternoon passed quickly as she helped her parents prepare for the party. After a quick shower, she changed into her favourite red dress with its large skirt and purple petticoat, and fitted bodice held in place by large straps. It always made her happy wearing this dress and she added her favourite purple hair accessories to her ponytail. Slipping her feet into her favourite sandals, she was ready for a night of dancing.

The guests started arriving at six o'clock, and the party was in full swing within thirty minutes with the families dancing to juke box favourites with their children. Some of the men stood around the BBQ, as her dad grilled the meats.

Some of the women sat in the air-conditioned room sipping champagne.

The casual but warm atmosphere ensured everyone was enjoying themselves. It was how so many parties over the years had been, filled with friendship and a strong camaraderie.

Her sister and some of the other twenty-somethings had yet to arrive, which didn't surprise Taylor. But what did surprise her was that Luca wasn't there.

Amber, in a halter neck black dress, which showed off her slim body to perfection danced up to her. A large grin made her look even prettier than she was. "I may not have anyone to kiss at midnight, but I'm having fun," she chuckled. "Even if this is a G- rated party."

She tugged her friend towards her, and reluctantly Taylor danced to "Shake your tail feather."

A few songs later and Taylor was breathless from the dancing and singing. "Thanks, Amber, for forcing me to join you. I'm having fun."

Amber waggled her eyebrows. "Told you."

Jason Williamson paused the music and spoke into the microphone. "Dinner will be ready soon, but we have a special guest who's here to entertain us," he said.

Everyone looked around as the music sounded, very loud. Some of the younger children covered their ears but Taylor could feel her brow furrow as Elvis's "Burning Love" played.

"Please welcome, the King," he announced in a grand voice.

Within seconds, an Elvis impersonator ran into the room and onto the low platform that had been set up. In Elvis's trademark white jumpsuit, complete with rhinestones and multiple rings on his fingers, the man looked like Elvis, even wearing a 1970s hairpiece, before lip-syncing to the song.

Everyone started dancing and cheering Elvis on, enjoying the festivities.

Taylor looked around the room, hoping to see Luca but he wasn't there. Shame, because he'd love to see this. Turning around, she watched the performance when she caught the eye of "Elvis." He grinned at her and her belly flip-flopped.

Doing a double take to ensure her eyes weren't making a mistake, she jabbed her friend in the ribs. "That's Luca!"

"Oh-my-goodness!" her friend cried out. "I can't believe that's him."

Neither could Taylor. Luca had dressed as his idol and was singing and dancing in front of his family and friends. Knowing his unassuming character, she was shocked that he'd do that.

Amber nudged her friend. "How good is Luca?" she yelled over the music.

Shock froze her muscles and Taylor couldn't dance, clap or do anything as Luca performed to the song. At the end, everyone cheered before the next song came on, a ballad. This time he looked at her and sang the lyrics of "The Wonder of You."

Her eyes widened, her heart thumped wildly against her chest as Luca publicly told her and everyone else at the event that the only one who understood him was *her*.

She choked back disbelief as he told her through the lyrics that her kisses and love were everything to him.

There was no denying what he'd done. This was a public declaration of love that could not be misinterpreted as the product of too much alcohol.

Her gaze left his for a moment and she could see her parents holding hands and watching her. Betrayed by them. They knew about Luca's plan.

Returning her gaze to Luca, she realised what he'd done.

He'd let down his mask, revealed himself to her in a way that was not easy. But he had done it. *For her.*

Love, appreciation and gratitude welled in her belly. As soon as he finished with Elvis's trademark "thank you very much," she literally pushed everyone out of the way and leapt onto the small stage, throwing her arms around his neck.

He caught her around the waist, and unable to help herself, she kissed him. Kissed him in front of everyone, not caring who saw or what they thought.

Eventually the wolf whistling reminded her this was a family event and her father came up and touched her shoulder. "Perhaps you two should go somewhere private to talk?"

Hand in hand, they walked to her room, a smile stretched across her lips, still unable to believe what he'd done. "I don't know what to say," she said.

"Tell me you love me," he said, holding her close.

"What?" she gasped, not expecting him to say that.

"Tell me you love me," he murmured against her ear, before his lips ran against the length.

She looked at him and blinked rapidly. "I thought I'd lost you as a friend. I humiliated myself in front of you yesterday and now you want me to tell you that I love you?"

"That's about right," he said, before his fingers trailed along the side of her face. "I just humiliated myself in a bigger way, so now you go first." His dark eyes sparkled with cheekiness and happiness.

"I'm surprised and staggered to find you telling me how important I am to you in front of fifty people," she said, as her heart raced with uncertainty. "What's going on?"

He drew her to the bed, holding her hands, his gaze locked on hers. "I've always loved you."

"But as a friend," she interrupted.

"Yes, as a friend. But after that initial kiss we shared, I saw you differently, but I was worried about hurting you and ruining our relationship. For the first time, ever, I thought about you romantically."

"You did?" she sighed, feeling her belly melt with joy.

"I did," he said with a nod. "But I was scared. One minute you're my friend, the next minute I'm thinking things that friends should not be thinking about each other." He kissed the tip of her nose. "I tried to squash my feelings for you, and then in the shop you told me you liked me, too."

"But you left," she said.

"I know. It was overwhelming. Everything happened so quickly." He stopped and rubbed his eyes. "I came to Melbourne to celebrate the holidays, not fall in love. I never expected to feel like this, and especially with you."

He brushed his lips against hers. "I needed to think and talk to someone. I spoke with my dad."

Like her needing the advice of Amber, he'd also reached out.

He ran his fingers through his hair. "I've never been in love and I didn't know what I felt, if it was real." He took her hand and placed it on his chest. "Feel my heart beating from nerves, joy and excitement."

She smiled at him. "What did your dad say?"

"He asked me questions about how I felt about you, and I realised that I want you in my life not just as my friend. You're beautiful, smart, funny, and I just want to be with you always." He paused. "I'm happiest when I'm with you. We laugh, we talk non-stop and you're a great kisser." He brushed his lips against hers.

As much as she wanted to kiss and not talk, she placed her fingers against his lips. "You know that I've had a crush on you forever, but you haven't had one on me. How can you suddenly be sure you love me?"

"I don't know." He drew back but held her hands. "But since that Christmas kiss, I can't stop thinking about you.

Something between us changed, and if my mum hadn't interrupted us on Boxing Day that afternoon, I would've made love to you and regretted nothing." He gazed at her, brushing the back of his fingers against her cheek.

"I can't explain it," he said in a low, husky voice. "All I do know is that I love you, not as a friend but," he paused, "as a woman. Later tonight, I want to show you how special you are to me. But for now, with fifty people outside, we'll keep it clean."

He kissed her and she kissed him back, loving the pressure of his lips on hers. They fell back on the bed and the kisses became heated till Luca stopped and broke away, their breathing coming in short bursts.

"You're killing me, you're so responsive to my touch and I want to forget that we're in a houseful of people and spend time with you." He lifted her hand and pressed hot kisses along each knuckle. "I know this is sudden, but I'm almost thirty. I know what I want in life and I want you. You've always been there for me and I can't imagine being with anyone else but you. You make me smile, you make me happy, you make me feel complete in a way that I didn't understand till now."

She placed her arms around his waist and held him tight, still quite unable to believe he was hers. Giddiness made her want to kiss him again and never let him go.

He sat back and gazed at her, love filling his dark eyes. "Taylor, my beautiful friend. You are the best thing that has ever happened to me. I love that I'm happiest when you're around. I love that my parents adore you. I love that you want a family. And I love that you're the one I want to spend my life with." He slid off the bed and knelt in front of her. "I've spoken to your parents but will you, Taylor, take this Elvis-loving scientist to be your husband?"

"You want to marry me?" Her heart rate quickened. "It's a bit soon. We haven't even dated yet."

He sat next to her. "Apparently, you had a crush on me and..."

She playfully punched his shoulder. "But once I get to date you, perhaps you'll bore the socks off me or perhaps you don't put the toothpaste lid on?" she said with a grin.

"Will you date me then? I have every intention of marrying you when you're ready," he said, pressing his lips against hers. "And can you give me an answer because I'm a little nervous here."

"Yes, but. . ." A concern of reality punched her in the belly.

"But what?" he asked. His fingers smoothed the skin along her forehead.

"But what about my business?" Worry and insecurity ate into her belly. "How will this work?"

"I don't know. We need to talk about that. I have a couple of ideas, which you may or may not like. You could sell your business or get your staff to manage it. Not really great options and I hate that you have to give up what you love for me, I really do."

"But even if I did, what would I do?" Her voice was high pitched and filled with anxiety.

"You can either work in a shop, like yours. Or, my preferred option is you focus on your social media and YouTube channel." He paused, while his thumbs caressed her pulse points. "You've done some tutorials on vintage inspired hair and makeup. Can you expand on it? Do tutorials for busy mums? Or for women with more time? What about how to look for bargains? How to mend clothes? I'm sure you can get a good following, and you could do what you do, but on-line."

The idea appealed but terrified her. "I'm scared," she said in a soft voice.

"Me too," he said. "But I want to do this with you." She could see real concern for her in his dark eyes. "I have a work contract for two years. If, after that time, you are not happy, we will return to Melbourne."

"You'd do that for me?" Her eyes widened, unable to believe he'd give up his career for her.

"I want to provide for you and I hope you'll be happy there. But if you're not, we'll come back," he assured her. "But I don't want to go another day without you in my life."

"I don't know what to say," she said before throwing her arms around his neck.

"Say yes and make me the happiest guy ever," he breathed into her ear. "We'll work through it together, darling." He kissed her thoroughly. "So, what do you say?" he asked, lifting his eyebrow.

"Yes, yes, yes. A thousand yesses," she said holding him tight. "I still can't believe you're mine and that my wish came true."

"It's a magical time of the year," he said, before pressing his lips against her. "As much as I want to be with you, *alone*, I think our parents are waiting for us." He stood. "Ready?"

"Ready," she said, jumping to her feet. "Thank you Luca for making my dreams come true."

"I should be thanking you. You're the best thing that has ever happened to me, and I can't wait to spend the rest of my life with you. My love, my best friend." He leaned over to kiss her again. "I love you."

"I love you, too," she said.

Hand in hand, they walked out to share the happiness of their newfound love with their parents, family and friends.

THE END

CHRISTMAS KISS IN LONDON

*C*an an online friendship lead to real-life romance?

EVERY DAY, Amber Webb, a counsellor in an In Vitro Fertilization clinic, helps couples seeking parenthood. With her own biological clock ticking louder, maybe it's time she started thinking about having babies of her own. The flirtatious guy she accidentally friends on social media could be perfect, if only he weren't younger than her, a party-guy surrounded by beautiful women, and living halfway around the world.

STUNTMAN DARCY HARRIS may be based in London, but his work on blockbuster movies can have him away from home for months at a time. That doesn't leave time for anything other than casual hookups. But the long-distance nature of his online friendship with an Australian beauty allows deep personal revelations they might not share in person.

. . .

WHEN THEY FINALLY MEET, can their online friendship stand up to in-person reality? She lives in Melbourne and he lives in London. He's younger and has a booming career ahead of him.   She wants to settle down and start a family. But can friendship turn to forever love when they share a snowy Christmas kiss in London?

DEDICATION

For those who love Christmas

CHAPTER 1

*A*mber Webb wished she didn't love Christmas so much, because if she was more like the Grinch, then she wouldn't be at this uneventful *Christmas in July* party, talking to this uneventful guy, drinking uneventful wine.

The premise sounded fantastic, a weekend away in the mountains, a delicious buffet Christmas dinner and lots of fun. Instead, she was stranded in budget accommodation that had been organised by someone who had no idea what event management was. Now, she was stuck with a group of people that she had nothing in common with. She'd tried to be friendly but it wasn't working. Neither was the alcohol.

Draining her glass, she pretended to be interested in whatever Darcy was saying to her. "You should look me up on social media." He pointed to her mobile phone.

Urgh. No thanks, she thought.

"Come on," he gave her arm a playful punch.

She eyed her arm, where he'd punched her, with narrowed eyes. She'd rather chew glass than spend any more time with this Darcy guy. Ugh. Taking a step away from his all-too-close presence, she started typing his name. Darcy

Tosser. She quickly removed the word Tosser before he saw it.

The obnoxious guy tried to see the phone's screen and she took a step away from him. "It's Darcy Hauris, H-A-U-R-I-S, make sure you spell it correctly. Not Harris." He leaned towards her, obviously trying to ensure she spelled it correctly.

She shifted her stance so her phone faced away from him. The screen blurred as the three glasses of the mulled wine dulled her senses. Blinking rapidly, she retyped his surname and watched it autocorrect to HARRIS.

"It's Hauris not Harris," he said, peering over her handset.

For goodness sake, she was about to whack him with her phone, with the mountain load of disappointment she felt from the Christmas promises she'd been expecting.

Enough already. She needed to get away from this loser. In that moment she decided to friend someone else so she and *Darcy Hauris* would never be "friends". Great idea, she thought.

She retyped Darcy Hauris into her phone, watched Hauris autocorrect to HARRIS, and then randomly friended the first Darcy Harris she saw. She placed her mobile in her purse. "All done," she smiled sweetly at the guy she never wanted to see again and made a beeline for the bar, away from Darcy the Loser. She wanted to drown her sorrows in another glass of cheap wine and commiserate on the loss of her romantic dreams for a special Christmas event.

If only her bestie, Taylor was here. Amber sighed with the weight of the world's problems on her shoulders. But Taylor was living with her fiancé, Luca, in America, far away from Australia, and far away from her.

* * *

A FEW DAYS LATER, on the other side of the world, Darcy Harris sat patiently in a chair flicking through his phone while his hair and makeup were being styled. As the lead stunt guy, he was not only proud of his achievements but loved connecting with his fans. Scrolling through social media, he *liked* a number of videos posted by blokes wanting to follow in his footsteps.

A post caught his eye. One of his followers was listening to his favourite band at a nightclub. . .in Melbourne. Narrowing his eyes, he clicked on the post and watched the short video of Rock Lint playing his favourite song, "You and Me." His favourite song and the one he loved using in his social media videos.

Rock Lint was a local band in Melbourne, Australia, virtually unknown in his hometown of London. He'd only found them by chance and now one of his followers was at a pub listening to them.

Amber Webb.

The name was unfamiliar to him, but he couldn't help but be impressed with her gorgeous smile in her profile pic. How had he not noticed her when she started following him?

She was in Melbourne and liked ice cream, historical dramas and watching cricket.

She wasn't like the usual followers at all. His interest was piqued and he typed a message to her hoping she was having fun at the concert.

* * *

THERE WAS nothing like listening to live music in a pub, Amber thought. The loud electric guitar sounds of Rock Lint seemed to reverberate through her muscles as Amber danced. In black, ripped jeans, chunky heeled boots, and tank top, she looked very different from the professional that she was, who attended all meetings and appointments in smart pantsuits and heels. Taking a sip from her bottled beer, she cast an appreciative smile at the aged décor and the eclectic group of fans who were enjoying themselves as much as she was.

The band finished their song to a loud round of applause and Amber melted into the background since she was on her own. Being a workaholic meant she had little time to socialise and the few friends she had, had crinkled their noses when she'd suggested coming out tonight.

A sharp pain hit her in the heart as she thought of her bestie, Taylor. Taylor would've come along, even though she hated rock music, preferring Elvis Presley's songs to Rock Lint.

A private message notification popped up on screen from Darcy Harris and she groaned, remembering the awful man from the Christmas event, Darcy-what's-his-name, and that she'd forgotten to unfriend the random Darcy Harris she'd friended in her attempt to get away from him. How embarrassing.

Opening the message and preparing herself to apologise, she was surprised to read the following:

Love Rock Lint, enjoy listening to my favourite band.

Amber stared at the message and nibbled her lip as she contemplated who this Darcy Harris was.

Checking his profile, she read he was a stuntman. Impressive. And so was his cheeky grin and his. . .whoa-impressive physique. He'd posted a number of photos of himself shirtless and her eyes widened as she took in his muscled torso, flat belly, and strong arms. Clicking on some of his shared videos she was dazzled by his stunts involving horse riding, jumping in and out of moving cars and Parkour. One video highlighting the best of his Parkour stunts left her breathless and impressed by his achievements. He seemed very young to be so talented.

At twenty-seven he was four years younger than her and her exact opposite. He came across as impulsive, irresponsible, and irresolute.

With nothing to lose, she typed a reply, *Having a fab time, they are a great band.*

Surprisingly, a reply came through straight away. *They are. Check this out…listen to the music.* He'd attached a link, which took her to a one-minute video of highlights of his career with Rock Lint's signature song "You and Me."

Amber grinned, her heart hammering hard in her chest. What to say next? What to say, what to say? Amber then typed, *Next time you're in Melbourne, you should see them.*

He replied, *Only if you come with me.*

A flirt? Amber smiled, unable to help herself. Darcy was everything she wasn't, and not only was he on the other side of the world, but he was younger. It's not like anything serious would happen between them. Someone that good looking and in the movie industry would undoubtedly have women throwing themselves at him. He wouldn't be interested in someone like her who preferred a night in with friends rather than clubbing. Since there was no chance they'd meet, she chose to flirt back.

Next time you're in Melbourne, look me up. Amber stared at the sent message, unable to believe she'd just written that.

An immediate reply popped up on screen. *It would be my pleasure. I'm working on a big movie, so we may be heading down under ;)*

Amber sucked in a sharp breath. He was coming here? No. Maybe. Ohmygawd. She was in over her head.

With trembling fingers, she wrote, *See you when you get here ;)*

Brilliant. Came the immediate reply and then *Gotta go, being called.*

Called? She wondered. Perhaps he was on set and was needed. Probably. Darcy Harris. She liked his name and she liked the sound of him.

Watching a couple more of his videos on social media, she was impressed with how easy and effortless he made jumping off buildings and diving into cars looked. Clicking through more of his social media posts, she whistled through her teeth, seeing the array of high-profile actors he'd worked with. And now she was friends with him, all because of that stupid Christmas in July function. At least something good had come of it, because the massive headache she'd woken up to the next morning had kept her off alcohol for the past two weeks. Until tonight. It only seemed appropriate to drink beer while listening to live music. How Australian of her.

Draining her beer, she pocketed her phone and made her way home, she had a big day of work tomorrow.

An hour later in bed, Amber intended to check on her patients' files and also clear some emails, but instead, she logged on to YouTube to watch more of Darcy's videos. He was right. Rock Lint was a favourite of his, their music featured in all of his stunt videos. She re-watched the high-lights video and was truly impressed by the ease with which he did his death-defying stunts.

She gasped when she noticed the time on her bedside clock. Had she really just spent almost two hours on this Darcy Harris guy? Hard to believe. Closing her laptop, she settled herself into bed and fell asleep, dreaming about a guy with chiselled abs, high cheekbones, and stunningly blue eyes.

. . .

THE FOLLOWING DAY, Amber was distracted and found it hard to focus on the couple in front of her sharing the pain of their IVF journey. Unable to summon up her usual compassion, due to her lack of sleep, she nodded appropriately and helped as best as she could.

Stupid of her to stay up so late watching Darcy's videos. Her patients needed her, and she shouldn't have wasted good sleeping time on the internet last night. What she needed was another strong coffee and a reminder that daydreaming about handsome, English guys was a waste of time. Hadn't she learned her lesson about smooth, good-looking men who could talk their way into her bed. Gah. She'd been so foolish.

And that was it…until she received another message from Darcy. *How's your day going? I just spent mine falling down a set of steps five times.*

He was cute, she had to give that to him. She liked the banter but was sensible enough to know nothing would happen between them. She'd seen the photos online of Darcy, always surrounded by good-looking actors. Each more beautiful than the other.

Taking a bold approach, she took a selfie, hair slicked back in a professional ponytail and in her conservative black suit. *This is me working, a little different from you.* She sent it, interested to know his reaction.

I didn't think good-looking lawyers liked rock music.

Good looking? Her? What a tease, she stifled a snigger.

She replied, *I'm a counsellor. I work with couples struggling to conceive.*

Back came his reply, *So glad. I prefer counsellors over lawyers. I bet you're good at what you do.*

She blushed at his reply, unable to help herself. *I try*, she replied.

One of the makeup artists I know is going through IVF. It sucks.

It did, she agreed. *Yes. I'm sorry about your friend. How's she doing?*

It's not easy for her as she's on set a lot.

Amber nodded, thinking about the difficulties of working away from the clinic when trying to conceive through IVF. She didn't know what to say. Not knowing the circumstances of his friend, she was reluctant to say something trite.

He replied first. *She's taking time off soon to focus on becoming a mum.*

That's a good decision.

She'll be happy to hear that, he said.

Are you sore? she asked, wondering if it hurt to fall down stairs when you were a stuntman.

A little, came back his reply.

I watched some of your videos. They're very good, she confessed, her cheeks burning.

Thank you. My brother creates and uploads all my videos for me, he'll be happy to know you like them.

She wanted to say something witty but it wasn't in her personality to be forthcoming and flirty. *How did you become at stuntman?* She really wanted to know. Over her nine years working as a counsellor, she'd met many men and women in a variety of careers, but never one in stunts.

It's 4 a.m. and I need sleep. I'll chat with you over the weekend. And then he signed off.

Disappointment filled her belly that he'd left, even though she understood that he needed to sleep.

Pushing aside her irrational thoughts, she reviewed her day before getting organised for the next four back-to-back meetings she needed to attend.

CHAPTER 2

*D*arcy was standing in the bar of yet another hotel, drinking more beers than he'd meant to. The day had been difficult for the crew, due to the lead actress's tantrums and insistence on re-takes. Running his hand through his hair, his gaze caught one of his fellow stunt guys and they raised their beers to each other thankful for the end of the day.

"Hi Darcy," Miranda said, snaking her way towards him. With her knockout curves and sex appeal, every guy on set was drawn to Miranda. Working in makeup, she knew exactly what she was doing when rubbing makeup on his legs or arms. She was the consummate blonde bombshell. She loved sex, or so he'd heard, and the thrill of the chase. He didn't know what appealed to her about him more, that he wasn't interested in her or that he was the stuntman for Ryan Gould, Hollywood's hottest star. Either way, Ryan could have her.

He didn't care that Miranda had worked her way through most of the crew; he just didn't find her overly made-up face and fake bee-stung lips to his liking. He loved sex, but he preferred women who were a little more tame and less...*out there*.

"How was your day? How's Ryan?" she asked.

"Busy and he's good," he said, hoping one of his stunt crew would come and save him. A quick peek and he saw his mates in fits of laughter as he tried to worm an escape from Miranda.

"I thought the actors mixed with the crew," she said giving him a sultry pout.

"No," he shook his head. "The actors are staying at The Cambridge, whilst the rest of us are staying here."

"Is Ryan—"

His mobile phone pinged, interrupting her. The alarm he'd set for himself reminded him to ring Amber in Australia. He'd worked out the time difference and hoped she'd be able to chat as it was around ten on Saturday morning there.

"Sorry, Miranda, I need to speak to my agent," he said before giving her one of his trademark smiles. "Bye."

He made his way out of the bar to the office space, a designated room with printers and computers. Finding a quiet corner, he leaned back in the chair, pulling out his mobile phone to message her. Forget it. He'd call her. She seemed nice enough and even though there was a roomful of people he could talk to, he wanted to talk to someone new, someone who didn't seem overly familiar with who he was.

Since he didn't have her number, he used social media to call and was delighted when she answered. "Amber, it's me, Darcy."

"Hi Darcy, I wasn't expecting you to call me. I mean, I know you said we'd *chat,* but I kinda expected you'd message me not actually call me," she said and he couldn't help but chuckle, hearing her so flustered. "I mean, it's nice to talk to you properly."

"What are you doing?" he asked with a casual tone.

"I'm lying in bed, reading my book," she said. "What about you?"

"I'm in a hotel in Northern England, having just finished work."

"How was your day? Did you fall down steps or do something death-defying?" she asked, her voice filled with interest.

"The movie is like *Mission Impossible*. Today, I jumped off a building."

"And you survived to tell me about it," she said with a chuckle.

"Very true." He liked her Australian accent. It wasn't too broad and she sounded friendly, like someone he'd like to hang out with.

"Are you working with anyone famous? Or is that a secret?"

"Ryan Gould," he admitted, expecting her to be as smitten as everyone else he worked with.

"Lucky you," she drawled.

"He's one of Hollywood's hottest stars," he exclaimed using his best American accent.

"Ho hum, he's a little too perfect for my liking," she admitted.

"Really?" Here was the first woman he'd met or knew, who wasn't clamouring to find out more about Ryan. "You're the only woman I know whose knickers are not wet because of him."

"I can't believe you just said that!" Her voice lifted a little in mock amusement.

He chuckled, pleased to see she was taking his jibe as it was intended…for fun. "Are you offended?"

"I don't know whether to be offended that you'd presume to know who I might find attractive or that you assume we've already developed such a bond that I would share such personal information." She paused. "This is our first phone call and you are already asking me what turns me on?" The light-hearted tone in her voice made him chuckle and he decided there and then that he really liked Amber and wanted to get to know her better. . .even if she lived thousands of kilometres away.

"Are you telling me that if Ryan asked you out on a date, you'd say no?"

She spluttered into the phone. "It's very unlikely that he'd be calling me, since he doesn't know me."

"I was telling him all about you today. He hadn't heard of INXS or Rock Lint, till I played some of their songs from my phone. He liked it. He also likes chocolate ice cream...like you."

"Rubbish, everyone likes chocolate ice cream and I don't believe for one moment that you wasted time talking to Ryan about me." She paused. "That's assuming you're even allowed near him," she said with her best school-teacher voice.

"I'm his stunt double," he announced with pride.

"Lucky him," she said, and his heart did an unexpected flip-flop.

There was a pause before she said, "Can I ask how you became a stuntman? It seems very dangerous."

"I train hard and still do every day," he said.

"Is there like a school you go to?"

"Yes, it involves four years of training, but I finished it in three."

"Wow," she said, sounding duly impressed. "What did you learn to do?"

"I learned how to ride a horse, a motorbike, how to skydive, climb, how to fight as well as trampolining and platform diving. I even had to work as an extra for a while to get my hours." He paused. Bugger, he couldn't believe he'd even mentioned that. "Worst sixty hours of my life," he said with disgust.

Being an extra was the lowest of the low. He'd moved on and would *never* do that now. He was the stunt of Hollywood's best, not some loser "extra" pretending to talk to someone in the background.

He'd worked hard and he was proud of finishing his studying earlier than his fellow learners.

"A film extra, too?" she gasped with mock horror in her voice. "Well I guess there's always the need to have someone so qualified being the person in the café background eating toast."

He spluttered into the phone, liking her sense of humour. "Did I tell you that I'm also a black belt in karate?" he asked, veering the conversation away from film extras.

She whistled. "That's very impressive. You must be a very handy boyfriend to have."

"Handy yes, but not such a good boyfriend," he said in a casual manner.

"Leave the toilet seat up, do you? Don't use coasters for mugs of tea?" She made an exaggerated uh-huh.

His lips quivered with enjoyment. "That too, but my work takes me around the world. It's not easy maintaining relationships."

"I wouldn't know," she said with an off-hand manner.

He ignored it and continued. "This movie is taking me to four countries in Europe, the Middle East and of course, here in England. I work most weekends so I can't just fly home, I'm often needed on set."

"Do you love what you do?" she asked.

The question took him by surprise because most people were interested in how many pounds he earned and which celebrities he knew. It seemed, yet again, Amber wasn't like everyone else.

"I do. I really love it," he said.

"Your poor mum must find it hard seeing her son doing what he does," she added.

"Mum knows me all too well. I was climbing fences from the time I was three years old. But she also knows I'm careful. I've been in this business for years; I don't take risks."

"I watched your videos and they're heart-stopping, I can't believe that's you jumping from building to building or diving into a car or taking part in those fight scenes."

"My brother, Blaine is really good at putting the videos together. Don't forget, you're watching all the best stunts I do in just over sixty seconds." He yawned and a quick check of his watch showed exactly how long they'd been chatting.

"I'm keeping you awake, sorry," she said.

"I like talking to you but it has been a long day," he admitted. "Can I call you tomorrow, same time?"

"Sure, I'll be out walking," she said. "Sleep well."

"Bye Amber," he said before disconnecting the phone. He rubbed his tired eyes with the balls of his hands, thinking about the delightful Amber and how easy it was to talk to her. The conversation flowed and he liked that she wasn't overly impressed with him as the lead stuntman working with Ryan. She was more interested in who he was, which was a refreshing change.

To his calendar, he made another note reminding himself to ring Amber, but he had a feeling that he wasn't going to need that reminder. He was looking forward to speaking with her again.

With sore legs, he made his way to his hotel room and collapsed on his bed, falling immediately into a deep sleep.

* * *

AMBER WALKED along the beach foreshore checking her mobile phone constantly, waiting for Darcy to call her. Silly really. He was involved in movies, well known and highly sought out for his incredible agility and no doubt, his trademark good looks. And not only that, he was years younger than her.

Having had her heart broken by a good-looking man, she was wary of them. Besides, Darcy was in England and she was thousands of miles away in Australia. But, she liked him. He was fun to chat with and the messages he'd sent made her happy about the fortuitous social media blunder she'd made in accidentally friending him.

Anyway, they were just friends. . .right?

And just to prove to herself that they were *just* friends and she wasn't trying to *snag him*, she wasn't wearing makeup and her hair was secured in a high ponytail.

The music playing through her headphones stopped and her mobile phone vibrated, Darcy? She smiled, seeing a picture of his handsome face appearing on screen.

"Hi Darcy," she said in a bright cheery voice. "Did you sleep well?"

"Yes, what are you doing?"

"Walking along the beach?"

"Is it warm?"

"No, it's freezing. It's winter. Hang on a minute." She tapped on the screen of her phone and took a selfie of herself with the grey waters of Port Phillip Bay in the background, before sending it to him.

"Nice pic of you," he said. "I thought it was always warm in Australia."

"We do have winter here," she said, a smile tugging at her lips.

"What else are you doing today?"

"After my walk, I'll clean my apartment, check my emails and then I'm seeing a movie with friends tonight. And you?"

"We're working today, I'll be doing a ratchet," he said.

"What does that mean?" She felt her forehead crinkle with interest as she continued her walk.

"I'll be harnessed and then yanked so it looks like I'm flying backwards to land hard against a tree."

"Ouch, sounds painful," she said.

"My neck and back will be padded, I'll be fine," he said with a dismissive tone.

"It sounds dangerous," she said.

"It's my job. I check everything and practice a lot." She could hear the pride in his voice.

"What made you decide to do this? It seems like an interesting career choice." She was fascinated to meet a real-life stuntman. It was so different from anything she knew, and she was keen to learn more.

"Why did you become a counsellor?" he asked.

Gah! "You answer a question by asking a question?" She hated that, she wanted to hear about him, not talk about herself. Besides, his life sounded a lot more exciting than hers.

"I'm interested in you," he said in a low voice that made her skin tingle.

How could she resist when he spoke like that, in a panty-dropping, come-hither voice? She shook her head to clear the naughty thoughts racing through it. Clearing her throat, she said, "You could say that it chose me." Well wasn't that the understatement of the year. "Both my parents are psychiatrists."

He chuckled in reply. "I can only imagine what dinnertime was like when they asked about your day."

The skin on the back of her neck warmed in reply as memories of embarrassment assailed her. Her parents analysed every-thing she said; they couldn't help it. Just because she recognised how their profession impacted their family life didn't make it any easier or better. "You could say that," she admitted.

"You didn't want to follow in their footsteps and be a psychiatrist?" he prodded. "Too hard? Too much studying? You wanted to be different?"

Bingo! Her jaw clenched as she remembered the disap-pointment in her parents' eyes when she'd told them she was studying to be a counsellor. They'd openly dissed her desire to work with IVF patients. A two-year graduate *diploma*? Really? You're so much better than that. Her breathing became shallow as she remembered the night of her gradua-tion ceremony, such a proud moment, and her parents hadn't been there.

"If I'd followed in their footsteps, I'd still be studying. It takes around fourteen years of University to become a psychiatrist," she said, focusing on facts and not the pain from the past.

Over the years, she'd realised that she couldn't change their behaviour and had accepted that they looked down on her career choice and also her. She was an intelligent woman who worked long hours, and devoted her energies to helping those in need, yet it wasn't enough for her parents. Her studying and work were something shameful, not something to be celebrated. Despite her insistence that she was okay with her parents' behaviour, she wasn't. It was all a show. The only person who knew this was Taylor, and she certainly wasn't about to reveal this to Darcy...no matter how kind and understanding he seemed to be.

She heard him whistle through his teeth. "So your parents are disappointed in you, but are you happy?"

Happy? She thought she was, she loved her work, most of the time, but something was missing. She wasn't sure what it was, but there was a spark missing in her life. "I love my job and I love helping couples. It's really rewarding," she said.

"That sounds like something you'd say in a job interview." He paused. "Do you really love what you do?"

Sometimes. Amber reflected over the sessions she'd worked this week. There were some aspects that made her wonder if she'd made the right career decision. "Yes," she said simply. "Now it's my turn, how did you become a stuntman?"

"Like you, it chose me. I had years of acrobatic and gymnastic experience. One day when I was around eighteen, my friend's hat blew off and flew into the Thames. For fun and also to show off, I did some jumps and flips to retrieve it—"

"Someone filmed it, put it on social media and you became world famous?" she interrupted. "Isn't that the way now?"

"It happens but that didn't happen to me." He paused. "After my impressive display of Parkour, a man came up and introduced himself to me. Jared Smitherson. Jared's a stunt coordinator and he's now my manager, but at the time he gave me his card and recommended I join the Register."

"Register?" she asked.

"Sorry, the Register is The British Equity Stunt Register, it's worldwide, recognised everywhere and has a list of registered stunt performers. It gave me the knowledge and skills for me to do what I do," he explained, but she could hear the love of his profession in his voice.

"That's very impressive, you must really love what you do," she said.

"I do. I love the stunts but also the adrenaline rush from doing what I do." His voice lifted and she could literally feel the excitement he got from performing.

Amber nodded, listening to him, and realised that his obsession with danger and risks was the exact opposite of her. Unlike him, she wanted safety and security, and a happy marriage.

Having dealt with infertile couples for so many years, one of her fears was an inability to get pregnant and not being able to have the children she desperately wanted. At thirty-one, her clock was ticking and she was hoping to find *the one* soon.

She wanted to find that perfect guy, just like Taylor had. She wanted to find love. She wanted to have a family. She wanted to shower her children with love, and support them with their decisions, even if she didn't always agree with them.

If her parents had approved of her career choice, perhaps they'd be closer and she'd spend time with them because she wanted to, not because she had to.

It was all wishful thinking but she'd sent out her "wish-list" to the universe, and Amber hoped that she'd get what she wanted. But Darcy didn't need to know that. They'd only been friends for such a short time. Besides, she was more interested in learning about him. "Does your family worry about you?" If she had a son doing such stunts, she'd worry about him.

"Yes and no. They know I'm careful and train, but they still get concerned." His voice was flippant and it stupidly annoyed her.

"You have a large family?"

"Yes," he said with an exaggerated tone.

"You say that like it's a bad thing." It irked her that people with loving families often didn't realise how lucky they were. She wished to be surrounded by a large, noisy family with aunts, uncles, cousins, and grandparents.

"I love my family, but it can be stifling," he admitted.

Stifling? She wanted to knock some sense into him. Instead, she gritted her teeth and said nothing.

"Amber?" His voice broke her thoughts.

"I'm here," she said still daydreaming of the perfect Christmas Day filled with laughter, joy, and friendship.

"Do you have a boyfriend?"

"No," she admitted. Her heart was still recovering from the betrayal of last year when Greg had deceived her for so long. How stupid and gullible she'd been.

"Someone hurt you?"

She hated that he knew the questions to ask. She didn't want to talk about it, even a year later, she was still embarrassed about her behaviour. "You could say that."

"Their loss," he said.

"Thank you." She paused and nibbled her lip before blurting out, "I think it's more his wife's loss."

"Ouch," he said.

"I can't believe I fell for the *we're-separating* line. You'd think that someone who works with people every day—I'm professionally qualified, after all— would have recognised a liar."

"What the eye doesn't see, the heart doesn't grieve over." There was a pause before he said, "Want to tell me what happened?"

"Not really," she said, even though she did. But she didn't want him to see her as the loser she'd been. He was world-famous, with a cult following of wannabes, whereas she was herself, a counsellor in Melbourne with a handful of friends.

She walked along the beachfront and took a lungful of air, reflecting on the simple pleasures of life. "I'm glad I friended you, even if it was by mistake," she confessed with a sigh.

"Really? I didn't realise." He sounded intrigued.

Her cheeks warmed at her blunder. *Why had she said that?*

"Amber?"

"Promise you won't laugh?

"I promise."

"Promise you're not crossing your fingers behind your back?"

"I promise."

"I-ah, um, was at this stupid *Christmas in July* party. They're popular here because it's so hot at Christmastime in Melbourne. It's nice to be able to eat baked foods and mulled wine at a Christmas party."

"That sounds so strange," he said.

"The party?"

"No, Christmas in summer," he chuckled.

"Last Christmas Day was so hot, we spent the day in pool," she said, reflecting on the happiness over those days, how Taylor had fallen for her best friend, Luca. The romantic in her, buried deep down, hoped it was the magic of Christmas that brought them together. Whatever it was, she'd hoped it would happen to her, hence her going to that dreadful weekend event.

"What happened at the Christmas in July party?" he probed.

"Ugh, it was awful. The organiser had no idea on how to put on an event and the only thing that saved me was the mulled wine." She lifted her eyes skyward, remembering the massive hangover she'd had from so much alcohol. "This guy who I wasn't interested in wanted to friend me on social media. His name was similar to yours, so in my hurry to get away from him I friended you instead."

"So you're not interested in me. You're not a fan?"

The sharp tone in his voice made her brow crinkle, and she wasn't sure if he was being serious or having fun at her expense.

"I hope you're joking," she said.

He chuckled. "That story is brilliant. It should be in a movie."

"It is funny, if you're not starring in it," she said, a smile teasing her lips.

"I've got to go," he said. "Enjoy the rest of your day."

"Thanks, Darcy. Bye," she said, before disconnecting the phone.

She'd talked to him for an hour. How had time passed so quickly? She liked his English accent and his dry sense of humour. An internet search had shown her countless sites, all dedicated to Darcy. He had thousands of fans who loved his action-filled stunts and his ability to make them all look so easy. How fortuitous, to meet him.

She wanted to keep talking. She wondered if her friend Taylor was awake. She really needed advice, and only her bestie could help.

CHAPTER 3

a quick check with the world time app she'd downloaded since Taylor had moved to the US showed it was early evening.

Her heart lifted with joy when her friend answered the phone and confirmed she had time to talk.

After the usual pleasantries, Amber blurted out, "I met a guy."

"I'm so happy for you. Tell me about him." She could hear the interest in Taylor's voice.

"He's a stuntman in England."

"Just a minute," she interrupted, "I thought you said you'd met someone."

"I have but he's just a friend, we met. . .we met online."

"I'm not going to say anything to you about being friends with a man," she said with a laugh.

"You're marrying your best friend," she said wistfully, remembering how Luca and Taylor had crossed the friend-ship line with a Christmas kiss.

"Tell me about this guy. A stuntman? Sounds interesting."

"Look up Darcy Harris," she instructed her friend.

"Okay, I'm at my laptop doing a search, hang on….Oh, he's cute." She paused. "How on earth did you two meet?"

Blushing, Amber filled in the details about the Darcy Harris and Hauris mix-up.

"Oh, that's too funny," Taylor said. "Oh my goodness, I'm looking at this video of him on YouTube. Wow!" She stopped, obviously watching it. "Is that really him?"

"Yep, that's his job."

"Hot and talented," Taylor said. "You lucky girl."

"We're friends," she insisted. "Don't start coming up with romantic scenarios just because you and Luca are together."

"I can only try," Taylor said, and they both laughed. "Shame he's in England."

Amber could feel her heart pick up a notch. "To be honest, it's better that he is. I mean, he is one of the world's most sought-after stuntmen. He travels non-stop. Even if we lived near each other. . ." her voice trailed off.

"What?" her friend asked.

"Seriously, look at him. He's so good-looking and has a social media presence that rivals the movie stars he works with. I mean, he's the lead stuntman for Ryan Gould. Ryan Gould!"

"I may have heard of him," Taylor chuckled into the phone. "Isn't he Hollywood's latest? He's hot."

"He is," she admitted with a sigh.

"Darcy and Ryan would have women throwing themselves at them. I mean, look at them. They're on set for months at a time. That life is so very different than ours."

"I have to agree with you," her friend said. "It's funny that you two met…but you're right, he's not the guy for you."

"What do you mean?" Amber asked, interested in why her friend thought so.

"You want someone stable, someone who will be there for you. After the way Greg cheated on you, I think you'd find it hard to trust again, especially a man who lives the lifestyle that Darcy does." She paused. "Honestly, you would not be happy being with him. He's not right for you. Besides, aren't you two just friends?"

"Well, we're friendly," Amber said, unsure how Darcy saw her. "We've talked a lot and I'd like to think we're friends."

"Enjoy the friendship. He sounds nice," her friend said.

"He is nice," Amber said with a sigh. Her heart grew heavy. Taylor was right. She and Darcy lived in very different worlds. Assuming that he was interested in her, and that was wishful thinking, then it would be an affair. And at thirty-one, she no longer wanted affairs. She wanted to find the one, just like Taylor had.

"Tell me, how are you settling in? I'm not going to ask if you've made friends because I'm sure you have," Amber said. Taylor was easy going and kind, and made friends easily. Unlike her, who was more reserved and quiet. She'd opened up to Darcy, and that was unusual for her to share so much personal information about her life.

"I've only been away for a couple of months," she said.

Amber's heart ached. It felt more like two years rather than two months.

"We've been looking at bigger apartments, so there is a spare room if you or our parents come to visit," Taylor gushed. "We think we've found the perfect one, and I'll send you pics soon. And since I can't work yet, while my visa is being processed, I'm doing some volunteer work."

"Of course, you are." Amber's smile grew as she thought of the generosity of her friend.

"There are a couple of local thrift shops. I sort through the donations, clean shelves and also set up displays."

"I'm sure you've made everything look amazing," she said marvelling at her friend's talents.

"The manager said their sales are skyrocketing—"

"Thanks to you, of course," Amber interrupted.

"It's nice to see a charitable organisation earning the money to help those in need." Amber could hear pride, along with self-worth and some embarrassment in her voice. "And we've booked our flights to Australia. We're having a small wedding in early January."

Amber squealed in excitement, ignoring the looks from others walking near her. "Ohmagawd, that's sooooooo exciting."

"Luca's parents want a large affair, but we've convinced them that we want a simple wedding."

"I can only imagine what they wanted," Amber rolled her eyes with amusement.

"We've booked the local church that the Bianchi's attend. Not only is it very pretty but it has a really nice hall. We'll have the ceremony, take pictures in the garden and then have an afternoon tea party in the hall."

"It sounds perfect," Amber said with a touch of envy. As much as she was thrilled for her friend, and she adored Luca, she was hoping that she would fall in love with someone, too.

"I'll need my bestie as my maid of honour, of course," Taylor continued.

"Thank you, it would be my honour and pleasure," she replied.

The friends continued chatting about wedding details.

"Luca is calling me. I'll speak to you soon. Love you," Taylor said.

"Love you more," Amber replied. *And miss you, too, more than you'll ever know.*

The emptiness settled in her belly, and Amber continued her walk home in the cold winter air, alone.

. . .

FIVE MONTHS. . .and hundreds of phone calls and messages between Darcy and Amber, later.

THE PHONE RANG and Amber knew it was Darcy without even checking the caller ID.

"Hi, handsome," she greeted him.

"Your boyfriend will be jealous if you continue to answer the phone like that," his clipped English voice filled her ear.

She grinned. "Andy didn't cope well with me having a male BFF. . .so he's gone." Her tone was light-hearted but her chest tightened as she recalled the recent fight she and Andy'd had. "You're always talking to him, I don't like it," he'd fired at her. "He's my friend," she'd defended herself. But Andy didn't care and soon the words had escalated, and he'd eventually walked out.

"Now I don't have a date for Taylor's wedding," she moaned.

"Pfft, you've got six weeks…plenty of time to find one."

She shook her head. "This from the guy who has women throwing themselves at him. You don't know what it's like for the rest of us mortals who are not blessed with your charisma and handsome DNA," she cooed at him.

"You deserve a spanking for that comment," he joked.

"And who's going to give it to me? You?" She blew a raspberry into the phone.

"You're a vixen," he said. "You come across as sweet and reserved, but underneath that professional exterior is someone who has a hidden naughty side. Tell me, are you wearing sexy or practical knickers today?"

"That's none of your business," she snapped, her cheeks still burning at his insights.

"I knew you loved lacy things."

"You are too cheeky for your own good, Darcy Harris. Your mother should've spanked *you* when you were little."

"The only spanking I want is from you, in your lacy undergarments," he said.

"Darcy, you are embarrassing me."

"Sorry, love, just having fun…at your expense. It's so cold here, the people are boring and I wish you could be here. It would be so much more fun if you could visit."

"I have a job," she said.

"So do I," he said in a sing-song voice.

"You deserve the cold weather as a punishment for your impudence," she added in her best schoolteacher voice.

"You're such a disciplinarian. Your ex, Randy—"

"Andy," she reminded him.

"Randy, Andy. . .whatever," he said.

"Are you saying that I drove him away," her brow crinkled with annoyance.

"No, he obviously can't handle a strong, self-assured woman like you."

"I can't believe we're having this discussion," she rolled her eyes. "I looked at the Outlander tours, they have availability over the Christmas period."

"That's because it's so cold that no one else wants to go. You do know that it's winter in Scotland then?"

"Yes, I do realise that," she replied in an I-can't-believe-you-said-that voice.

"What happens if you're stuck with a group of people who've all read the books and discover that you haven't. They may stone you for only watching the show on telly," he admonished her with a jovial laugh.

"First, I don't have time to read the books—have you seen how thick they are? Besides, it's a tour, it's supposed to be fun."

"Are you going to come to London to see me after the tour?"

"Yep, but only for a quick visit," she said. "I've got to be back in Melbourne for Taylor and Luca's wedding. Besides, I barely have two weeks of leave."

"Give me the dates you'll be here," he said. "I'll show you London. We'll have so much fun together."

"I think so, too. I want to do all the touristy things," she added. But aren't you booked to start a new movie in January?"

"Yes, we start mid-January, in France, I think," he said.

"Shame you can't make it for the wedding. You could've been my plus one," she sighed. "It would've been fun to have had you as my date."

"I could've parachuted into the church," he suggested.

"And upstaged the bride, my best friend? I don't think so," she said.

"As much as I would love to attend the Wedding of the Year, I have a film to do with Bruce O'Neill." He stressed the words, just to tease her.

"Bruce O'Neill? I love him. Perhaps I will visit you on set," she said in a cheeky manner.

"You most certainly will not. He shags every woman he can. I don't want to hear about him going after you."

"Is he any good?" she asked, stifling a giggle.

"Gah! How would I know? It's not like I've had sex with him," he said.

Amber burst out laughing. "You make me laugh."

"You're still not shagging him," he reprimanded her.

"Didn't you say that the actors stay in different hotels than the crew? You wouldn't know if I had a sleepover…in his room," she said.

"Not with this movie, we're all staying together. In fact, my room is next to his," he insisted.

"You're cute when you lie," she chuckled. "Okay, so the clinic usually closes over Christmas and New Year's, so I'll fly in just before Christmas, see you, then do the tour, come back to London for a day, then travel home. I need to allow a few days for travelling," she said.

"Haven't you left everything a little late? It's December, and you still haven't booked your flights."

"I can't book until I get my leave approved," she said, frustrated that her manager had still not signed off on her request.

"You said the clinic closes," he said.

"It does, but there's always someone available to help couples, especially over Christmas. If someone has a miscarriage or an IVF failure, they can need some counselling. In the past, I always did this and so my manager assumed I would do it again. She was not happy that I asked for leave."

"Someone else will have to do it this year. You, my love, are coming on a well-deserved holiday," he said with assurance. "Now go tell her you've *already* booked your flights."

"Lie?"

"Yes," he said.

"I've got a meeting with her this morning." She looked at her watch and her eyes widened. She was going to be late. "I need to go. I'll call you later, love you," she said.

"Love you," he blew kissing sounds into the phone.

It should be weird that he often said "love you" to her, just like Taylor did, but it wasn't. Over the many calls and messages between them, they'd become so comfortable with each other that blowing kisses and signs of affection had become the norm. She treasured her relationship with Darcy, and her recent ex, Andy, hadn't liked it at all. That's why he was her ex and she was still friends with Darcy.

Disconnecting the call, she tossed her mobile phone into her tote bag, grabbed her files and everything she needed before heading for the door. A quick check in the long mirror reflected the businesslike image she liked to portray. With her hair tied back, black pencil skirt, black stilettos and smart business shirt, she looked efficient and hard working.

All she needed was to get that leave form approved.

* * *

AMBER'S JAW dropped but words did not come out of her mouth. The shock of what her manager, Megan, had just said, floored her.

"They're making cuts to all areas of the business and the staff are now expected to work over the Christmas-New Year period or use their own leave. It will no longer be paid by the company," the older woman clarified with a stern voice.

"I've been with the company for nine years, and it's always been this way. The company paid for leave as the clinic was closed," Amber said, quite unable to believe that she might not be able to have the holiday she wanted. And she'd always been well compensated for working when no one else wanted to. A saving grace from parents who weren't into the whole "family Christmas gathering."

"This is a business. Counselling is provided free to the clients who are going through IVF but we still need to *pay* you and the others. A decision has been made, and that's final. Since you've always worked around Christmas time, I expected you to do so this year." Her manager's clipped tone left her little doubt that there was no negotiation. She had to fit in with the business if she was to keep her job. That meant she'd have to change her plans and leave in the next couple of days. Was there a tour in mid-December? Were there flights available? And what about her clients? They needed and relied on her.

"B-but, I put in a leave request." For the first time in years, Amber felt her cool demeanour slipping and she was fired up. "I've booked my flights," she lied.

"That's your problem," her manager sniffed.

"You can have leave now and be back on the twenty-fourth of December to manage the calls we get over Christmas."

"That's it?" Amber's eyes widened.

"I think that's a fair compromise. One of the other counsellors will need to manage your workload while you take your leave," her manager said, making Amber squirm despite the cold air-conditioning of the building. "Make a decision, I'll give you till the end of the day to let me know. That will give you time to speak to the airline to change your flights."

Amber's chest tightened, resentful at how she was being spoken to, as disappointment crashed over her. The wintery Christmas she'd been looking forward to this year would not be happening. She stood on shaky legs and walked to her office.

Closing the door, she collapsed on the sofa as questions badgered her brain. What to do? Spend two weeks in London? With Darcy?

Over the past five months, they'd become firm friends, talking regularly, and the empty void in her heart had started to fill. Darcy had been a wonderful person to talk to. Thanks to technology, they could talk all the time, face to face, despite having never met. The decision to go to the UK hadn't been taken lightly, and she was reluctant to fly to London just to see him.

Just because they were long-distance friends, their relationship might be different when they were face to face. He was famous, well received in his circles and she was...she was her. Darcy loved the thrill of excitement of putting himself in danger, going to movie premiers and surrounding himself with the elite in the industry.

She hated all of that. Unlike him, she was reserved and she wanted to find someone special and start a family in the next couple of years.

And that's why falling for Darcy was wrong. She had started to like him as more than a friend months ago but had kept those feelings in place. Nothing could come of it… assuming he was interested, which he wouldn't be. He was surrounded by beautiful women on set. She'd heard about the antics the crew got up to; he'd told her everything. She wasn't a prude, but that lifestyle was not for her.

Which is why she'd decided to do the tour. It was an excuse to get to the UK, have a holiday, but also see Darcy without looking "desperate" or like she'd travelled almost thirty hours to see him.

She rose, walked to her desk and fired up her computer. Crossing her fingers, she hoped there were flights available for when she needed them.

* * *

ON THE OTHER side of the world, Darcy was enjoying a beer with his co-workers. The movie was finished and he was about to return to London.

"We're heading to Ibiza for a couple of weeks. You should join us," his friend Ethan said. "Sun, beer, women."

Darcy ran his fingers through his hair. He'd been planning on returning to London for three weeks. He and the others were tired after an intense filming schedule and numerous stunts. Spending time with his mates in the sun would be far more fun than London. Amber wasn't due to arrive for three weeks, so he had plenty of time to relax before meeting her.

A smile touched his lips. He couldn't wait to meet her in person. He loved their chats and hoped they would have as much fun together, as they did over the phone.

"I need a new mobile," he said. His phone had accidentally fallen and been trampled on by a horse, and he'd been so busy that he hadn't had a chance to get a new one.

"Don't be daft. You can get one at the airport, idiot," Ethan said with a laugh before slapping him on the back.

"We've been freezing for the past two months here in Cotswolds," Ethan slapped the back of his hand against Darcy's chest. "I can't believe you're thinking about whether to go or not. We've earned it, we deserve this break."

He was right. They'd been on set for months for a historical drama, and he'd been working hard.

It may not be swimming weather, but it would be nicer in Spain than London. Besides, he'd be with his friends. "I'm in," he said.

CHAPTER 4

*A*mber stood on the sidewalk and looked up, excitement zipped up and down her arms. She was here in London. It was bitterly cold and a far cry from the hot, summer day she'd left in Melbourne, but she couldn't be happier. She was strolling along Oxford Street and couldn't help but admire the stunning display of Christmas decorations. It was stunning and everything she'd imagined.

Everything was awash with beautiful lights; the buildings, the trees, and even the sign posts. Since it was dark early, the street looked glorious and Amber loved it all. She smiled watching the red double-decker buses drive past as well as the black taxis, shaped differently to the taxis in Australia. It may be corny, but she loved all things British and her heart tripped over in excitement as her gaze darted around the street, taking it all in.

Despite the cold, the streets were filled with pedestrians, and even that made Amber happy. She couldn't imagine what could remove the smile on her face, she was so happy that she was literally bursting with joy.

Despite the exhaustion of travelling for thirty hours to

get here, Amber walked gaily along the street. Using her mobile phone, she took pictures of the decorations. She'd find a pub to have dinner and then return to her hotel for some much-needed sleep.

If only Darcy was with her, sharing her excitement but he was on set, with a broken phone. He'd messaged her from his friend's mobile and promised to let her know as soon as he had a new phone. They hadn't spoken for a week, and she missed their talks and messages. She'd sent a message to his friend, asking Darcy to call her. She needed to let him know that she was here in London.

A message popped up on screen and she grinned seeing it was from Darcy. Her heart lifted with excitement; she could tell him she was now in London. They could meet. . .finally.

She opened it, and her heart sank. He'd sent a picture of himself lazing on a lounge, beer in one hand, and his arm around a friend. They were warmly dressed but there was a large expanse of gloriously blue water in the background. Her brow furrowed—that didn't look like England. Her heart pounded against her chest as she read the message. "Finally back online, and having a well-deserved break in Ibiza. See you soon in London."

Amber swore under her breath. He was in Ibiza, the world's biggest party town. Tears filled her eyes. She was a fool to think they could be any more than friends. Stupid. Stupid. Stupid. She should've stayed in Melbourne and not taken a risk, flying to London. Every time she stepped outside of her comfort zone, things went pear-shaped. She should've learned by now. Look at the issues she had with her parents, the disastrous, ill-advised affair with Greg, her ex-Andy, and now this.

Looked like she was spending two weeks on her own in London, she realised with a resentful sigh.

Moving to the side, to avoid the pedestrian crush, she

leaned against a shop window. She'd missed out on the Outlander tour, but there were other tours to do. She had the whole UK to see, not just London, she reprimanded herself. There was so much to see. Pushing away her disappointment, she tugged off her glove so she could ring Darcy. He answered immediately.

"I've missed you," he said, not bothering with pleasantries.

She bit her lip, not wanting to say something sour about him being away and it was unlikely that he'd even given her much thought when he was partying with his friends. Taking a reassuring breath she said, "I've been meaning to talk to you about my trip"

"Please don't tell me you're not coming. That witch of a manager should've approved your leave."

"She did," she said with a dramatic sigh.

"That's good," he said. "For a moment, I thought I wasn't going to see you."

Well, you may not, she thought. "There were conditions with my leave approval. I wanted to tell you, but you've been off-line for a few days. I did send a message to your friend."

"Ethan? I'll kill him," she heard the harsh frustration in his voice. "Tell me, is everything alright?"

"Yes, but um, I-um, need to tell you that I'm in London. In fact, I'm walking along Oxford Street now."

"What?" he almost shouted in the phone. "You're in Oxford Street? Right now?"

She tried to make light of the situation. "I know it's the touristy thing to do, but it's—"

"You're in London?" he continued shouting. "What the hell are you doing in London *now*?"

She wasn't sure why he sounded so angry, so she used her calm voice to explain. "The company is going through a restructure, and they would not budge on the leave request. It was either take the leave now or leave my job," she quipped. "I can't afford to lose my job just so I could see you and have the wintery Christmas I always wanted." She paused. "My flight home leaves on the twenty-second of December, which means I'll be back in Melbourne to work over the Christmas-New Year's period."

"But you work every year. They couldn't have someone else do it?" he barked into the phone.

Her chest tightened with the disappointment of being coerced and bullied into working. "As I said, it was work or be fired."

"I'm sorry, darling, that's terrible." There was genuine disappointment in his voice.

"I know. I did try to tell you, but then I was flying here. I'm sorry that I'm missing you. Perhaps you'll come to Melbourne one day and we'll meet—"

"Are you kidding me?" he said. "I'm flying to London tomorrow."

"B-but, you're with your friends. Don't you want to stay in Ibiza?"

"Of course, but if the choice is Ibiza or you, I take you," he said.

She blushed hard, and she was glad they were not talking via a video hook-up, so he couldn't see how his words affected her.

"Where are you staying?"

She mentioned the name of the bed and breakfast she was staying at in Earl's Court.

"You're not staying there. It's a dump."

It wasn't The Ritz London, but it was in her price range. "The rooms are clean. It's fine," she said with a dismissive voice.

"You'll stay with me," he assured her.

What?! Her heart skipped a beat. Stay with him? In his apartment? "I-I d-don't think—"

"Amber, I have a large two-bedroom apartment in Greenford. I'll send you the details with the codes to get in. You're staying with me, and that's final," he said with such determination that she didn't bother arguing it. It would be pointless.

The thought of living in his apartment for a few days thrilled but also worried her. She decided to focus on the practical side, rather than worry about the maybes. "You're so bossy," she said in a playful voice, which she hoped wouldn't betray the nerves rolling in her tummy.

"I can't believe you're staying in Earls Court," he said in a manner that made her lips press together.

"What's wrong with Earls Court? It's full of Australian and New Zealand backpackers," she said. She wasn't a backpacker, but so far everyone she'd met had been very friendly and it seemed the area to live in.

"Exactly," he said with an exasperated sigh that made her bite her lips to stop from giggling. "You're here to see *me* and London," he pointed out to her in his clipped English accent. "Not, be running around with students and drinking till late at night."

"I may find Mr. Right amongst one of them."

"You'll probably find a ton of guys who want to bed you, my darling, now just listen to me. . . I'll get Polly to make up your room, get the heating on, and fill up the fridge before you arrive tomorrow. Can you get there at around midday?"

"Sure, but I don't want to put you out," she added, even though her arrival hadn't seemed to be an imposition on him.

"You're my favourite Australian—of course, I'll look after you," he said, and her heart warmed. "I'll text you the address and security codes now."

"That's really nice of you, Darcy. I don't—"

"I'll message you the details," he said in a decided voice

that reminded her that this is what he wanted. And it was silly to argue. He was her friend and had invited her to stay in his home. She should accept and be thankful not to be staying in the boring bedsit.

He continued. "Tomorrow, get the tube to Shepherd's Bush, then from there, you get the train to Greenford. There isn't a direct line from London. Then get a taxi from the station. It's only five minutes away."

"I don't want to—"

"See you tomorrow." His voice was friendly but determined before he ended the call.

Amber's heart lifted with anticipation and excitement. She was going to see Darcy tomorrow. Finally.

Staying at his apartment would help her financially and she intended to use her accommodation money to buy lunches and take Darcy to the theatre. But, they would be together, living in the same place. Would that be awkward? No. They'd spent hours talking. She adored him. They just needed to behave the way they did on the phone when they were together. She was sure everything would be fine. What could go wrong?

With that resolved discussion with herself, she pocketed her phone before continuing her walk, admiring the Christmas lights.

* * *

AMBER HAD WALKED from the station to Darcy's apartment, dragging her suitcase with her. It would've been easier to catch a taxi, but she'd been enchanted with the prettiness of the town and wanted to see it now, rather than later. Her steps were slow but despite the cold and her suitcase, she marvelled at the architecture that seemed so *English* to her.

She admired the rows of houses, all the same, along the

street. And the red double-decker buses. Darcy lived in a nice suburb but it was so different to Melbourne, and where she lived. There were more apartments, the houses seemed smaller and there were plenty of apartments above shops.

And just when she thought it couldn't get any better, she found his apartment. A retro warehouse, built in the 1930s, had been converted into sleek modern but art-deco-inspired apartments. Not only was the building, the entrance, and stairwells stunning, but so was Darcy's apartment.

Since she'd arrived she'd looked around his apartment, at his photos, and the souvenirs on display. Did he have secrets he'd kept from her? Was there anything that he'd not told her? Nope, he seemed to be exactly how he was, a man who loved his family and worked incredibly hard.

Large windows framed the garden and parks outside, and Amber grew excited to be staying here. It was definitely much brighter, larger, and nicer than the bedsit in London.

As promised, the heating was on, the fridge was full of fruit, vegetables, deli meats, and cheese, and the spare room had been made up for her. Although eager to see more of the beautiful town, Amber had accepted that she needed a break before doing so and had made herself a cup of tea and helped herself to a homemade biscuit. Settling in the wing-backed chair, facing the window to admire the view, she blew out a long breath. The exhaustion of the long flight from Australia, the tiring walk hauling her bags, and the jet lag washed over her in a heavy wave and she closed her eyes. Reminding herself that she had barely two weeks of leave and couldn't afford to spend the time sleeping, she was reluctant to have a nap.

But within seconds, she fell into a deep sleep and her tea remained untouched and grew cold.

* * *

Darcy let himself into his apartment, excitement bursting from every cell. He'd been fortunate to be able to book a seat on an early morning flight and had arrived home sooner than he'd expected. He'd had barely three hours sleep but didn't care. Amber was here. He still had to pinch himself that the fun Australian he'd met by chance was in England. After the endless getting-to-know-you chats, she was *here*.

Walking in he said, "Amber?"

There was no reply and he felt the skin between his eyebrows crease. She'd gone out? His excitement deflated. After dumping his bags at the front door, he strode in and saw her asleep in his favourite chair.

With her eyes closed, her glasses sitting oddly on the bridge of her nose, she was still pretty and he took a moment to admire the long dark blonde hair that fell in loose waves over her shoulders. It was so much nicer than when she had it constricted in a tight bun.

He squatted beside her and touched her hand. "Amber, wake up," he whispered.

She stirred and he smiled as her eyes fluttered open. "Hello Darling," he said.

Her eyes opened and she jerked back in surprise. "Darcy, when did you get here?"

"Just now," he said.

"Goodness, I fell asleep." She fixed her glasses before looking at her watch. "For two hours," she said, obviously annoyed at herself for sleeping so long.

She rubbed her eyes, then stood, before wrapping her arms around his neck. "Hello, you," she said.

His arms came around her slim waist and he held her tight. How many times had he thought about her and what it would feel like having her this close? He breathed in the honeyed apple scent of her hair and tugged her close. It felt so right to have her in his arms.

He started to take a step back, thinking it was a little inappropriate to hug for so long, but she held on tight. "I'm so glad to finally meet you," she murmured.

"Me too, darling, me too," he said. And he was happy to see her. . .finally.

She took a step back and they looked at each other, as though seeing each other for the first time. Despite the hours of talking, video calls and messages, she looked different in real life. Not only prettier, but he could see flecks of green in her brown eyes. And she was tall. Not as tall as him, but she reached his shoulder without heels.

Her lips pressed together in concentration. "You look like you have a million thoughts going through your head."

Caught. He could lie or tell her the truth. He decided to go with both options. "I didn't realise how tall you are, and I have to be honest, you look even better than your photos."

He caught her blush of unease. "I know, I'm too tall and too thin"

"You're beautiful as you are," he replied with honesty. "I simply didn't realise you were tall."

She pressed her lips together with frustration. "Sorry I didn't mention it, I'm sick of all the stupid giraffe, basketball and weather jibs I've endured over the years." She rubbed her arms.

"Sorry, weather jokes, that doesn't make sense," he replied.

"Ohhh, you sound so English when you say that," she chuckled. "Over the years I was often asked, 'What's the weather like up there?' or 'Do you play basketball?' Like I would play basketball just because of my height."

"People are rude," he said. "Now, I just need to unpack and get ready to take you out. Why don't you have a cup of tea?" His gaze directed her to the cold one sitting on the side table. "I won't be long."

* * *

DARCY'S FINGERS trembled as he unzipped his bag and tossed the clothes into a laundry hamper. Amber was beautiful, stunning, and her smile was making his tummy turn like a tumbleweed in the desert. Because they were friends, she'd often answer the phone brushing her teeth, without makeup, wearing her glasses, or in pyjamas in bed. The comfort and ease between them was so great that he'd divulged things to her that he would never tell a girlfriend. But since she was a friend and so far away, he'd shared with her tidbits that he usually kept to himself.

And now she was here. Here in England and here in his apartment.

He rubbed his face, still quite unable to believe he was about to spend time with Amber. She was the best female friend he'd ever had, and he just adored her.

Nerves jangled in his belly and he felt as awkward as he had on his first date as a teen. Their relationship had developed using technology, not face-to-face. Things could be hidden, but now he felt exposed and raw. Would they get on as well face-to-face? And would she like him, as he was.

He was four years younger than her and knew that they were at different places in their careers. Unlike her, he was not interested in settling down and had never been in love.

Apart from the obvious fact that they lived in different countries, there were a host of other distances between what they wanted in life. It was why they were only good friends, even if he was attracted to her. He'd have to be dead not to notice how gorgeous her lips were, her smile and her large dark brown eyes.

HALF AN HOUR LATER, he joined her. "Ready?"

She stood. "Depends on where we're going?"

"I've booked tickets to the theatre, and we'll have supper first," he announced. He'd been fortunate to find a pair of tickets for one of the city's most popular musicals.

"Is this okay to wear?" She pointed to herself.

He admired the knee-length dress she wore teemed with knee-high boots. "You look great."

She smiled. "Thanks, that sounds fabulous. Are we going now?"

"Yes, we'll drive to Shepherd's Bush, park and then catch the tube in," he said.

"I can't wait," she said, a wide grin across her face that showed she was as happy as he to be together tonight.

A FEW HOURS LATER, they walked together and he noticed how Amber kept looking up, rather than at him. "Is something wrong? Have I got something between my teeth?" he teased.

"Not at all," she said with a smile, and threaded her arm through his. "I just can't believe I'm here in London. It's so festive with the Christmas lights, and I feel like I'm in a winter wonderland."

"Are you going to start singing the song, 'Winter Wonderland'?"

"I'm tempted...but I won't because I have such a bad singing voice," she taunted him.

"After I took you to the theatre?" His hands pressed against his heart as though she'd wounded him.

She chuckled. "That show tonight," she sighed loudly. "It was so good." She stopped walking and faced him. "This has been the best night. I love the pub where we had dinner and the musical was so wonderful. I'm so happy. Thank you for everything." She hugged him tightly.

He held her close and they stood there in each other's arms, despite the biting cold and people brushing past them on the busy street.

Wiping away a cold drip on his cheek he looked up to see light flurries of snow. Ugh, he grimaced. More cold weather.

"Darcy," she tugged at his sleeve. "It's snowing," she said lifting her eyes to watch the snowflakes fall. Tugging off her glove she raised her hand as though trying to catch them. "This is magical. I've never seen snow before."

"Never?" Surprise at her statement made his eyes open wide.

"It doesn't snow in Melbourne and I've never been a traveller. I didn't even take a break between finishing school and doing my diploma to see the world, as so many do," she confessed in a low voice. "And I work a lot."

"Your company has taken advantage of you, making you work every Christmas," he added in a frustrated voice. How unfair that it had taken her years before she'd had the opportunity to travel. He, on the other hand, had a passport filled with stamps from the years of working in different countries.

"I'm going to make a wish," she said.

He watched her close her eyes and it was as if he could hear her wishing for something special to happen to her. He intended to make sure they had a fabulous time together and she'd return to Australia reinvigorated from her time away.

* * *

IT WAS STUPID, romantic, and total lunacy for her to wish that Darcy would kiss her under the soft drizzle of snowflakes. They were friends, and she was pragmatic enough to know that nothing could happen between them. They were so different. Not only was he a risk taker, but he loved to be the centre of attention and attend as many parties as he could. He was younger than her and working hard in his profession to establish a name for himself.

He'd ribbed her about her preference for *parties* that involved drinking wine, eating chocolate, and watching the telly in her pyjamas.

She didn't need her high IQ to know that guys like him dated hot actresses, not lonely workaholics. She'd seen the admiring glances from other women tonight. Women either discreetly looking at him from under mascaraed lashes or were more upfront with him. A couple of women had even slipped him their numbers with a cheeky wink.

Unlike her, he'd laughed at the attention, not at all embarrassed, while she'd been mortified. She'd been shoved aside by women all too eager to flutter their lashes at Darcy.

She couldn't imagine what it would be like if he was her boyfriend. That incessant, unwelcome attention would upset her. It's not like she could shout out, *back off, he's mine*, because they were just friends.

Taking a step back, she admired the square cut of his jaw, his blue eyes, and dark hair. He really was the most handsome man she'd met and had a lean, well-defined body from years of weights, gymnastics, Pilates, karate, and healthy eating.

"I hope your wish comes true," he said.

So do I, she prayed.

"Let's get a drink. There's a brilliant pub nearby," he suggested.

"That sounds great," she said, looping her arm through his. "Let's just hope your female admirers aren't there."

He rolled his eyes. "Sorry about that. I guess trouble follows me."

She chuckled. "It certainly does."

CHAPTER 5

"*G*reat choice, I love this pub," Amber said, her gaze taking in the polished wooden bench top, the wooden bar stools, and the wooden beams which had been decorated with festive tinsel.

"Don't say it," he gaffed, raising his hand towards her.

"It's so English," she chuckled. "I'm sorry, I think I've said it a million times and it's only my first day here."

He shook his head in mock disbelief. "It's a pub."

"No, it's not, it's so different to ours in Melbourne. The lighting, the polished wood, the roaring fire. I just love it." She paused. "Go on." She rolled her wrist in the air to encourage him to finish what he's been saying. Amber sipped her wine as Darcy related yet another amusing story about his work. "You must see so much action on the film sets."

"You can't even imagine some of the shenanigans that go on," he said before taking a sip of his beer.

"I love that you love your job. You really do," she said.

"Best job." He grinned.

"Despite the cuts, bruises, and broken bones?"

"Definitely," he said. He looked at his watch. "It's getting late. Is there anything you specifically want to do in London?"

"I do want to see all the tourist sights. Buckingham Palace and the Changing of the Guard, Tower of London and Tower Bridge, Big Ben and Parliament House, British Museum, Piccadilly Circus and Trafalgar Square, Westminster Abbey, St Paul's Cathedral, Churchill's War Rooms, Convent Gardens," She ticked them all off on her fingers.

"You'll need more than two weeks," he grinned. "We'll take the tourist bus around London and we'll see as much as we can." He paused. "I thought you might like to go for an overnight stay and see Bath."

She clapped her hands in delight. "I would love that."

"We'll visit everything quickly, especially the museum, so we can fit it all in," he said, draining his beer. "Another?" He pointed to her almost empty glass.

"As much as I love sitting here with you, I think we need to get back. I want a good night's sleep if we're going to be walking all day tomorrow."

"And every day after that, till you leave," he added. "I'll check the times for Buckingham Palace and work out a schedule to fit in as much as we can. And I'll book for us to go to Bath in a couple of days."

"My own personal guide," she fluttered her lashes at him, like all the annoying women tonight.

"Flattery will get you everywhere, Amber." He stood and held out his hand to her. "Let's go."

* * *

THEY SPENT the next three days visiting all the sights she wanted to see and took the usual tourist photos. Thanks to all the talks they'd had over the past few months, there were no uncomfortable pauses and Amber was the happiest she'd ever been.

They walked non-stop, used the Tube to get around London and laughed…a lot. She never wanted her time there to end.

"I wish I'd travelled more when I was younger," she confessed as they stood waiting for the guard to change at Buckingham Palace.

"You're here now," he said.

"I know. But I've never had a lot of friends, and I was scared to travel on my own." She sighed. "If I analyse myself, I would say that my parent's lack of acceptance of me and my work made me feel inadequate. If they'd encouraged me, perhaps I would've had the confidence to see all of this sooner."

"Don't be hard on yourself," he said.

"This from the guy who has women throwing themselves at him, has worked and travelled to more countries than I have fingers, and is establishing his own business," she said.

He gave her a playful punch. "Shhh, that's a secret. I wouldn't want my agent to hear that."

A smile tugged at her lips. "Your secret is safe with me," she whispered in reply.

"What guy doesn't want women throwing themselves at him?" He lifted his eyebrow in amusement.

"You know what I mean. I couldn't handle dating you and having these women coming up all the time," she confessed.

"Really?" His forehead creased with concern. "I'm sorry if it makes you uncomfortable."

"If we were together, and this is just hypothetically speaking," she stressed the word *hypothetically*. "Yes, I have to be honest, I would not like these women intruding on our time together."

He rubbed his hand across his forehead. "I think I've been

in the industry for too long. I've forgotten what it's like." He paused. "I'm sorry."

"It's fine. You don't have to apologise, I'm just saying…" she added.

She looked towards the palace. "Do you think it will be starting soon?"

"Are you changing the subject?"

"Not at all. My feet are freezing." She stomped her feet a few times to prove her point. "I'm hoping we can see this so we can start moving again."

"You're a terrible liar, Amber." He paused. "There's still time to talk. Tell me, is there any other reason you wouldn't date me?" His tone was serious and Amber looked at him with surprise.

"Where's this coming from?" She wasn't sure why, but talking about them being together as a couple made her feel uncomfortable and squirm in her sensible walking shoes.

"Nowhere, just asking." There was innocence sketched across his face, but since he was an actor as well as a stunt-man, Amber wasn't totally convinced there wasn't a reason for him asking.

Since he'd asked, she'd tell him, even if he didn't like the answer. "I would like to say that I adore you—"

"But," he interrupted.

"But, you're younger than me and not interested in settling down or starting a family soon. You work in an industry that makes me feel uncomfortable. I know I sound like a prude—I have nothing against consensual adults having sex, but the lies and cheating that go on in your world are not for me." She stopped for a moment and then said, "We are just too different. We're great as friends, but I can't see us as anything more. And I wouldn't want to do anything that would jeopardise our friendship. I don't think good sex would be worth it," she added.

"So you think I'd be a good shag, huh?" He gave her a playful jab on her arm.

"It was written on the back of the toilet door at the pub last night," she lied.

He burst out laughing, and a few people looked at them. Amber's cheeks burned hot, but Darcy didn't seem to care. He leaned close and whispered into her ear. "I think you're over-estimating the number of women I've slept with…and just so you know, I am a good shag."

This time it was Amber's turn to burst out laughing, and she felt giddy with joy. She loved him, she really did. No guy had ever made her feel so happy and been so interested in her. And yet again, she thanked the magic of Christmas, even if it was *Christmas in July*, that had brought them together.

The joy he'd brought to her life was special; it was real and alive. The empty pit of loneliness in her heart was closing, and Amber was already dreading the day when she would have to return to Australia. They might not be lovers, but Amber was already falling for him. He was the wrong guy for her, but her heart had missed that memo because she now had strong feelings for him, and, despite what she's said, they didn't involve friendship.

* * *

THE FOLLOWING DAY, they left early and drove towards Bath along the M4. Instead of the two and a half hours a direct drive would've taken them, Darcy took detours, taking them to the historical areas of Reading, Swindon, and Chippenham. If he was bored by the abbeys, stately homes, historic village streets, and museums, he didn't show it. Hand in hand, he showed her a side of England that was both picturesque and interesting, and she was absolutely delighted. "I can just imagine them filming historic movies here," she said. "If you remove the cars, signs, and lighting, it's like it was a few hundred years ago. I love the architecture and paving on the streets."

If he was amused by her captivation and glee, he didn't say anything. She took heaps of photos and bought lots of souvenirs including tea towels, fridge magnets, hand knitted tea cosies, and two cushion covers.

"I hope this all fits in your suitcase," he said, removing the large bag from her hand and holding it. If not, I'll post it to you."

"Thank you," she said.

Back in the car, on their way to Bath she said, "I thought London was amazing, but this has been even better," she said, not even bothering to hide her delight. "Thank you for the most brilliant day."

They were driving towards Bath, and almost there. He turned to her and gave her a devastating smile. "You're welcome," he said.

The air in the car became too warm all of a sudden, and she opened the window to let some air in to cool her face.

"It's cold outside," he said, as the interior of the car cooled down.

"Sorry, I was feeling a little off, motion sickness I think," she lied.

"Shall I pull over? Do you need to walk outside?" he asked, his voice filled with concern.

"No, I'm fine. There's only a few more kilometres to Bath," she said, as they passed a road sign. "You know, I don't understand why you use miles, when England has a metric system."

He shook his head. "Who knows? At school, I was taught to do calculations in kilometres, but road signs have miles. Cooking oil is sold in litres but beer is in pints." He shrugged. "I don't know why."

"That's very strange," she said. "But anyway, today was amazing. Thank you for taking me to all those historical places. It was fascinating. I meant to ask, have you worked in any of them?"

"Yes, and yes to a number of other places in England," he said.

She nodded and looked out the window as they drove into Bath.

"I'll drive around so you can see Bath before we check in to the hotel," he said. "This is typical of the housing," he pointed out.

She took in the houses side-by-side, all the same. "It seems that the town's architecture is the same, they've used a honey coloured stone," she said peering out the window.

"Yes, it's been used extensively, even the Abbey is the same colour."

"Wow," she said.

"We'll walk around here tomorrow but have a look at this now," he said.

This, turned out to be thirty or so homes built next to each other in a sweeping crescent, around five hundred feet, in front of a large green lawn.

"This is the Royal Crescent and was built sometime in the 1700s, I don't remember the exact date. It's an example of Georgian architecture."

The skin creased between her eyes as she looked at him with amazement. "How did you know that?"

"You'd be surprised by the things I remember. I've worked on a lot of historical movies and tele-movies. I don't know. I just remember seemingly unimportant facts."

"Well, it's interesting to me, thank you," she said with sincerity. "I can't wait to see this during the day. It's so beautiful."

"And we'll also visit the Roman Baths."

"As in what the Romans built?"

"Yes," he said.

"I can't wait." Her sigh was filled with contentment.

"And the day after tomorrow, we're doing a Jane Austen tour," he said. "She lived here for a few years and wrote a couple of novels."

"You remembered," she said, pressing her lips together so she wouldn't dissolve into a puddle of emotion. A couple of months ago she'd caught a cold and had spent two days sick in bed watching Jane Austen movies. "That's so thoughtful of you. I didn't know she lived here."

"There's a tourist centre, then we're doing a walking tour and after we'll find somewhere for afternoon tea."

Her heart fluttered with excitement. "That sounds amazing. I'm sorry if it's going to bore you but I can't wait."

"I'll be with you, so I don't mind. You're the quintessential tourist and I'm really enjoying your excitement. It must be why even *I'm* enjoying all this historical stuff."

"You are the best Darcy, and so thoughtful. Thank you."

"Tomorrow, we'll walk around, see the Abbey, the town, and the Baths," he said.

"You must be tired after all that driving," she said. With the occasional drifts of snow and cold winds, she was happy that he'd driven today.

Soon enough, they were checking in to their hotel and Amber's eyes widened in astonishment at the old-world charm of the stately hotel. This place was definitely out of her price range and her belly rolled with concern about the cost of staying here.

She snapped out of her thoughts as Darcy's voice became more insistent. "That's not appropriate," he said.

"What's going on?" She noted the annoyance that had tightened the muscles around his jaw.

"They've made a mistake with our booking, and to

compensate, they've given us a suite," he said with a serious look in his blue eyes.

"And the problem is?" she whispered. A suite? She couldn't wait to see it.

"There's only one bed," he whispered back. "They've offered us a trundle bed but for the price I'm paying, I don't see why I should have to sleep on a child's bed."

"Excuse us," she said to the receptionist before tugging him to a corner. In a low voice, she said, "This place is a little out of my price range but if they're giving us a suite, let's take it. I'll sleep on the fold-out bed. You drove all day."

"I don't think—"

"I'm sure the trundle bed in a suite will be far nicer than the bed and breakfast I was staying at in London," she said with determination. "This place is amazing! I want to stay here," she insisted with a pleading tone. "In fact, the carpet is so plush, I'd sleep on the floor."

He kissed her forehead. "You don't have to do that." He paused. "This was my Christmas present to you. I wanted it to be perfect."

"The past few days have been perfect. Today was perfect, and I'm sure tomorrow will be, too." She took a deep breath. "I've never seen a hotel as beautiful as this and I would love to stay here."

"They have their own spa and indoor pool," he said.

"We're staying here, that's final," she said. Her eyes widened even more, when he showed her the photo of the spa in the hotel brochure. "That looks incredible."

"You have to swim naked," he paused for emphasis, "just like the Romans did." He chuckled in her ear.

She punched him, hard. "If you want to get into my panties, you don't have to get me to swim naked or convince me to share a bed with you, you only had to ask," she said before biting her lip, unable to believe she'd blurted out something so cheeky and naughty.

He sucked in a sharp breath. "You're playing with fire, Amber Webb," he whispered into her ear.

She lifted her chin in a provocative manner. "Can you hurry up? I want to see our *suite*."

Within minutes, they'd unlocked the door and walked into their room. Amber's heart almost stopped at the beauty of it. She whistled through her teeth. Stunning, opulent, lavish, tasteful, were words that came to her as she marvelled at the room they were to be staying in. Fresh flowers, mood lighting, Christmas music playing the background, fluffy pillows, and plush carpet. She wanted to groan with delight. This was one of the most beautiful rooms she'd seen. "I never want to leave here. It's so gorgeous," she said, walking around the suite, admiring the perfectly wallpapered walls, the perfectly hung painting, and the perfect little touches—like chocolates and wine, to welcome them.

"I wouldn't mind a swim," he said, stretching his arms above his head. "It's been a long day."

"I didn't bring bathers," she said. "I'll sit on the side and watch you."

His lips pressed together and he lifted a brow as he said, "I can't believe you said that. I don't think so."

She took a step back. "I have to swim naked?"

"Would I do that to you?"

"Maybe? No," she stumbled over her words, still unsure if he was teasing her or being serious.

"Let's unpack and then you can check the bathroom, there should be a package for you," he said with a more serious tone.

"A present for me?" Her heart jumped up in excitement.

"It's not really a present, just...just go and open it." He pointed to the ensuite.

She literally sprinted to the bathroom but stopped and gasped as she entered. It was almost the size of her living area in her Melbourne apartment. "I want to live here," she called out. "I never want to leave."

On the vanity was a basket and some bathing suits, neatly folded in it. "Darcy, you organised bathers. Thank you!" She rushed to him and threw her arms around his neck, pressing her lips against his cheek.

"I assumed you didn't bring any," he said, holding her close.

"I didn't expect to be swimming during winter in England," she laughed. "Let's go," she moved out of his arms. "Forget unpacking. I want to go downstairs." Excitement burst from her every pore. She snatched the brochure from his hands and read. "There are two natural thermal pools, blah blah blah, four-story glass atrium, blah blah blah."

"What's with the blah, blah, blah?"

"The details, come on, let's go," she insisted. "I'll be ready in five minutes."

A few minutes later, Amber stood in front of the mirror staring at her reflection. Of the three bathers, only the black bikini fit well and pangs of self-consciousness flooded her, which was silly. Friends wore bathers and swam together, so why were her fingers trembling? She wanted to dismiss the reason but she couldn't. She wanted him. Wanted him more than she'd ever wanted a man. It didn't matter that they couldn't have a future together or that if they went from friends to lovers, it would mean the end of their friendship.

She knew what she was like. She would struggle to remain friends with him if they made love. She'd had a few boyfriends over the years and wasn't into casual sex. But she wanted to take a chance and just enjoy the moment. Could she do it?

But what if he didn't respond? How mortifying would

that be? Her cheeks burned, just thinking about it. She shouldn't even think about it.

What if Darcy only liked her as a friend? But then she remembered how tightly he'd held her, how his lips had lingered on her cheek when he kissed her, and how his gaze sometimes found her soul.

Should they give in to chemistry? What about their friendship?

A loud knock at the door startled her. "I thought you said you were going to be quick," he said through the door.

"Sorry, coming now." She grabbed one of the fluffy cotton robes and tightened the belt around her waist. With her hair tied up in a messy bun, and the provided slippers on her feet, she stepped out of the sanctuary of the bathroom.

*D*arcy's eyeballs almost fell out of their sockets when Amber shrugged out of the hotel terry-towelling robe and walked towards the pool. The triangles barely covered the bits they were supposed to and he was struggling to keep his thoughts in the friend-zone. Hell, he'd been battling with the whole friend issue since she'd arrived.

He was going to embarrass himself if he removed his robe. He swore under his breath. "Back in a sec," he said and headed to the lavatories. He needed a few minutes to calm his libido before he did something stupid like kissing her. Not just kissing her but kissing and tasting the soft skin along her jawline and down to her shoulder.

He moved his thoughts from Amber's delectable body to his recent stunts on the latest movie. Thinking about the pain of falling off a horse in period costume, being pushed down a staircase and having to deal with bruises on his thighs and buttocks was the calming agent he needed.

Back in the atrium, he realised it was just him and Amber in the spa area, and he assumed most of the other guests were either having dinner or getting ready for dinner.

Within seconds, he was in the pool and he took a few minutes to accustom himself to the soothing, warm waters. "This is what I need after a day of work," he said before floating on his back.

He stared up at the high ceiling and a sense of peace settled over him. He couldn't remember the last time he'd relaxed like this. Time between being on-set was usually spent with friends, and they either drank too much beer or chased women.

Closing his eyes, he was overcome with emotion. He wanted to be with Amber. He didn't want her to return to Australia; he wanted her to stay here, with him. Drinking and partying with his friends just didn't hold the appeal it once did, and he was gripped with fervour that was new, raw and disturbing.

He'd never spent as much time with a woman as he had with Amber. They'd talked non-stop, gone sightseeing, and had fun. His thoughts had strayed into dangerous territory over the past couple of days but he didn't want to hurt her.

She wasn't into casual sex. If he crossed the line from friends to lovers, it would have to be more than just a shag. She wasn't the type of woman who had sex for the fun of it.

Thoughts of him and Amber in bed, tumbled through his brain and he quickly rolled over in the water so he was no longer floating on his back, before he embarrassed himself.

Swimming over to her, he found her seated, head resting on the side of the pool, eyes closed. "This is so relaxing," she murmured.

His gaze took in the black bikini and he knew he was a goner. Perhaps he should wait for her in the iced pool? He shivered and considered going with the sauna option instead. "I might have a sauna," he said.

Her eyes fluttered open. "We just got here. Is there a problem?"

Yes. "No, I thought it might be more relaxing," he lied.

"Something is bothering you. Do you want to talk about it?" she asked in a soothing voice, as she moved towards him. She reached out to comfort him, but her hand ended up on his thigh.

He cleared his throat, before running his fingers through his hair. Inching his bottom away until her hand fell and no longer touched his skin. He missed the warmth of her hand, even though it wasn't a good idea for her to rest it there.

"Have I done something to upset you?" There was genuine concern in her large brown eyes.

He shook his head, a tightness ached in his chest. "Not at all, it's me."

She blinked rapidly. "I told you how the most humiliating moment in my life, was when my father caught my boyfriend and me having sex. Urgh. That was awful." She paused. "I think we've gone past the point of not being able to tell each other things."

"I want to kiss you," he blurted out. If he'd thought about it, he wouldn't have said it. The words just tumbled out and there was no way to un-speak them. Bugger.

Her jaw dropped, and her mouth formed a perfect O.

"We're friends and I don't want to make you feel uncomfortable but I'm feeling things that I shouldn't be feeling for you," he said in a low voice. He rubbed his chin. "I'm worried that I've already ruined our friendship, just by saying this." The heat in his body rose as he waited for her to reply.

She bit her lip and stared at the wall behind him.

He swore under his breath. He'd blown it. He should've kept his mouth shut. "I'm sorry, I should've—"

"I'm attracted to you. I want you to kiss me. And, um, I-I'm also scared about crossing the line," she said, the words tumbling from her lips. "Is it hot in here, or is it just me?" She looked around before blowing a long breath out. "What do we do?"

He inched towards her, sat next to her in the pool, the water lapping their shoulders, and took her hands in his. "We pretend this never happened or we kiss."

"I can't pretend." Her voice was scratchy and her breaths came in shallow bursts.

Deciding he'd lead and let her either follow him or call a halt to it, he placed his hands under her armpits and he lifted her so that she sat astride his lap. "Tell me to stop, and I will."

She was so close, their breaths mingled.

"Amber," his finger trailed along the softness of her cheek. "I've never wanted to kiss someone as much as I want to kiss you."

"Me too," she replied, her eyes drowsy with desire. "Can I blame the madness of Christmas?"

"No." He didn't want there to be a reason for them to have kissed. "If we kiss, it's because we want to. There's no blame. We do this together," he paused. "Or I'll go and sit in the spa, over there." He pointed to the room near the entrance.

She nodded slowly. "I'm worried about making the wrong decision," she confessed. "I'm scared about losing you. Every day I deal with conflicting couples, so you'd think I'd know better. But I seem to sabotage my own relationships. Every. Single. One. Of. Them." She stressed the words for emphasis.

His belly knotted with regret and gratitude. He was disappointed at not being able to taste her lips. And relieved that she'd made the decision between them.

The decision was made. They should stay as friends because if she wasn't sure about the kissing, then it meant it wasn't the right thing to do.

She started to slide off his lap away from him, so she stood in the pool facing him but with enough water between them so he couldn't reach her.

The choice had been made and he let her go, reluctantly.

He could see her smile wavering and a pensive expression in her eyes.

It was the right thing to do. "It's better this way," he said, not believing a word. A painful lump became stuck in his throat as his limbs felt as heavy as wet cement. His chin lowered to his chest and he closed his eyes, breaking eye contact, as his shoulders slumped.

AMBER WANTED TO APOLOGISE, explain, as she stood before him. But the words were stuck in her throat. How to explain years of bad relationships, not just with her boyfriends but also with her parents. She squeezed her eyes shut as a dull, heavy feeling settled in her chest.

Despite being able to successfully help others with their relationships in her professional world, she'd always done badly when it came to herself. She had few friends, little family and was so lonely.

Darcy was the best thing that had happened to her, and now she was about to destroy that, too. No, she told herself, she wouldn't do it.

With determination to prove to herself that she was worthy of him, she walked towards him.

"Darcy," she said, in a soft voice. He looked at her, and she stared into the blueness of his eyes, filled with sorrow. "You are the best thing that has ever happened to me. I treasure and value you more than my own parents. I love you with every fibre of my being, and I'm so scared of losing you."

She stopped and took a deep breath to steady the trembling in her heart. "We found each other through social media, like the same music and have so many shared interests. I have to confess that I opened myself up to you, told you secrets I would never tell a boyfriend, because I never expected there would be any romance between us.

"You're four years younger than me and are at a different stage in your life. I'm ready to settle down, have a family whereas you...you're famous and work with Hollywood's elite." She licked her dry lips. "You were my un-perfect guy. You became my best friend, because I knew we'd never be more than friends."

His head nodded and she could see remorse and sadness in his eyes. His shoulders sagged as he leaned against the pool edge. "I know, me too." He paused. "Unlike you, I'm close to my family, but I've never been in love. I've never met someone I'd give up my career for. Some of the shows and movies I've worked on were about that type of love, but I never believed in it."

"And what do you believe in now?" she asked, almost too scared to hear the reply.

"If I didn't love and respect you, we would've had sex by now," he said with honesty. "We are attracted to each other, but I don't know if it's physical or if there is more to it." He lifted a brow. "You're the counsellor, you should know more than me."

She threw her hands up in frustration. "That's the problem, I'm good at helping others, terrible at helping myself."

His lips twitched with amusement.

"It's not funny, Darcy." She pouted.

"If we were a couple that you were talking with, what advice would you give them?" His brow furrowed with curiosity.

Her finger tapped her lip. "I'm not sure. But I would not advise making hasty decisions."

"Good idea, what else?" he asked.

"I'd get them to talk through their issues," she said.

"I'll go first," he said, and she stifled a chuckle, that he was so eager to talk with her.

"We're friends, and as you said, we can't be more than friends for all the reasons you've mentioned." He lifted his hand and ticked them off his fingers. "Different countries. Different aspirations in life. Different expectations. Different backgrounds." A slow smile stretched his lips. "Have I missed anything?"

She shook her head.

"The main issue that I see is that if we kiss, things will change." He placed his hand on his chest. "I don't think I could like or love you any less than I do now. I'm going to say that I believe we can kiss and remain friends after you return to Australia. The decision is now with you."

"You rat," she said. "You made it sound so simple. You've left out feelings and emotions."

"You're the counsellor," he teased. "That's your job."

"You once told me that you're a good kisser," she said, as determination gave her the boost of confidence she needed.

"I am," he said, sitting straighter, his eyes sparkling with mischief.

"I want to see if you're as good as you make out to be. I think you were exaggerating," she said with a dismissive toss of her hair.

"You want to do an experiment? Prove you're right?"

"Something like that," she moved towards him so she stood in front of him, the warm, thermal waters lapping at their skin.

"Are you going to rate me?"

She nodded. "Yes, I'll give you a mark out of ten." She inched closer.

"And what if I'm right? That I'm a good kisser."

"Then I'll kiss you again, because, who doesn't want to be kissed by someone who knows how to do it well?" she asked leaning forward so their mouths were barely an inch from each other.

"I like to win," he said.

"I know. It's what makes you so good at what you do," she replied in a soft voice.

Their gazes locked and he placed his hands around her slim waist.

For a moment, the whole world could have stopped turning and neither would have noticed. Their focus was completely on each other. Their breathing grew irregular, and Amber was sure he could hear her heart thumping against her ribs.

In perfect synchronisation, they leaned in and their lips touched. Their first kiss. With one arm anchoring him to her, the other hand came up so his fingers could trail along her jawline.

She shivered in anticipation.

"Your skin is so soft," he whispered, before his hands came and cupped her cheeks and he kissed her. Not a brush of his lips but a proper kiss that made her moan with delight.

His lips were soft and he kissed her like she was the most beautiful woman.

Her arms involuntarily came up and locked around his neck as she kissed him back. Together, in the pool, they kissed, and kissed, and kissed.

Breathless, his lips moved along her jawline to nibble and taste her skin. Her body zinged with anticipation and her blood surged through her as he licked the rim of her ear before sucking the lobe.

She closed her eyes as the sensations flooded her body. Soon enough, his lips were on hers and he deepened the kiss and he kissed her with a passion that she'd never felt before. His tongue swept into her mouth and she groaned in reply.

Her body hummed in delight as he kissed her till she was breathless and so desperate for his touch.

She wanted to cry out when he pulled back from her, and despite wanting to remain cool about the whole kissing-her-friend thing, she knew she was grinning like an idiot. As much as she wanted to keep her emotions under lock and key, she couldn't.

"That was...that was amazing," she said with an eagerness that made her want to cringe.

"It was," he replied, as his fingers stroked along her cheek.

"I was expecting a smart answer from you," she admitted.

"And usually, you'd have one, but, um, I don't know. I'm lost for words," he confessed.

Her eyes widened with surprise. "Really?"

"Yes, really," he said. "I don't know about you, but I'm turning into a prune." He lifted his hand showing the skin to her. "Let's get out of here."

They walked out of the pool, hand in hand, and donned their robes.

"I'm starving but can't be bothered going out to eat," she said.

He grinned. "Same. Why don't I order in?" He walked over to the courtesy phone after she nodded. A quick call, and he returned to her with a satisfied smile. "We've got half an hour. You go upstairs and have a shower, I'll have one here," he pointed to the changing area.

"You're so efficient," she said. "I'll see you up there."

He brushed his lips across hers and she shivered in anticipation. "See you soon."

* * *

AFTER HER SHOWER, Amber wondered what to wear. They'd crossed the line between friends, and instead of berating herself, she'd been singing and dancing, taking more time than usual in getting ready. Not wanting to appear over eager or too enthusiastic, she'd donned her fleecy pyjamas, her hair was twisted in a messy bun and she was wearing her glasses, just as she had when they were in London.

That kiss. Goodness. That kiss had rated eleven out of ten, and she could still taste his lips on hers. He certainly knew how to kiss. She pressed her fingers against her mouth. She wanted to kiss him again, and again if possible.

A knock at the door brought her to her senses. "Amber, hurry up, you've been in there for ages. Supper's ready."

Giving herself a quick once over, she smiled at her reflection. She couldn't change who she was. A kiss wouldn't do that. Besides, it was not like he was suddenly going to change his career so they could start a family. The likeliness of that happening was about the same as him spending Christmas in Australia with her...in other words, it wasn't going to happen.

She walked out of the bathroom and into the living room, where she gasped. "You've outdone yourself, Darcy," she said, admiring the indoor picnic he'd built. With a blanket and pillows and candles in the middle, he'd cleverly devised a cosy, intimate eating experience for them. It was special, wonderful and romantic. "This looks lovely." It was more than lovely; it was beautiful but she bit her lip, not wanting to gush. She was still unsure how to behave around him now that they'd kissed.

In boxer shorts and a T-shirt, he'd opted for the same casual look as her.

She chuckled at the background music playing softly. Not smooth but heavy rock. Rock Lint. The rock band's music that had brought them together on social media a few months earlier. "Nice touch with the music, Darcy."

He grinned in reply. "Sit," he gestured to the pile of pillows he'd organised for her.

"This looks amazing. You ordered finger food," she said, admiring the number of small plates with artfully arranged food.

He lifted his brow with amusement. "I can assure you that no fingers were harmed in the preparation of tonight's supper. On offer," he pointed out each dish. "A selection of cheeses with local chutneys and biscuits, samosas, wild mushroom risotto, sautéed scallops, and a salted caramel tart."

"I'm salivating. It looks and smells delicious," she said, helping herself to a portion of risotto and some scallops.

He poured them each a glass of champagne.

Placing her plate next to her, she lifted her glass and clinked his.

"To friendship?" she suggested.

"No, to you. Thank you for coming to see me. These past few days have been so much fun, and I have enjoyed every minute," he said.

"Even the museums?"

"Even the museums," he said with determination. "Sightseeing with you over these past few days has been brilliant."

"It has. I'll drink to that." They each sipped champagne before eating.

"You forgot to give me my mark," he said seemingly innocent while nibbling on a samosa.

"You beast," she chuckled. "You're so competitive."

He shrugged. "It's a guy thing."

"I'm busy eating," she said making a show of stuffing her mouth with scallops.

He shook his head. "You know how to stifle a conversation."

"Sorry, I can't hear you, I'm eating," she joked with him.

After everything had been eaten, and most of the champagne had been drunk, they lay next to each other on the pillows, watching the flicker of flames in the fireplace.

"This hotel is amazing. Thank you for dinner. I loved it," she turned to him and kissed his cheek.

"Amber, there's something we need to discuss. There's only one bed—"

"The bed is massive. It's so big, we'd need megaphones to be able to talk to each other from either side. I can confidently say that we could comfortably sleep on a side, and there would still be a wide berth of bed between the two of us."

"I didn't want you to get the wrong idea," he said.

"I think it's a great idea, to share a bed," she said before brushing her lips across his.

"Amber, I don't want you to regret anything in the morning."

"The only thing I'm going to regret is not seizing this moment and enjoying it. I want you and you want me."

"We drank a lot of champagne," he said.

She dismissed his concern with a wave of her hand. "I know what I'm doing and saying."

"Are you sure?" he asked softly.

"I'm sure," she replied, confident in her decision to spend the night with him. Their kiss had been earth-shattering, and she wanted more. She was sensible enough to know that this was a one-off and they'd have to go back to being friends after. But she wanted to break out from her shell of being the responsible one. She'd been like that for years and what had she got? Few friends, little contact with her parents, and only a career to keep her company. And now, that career could go. With the shock of her manager's announcement of budget cuts, she'd been preparing herself that she might be looking for a new job next year.

She was breaking out of her comfort zone and she was going to enjoy every moment of her time with Darcy.

She was thirty-one, she'd had boyfriends. She wasn't so naïve as to expect anything from him. She wanted to give in to temptation, be naughty. His kisses made her knees weak. She didn't want to look back and wish she'd been more bold.

Next week, she'd return to Australia, heartbroken but at least she wouldn't be filled with regret.

Taking charge, she shifted herself so she sat astride him. "I want you, just like you want me." She brushed her lips against him. "We're friends. No regrets."

"I want you with every fibre of my being," he said. "But I want to make sure this is what you want, too."

"This is what I want," she whispered in his ear, before kissing it. "I'm sensible enough to know *how it is*. But I really want this—"

He captured her mouth with his and kissed her with a passion that made her thankful for her decision.

"You are so beautiful," he said, laying her down on the pillows. He removed the elastic and untied her bun. "I like you with your hair down," he said, kissing away any protest.

"Just so you know, your kissing is an eleven out of ten," she said before he captured her mouth in another devastating kiss.

CHAPTER 7

The following morning, Darcy woke and found Amber cuddled beside him. During the night, they'd shifted, moved towards one another and slept in each other's arms. Darcy sighed, unable to believe how perfect they fit together. Their coupling had been incredibly wonderful and he didn't know how he was going to let her go next week.

They belonged together, not for a fling but for the long term. He didn't know how he was going to convince Amber, but he was going to find a way. She was correct in that there were a lot of differences between them, but surely they could overcome them. They needed to talk.

But for now, he needed to exercise. He was due on set in a few weeks in France, and he couldn't afford to compromise his fitness.

"Amber, darling," he whispered in her ear.

She murmured in her sleep and he was ready to ditch the exercise and make love to her again. No. She needed to sleep.

With reluctance, he untangled himself from her. Got out of the bed, and wrote a note, leaving it beside her on the bed.

The room was a little chilly, so he started the fire and then changed into his workout gear, before heading downstairs.

Two hours later, after a punishing run and weight-training session, he walked into their suite, hot and exhausted.

"Good morning," she said, curled up in a chair, reading a book. She greeted him with a warm smile but remained seated. "How was the gym?"

He ran the towel over his face. "Tiring."

She looked radiant and beautiful, despite wearing jeans and a warm sweater.

"I've had a coffee, but I'll make you a cup of tea while you shower. There's some fruit for you, and then we can go out for breakfast." She pointed to the low table where a complimentary bowl of fruit sat. His gaze took in the cleaned room, noticing the pillows and throw rugs had been folded and returned to where they belonged. It was like last night hadn't happened. Even the plates had been put away.

A niggle of worry wormed its way into his belly. "Is everything okay?"

"Yes," she added brightly. "Everything is great."

"I won't be long," he said, his belly full of trepidation.

After a hot shower, Darcy shaved and then dressed. Something was going on and he was worried about what she was going to say. Obviously, things had shifted between them, and he could tell even though she appeared happy and relaxed this morning. It seemed she was comfortable with their no-regrets agreement.

He sat across from her, now dressed, his feet in warm socks, as he drank the large mug of tea she'd made for him. Hot, strong with a splash of milk. The tea was exactly how he liked it.

She looked at him. A tiny smile on her lips gave way to a bigger one. She sat straight in her chair and he could literally feel the excitement bursting out of her. "I just want to say that last night was amazing. There are no words about how great it was. And you don't have to worry about me becoming all clingy and needy with you."

He didn't know whether to be happy or disappointed about that. But he was relieved so far about where the conversation seemed to be heading.

"If you were older and ready to start a family, I'd ask you to marry me because *connection*"—she pointed from her to him—"doesn't always happen. I wish things were different but they're not. I still want you in my life." She paused. "Do you remember when you were fourteen, and you decided that you didn't want to be a professional gymnast?"

He nodded. He'd subconsciously sabotaged his team's success at the interschool finals. Instead of placing first, they'd placed fourth. His teammates were as disgusted with him as he was with himself. But it was in that moment, he knew he didn't want to commit to training every day and spending every second of the weekend either training or competing. At the time, his parents had been disappointed that despite his talent, he no longer had aspirations of making the English Olympic Team.

"I've had one of those moments," she leaned towards him. "I've been living a life half lived. I realised this morning that I can't expect to get happiness with a husband and children. It doesn't work like that."

Worry made his heart beat quickly, as he wondered where the conversation was going to end up.

"I've stayed in a job to prove myself right against my parents. They wanted me to follow in their footsteps, and I didn't. I did what I thought I wanted, not what I really want- ed." She banged her fist against her breastbone. "I don't know what I really want to do. I have issues with my periods and I'm scared that I'm going to need IVF to have children. I hate

IVF. It scares me. I've been surrounded by it for years…and I don't know if I have the strength to go through it."

"Amber, you are so strong and courageous. I know you can do it."

"Thank you, Darcy." She paused. "And I've been thinking about us. You're about to be in ten different locations over the next year, you're going to be busy." She raised her hand to stop him from speaking. "Let me finish. I know you'll always have time for me, but I need to find out what *I* want."

She sipped some water before she finished speaking. "I don't know what I'm going to do next year, but I'm going to consider foster care, writing a book, doing dancing lessons, making new friends, and being true to myself."

He shook his head with the incredulity of the situation. "That is some revelation you've had."

"It's all thanks to *you*," she said with pride.

"No, this is about you, not me." He couldn't see how this was about him, when she was making the most inspiring changes to her life. He was in awe of her courage.

"Darcy, last night in the pool when we kissed, I felt like I'd stepped off a cliff. I did something that was so unlike me that I still can't believe it. But this morning, I realised that to get what I want, I need to go after it…I can't expect it to fall in my lap." Her voice was filled with imposed determination.

His heart was close to bursting, he was so proud of her. She'd changed in such a positive way that it took all of his willpower not to lift her in his arms and kiss her again and again.

"I don't know what to say," he said, a little confused, and also overwhelmed with such a momentous change.

"Just wish me luck, and then take me out for the day, so we can celebrate," she said.

He stood, lifted her by the waist and swung her around. "Good luck, Amber."

* * *

FOR THE NEXT FEW DAYS, they walked hand in hand, kissed a lot and savoured the nights in each other's arms. Back in London, with Christmas a few days away, the streets were filled with pageantry, and they spent every moment together.

Even though she was leaving soon, they didn't talk about it, but rather focussed on being together. They talked and laughed. The lovemaking and kissing hadn't torn them apart, but rather had brought them a closeness that was disturbing him. How could they say good-bye?

Despite her conviction in changing careers, Darcy was worried. Her best friend, Taylor, was in America, and she had little family support. The change in her was so dramatic that he needed to assure himself she would be okay.

Each time he raised the issue with her, she brushed his worries aside before kissing him. It was her tactic for ensuring that the difficult decisions would be decided on her own, in Australia.

And then finally the day came when at Heathrow Airport, they stood outside Immigration, and he held her close. He couldn't say good-bye. He'd fallen in love with her, he was sure of it. He'd never felt like this before, and he couldn't bear to wake up tomorrow alone in his apartment. "I'm going to miss you," he said, his face buried in her shoulder.

"I'll miss you more," she said, tears running down her face.

"Stay with me, don't go home. Please." He, who'd never begged a woman for anything, would lay on the floor and plead if it would help.

"I have a job, responsibilities to return to. I can't stay here. What would I do? You're on set in three weeks, and you'll be away for months at a time. Do you want me to sit in your apartment, waiting for you?"

He blotted her tears with a tissue. "I know. You're being the responsible one. I'm thinking with my heart."

"I love you so much, but we need to go back to how things used to be," she said.

"Are you joking?" His heart was being ripped apart with her leaving him, and she expected them to be friends again? He could barely breathe for the pain that was squeezing his ribs so hard.

"We have to, otherwise I'll fall apart," she said. "We both know a relationship between us can't work. I've accepted it." She blew her nose. "I'm not saying good-bye, I can't, but I'll call you when I land in Melbourne."

"That's a day away," he said wistfully, thinking about the long flight she had ahead of her.

"Merry Christmas," she said. "At least I can say it to you in person. I wish I could've enjoyed dinner with you and your family, but I have to get back to work in a couple of days."

"I know, I know," he repeated. "Have a good flight." It sounded trite. He just wanted to pin her to him so she couldn't leave.

"I'm going to watch a stack of Christmas movies on the plane," she pointed to her tablet.

"I don't want to say good-bye," he said.

"Me either," she said, before pressing her lips against his. "Love you." She picked up her bag and turned to wave at him before entering the Immigration hall where he was forbidden to enter.

His heart ached and he rubbed his palm over his chest, wondering if he'd ever feel happy again. She disappeared from sight, and he rubbed his eyes.

Shoulders stooped, he turned and walked out of the airport so he could drive home.

* * *

CHRISTMAS DAY in Melbourne and the summer sun was burning bright. The early morning weather predictions were that the day would be scorching hot and encouraged everyone to stay indoors or under cover.

Luca and Taylor had surprised their parents with an earlier-than-expected arrival from America, and Taylor had invited her for lunch. "Mum and Dad are hosting, they'd love to see you."

"They won't mind me coming over?" She didn't want to appear too eager, but she loved Taylor's family and wanted to see them.

Taylor laughed. "They adore you. Of course, you should come over." Her friend paused. "I think I'm jet-lagged but I just realised that you're not working, why?"

"I've resigned," she said brightly. Leaving her job had brought a sense of relief and excitement about finding a passion and purpose in her life. She still couldn't believe she'd left. After all these years, she'd left a well-paying job to find meaning and happiness. Even if she didn't know what she was going to do...and she was more than a little scared.

"Goodness, you need to tell me everything and I mean everything. Come over soon. I want to see you," Taylor said before ending the call.

Placing the phone in her tote bag, Amber caught her reflection in the mirror and stood for a moment to admire the outfit she'd purchased yesterday.

She'd decided to donate all of her tailored pencil skirts and sharp work gear. Gone were the days of tight clothing, akin to having a boa constrictor for a skirt.

She teamed the new floral dress with wedged sandals and smiled at her reflection. She looked good, not because of the new clothes but because she was making decisions that would bring her happiness.

The one decision she'd made that hadn't brought her

happiness was walking away from Darcy. Since she'd said good-bye to him she'd wondered if she'd made the right decision. Should she have left him? And now that he wasn't returning her calls, perhaps it was too late? Every moment since she'd kissed him good-bye had pained her.

Had she allowed the sensible side of her to make a poor judgement?

She removed her mobile phone so she could send Darcy a picture of herself in her summery dress. It was Christmas Eve in London and she wondered what he was doing. "Enjoying Melbourne's heat. How's the snow?" she wrote alongside the picture of her.

She hadn't heard from him lately. He'd messaged her, apologising and saying that there was limited coverage where his parents lived and he couldn't speak to her till after Christmas.

A quick glance at her watch told her she needed to leave. She was anxious to see Taylor. She'd missed her so much over the past few months.

There was a loud knock at the door and she looked up in surprise. Who could it be? On Christmas? She chuckled to herself, the best way would be to open it and find out.

She swung open the door with a joyful, "Merry Christmas" expecting it to be a neighbour and her eyes widened and she gasped. "Darcy, what are you doing here?" She stopped. "Is that really you?"

He reached out and tugged her close. "It's me, darling. I came to see you."

She snuggled in his arms. "I can't believe you're here. Why are you surprising me like this?"

"May I come in?" His clipped voice sounded so very English, making her wonder if everything was okay.

"Of course." She held the door wide so he and his suitcase could come into her apartment.

"Thank goodness you have air conditioning, I'm melting in this heat," he said, standing in front of the cooler. He wiped his hand across his brow and stood in front of the unit belting out cool air.

"How did you get through the security?" Her eyebrows came together with curiosity.

"Taylor, she gave me the code. I hope that's okay," he confessed.

"Taylor knows you're here?" Her heart leapt into her throat. Taylor knew but had said nothing to her ten minutes ago.

"Of course, she invited me to lunch at her parents'," he joked.

"Stop." She placed her hand against the wall as a wave of dizziness hit her. "I feel like I'm in the Twilight Zone here. What do you mean, you and I are going there for lunch? That doesn't make sense."

"Shall I start from the beginning?"

"Please," she said, feeling light-headed.

He took her hand, and they sat next to each other on the sofa. "Your apartment is nicer in real life." He gave her a cheeky wink before clearing his throat. "When you left, it was like a piece of me had been cut out. I knew that I couldn't go back to how things were. I know it's what you wanted, but it's not what *I* want." He stopped and took some deep breaths. "I didn't know what to do, so I visited my parents and told them everything. How we met, how you came to England and how you left. They've been happily married for over thirty years so I value their opinion."

She was fascinated and a little jealous that he had such a warm and close relationship with his parents. She would never seek hers out for advice on love...or anything. "What did they say?" she asked, so curious and eager to know more.

"They confirmed what I suspected," he said flippantly.

"What? Stop being silly with me. I want to know," her voice lifted, wanting to hear what they'd said to him. Was this why he'd flown halfway across the world to see her?

He lifted his hands, palms facing her in a defensive manner, but she knew he was teasing her. Then a serious look crossed his eyes, and the playful manner departed. "Amber, I'm in love with you, as in serious, wanting-to-be-with-you-forever love."

The breath expelled from her lungs in an ohhh, and her insides melted with adoration as he delivered his declaration. She wanted to say something but couldn't as shock, amazement, and unexpected joy clogged her throat.

He continued. "We became friends, and then we became lovers. But I can't imagine my life without you. I can't just be your friend." He said with honesty. "I want you, in my life, in my bed, with me for always. And we can't do that if you're here and I'm over there." His voice lifted with emotion. "I've got some ideas…wait a minute, no. We have to stop," he said, as a startled look crossed his eyes.

"No, keep going." Her nerves went haywire, seeing the grave look on his face. "What's the matter?" she asked.

"Um, before I go on, I should make sure that you do love me, I mean, like the way I love you?" The cuteness of his question was in stark contrast to his determination displayed only recently. How did someone so handsome, so confident and so self-assured not know that?

She decided to tease him. "I love you as much as I love chocolate."

His eyes widened and she could see the amusement in his eyes. "That's not enough," he said, playing along.

"Okay, okay. I love you as much as I love coffee," she tried.

"Minx," he said before he tugged her towards him and kissed her. Really kissed her. Kissed her till she was breathless. Kissed her till she clamoured onto his lap and started undoing the buttons on his shirt.

Then he stopped and pulled back. "Tell me you love me," he said, his eyes flushed with desire.

She yearned for his touch and her lips craved to be kissed. Forgetting the playful moment, this was the time to tell him how she really felt. "I love you, Darcy. I love you so much that I physically ache for you. Every morning I reach for you in bed and wish you were here with me. I wish there was a way we could be together because I wish I could be with you for the rest of my life. Not just as a friend, but as my lover. I'm so in love with you that I can't think straight." She leaned in and hugged him hard. "I don't know what to do, but what I do know is that I love you so much."

He held her close and soothed her by running his fingers through her hair. "I looked at a lot of possibilities, including me moving to Australia but unfortunately, there isn't enough work for me here. I need to stay in England, and close to Europe. If we're to marry, I need to look after and provide for you."

"Did you just say marry?" She sat up in his lap, her pulse skittled at the mention of the word *marry*.

He gave her a cheeky wink. "I may have." He took her hands in his and kissed the knuckles. "Amber darling, just listen, please."

"Okay," she agreed reluctantly.

"As you know, my job will always require me to travel. But what I can do is refuse the big movies where they film in up to ten locations over twelve months. If I can, I'll try and restrict to working in movies that are filmed in the UK, and I can act in commercials. Commercials pay well—it's not as fun as stunts but it's a good living." He paused. "Come and live in England with me, I will always have to travel, but I'll try not to be away for too long. And for some movies, you'll come on set with me. And in two to three years, I'll have enough money for a house, and we'll find something we love and settle down."

Flutters of surprise filled her belly. "You'd cut your career down for me?"

"It's more of making changes so we can be together. And when we have a house, we'll have the family you've always wanted." He paused. "Can you wait a couple of years?"

Her heart hammered against her chest. Everything sounded perfect and she wanted to yell out yes. Except there was one detail he'd forgotten. One of the most important issues to be addressed. "What will I do? I don't know if my qualifications are recognised in England," she said with a shrug of uncertainty.

"I'm sure you can work as a counsellor. You've got years of experience to help couples and women in need." He lifted her hand and pressed a kiss to her wrist. "But I was thinking you should write a book. A book to help those infertile couples deal with IVF."

"Me?" She pointed to herself. "Write a book?"

A smile twitched his lips. "You said yourself you wanted to look at foster care, dancing, writing a book and making new friends."

"I can't believe that you remembered me saying that," she gave him a playful punch to his shoulder.

He ran his fingers down the side of her face. "Amber, you have years of experience and knowledge. An electronically published book has the opportunity to be available to women all over the world. We'll find someone to help you write and publish it, and perhaps you can start a blog? I want you to have meaning in your life," he said. "What do you think?"

"I love the idea as much as I love you," she pressed her lips against his. "You've thought of everything."

"I want you to be happy," he said, and she could hear the sincerity in his voice. This was about them, not just him.

"I love your apartment and I love where you live. It's nicer than London, which is too busy for me," she said. She really liked the suburb he lived in, with its eclectic mix of old and new. When she walked from the train station to his apartment, she'd admired the suburb and felt at ease.

"We'll do things together and we'll make new friends. Tomorrow, we'll visit your parents."

"Ugh," she rolled her eyes. "I'd rather just be with you."

"I need to meet them and I want to seek their blessing to marry you," he said in a low but insistent voice.

She fired him a cranky look. "Shouldn't you ask me first?"

He gave her a dazzling smile that made her heart flip-flop. "I left my family's Christmas lunch to be here with you. I do need to speak to your parents as I'm taking you to England to live with me. Then, I need to introduce you to my family. They'll love you, how could they not? And then once you've emigrated, I'll find a romantic way to propose." He paused. "But just so you know, it will happen." He kissed her. "You're the best thing that has ever happened to me. I want you in my life, always, and if I have to make adjustments in my work, then I'm prepared to. I will do everything to make you happy. We'll travel around the UK and Europe when I have time off between movies."

"You've made my Christmas wish come true," she said. "I don't even know what to say. I left you heartbroken, and now you're here giving me your love, an opportunity to change my life and to find meaning and purpose. Yes, yes, yes. I can't wait to spend my life with you." With a long exhale, she confessed to him. "With Taylor living in the US, I've felt empty inside and needed a new career path. During the flight home I thought about what to do and as soon as I was in

Melbourne, I resigned from my job. I'd been there too long and wasn't happy anymore."

His mouth fell open. "What? Why? What were you going to do?"

"I had no job to go to. All I knew was that I needed to take a step toward making myself happy."

"B-but to leave?" He shook his head with disbelief.

She folded her hands in her lap, remembering that moment she'd walked out of the clinic, alone and unemployed. "Our time together showed me what happiness was. I wanted that for myself," she said, her hand pressing against her heart. "I knew that I needed more in my life."

He lifted his chin and gave her a *knowing* grin. "Do *I* and my suggestions make you happy?"

Her eyes filled with joyful tears. "They do. No one has ever given me such a thoughtful and considerate gift. The gift of life, of being true to myself."

His hands cupped her cheeks and he looked directly at her. "Darling, only you can do that, and you did do that. You're the most sincere, beautiful, honest woman. I think I just fell in love with you a little more."

She stifled a sob. "But look at what you did for me, for us. You made changes so we could be together. I'm so lucky to have you." She hugged him, holding him close, so thankful that this beautiful, considerate man had chosen *her*.

He shifted so he could gaze at her. "Merry Christmas, my beautiful Amber. You make my life complete."

"Merry Christmas, Darcy, my one true love. I can't wait to spend my life with you."

They sealed their love with a kiss and turned up later than expected at the Williamson's Christmas lunch.

THE END

ACKNOWLEDGMENTS

Dear Reader

I love writing holiday stories and couldn't wait to write another this year. I already knew and loved Amber, who was such a good friend to Taylor in Christmas Kiss, New Year's Wish, so it seemed only natural to give her a HEA (happily ever after).

But I needed a hero, someone so different from her. During the time I was creating a hero, my husband introduced me to his new friend, Jared Cohen, who has spent years as a stuntman. Wow! I was fascinated by his career and insights into the movie-making business and ta da, I'd found the perfect hero guy for Amber.

Thank you, Jared, for helping me create Darcy Harris, and answering all my questions.

I often talk about finding inspiration for the books I write. There are ideas everywhere, and they are perfect for my holiday books. As soon as I saw this video, I knew I had to use it; it was the perfect way to have Darcy and Amber meet - https://www.facebook.com/georgehtakei/videos/211878956093904/

If you want to be captivated by the wonderful places in England, where most of the book is set, head over to my Pinterest page - https://www.pinterest.com.au/joannedannon/inspiration-behind-christmas-kiss-in-london/

And if you're interested in the type of stunt work that Darcy does, check out Chase Armitage (who I used to create Darcy) who is incredibly talented and whose videos are breathtaking, and fascinating viewing – https://www.youtube.com/watch?v=e1vaYr-mCzk

I am blessed to have a brilliant support team and I want to thank my editor, Jena O'Connor for her incredible insights and awesome editing. Thank you, Janice Owen and Kat Sheridan for making my book shine. For the talented Erin Cawood, for her gorgeous artwork, and for my writing besties, who are so supportive and always there for me – thank you, Charmaine Ross, Lexi Greene, and Tracey Pedersen!

And thank you to my awesome author friends, Helen J Rolfe and Khardine Grey, for their help with this book.

I hope you enjoy Amber and Darcy coming together. It has one of my favourite tropes, friends to lovers.

Wishing you a magical Christmas and a very Happy New Year.

With love, Joanne x

CHRISTMAS KISS: BUT ONLY FOR THE HOLIDAYS

*C*EO Leo Turner: handsome, intelligent, all-around nice guy, recently single, and needs a plan.

CHRISTMAS IS JUST around the corner and the residents of Mono Melbourne retirement home are already conspiring to set him up with one of their granddaughters. What better way to make it through all those Christmas functions than to have a fake girlfriend? And who better to play the part than a woman he'd never fall for, Jenna Williamson.

SUPERMODEL JENNA IS STUNNING, sparkling, selfish and not interested in settling down—the perfect candidate for a one-month assignment.

EVERYTHING IS PLANNED PERFECTLY...OR so he thinks.

. . .

BUT WHEN CHRISTMAS kisses get heated, Leo realises not everything in his life can be meticulously organised.

CAN a dash of Christmas magic make this "arrangement" permanent?

DEDICATION

For my readers, thanks for reading my books xxx

CHAPTER 1

*J*enna Williamson rubbed her eyes, and wished she could rub out all the misfortune that had befallen her. Not only did she now have to live with her parents *at age thirty-one*, but she didn't have the money to pay the legal fees for her apartment.

Back in her childhood bedroom, she fell back on the bed, her head resting on her pillow. The stylish apartment with its majestic city views she'd so carefully invested all her money in had turned out to be a dud thanks to the builder who'd used cheap cladding that was not compliant with Australian building regulations.

The tenants were filing a class-action lawsuit against the builder, but in the meantime, the clean-up bill was going to eat into her savings. She also needed money for the class-action. Her stomach tumbled with angst at having to ask her parents for help. Bad enough she had to live with them while the fire systems and dangerous combustible cladding was being removed from the apartment block.

The cladding was supposed to provide thermal insulation and fire resistance. But the shoddy products used by the builder meant there was a potential for fire to spread quickly upwards on the building. For now, it was considered too dangerous for her, and the others, to live in the building.

She sighed with desperation at how awful things had become over the past couple of months.

And it was almost the holidays, a time of fun and a time to relax with friends over summer days and nights. She'd soon have to pretend she was happy, if only to keep her parents from worrying.

It was December which meant their neighbours, the families of Clarendon Close, would come together and celebrate the holidays together as they had for many years.

Inevitably she'd get the same comments; "You need to find someone special" or "Your biological clock is ticking, you shouldn't leave having babies for too long."

She was thirty-one, not forty-one, plenty of time. But she wasn't interested in having a baby. Was that so wrong?

The idea of sleepless nights, toddler tantrums and baby spew made her feel queasy. She'd accepted over the years that she just wasn't maternal. Shame no one else could accept it.

And now that she was living back with her parents, they'd been hinting, not too subtly, about partnering her up with sons of their friends. She pressed her lips together in frustration at her parents' clumsy attempts at match-making. She loved them but there were times she wanted to *kill* them.

A quick check of her mobile phone reminded her that she had her youth mentoring sessions soon, and she needed to drive there and not be late. As a stickler for being on time, she needed to impart her knowledge on her young charges with actions and words.

She'd recently started night classes, studying all she could learn about starting and managing a small business. She planned on modelling as long as she could, but needed something long term. Mentoring up and coming models, was the perfect idea. Not only could she impart her knowledge but she had the know-how to help aspiring models blossom into international stars.

The weekly one-hour sessions, she ran, were free, but where the young men and women needed more one-on-one support, or for her to represent them, then she charged. Her fees and rates were reasonable, and on the lower side compared with other talent agents.

She stood and walked slowly to the en-suite bathroom to fix her hair and makeup.

As a model, she was always dressed immaculately, and her makeup flawless. A shudder of revulsion ripped through her at the idea of being seen in public not looking her best.

Within minutes, her makeup was perfect, and her long blond hair was tied in a messy bun.

Dressed in skinny jeans and a tank top that highlighted her slim physique, she added uber cool sunnies, a tote bag, and wedge heels. Smiling at the mirror, she appraised her look; it was flawless, casual, and oh-so-gorgeous.

Blowing herself a kiss to reassure herself that life could only get better, she waltzed outside to her beloved convertible. Starting the engine, she drove to the youth centre where she met up with aspiring teen girl models each week.

* * *

LEO TURNER SIGHED and ran his fingers through his hair. Unbelievable. It was December, and the retirement home he managed had a number of functions over the next month which he would be expected to attend. . .with his girlfriend.

The problem was that said girlfriend had ditched him for a bad boy.

You're so boring, Leo. He could still hear her teasing in his ears.

Sure, he worked hard, but he was thirty-three and in charge of one of Melbourne's largest and most prestigious retirement homes, Mono Melbourne.

He was the youngest general manager of their homes, and he was determined to show the Executive team that they had not made a mistake in hiring him.

And what Cailah hadn't seemed to understand was that his lavish apartment, with its beachside address, had been achieved from hard work, and long hours including weekends.

I need a man who'll take risks.

He wasn't a man who took risks. Everything about his life was checked, organised and risks were mitigated.

He didn't ride a motorbike, have sex in public places or hang out with questionable people.

He'd thought everything between him and Cailah had been perfect, until she'd just dropped her bombshell that she was leaving him for a bikie who Leo could only describe as a *bad boy*.

He'd been planning on asking Cailah to marry him. He thought she was the one.

Obviously, he'd made a massive mistake, and the sting of it still hurt four weeks later. It was early December and he had no intention of turning up "single" at the holiday parties. For the past two years, the residents had been trying to set him up. He'd had enough. Enough bad dates to last him a lifetime.

This morning, he'd been introduced to Kate. Kate was pretty, and seemed very nice but she was still studying at University. He was tired of the residents introducing their granddaughters to him. It was exhausting, and frustrating.

They took his rejection of their granddaughters as a personal attack on them, which was ridiculous.

He'd gone on dates with some. But most were too young for him, couldn't they see that?

Obviously not, he sighed.

He needed a break.

He needed a fake girlfriend. Yes!

He snapped his fingers at the thought.

Someone who could act. Someone beautiful. Someone who wasn't interested in marrying.

But who?

Leo racked his brain. Surely one of his friends could play his endearing girlfriend for the next month?

No. Most of his friends were married or in long-term relationships.

He scratched his head. A childhood friend?

There was always Jenna.

Oh, God. He shuddered at the idea of being with her. Selfish, opinionated, and rude were her most endearing qualities.

No. He'd have to find someone else, even if he had to pay an actress.

Jenna would be the worst person to play his girlfriend. She hated babies. She hated old people. She hated sick people.

She didn't seem to have a compassionate bone in her body and would be the least likely person he would date. She'd hate it here. The retirement home was stylish, modern, and classy. It was aimed at senior citizens who were young at heart and wanted independent living that also provided a 24/7 dedicated nursing team, social events, exercise classes, and a range of holistic services to keep them healthy, strong, and vibrant.

He loved the home, and its residents. It was the place he'd love his parents to retire to.

They even had a wing catering to those who were no longer able to live on their own, whilst a separate wing provided respite care.

He leaned back in his ergonomic chair and ran his fingers through his hair. With only one day left, he needed to find a date who could pretend to be his ex, Cailah.

No one needed to know that Cailah had left him four weeks ago for a guy called Racer, who looked like he belonged in an outlaw motorbike gang.

He couldn't work out how sweet Cailah, the woman of his dreams had met up with someone so unlikely. And then ditched him.

He blew out a frustrated breath.

It seemed the silly season had started early.

Hours later and a gazillion internet searches later, Leo's head rested in his palms, his elbows on the desk feeling defeated. He blew out a long breath at the realisation that finding a fake girlfriend was easier in theory than in reality.

The first event was tomorrow night and there was no way he could find someone by then. . .who could also be available for the next month. He needed more time and there wasn't any.

Perhaps he should just admit he was single? An effective solution, and then he wouldn't have to worry about pretending.

Running his fingers through his hair strengthened his resolve.

He had this stupid, romantic idea that he'd know the right woman by her kiss. If the kissing worked, then surely other areas would, too.

And Cailah?

Her kisses had been fine. . .till she'd left him. Perhaps his ideals should be shoved aside and confined to teen romance movies.

Gah! He disgusted himself.

A knock on his office door had him looking up. His executive assistant Marc walked in. "I've got a ton of questions I need to go through with you."

He gestured to the chairs on the other side of his desk, inviting Marc to be seated. He liked Marc—keen, smart, and competent. He was only twenty-four, but he was the best assistant he'd ever had.

Over the next hour, they discussed and finalised outstanding issues.

At the end, he rubbed his chin and wondered if he should confide in his extra-ordinary assistant. Surely Marc would be discrete, but he would also understand the issues he dealt with at the home.

Clearing his throat a couple of times, he took a deep, much-needed breath. Standing, he walked over and closed the door to his office and faced the young man.

Marc's face whitened with worry. "Am I about to be fired?"

"No." He gave him a reassuring smile. "You're the best assistant I've ever had."

Marc's lips struggled to smile.

Deciding to be honest and upfront, he said. "I need your advice."

Marc's shoulders slumped and a breath of relief escaped his lips. "Sure, I hope I can help you."

"As you know, some of the residents here love a good romance, and are determined *match makers*," he started to say and stopped when Marc's face started to redden.

"I didn't want to say anything, but, um, b-but, Mrs Weddon and her friends want me to meet their granddaughters." He rubbed his eyes. "My girlfriend and I recently broke up, well, she left me. I'm really not in the mood to start dating again. Rose and I were together since high school, and um, this is embarrassing to admit, but I'm heartbroken. I don't want to date someone else, especially not now."

"I didn't know you'd been together for so long." He stroked his chin, listening to Marc's tale of woe. It was similar to his. Perhaps his assistant would understand his dilemma.

"Yes. Since we were sixteen. She's been the only girl for me." Marc sighed with exaggeration.

"What happened?"

"She wants to travel, live overseas, see the world." Marc threw his hands up. "But to do that I need to leave this job, rent out my place and follow her."

Leo was sure his heart skipped a beat. Lose Marc? No way. It was bad enough when Marc was on leave and he had to work with the temporary staff he'd organised. *Let Rose go and find herself*, he relied on his assistant.

Marc straightened his shoulders. "Back to you, what do you need help with?"

"I need a girlfriend," he said. Straight to the point and succinct.

He expected Marc to chuckle, but he didn't. "Cailah?"

Leo shook his head. His assistant knew only what he needed to know. He and Cailah weren't together.

"Surely you have a friend you can ask?" Marc's brow became furrowed as he thought intently about helping him. "Don't ask an ex, that will get you into trouble."

The two men chuckled.

"I have a friend but I don't think she'll do it," he confessed in a low voice.

Marc's shoulders straightened. "Then find her weakness and use it to your advantage," Marc said with confidence.

Leo's eyes widened at the assertive tone of his EA. "You're not usually so ruthless."

"You know me," he shrugged. "I'm a softie, but if you turn up single tomorrow night at the Carols by Candlelight Mrs Weddon will be introducing you to her granddaughter, who's studying medicine at the University of Melbourne. However, according to her grandmother, she is smart, pretty, and currently single." Marc said with a flourish of his hand.

Leo shook his head. The idea of dating a uni student made him want to punch a wall. Seriously? He was in his early thirties, not his twenties. "And what about you?"

Marc's face suddenly looked sunburned. "I, um, have two options. I either pay my cousin to be my girlfriend, or my best mate, and pretend we're gay."

Leo sniggered. "Those are your options?" He dramatized his voice for effect.

Marc nodded. "My mate will do it for a couple of beers and a game of pool. My stupid cousin wants a few hundred dollars so she can see some stupid band. Stupid. I think I may go for the gay option, my mate won't let me down." He paused. "And I'll have a better time with him."

The two men chuckled.

Leo ran his fingers haphazardly through his hair. "Can you believe we're having this discussion? I mean we're strong, smart men. . .and we have to pretend."

Marc nodded in reply. "I know. But Mrs Weddon is a force of nature, and always gets her way."

"She does indeed." Leo nodded slowly. The memory of Mrs White introducing Kate to him this morning invaded his thoughts. Mrs Weddon wasn't the only one around here that was determined to marry him off.

"Your cousin, maybe she'd be interested in me?" he asked with hope.

"Um, she's eighteen," Marc said, his ears becoming red.

Leo wanted to punch a wall. He was not going to *pretend date* an eighteen-year-old. He wasn't that desperate.

That left Jenna.

He tapped his finger against his lip as he considered approaching her.

His smile grew.

He'd find her weakness, and use that to his advantage. He could do that. Surely?

JENNA WAS SITTING on the sofa, laptop on her thighs reading her emails. Her savings had covered the cost of fixing the cladding. One of the residents had used a family friend to expedite the process, and she could return to her apartment in February, eight long weeks away. That meant she had to remain living with her parents till then.

If she rented her apartment out after February and continued to live with her parents, she could save the money she needed for her contribution to the legal case. The residents of her building had all agreed to collectively sue the builder for the breaches to the building code. If they won the case, she'd get a share of money which would financially help her after using her savings towards her share of the cladding fix.

But she couldn't rely on a win. And it would take time before the case went to court.

She'd been caught up in a mess that was not of her making, yet was impacting her financially.

For now, she'd have to suck it up and live with her parents. She'd lose her independence, but she had no alternative.

A headache grew in the base of her head and spread down her neck, and she tried to massage it away.

The doorbell rang, and she looked up in surprise. Her parents were out, and she wasn't expecting anyone.

Probably someone selling something. She was going to ignore the caller, but curiosity got to her, and she walked to the front door and opened it.

Her jaw dropped when she saw it was Leo.

Leo!

The guy she loved to rib. His personality was like paint drying. While she loved to socialise and meet new people, Leo was always working. So dull.

"What are you doing here?" She crossed her arms across her chest, her eyes narrowed with interest.

"Good evening, Jen," he said, using her hated abbreviated name.

"It's Jenna," she snapped, not inviting him in.

"I know," he said with a sparkle in his eyes and a cheeky smile.

Damn him.

She shifted her stance. "What do you want?"

"I'd like to be invited in so we can chat," he said with such politeness that her jaw dropped.

"I'm busy," she said with a flick of her hair.

His gaze travelled from the tips of her toes, along her bare legs, across the tiny shorts and tank top she was wearing. Their gazes clashed, and she shot him a look of defiance.

"I can see that." His chin lifted as his gaze took in her casual clothes that screamed *I am staying home tonight*. "Now stop playing games and invite me in so we can talk." He paused. "Or I could talk loudly so your neighbours can hear. I mean, it's a beautiful summer evening, and there are people out watering their gardens. I did say hi to the Bergmans on my way here."

Jenna's lips pressed together with annoyance, reminding her why she didn't want to live at home. The close-knit society of Clarendon Close was stifling. Everyone knew everything. By tomorrow, everyone would know that she and Leo had spent time together tonight while her parents were out. She let out an exaggerated humph. "Come in." She turned around and marched into the house, not bothering to see if he was following her.

He did, of course, hearing the soft click of the latch as he'd closed the front door behind them.

Plonking herself back on the sofa where she'd been, she didn't bother to offer him any refreshments. Her rudeness surprised her, and she dismissed it as the result of her surprise at his visit, and her general dislike for him.

He sat opposite her on the sofa that her dad preferred, and her breath hitched as she gazed at him. Reluctantly she admitted to herself that he looked really good in his suit. His knotted tie had loosened, and the top button was undone which gave him an appealing look that she was shocked to acknowledge. . .even to herself.

With his dark hair mussed, like he'd been running his fingers through it, and his dark eyes, he was the kind of guy she would've been interested in, if he wasn't Leo, and so *boring*.

He leaned back into the sofa, stretching his muscles and looked. . .tired. There were faint lines around his mouth, and there were shadows under his eyes. Rubbing a hand across his face, he suddenly sat up, his arms and elbows balanced on his knees. "Sorry to drop by unannounced, but I have a favour to ask."

"Ask away," she said, her hand did circles in the air, encouraging him to continue.

He cleared his throat. "I need your help with a delicate matter," he said in a low voice.

"What is it?" she asked, interested in knowing what he wanted. It had to be important for him to come out to see her. Why couldn't his question have been addressed via a phone call?

He cleared his throat again. "I need a fake girlfriend for the holidays," he said with clarity and purpose.

"And?" She pretended to yawn, looking bored.

"And, I'm hoping I'm looking at her," he said, his gaze meeting hers.

Her body stiffened and she glared at him. "Have you been drinking?"

"Not at all. You'll be perfect. You have no interest in dating me." He made quotation marks in the air. "I'll need you till New Year's Eve."

"What about my looks, my personality, my ability to hold a conversation," she fired back at him. She didn't know whether to be insulted by his comment or not.

"I need a fake girlfriend, and I need *you*," he said with a determined voice. "And I'll pay you."

Her teeth ground together. "I'm not for sale." How dare he think he could waltz in here and assume she'd be at his beck and call.

"Everyone has a price. . .even you," he said with a chuckle. "And even me."

"*D*on't you have a girlfriend?" Her voice sounded stupidly shrill. "Or are you into kinky things?"

"No and no." He leaned forward, his chin rested on his hands. His elbows still resting on bent knees. He considered toying with her about the kinky part but made a split decision not to. He didn't have time. With an important event tomorrow night, he needed her agreement now, so he could go home and have dinner. Having been at work since 6am, he was fed up, and not in the mood for Jenna's games.

"Cailah and I are. . .on a break." More like a permanent break, but Jenna didn't need to know that. "I have a number of work functions to attend and I'd like you to be there with me."

"Sounds boring," she said.

He got the reaction he'd been expecting. Of course, anything to do with him was *boring*. He flinched as though he'd been struck. Taking a deep breath, he went into his manager mode so he could convince her to accept the part. Generally, he loved a challenge but tonight he was tired and just wanted to get this over with.

"The parties may not be as fun as what you usually attend, but it's still an opportunity for you to glam up. Besides, many of the people you'll be mingling with are wealthy or have wealthy, *single* sons." He paused for dramatic effect, hoping to entice her. "You never know who you may be talking to. The Jengeests are residents at Mono Melbourne."

Jenna gasped in reply.

He'd mentioned a wealthy couple who'd owned one of Australia's best toy companies, who were now living at the home. The "carrot" he'd used to bait her seemed to be working as he noticed she was sitting straighter and there was interest in her gaze.

She pressed her lips together as though considering his proposal. "Is that it?"

"We have a lot of people at the home, some have been pillars of the community. I can introduce you to them. I also know who has sons, unmarried of course." His voice was clipped, and efficient, the way he conducted himself in business. This was a business arrangement after all.

The skin between her eyes crinkled. "How can I, as your girlfriend start dating?"

"This is a short-term arrangement. All you need to do is dazzle people, as well as be a supportive girlfriend for one month. After that, we break amicably and you can follow up on leads, shall we say?" He leaned back into the sofa to watch her reaction. She was going to accept, his gut told him. She was shallow, interested only in herself. He had no doubt that she'd jump at the chance to be his fake girlfriend.

"Let me finish by saying that I will pay you for your time." He made a show of looking around the room, reminding her that she was living with her parents for a reason. "I'm sure you could use the extra funds, especially as fixing the cladding on your building will be very expensive."

His parents had casually mentioned the apartment issues

Jenna had been dealing with, especially as they were close friends with Amy and Jason, Jenna's parents. Not much stayed private amongst the residents of Clarendon Close.

The smug look drained from her face.

Jenna then leaned back on the sofa, mirroring him but unlike his relaxed posture, he could see her muscles were tight and rigid.

Wearing tiny shorts, her long legs were on display and Leo took a moment to admire the toned length of them. Jenna was stunning. Always had been, and always would be. From a young age, she'd been the domineering sister, the one who bossed around the kids when they played together, all those years ago.

Despite her beauty, he'd never been drawn to her. Her egotistical replies and bossy nature had never appealed to him.

He'd preferred to date women who had a sweet nature, women liked Cailah. He sighed with despondency. Shame she preferred some bikie dude with tatts, who probably was into rough sex. He swallowed hard, pushing away the loss and hurt of their breakup. He needed to focus on getting Jenna's agreement and managing the events during the holiday period, not wallowing in pity.

"What about our parents?" Her head cocked to the side with curiosity.

He'd forgotten about that. "What about them?" he replied in a soft voice that didn't betray the spike of concern in his belly. What would his parents say? And the Williamsons, her parents? "We'll make up a story, and after New Year's Eve, we'll say we tried but it didn't work out." That suggestion worked for him, and he hoped she liked it, too.

She nibbled on her lip in contemplation.

"Come on, Jenna, it's not that bad. It's a few dinners and some events over the next month. We'll attend the Clarendon

Close Christmas Party as a couple, and in the new year, we'll break up. Besides a few kisses and holding hands, it'll be a piece of cake," he said with determination.

"Kissing?" She sounded surprised, almost shocked at the suggestion.

"Of course, a few kisses, otherwise no one is going to believe that we're together." He was surprised that she seemed so *scandalised* at the idea of them being a couple. Did she really not like him? Had it been a mistake to ask her? Probably, he realised with dismay.

"Can I still rib you?" Reminding him that she was a *prima donna* and the last person he'd ever truly fall for.

"If you didn't, they'd know it was a show," he said with a humph. For years he'd been the source of her jokes, and he'd hated it. And since last Christmas there had been plenty of jokes around him "dating" one of the residents. But for now, he'd rather her smutty remarks than having to deal with the Mrs Weddons of the world.

Even his EA, Marc, agreed with him. These older women were a force on nature, and he didn't know how else to protect himself from them.

"I don't know," she said slowly, crossing her arms as though in deep consideration.

Fatigued, drained, annoyed, he snapped. He should've known Jenna would be the uncompromising tease. Jenna was selfish and would never do anything to help someone out. . .even for some much-needed financial help. He was stupid to have thought otherwise.

"Forget it," he fired at her. Standing, he stared at her. "I'll see you later."

"But you didn't get what you came for," she said hurriedly, before standing.

"I did, and you've just reminded me why I should've asked Ruby Bergman instead of you. She's a lot more sincere and easy-going than you." He cursed under his breath. "At least I won't have to deal with your prickly nature." His stomach hardened with frustration.

"Ruby?" He could hear the disbelief in her voice, which made him smile. Jealous? Or annoyed there was competition?

He spun around to face her. "Yeah, Ruby." His chin lifted with impatience. "The girl who used to live across from this house who's *also* grown up," he said with an exaggerated head shake.

"But she's dating someone. . .seriously." She stood in front of him. Even with bare feet, she reached just past his shoulders. Her height and slim build made her the perfect model, plus her attitude. Yep, the attitude that she'd had since she was a girl.

"Yeah, I know that. But we'll work around it. We'll be upfront with her parents, and explain it all. It's more work for me, but at least she won't give me as much grief as *you*." He spat out the word *you.*

He hadn't considered asking Ruby since he knew she was engaged or with someone serious. The issues were harder to resolve with Ruby but with Jenna toying him, he didn't care. He was fed up and couldn't pretend otherwise.

She'd always been like this, even as a teen. Baiting and teasing him. Even though she needed the money, she was stalling.

"See you at the Clarendon Close Christmas party," he said with a wave. "I'll see myself out."

He'd taken three steps towards the front door when she cried out. "Stop. I'll do it."

With his back facing her, a surprised smile stretched across his lips. He'd been ready to leave, tired of her games. He didn't care why she'd changed her mind but he was relieved. Turning slowly to face her he said, "Okay, let's do this."

* * *

JENNA'S HEART beat so rapidly that she was sure Leo could see her chest moving from the thump-thump of her heart. Darn him, and darn her for needing to agree to this stupid proposal.

He walked over to her and stood so close she could see the tired lines around his eyes. "Thank you," he said.

She hadn't expected that. In fact, she'd been expecting him to gloat or do some silly macho victory dance around her.

"It's late and I haven't had dinner. I'm going to make myself a cup of tea," he said, rubbing the back of his neck as he walked towards the kitchen.

A wave of concern and thoughtlessness washed over her. She should've been a better hostess. "There are some left-overs from tonight. Mum made dinner not me, so it's edible."

"Thanks, I'd appreciate some of Amy's home cooking," he said with honesty.

A FEW MINUTES LATER, she'd warmed up the leftover chicken and vegetable stir fry, and rice that her mum had cooked. She'd even poured them each a glass of wine.

She sat opposite him and watched him as he ate with gusto. It was late, and he'd obviously missed dinner. They weren't friends, and had never shared camaraderie, as he had with her younger sister, Taylor. But then, everyone liked Taylor.

She may have agreed to his request but that didn't mean she'd just go along for the ride. She needed to know more and understand why Leo needed a fake girlfriend. Her pride insisted on knowing why he'd chosen her. "Can you tell me why you need me?"

He finished chewing and lowered his cutlery. "Yes, but our agreement is *not* to be shared with anyone. If you tell any of the residents or anyone we know, the deal is off. I'm only paying you if you keep your end of the arrangement."

That sounded reasonable. She also didn't want people knowing she was "dating" someone because it would hope-fully stop her parents trying to match-make her with their friends' sons. It was in both their interests that they worked together, rather than against each other. Placing her hand over her heart, she said, "Promise."

He cocked his left eyebrow sky high. "You already know the answer."

She sipped her wine, and pondered the reason. Placing the glass down, she snapped her fingers. "Do you really get that much grief at work from those sweet little old ladies? I thought you were joking."

"No, it's not a joke, and there is nothing *sweet* about their keen-ness to match-make me. So, to answer why I am doing this, it's easier to have a partner, especially over the holidays when there are a number of events I have to attend." He sounded so despondent, and she was surprised to hear this was taking an obvious toll on him.

For the past few years that he'd been working at Mono Melbourne, she'd enjoyed ridiculing him, especially at the yearly Christmas parties. Leo had seemed to take it in his stride and had laughed it off.

Her heart sank with the realisation that she may have hurt him. And not only had he endured her ribs, but everyone else's. . .and that was thanks to her leading the charge, so to speak. "No wonder you were with Cailah for so long," she said softly under her breath.

"What did you say?" he asked her, his face marred with annoyance.

Crap. She hadn't realised she'd said that out loud. She hadn't really like Cailah, she just seemed too false. Ironic since his new girlfriend, *her*, would also be false. "Sorry, I honestly didn't see you two as compatible."

"Really?" he lowered his cutlery and glared at her. "Tell me why."

She squirmed in her seat, uncomfortable in talking about his ex, and her opinion of Cailah. "We don't need to get into this, do we?" she asked, hoping he'd let it go.

"Yes, we do. As my *girlfriend*, we can't have secrets from each other." He was not happy with her and her blunder. She could see annoyance blazing in his dark brown eyes.

"Um," she stumbled over her words, feeling self-conscious and embarrassed. "I just didn't see you as compatible, I don't know. You just didn't seem to complete each other." She shrugged, feeling silly. There was something about them as a couple that didn't seem to jell. She'd initially dismissed it as Leo not being good enough for Cailah. But she was biased *against* him, so what did she know?

He continued to eat his meal, while she watched and sipped her wine. It gave her a few moments to reflect on what they were doing. Was this the stupidest thing she'd ever done?

She may be a model, but she was savvy and had a strong business acumen. She read all her contracts, and had been careful with her money. Having to deal with the cladding, the builder's issue, frustrated her, because she had no control over it. It was out of her league, and she hated that. "Will anyone know our relationship is fake?" she asked, rubbing the middle of her forehead with confusion.

"No, not even our parents," he replied with a sincere tone. "Our relationship is just for work but I think it will be better if we just do this properly, and just appear to be dating for this month. What do you think?"

"Yes, I think that would be easier." She paused reflecting on the situation. "How did we meet?" She scratched at her ear, as she looked at him.

"When your family bought this house," he said with a smug smile.

She chuckled at the silly reply. "You know what I mean."

"Let's try and keep it as truthful as we can. I'll say I ran into you when visiting my parents, we went out for a drink to catch up and it went from there." He gave her a confident grin.

She nodded, thinking about his suggestion. "That would work."

"Let's not complicate things." He finished eating, wiped his mouth with the serviette, and then took his plate to the sink, filling it with water. "Thanks for dinner." Returning to the table he said, "Tomorrow is the first event, Carols by Candlelight. It's an informal event, a picnic in the gardens. The residents have been encouraged to invite and bring their grandchildren and families. We have school students singing, and of course, a visit from Santa."

"Sounds like fun," she said with honesty, thinking back to when she and her sister Taylor were young, and her parents took them to the local school or park for such events. Those family times were special and important to her, and a pang of longing swept over her.

"You suddenly look unhappy. Are you okay?" he asked, concern filled his voice.

She shifted in her seat. "I was thinking about us going each year to family events, and I thought of Taylor."

"You miss her?" There was genuine concern in his question.

"I do. When she lived in Melbourne, I really never made

the effort to spend time with her, or even visit her shop. I was always busy." She sighed with sadness. "And now she's living in America, I keep wishing I'd been a. . .better sister."

"But you're not like that, are you?" he said. It was a statement, more than a question. "The world revolves around you. You've always been like that, and always will be."

She ran her hands down her top, smoothing out the wrinkles, surprised at his honesty. "Do you hate me?"

"No, I don't hate you. But you always put yourself first, even before your sister." He leaned back in his chair, his hands supporting his head.

"And yet, you asked me to be your fake girlfriend," she said wrinkling her nose.

"It's a business agreement," he said simply. "It will work because we already know each other. We each have our own reasons for this *temporary* arrangement."

She could see his confidence in the straightness of his shoulders and in the definitive way he spoke.

She considered his honest reply, but it didn't comfort her. In fact, it made her feel uneasy about their relationship.

"Don't overthink it," he said, seemingly reading her thoughts. "We're helping each other. I get a breather from the residents, and you get some much-needed cash. It's a win-win situation."

"Fine, you're right," she said. "But I don't want your money. Dating you will give me a breather from my parents trying to find *me* someone special." She made quotation marks in the air when she said special.

"So you know what it's like?" he said.

She nodded slowly.

"We know each other, and that will make it easy for our *relationship*. It will be more natural." His chest thrust out with certainty.

She nodded with unease. "When did we start dating?"

"Are you seeing anyone?" he asked. "I never checked."

"No. And I would've told you," she said.

"I was going to ask you to pretend to be Cailah, since no one at the Home knows we broke up. But I don't like deceit." He paused and scratched his chin. "Let's say we started dating three weeks ago?"

"Well, I've been living here for a couple of weeks, so that works well," she affirmed with a smile. "We'll align our stories especially because of our parents."

"Tomorrow night, you just need to turn up at seven o'clock. It's supposed to be a warm day. Don't forget the insect repellent. And also, is there anything you don't eat? Any allergies?"

"No, whatever you organise will be fine for me," she said, knowing she wouldn't eat much. In her early thirties, maintaining her figure and staying slim was getting harder each year.

Leo yawned, and he covered his mouth with his hand. "I'm sorry, it's been a long day. I'd better be going."

"Sure," she said. "Don't worry, I won't let you down." Her chest expanded with certainty, knowing she could play the role perfectly.

He did a finger gun salute at her. "I know you won't." He stood, pushed in his chair before rubbing his eyes with his fists.

A faint five o'clock shadow gave him a sexy look, especially with his messed hair. She caught herself staring. She'd never thought of Leo as anything but boring. But in his suit, and with his impressive height and slim waist, she realised that he was good looking. How had she never really noticed before?

"I'll text you the details, don't be late," he instructed as they walked to the front door. "Oh, by the way, we need to practice." He stopped and turned to face her.

"Practice what?" she asked with surprise.

"Kissing," he said with a nonchalant manner.

"Here? Now? Kiss?" She heard herself gasp.

"I don't think our first kiss should be in front of others, do you?" Unable to believe she'd have an issue with a practice kiss.

"But aren't you just going to kiss me on the cheek? Hold my hand? Do we really need to be. . .intimate?" She knew she sounded pathetic, like a silly teen, but she wasn't ready to just start kissing him. In all the years that she'd known him, he'd been the boring guy, the one least likely to be kissed by her. And that attitude hadn't changed even over the past few years.

She didn't want to be *bad-kissed* by him. She wasn't attracted to him, even in his tailor-made suit, right?

"Jenna, these games have to stop," he snapped, his face filled with defiance and resentment. "It's a kiss for goodness sake. I'm not asking you to parade naked down the street singing 'I am Woman.' I'm sorry that the idea of kissing *me* is so repulsive to you." His eyes darkened with annoyance, and the skin around his jaw was tight. "No wonder, I've never entertained the idea of kissing *you*."

"What?" Surprise at his strong words and his statement made her eyes open wide. "You don't want to kiss me?"

"No, you're probably the type of woman who'd rate a man on the first kiss, never allow for mistakes, and would expect him to do your bidding. . .like a dog." He took a step away from her, his face pained with blame and disgust.

"Wow, that's mean," she fired at him. She knew she was selfish and a perfectionist. But that was why she was so successful in her career. Being a perfectionist and working hard had made her stand out from other models. There were plenty of beautiful women, but she was tough on the inside and out.

"It is mean. . .but it's true. You're hard and tough— there is no sweetness about you." He crossed his arms and gave her a steely look.

"And yet you still want to date me?" She leaned back against the wall, watching the confusion cross his face.

"It's a business arrangement. I would never date you, for real," he said with a determined look in his eye.

For some inexplicable reason, she wanted to know more. "Why?"

"Because. . .we're just not compatible." He waved his hand in the air for emphasis.

She narrowed her eyes. "But we're expecting others to accept it."

"Yes, which is why we should kiss. Get the ick factor out of the way. We can't have this conversation in front of others." Still unable to believe they were having this conversation.

She waggled a finger at him. "You think kissing me is icky?"

"No. But you think that about me." He challenged her, his arms crossed again over his chest.

She paused, unable to find a retort. He was right, darn him. They needed to kiss, practice so when the time came in front of others, it wouldn't be so new. After all, real couples kissed all the time. "You're right, we should practice."

He didn't look smug or fire any more banter at her. He simply nodded and took a step towards her. Taking her hand, his thumb drew lazy circles around the pulse point of her wrist. He stepped closer, and her pulse skittered with nerves.

She and Leo were about to kiss.

Her heart thudded against her chest with the realisation. They. Were. About. To. Kiss.

His right hand came up, and his knuckles traced the

length of her face. The graze of him against her face was soft and tentative. "May I kiss you?" he whispered.

She nodded, her voice suddenly constricted with emotion.

His hands came up and cupped her cheeks, his thumbs traced the skin along her jaw. He moved forward so she could feel the warmth of him through his clothes. Moving even closer to her, he moved his mouth towards hers, and she held her breath in anticipation of his bad kiss.

His lips brushed hers. And then he stopped. Then he came back and brushed them again.

She could barely breathe. Surely the next one would be bad?

He dropped one of his hands to rest on her hip. The other hand tangled into her long hair as he gently massaged her scalp.

A groan sneaked out from her lips, and she placed her hands on his shoulders, as she moved in and kissed him.

The kisses started slow, as they explored, getting to know each other. Her eyes closed, and she revelled in his soft touch as their lips met.

Her hands slipped from his shoulders and ended up resting on his chest, an impressive chest, she could feel through the cotton of his business shirt.

He pulled her to him, anchoring her as he opened his mouth and deepened the kiss. She responded, unable to help herself. She wanted more, craved his touch.

Goodness, the man knew how to kiss, she realised with surprise.

He kissed her and then his tongue swept through her mouth, and she welcomed him in. Their tongues danced intimately around each other, and she heard his groan, or was that hers?

He tasted of confidence, strength with a dash of dry white wine.

Pressed against her, she could feel his hard body, and her fingers explored his chest before moving downward to hold him around his waist.

She wanted to say something, but she was in a vortex of want and need, so strong that she'd never experienced anything so amazing.

A key in the door, made her ears prickle. Then she heard the door opening, and she tore her mouth from Leo's as she opened her eyes to see her parents' faces. Wide-eyed, filled with surprise, their mouths were in an O shape.

"Um, sorry we interrupted you two," Amy said.

Busted.

Jenna's heart thundered against her ribs from embarrassment, whilst only seconds ago it had been in response to Leo's amazing kissing technique.

Looks like their fake relationship was now on. There was no backing out. Her parents had caught them *making out*, which meant everyone in Clarendon Close would know about it tomorrow.

She may be in a fake relationship with Leo, but based on how he'd kissed her, it wasn't going to be a hardship. In fact, she was looking forward to more kissing.

CHAPTER 3

*J*enna strode into Mono Melbourne and felt eyes on her. Normally she thrived on it, loved the attention, but this evening, she was nervous, edgy, and concerned.

She was out of her comfort zone, being amongst retirees and the elderly. But that wasn't what was making her tummy roll with confusion.

It was that kiss.

That kiss she and Leo had shared, which had kept her up most of the night. Only in the early hours of the morning had she finally fallen into a tired sleep. Makeup, her best friend, had ensured her skin was glowing, and she was looking perfect.

Her parents were delighted at finding out that she and Leo were "dating." Their unexpected arrival and intrusion into their practice kiss had been disconcerting and welcome at the same time.

After respectfully greeting her parents and briefly chatting with them, Leo had left. And she hadn't spoken to him since. And here she was, playing the role of girlfriend for his work colleagues and the residents.

With the weather still warm, she'd dressed in a maxi dress that showcased her height and slim figure, and had paired it with flat-heeled sandals. She always looked her best, and was used to turning heads, looking impressive in whatever she wore.

Having been directed to the garden, she gasped at the prettiness of the set-up. Strings of twinkle lights created a picture-perfect scene complemented with the warm glow of candles in hurricane lamps.

The sun had not set, but *thanks* to daylight saving, it would not be dark for another couple of hours. However, the surrounding buildings had resulted in long shadows cast over the gardens.

Looking around, she caught Leo's gaze, and he smiled when he saw her. Excusing himself from the person he was talking to, he grinned as he walked over to her. "Jenna, you look beautiful as always," he gushed before pressing his lips against hers.

She relaxed into the brief kiss, and returned a smile to him. "Hi, Leo."

"Can I get you a drink?" He pointed to a table, piled high with bottles of soft drinks, juice, wine, and beer.

"Yes, thank you," she said. Taking his hand, she leaned in to whisper. "I'm nervous."

"I can't tell by looking at you. And just so you know, I am too," he confessed in a low voice.

Her gaze took in his casual look. Dark denim jeans and a short-sleeved shirt, he looked really handsome and she wondered why she'd never thought of him like that before. In all the years that they'd known each other, she'd never looked at him in a romantic way or even considered dating him.

She'd treated him terribly, like a game for her own plea-sure, and it reminded her of a cat toying with a mouse before it killed it. Yep, she'd been like that.

And now everything had shifted. The guy she loved to hate was her "boyfriend" and even worse, his kiss had been mind-blowing, so unexpected that she longed for more.

Taking two glasses of sparkling wine from the table, he handed her one and smiled. They clinked glasses, before he whispered in her ear, "To us, and a happy holiday month."

Her breathing quickened unexpectantly as he said "to us," and all she could think about was how good his lips had felt on hers.

She replied with only a smile before she sipped her drink, needing the *dutch courage* to pretend he wasn't having any effect on her. The lemony scent of his aftershave and the smile he gave her was making her skin tingle with need.

"Everything looks beautiful," she said, casting an admiring look around the garden.

"We've got picnic blankets and dinner organised for everyone, and for some, everything has been set out on tables with chairs. It depends on the resident's mobility, and the families' preferences," Leo explained.

Everything had been meticulously planned, she could see. From the family-friendly layout, to the way that families were encouraged to spend time with the residents. Children ran around, happy, smiling, and even a small petting zoo had been set up for the younger children. She could see children grinning; holding, cuddling bunnies and other small animals.

She felt like an intruder amongst all the happiness, like she didn't belong. Not only was she a fake girlfriend, but she'd never really wanted a family. She didn't hate kids, but it just wasn't what she wanted.

Unlike her sister, Taylor, who loved holding other

people's babies, she avoided it, not wanting spit or, even worse, baby vomit on her. She shuddered at the thought.

But in this family enriched environment, she had an appreciation for why couples chose to have children. . .but it wasn't enough for her to want one for herself.

"Um, so where are we going to be?" she asked, looking around.

"There are some tables over there, for families with older or no children, that's where I've organised *our* picnic," he said, pointing to an area away from the small children.

"Can we go there now, or do you need to welcome people?" She was curious to see the space organised for them, and was happy to wait alone for him if he needed to work.

"No, I'll come with you now, however, I will need to work later on," he said, taking her elbow and leading her to a more secluded space.

She gasped when he brought her to their picnic area. It was the type of set-up that belonged on Pinterest and should be shared over and over on social media. From the pillows to the candles in jars, it screamed romantic.

"May I take a picture?" she asked, desperate to want a copy of it for herself.

"Of course," he said, standing to the side.

She snapped photos using her phone, still surprised at how beautiful everything had been set up. "This is a lot more professional than what I had expected," she confessed. A quizzical look crossed his eyes and she realised her blunder. "I didn't mean it like that. I meant, I hadn't expected this for a carols evening."

"Our residents expect quality. It's why they spent a lot of money in buying into this village. We want them to enjoy something special, and with their families," he replied in a business-like voice.

"Well, it's really nice," she gushed, mentally kicking herself over her gaffe.

"Shall we?" He pointed to the blanket then and placed their glasses on a low table, before they sat down. "We have time to eat before we start singing, and then in about an hour, Santa will be dropping by for more songs and gift-giving."

Conversation milled around them, but she was totally captivated by the man in front of her as he expertly set up their picnic. The low table was covered with a selection of mezzes including crackers, cheese, mini frittatas, stuffed vine leaves, dips, and three-fingered sandwiches. There was also fruit and petit-four, a selection of bite-sized cakes and pastries that made her mouth water.

Her stomach rumbled and she ate from the platter avoiding the carbs, and the desserts. The food was delicious and she enjoyed every mouthful, despite not tasting the lemon tart she so desperately wanted. But her figure was her income, and she couldn't afford to gain any weight.

"Is this the type of work you did before you became the boss?" she asked, curious to know more.

"You could say that. As the event manager, I did a lot of events but I showed them how I could run a budget, and manage staff. It was one of the reasons I was able to take on the manager job, which is a lot more stressful than the event manager role," he confessed.

"Do you like what you do?" she asked, taking a sip of her sparkling water.

"I do. It's long hours but I find it really rewarding, and I love being around the residents. There's so much history, and the stories they tell. . ." he chuckled. "I sometimes wonder if they're embellishing them or not."

"Probably not. . .they were young once, too," she said with a wink.

He gave her a dazzling smile. "I think you're right." He leaned over and kissed her cheek.

She felt her skin warm, and knew it wasn't from the weather. It was Leo. Everything about the past day had made her see him in a different light. It was like her whole world had shifted, and everyone was comfortable except her.

A quick glance at his watch had him saying. "I need to work, back soon." He stood, then leaned down and brushed his lips against her. "You may or may not have people interested in who you are coming to talk to you. Remember, we've been dating for three weeks. Go with the *friends to lovers* angle for our relationship, it makes sense," he said to her in a low voice, before he straightened and walked off.

Her lips were still tingling from his kiss, and she gulped the remaining water in her glass to cool her dry, parched throat.

She packed away the remnants of their picnic, but slipped the sign, written in a pretty script font, saying "Leo and Jenna" into her purse. She wasn't sure why she kept the pretty paper sign but she did anyway.

She watched Leo oversee the staff. Standing straight, a smile on his lips, she could see he was in charge, directing people, answering questions, looking impressively handsome.

Her breathing grew rapid as she admired his lean body, sharp cheekbones, and dark hair. Again, she asked herself how she could have seen him as anything but impressively good-looking before?

A figure suddenly blocked her view. "Hello," an older lady said.

"Oh, hello," she replied and stood feeling it was rude to sit on the ground and look up. "I'm Jenna Williamson," she held out her hand.

"Margaret Weddon," the woman replied. "You're Leo's. . .friend."

"Ah, yes, I'm his girlfriend," she said with sincerity. Her breathing grew rapid as this was the first time she would play the role of girlfriend, and she was on her own. She could do it, she reassured herself with a deep breath.

"You are beautiful," came the reply as a pair of blue eyes stared at her.

"Thank you." It took every bit of willpower not to step backwards, away from the invasive gaze. But she stood firm and lifted her chin in defiance.

And then the questions started.

How long had they known each other?

How long had they dated?

What did she do?

Who were her parents?

Did she have siblings?

A light, a darkened room, and a chair may have made Margaret happy, but Jenna was overwhelmed with the verbal badger. Determined not to show any weakness or crumple beneath the pressure, she smiled and answered all the questions with determination.

"So, Margaret, is your family here?" She tried to deflect the conversation away from her, but the older woman was too clever for her.

"Yes, over there." She pointed to where everyone was seated, and not to anyone in particular. "What type of modelling do you do?"

Suddenly they were interrupted by Leo's voice over the microphone advising that they would start the carols soon. Families gathered together, and Margaret thankfully left.

Jenna blew out a long breath and collapsed on the picnic blanket, feeling like she'd been interviewed by security border patrol.

After taking some steadying breaths, she realised now why Leo had asked her to be his fake girlfriend. If this is what she'd been through, she could only imagine what he went through *all the time*. Yet, he'd never complained about it. He only saw the good in people.

It made her feel bad, yet again, about all the things she'd taunted him about over the years.

It was the holiday season, and perhaps that's why she'd had an epiphany. But she decided, in that moment, to be the best fake-girlfriend she could for him. He deserved it.

The host, a handsome man in his mid-thirties, stood on a small stage, microphone in hand as he introduced himself, made jokes, and entertained the crowd.

She found herself smiling and enjoying herself. Then everyone was encouraged to sing as the music blared from the speakers.

A mixture of traditional carols and Christmas songs were sung before a school choir performed an excellent rendition of "Rudolph the Red Nosed Reindeer" and "Come all ye Faithful."

Jenna found herself happy and singing along, feeling the magic of the holiday season wash over her as pleasant and welcoming as the warm, summer, evening air. It had been many years since she'd sung a Christmas song, and she reminisced about the family times when she and Taylor were primary school-aged.

Leo returned and sat next to her. "Enjoying yourself?" he asked in a low voice.

"Yes, it reminds me of when Mum and Dad would take Taylor and me to community events, when we were kids," Jenna said with a grin.

"Good memories?" It was a statement, not really a question, because he knew she'd had a happy home life growing up.

She nodded. "Yes, definitely."

"Me too," he said. "And then we started the Clarendon Close Carols night."

"Yep, we took turns hosting that each year, and then Christmas parties, and of course New Year's Eve." Her voice was whimsical as she reflected over the past twenty years.

"It was a good place to grow up," he said, his voice filled with grateful longing. "A street full of kids and parents who genuinely liked each other."

She stifled back nostalgic tears, remembering how the families had bonded over the years, and there hadn't been any fights amongst them. "And then we all grew up–"

"And the kids had kids." He cocked his head to the side recalling what she knew.

"Yep," she said. She took a deep breath as a spike of unease hit her chest. She wasn't one of those "kids" who wanted kids, preferring to be a leader, a career woman, an opportunist. Settling in suburbia with 2.2 kids and a white picket fence wasn't for her. "You want this?" Her arm swept towards all the families, together, united and happy, enjoying time together.

His eyes brightened in reply. "For sure. I always assumed that I'd find the right woman, get married and have a family, just like my parents. You and I are the same, in that we were both raised by parents who loved and provided for us." He paused. "Not everyone is as lucky as we were."

She nodded, reflecting on how happy her childhood had been, and how loving her parents were then and now.

A shallow sigh slipped from her lips. Unlike Leo, who helped others with genuine care, she'd never done any community work.

But then she had a great idea for a business, assisting up-and-coming models. But the drive had stemmed from a selfish point of view, not philanthropic.

But then it had become personal.

Some of those girls needed help, help she had no idea how to begin.

They were troubled teens who turned to her, desperately needing more than career advice.

And a year later, assisted by her sister's friend, Amber, she'd been able to not only provide direction but valuable help to some of the girls.

"Jenna," he said, interrupting her thoughts.

"Huh." She turned to face him.

"Just checking to see if you were okay. You seemed a million miles away, lost in your own world." His face was close to hers and in the evening light, she could see the concern in his eyes.

"Fine, sorry, just thinking," she said, waving her hand to dismiss his worry.

"Okay. I have to get Santa ready, back soon." He brushed his lips against hers and she felt herself shiver in response. It was part of the arrangement, the need to portray a loving couple but each kiss, each touch, each soft word was causing havoc on her senses. But she was unexpectedly craving more kisses, more touching, more words.

She took some steadying breaths before she stood and walked to the drinks area and drank another flute of sparkling wine.

No man had ever had such an effect on her, and Leo was the last guy she'd expected to like. His kissing literally "rocked her world." She didn't want it to be this way. Of all men, why Leo?

There was no answer, of course. She could play a role, it was her job to do so.

The music became louder and children started screaming out "Santa," and then the large man in the red suit appeared, waving.

It was silly, entertaining fun, as Santa and his helpers distributed gifts to the residents as well as the children. They weren't random presents but obviously chosen with care, as the presents each had names written on them.

And then Santa stood in front of her. "You're Jenna?"

She nodded, apprehensive as to why Santa wanted to know who she was.

"Ho, ho, ho, Merry Christmas," he said in a low voice, sounding exactly how Santa should sound.

A man, dressed as an elf, handed her a gift, beautifully wrapped in festive paper with a large red bow.

"T-t-thank you," she said, happy to be given the present but embarrassed that she was the only non-resident adult to receive a gift so far.

Soon, all the gifts had been given out, and Jenna returned to the picnic area where she and Leo had been. It was dusk, and many families were saying goodbye to grandparents, and friends. It was time to go.

She collected her purse and tidied their area up. Unable to help herself, she sat on the blanket and carefully opened the present, curious to see what Santa had given her.

She gasped when she saw it was a bottle of her favourite perfume. But how?

Leo had only asked her last night.

"Lucky you," a voice said. Looking up, she saw Margaret, flanked by three other older ladies, standing in front of her.

"Yes, it is a lovely gift," she said, not wanting to reveal how special and meaningful it was. Leo had gone to a lot of trouble she realised. The women behind Margaret stood there but no one introduced themselves, so Jenna simply smiled at them.

"Someone likes you," Margaret scoffed.

"Yes, I think Santa had some help from Leo. It's my favourite perfume," she gushed, hoping Margaret would see her as the adoring girlfriend of Leo. "I'd better get going." She placed the bottle and wrapping carefully in her handbag and stood. "Nice meeting you, Margaret." Despite the tough questions, she sort of admired the older woman in her resilience and determination.

"You, too," the woman said with a lift of her chin. "See you later."

"Goodbye." Her gaze took in the four women before she walked away to seek Leo.

CHAPTER 4

*T*he following Saturday night, Jenna and Leo met secretly at a small park a few streets away from Clarendon Close, before they were due to attend the Bergman's Chanukah party.

This would be the first time they'd have to put on a show in front of those they knew, and it would be a big test of their "relationship." The people at the party were the friends they'd grown up with.

"I know I don't have to tell you how important tonight is," Leo said with conviction. "We need to stay in character, it will help when we have my work functions. If we make mistakes tonight, then there's a good chance we'll make mistakes at my work events."

"Yes, yes," she said pretending to yawn. "These are our friends, they've known us since we were young, so there's no room for *mistakes*."

Grinding his teeth in frustration, he said with an authoritative voice. "And the parents will be there. They'll all be surprised that we're together, so we need to be careful."

"The Carols by Candlelight went well, didn't it?" Jenna's

voice was light and breezy, in full belief that everything was fine.

Leo didn't think so. Feedback from his assistant Marc had confirmed what he suspected—the residents had been impressed by Jenna's beauty but didn't see them as "together." In fact, Marc had overheard some women gossiping about Leo being too good for Jenna, and that he deserved a more kind and understanding girlfriend. Mrs Weddon had recommended her granddaughter, of course.

Marc had hinted that a couple of residents believed his relationship was a farce and were angry about his dishonesty with them.

Leo thought back to that moment and wished he'd been honest upfront, and just been the *single guy* at the events. Less worrying, less stress, less. . .everything.

But it was too late. He'd asked Jenna to play a role and they needed to try harder, which was why tonight was so important. If their friends didn't believe in them dating, then the residents wouldn't either.

"Right? I'll have you know I do part-time acting, as well as modelling. I know what I'm doing," she added.

Her confidence didn't assure him. "You need to act. . .harder, okay? You're playing yourself too well," he blurted out with a wince.

Crossing her arms, she glared at him. "What's that supposed to mean?"

He avoided her grouchy gaze.

"We're in a new relationship supposedly having lots of sex and spending lots of time together. It can't just be me kissing you. You need to play a part. You need to act like you enjoy being with me," he said, his voice filled with frustrated annoyance that he had to spell it out for her.

A quizzical look crossed her eyes, and he wasn't sure what that meant.

He ran his fingers through his hair with frustration. "Tonight we'll probably be playing the dreidel kissing game. You need to say things like 'I hope it lands on me, so I can kiss Leo' or something like that."

A look of disgust made her step back. "That's stupid."

He muttered a swear word under his breath. "People in a haze of lust say things like that. Now listen," he instructed. "You need to step up and act more lovey-dovey around me." He felt the skin between his eyes crinkle in annoyance. "Just act, okay?"

"Fine," she snapped. But he was wary of her agreement. She was too self-assured, and didn't like any form of criticism.

He blew out a long, exasperated breath. "Our parents will be there, and if we can convince them that we're together, then everyone at work will believe it, too," he said.

Her lips pressed together, as though she couldn't believe that her acting skills weren't up to par. "I acted well," she snapped.

"Not well enough. You've had boyfriends before, just be like how you were when you were in love with one of them," he muttered.

Her mouth opened, then she snapped it shut.

"What? What were you going to say?" He pointed a finger at her mouth. "Don't say 'nothing,' I know you. You're hiding something from me."

"Fine." She fired him a look of disdain. "I've never been in love. A lot of the men I work with are gay, and the others just want sex, nothing permanent." She straightened her shoulders. "I've just never met the right guy. So, I can't look like I'm in love, when I've never been in love. Okay?"

"Okay, we'll work on it," he said in a straight forward voice, his fingers tapping against his thigh, as he thought about what she'd just said.

She glanced at her mobile phone. "We need to get going so we're not late."

"We're going to be late, and you need to look the part." He flashed her a knowing smile.

"What do you mean?" She blinked rapidly.

"Do I have to spell it out?" He leaned back on the bench, keeping his stance casual, but confident.

"Yeah, you do, I'm not following." She looked genuinely baffled at his question.

"For someone as clever as you, you're not really astute when it comes to relationships," he said in a low voice, surprised that this supremely savvy, strong-willed and self-assured woman was seemingly so inexperienced.

Tilting her head with contempt she said, "I told you, I haven't really dated much. My career is more important to me."

"That's fine. But for now, I need you to pretend that all you want to do is be with me, and I when I say *be*, I mean have hot smoking sex, where the neighbours hear you screaming my name." He gave her a fierce look that told her this was how things were going to be done. He was in charge, and she needed to follow his lead.

Her lashes fluttered with understanding. "Fine, whatever, come and kiss me," she said in a bored voice.

Irritation threaded up and down his spine. "And this is why we need to practice," he fired at her. "*You* need to seduce me. You need to come and kiss me, not the other way around," he snapped. "You need to be a loving girlfriend, you need to play the part."

"But–"

He drew his hand in the air horizontally to silence her. "No buts. You need to take the lead, not me." He rubbed the back of his neck, feeling the start of an irritating headache coming on.

* * *

Jenna stood and looked at Leo in the early evening sunshine, horrified that he believed that her acting skills were lacking. She was sure that she'd portrayed her role well and was irritated that he, and his assistant, didn't think so.

And now she had to kiss him. Whatever.

She stepped towards him and admired the strong definition of his cheekbones, his brown eyes and full lips. There weren't many men that she had to look up to, and she liked that Leo was tall. A rarity amongst the designers and photographers she worked with.

Taking another step towards him, they were so close that there was only a distance of a few centimetres between them. She took a moment to inhale the scent of him, warm, masculine with a hint of spice.

Her hands came up and pressed against his pecs. They were hard and defined, thanks to the daily jogs she knew he did.

Her fingers trailed along the length of his chest and then down his arms. They were equally impressive, strong and muscular. "You work hard to keep yourself fit?"

"Just like you do," he said, but his voice was less assured than it had been a few minutes ago, and she wondered if her touch was affecting him. . .the way it was making her tummy tumble with anticipation.

Her fingers continued to touch and learn all the peaks and troughs of his torso, and she could hear his breathing grow rapid. Running her fingers down the side of his face, she stood on tiptoes and brushed her lips against his. She did this a few times before he responded, but she could feel him holding back.

He wanted her to take the lead, and this annoyed her as

much as it interested her. "Enjoying yourself?" she whispered.

"Yup," he said softly.

Her hands came to clutch his neck, to bring him closer to her, and his hands came around, settling on her hips.

And then she kissed him, the way she'd been wanting to kiss him since he'd organised for Santa to give her a bottle of perfume. Pressing her mouth against his, she kissed him, loving the feel of his soft lips and the rasp of his five o'clock shadow. "You didn't shave."

"I decided you like a bit of stubble," he said.

She ran her fingers down his cheek. "I can live with that." And then she opened her mouth and kissed him hard. The way she'd been thinking about since the other night.

There was no sweetness or playful kisses, she kissed him the way lovers kiss. Not because he'd told her to, but because she wanted to.

His mouth opened, and her tongue swept his mouth. Their kisses became greedy and wanting.

Tugging her close, his hands cupped her bottom as his hands secured her close to him.

Her arms had come around his neck, not wanting to let him go.

They kissed and kissed and kissed.

Then his mouth made his way to her neck and he licked, sucked, and bit the length all the way to her bare shoulder.

Her head fell back as his mouth claimed the skin along her shoulder, and then back up to her ear. His tongue licked along the rim of her ear before he sucked the lobe.

She cried out in delight as his hand pushed her hair aside and his tongue tasted the skin behind her ear. Then they were kissing again, and her hands went up and under the cotton of his black T-shirt as she touched his abs.

"Leo," she sighed.

His hands roamed her back, and her nipples tingled with delight begging to be tasted and sucked. She'd ditched her bra tonight in favour of the simple green strapless dress she wore. But it also meant that there was one less barrier between her and Leo, and she desperately wanted him to tug her top aside and feast on her. Their breathing grew rapid, and his hands threaded through her hair, messing up the perfect *do*, she'd spent time on.

His hands pressed against her back, as they continued to kiss, and her heart pounded with anticipation. Forgetting they were in a public space, she wanted him to take her, here, and now.

The excitement and anticipation throbbing in her veins made her feel wild and wanton. She could feel his hard length pressing against her, and she knew he wanted her as much as she wanted to him.

"Leo, take me," she begged before his mouth plundered hers.

A few more heavy kisses, and she was sure she was about to self-combust from the passion between them. A dull ache had settled between her legs, and she longed for him to touch her, and take her to dizzying heights.

Then he paused and looked at her. His breathing was unsteady and she could see the desire in his eyes. He wanted her as much as she wanted him.

But instead of him acknowledging that, he said, "That's better."

"W-what?" She wasn't sure what he meant, but her body was still humming in anticipation.

"Now you look like you want me," he said with supreme confidence.

"Is this some kind of joke to you," she said, her fingers tracing her swollen lips.

"Not at all. Now you look like a woman who's in love," he said simply. "Come on, let's go."

"No, I need to fix myself up," she said, horrified that she'd attend the party with smudged makeup and her hair in a mess.

"You look exactly how you should," he said. "Sexy, hot, and looking like you're getting plenty."

Her jaw dropped and she was sure her mouth looked like a goldfish. But nothing came out of it.

"Come on, now you look like my girlfriend," he said, brushing his lips against hers, before he took her hand and led her to his car.

* * *

LEO WASN'T sure if he was physically able to drive his car a few streets away to the party. His heart was thumping hard against his chest, and he had an uncharacteristic urge to throw her over his shoulder, and take her to his old room in his parents' home and make love to her.

Her kisses and reaction to him had been like dynamite, and he didn't know if he could control the shake in his hands, thanks to the want and need pumping through his veins. He wanted her that much.

The teasing and kissing had been for real. He needed her to look the part, not like a *beauty*. But when their tongues had met, the fire inside of him had burned hotly, and he longed to touch her and make her his. But that wasn't going to happen. Not only had they been in a public area, a kid's playground, but he had no intention of making love to her. . . ever.

Sex would make things complicated. She was a means to an end, and he didn't want to hurt her.

She may have driven him crazy over the past few years,

but he was still honourable enough that he wouldn't sleep with someone who he was not in a relationship with. It may be implied, but he wasn't going to take advantage of her.

Some deep breaths helped settle down the hormones racing through his body, and by the time they reached the Bergmans', he needed a beer or three. She'd gone bra-less tonight in her summery dress, and the knowledge had left him aching in ways that he shouldn't be. . .especially at a family event.

At the party, they greeted everyone. "Sorry we're late," he said to Gabe Bergman, who was his age.

"I can see why," Gabe gave him a knowing grin, before clapping him on the back. "Good to see you."

As usual, Sue and Saul Bergman had outdone themselves with the dinner buffet, and the party was in full swing.

After dinner, a movie was organised for the children, and the adults talked amongst themselves. The parents in one room, the grown-up children in another.

"No kissing games this year, no one is single anymore," Gabe said looking at Leo.

"How about truth or dare?" Ruby, his sister, suggested.

"We're not teens anymore, we don't have stupid stuff to share," Gabe said. "Besides, we have to be responsible, as some of us are parents."

They all chuckled together, before they sat around the table.

"Let's talk about Leo and Jenna," Gabe suggested.

"Let's not," Leo said, before putting his arm around Jenna, and kissing her shoulder.

"I would never have guessed you two would get together," Ruby admitted.

There were nods and agreement from the others.

A knock at the doorframe had them all looking up. "Dessert is served, and then we're dancing."

"Uggh." Ruby cried out. "We're becoming old and boring."

"Speak for yourself, I love dancing...especially with Jenna," he said to the sound of others pretending to vomit from his words. He laughed them off. "Come on guys, we're in the honeymoon stage. I like everything about her."

There were more fake dry retching sounds before everyone laughed.

Brushing his lips against Jenna's, he then whispered, "Come on, you can watch me eat dessert before we dance."

LOUD MUSIC, a compilation from the 1960s, 70s, and 80s blared from the sound system and the couples danced in the living room.

The children were jumping up and down on the spot in a group, and Leo danced with Jenna away from the commotion. "Do you miss eating chocolate?"

"Of all questions to ask, I didn't expect that one," she chuckled. "But yes, I do."

"Don't worry, I know your figure is important to you. It's a shame that you have to deprive yourself," he said with an accepting smile.

They danced slowly, in each other's arms even though the music was upbeat.

"It's how it is," she added, as though favourite food deprivation wasn't that bad. For him, it was. He hated the idea of her almost starving herself for her career.

"What did you think I was going to ask?" he prodded, pretending he had no idea.

"Don't play daft, you know exactly what I was thinking." She gave him a playful punch.

"Was kissing me that bad?" He gave her a playful grin.

"No, but it feels so weird that we're together in front of

everyone," she confessed, looking around at the families they'd known for so many years.

"I know, it's the same for me. I mean, our parents are over there." His head nodded towards the other side of the room. "But just so you know, you've played your part amazingly well tonight. Thank you."

She didn't say anything.

"Everything okay?" His eyebrows came together, and she could see concern in his eyes.

"It's ironic that no one is badgering me about settling down because I'm with you. We're not real, but they don't know that," her lips parted with wonder.

His mouth dried and his chest tightened, thinking about their arrangement. "You should enjoy the break, because next year you'll have them asking you again when you're going to settle down." He gave her a cheeky wink to lighten the mood. It seemed to work as she gave him a small smile.

"Since Taylor and Luca are happily married, I have less pressure on me. But I know Mum and Dad want me to find someone," she confessed in a low voice, looking around to see if anyone could hear them. Unlikely, since they were dancing away from the others.

"And the problem is?" He lifted his brow, curious to know more.

"I'm not really the mothering kind," she said with a grimace.

"You don't say," he said in mock amusement.

"I'm being serious." She gave him another punch to his shoulder, this time it was a little harder as she threw her frustrations at him physically.

"I am being serious," he acknowledged with a smile. "How many times have I heard you refer to kids as brats? And in all the time I've known you, I've never seen you play or socialise with one."

She'd never held or helped one of the new mums who needed a hand. She'd always shuddered, telling them she was allergic to babies.

"Children and I are like oil and water; we don't mix," she said with determination. "What about you?"

"I like kids." He did. Over the years, he'd enjoyed playing backyard cricket, and toddler tantrums never fazed him. "But for now, my career is my focus," he admitted. Since being promoted to his new role, his focus revolved around managing the Centre, maintaining his fitness and seeing his friends. With his long working hours, he knew he didn't have the time to devote to a wife and a family. Perhaps in a few years?

"As is mine." She sniffed, reminding him that her career was just as important as his.

He twirled her around, before giving her a playful kiss. "Tell me. Have you thought about doing something more than modelling and acting? I have to be honest, I think you're a talented model, but not so much an actor."

She glared at him. "I'm an extra, and I get paid well for what I do."

"Jenna, you love the limelight, you can't be happy in the background. That's not you." His voice was firm with certainty. "It's why you're such a good model, you love the prominence you get in the spotlight."

Raising her brow, she reflected over what he said, before admitting. "You're right. I don't like being *behind* the star. I want to be the star."

"So, what are you going to do about it?" he asked capturing her gaze.

CHAPTER 5

*J*enna wasn't too sure whether to tell Leo the truth about her mentoring program, which was silly because they were "dating" and he needed to know. . .didn't he?

"When you think too hard, you get these worry lines between your eyebrows," he said, as his fingers brushed away the creases. "Are you working out a story to tell me? Hiding the truth from me?"

"Now why would I do that?" she fired at him, hoping her eyes wouldn't betray her. That was exactly what she'd been thinking.

"You have this cool, ice-queen exterior that suits who you are. But underneath, you are totally hot," he said.

"You sound surprised," she said.

He twirled her around before dipping her. Back in his arms so their gazes met, he said, "I've known you since you were aged in single digits, and you're still the same. But at the park. . .the way you responded showed me a side I was surprised to see."

"Really?"

"Yes, really," he admitted. "You may be outrageous in some of the things you say and do, but you've never been a tease or a flirt. But you usually do that with a crowd. When it's just you and me, you're different."

"I'm being polite, you annoy me." She stuck out her tongue at him.

He chuckled. "You're not polite to me, and you annoy me, too."

"You're stuck with me till New Year's Eve." She sighed dramatically.

"If you kiss me like you did at the park, I may keep you on longer as my girlfriend." His voice sounded raspy and full of need.

"I don't think so. You're too dull for me." She made a show of yawning.

"Then next time we make out in a public place, you might remember how dull I am before you ask me to *take you*," he whispered in her ear.

Her chest tightened as she remembered that moment when she'd forgotten everything around her, and all she could focus on was the want and desire pumping through her veins. All she'd wanted at that moment was Leo. Leo and his amazing kisses, and the touch of his fingertips all over her body.

"If you keep looking at me like that, I'm going to take you outside, find a dark spot, and kiss you senseless," he said. His eyes had darkened, and she could see the need. It was exactly how she felt.

Shaking her head to push away thoughts of them kissing, she said, "All this talk about kissing is making me thirsty. Let's get a drink?"

"Sure," he said, taking her by the elbow and leading her to the kitchen.

After each having a glass of water, he said, "Do you find

me so boring that you couldn't date me after the New Year."
He paused. "Not that I mind. I'm asking for a friend."

She laughed at his silliness. "I don't think we're compatible."

"You're right. We are different. I mean, you don't give back to the community–"

"I do," she snapped in reply.

"Ha, I knew it," he said, pointing at her. "I knew you were hiding something from me. What is it?"

"Well, if you must know, I started a course to help aspiring models. Teaching them how to walk, pose, hold themselves and of course apply makeup."

"But?"

"Some of these girls have serious issues, I mean they're young, in their teens, and some of them have such crappy lives," she said, reflecting over what she'd learned over the past year. "I rent out a room at a local Church, and once a week, we meet."

"You mentor them?" he probed, looking interested in what she was confessing to him.

"You could say that." She leaned back, her bottom pressed against the benchtop, her arms lose by her side.

"How do you know what to say?" His forehead creased with wanting to know more.

"Amber has been helping me," she admitted. Asking Amber had been a stroke of luck, and she'd been fortunate to have someone to guide her through how to manage difficult issues such as angst and rejection.

"Amber, your sister's friend? But isn't she in London?" He scratched his chin.

"She is. And she even wrote an article for me. I paid her of course, and I've distributed it amongst the girls. It talks about self-esteem and being a young woman in the twenty-first century," she boasted, proud of what she'd achieved so far, again thankful to be able to gain Amber's insights.

"That was a good idea, that sounds very wise in helping them," he praised, with a smile filled with admiration.

"Thank you." Her heart warmed in reply to his recognition of her work. "Amber's background is dealing with IVF couples, but she really knows a lot about family break-ups and working through such issues."

"Taylor must miss her, they're such good friends," he said, his voice filled with genuine sympathy for two best friends that were no longer living in the same city.

"She does. They're in separate countries but I know they talk all the time, and send each other endless messages." A tiny worm of envy threaded through her belly thinking about her sister and Amber. They were such firm friends, and more like sisters. Jenna wished she had that relationship with her own sister. . .or even with a friend. But she didn't. Her commitment to her career and the long hours she often worked meant she hadn't developed long-lasting relationships with friends.

"Isn't she getting married to some English guy?" His head tilted to the side.

"Yep, their wedding is in late January." Her lips parted slightly in resentment that everyone around her had found awesome guys to settle down with, and she hadn't. She may not have a plus-one at the wedding, but at least she'd look fabulous. She'd scored a sample dress from a local designer, which could only be described as a "show stopper."

"Are you going?" His left eyebrow lifted.

"Yes. Not only will I get to see Taylor and Luca, but I'm hoping I'll meet some gorgeous English bloke." Her voice was filled with silliness but deep in her heart, she hoped to find someone special. And if she had to live overseas, like Amber, then she was prepared to do so.

"You don't really care about Amber, you just want to find yourself a good-looking guy, like she did." He released a smug sigh.

She was about to fire off a crude remark when she saw the twinkle in his eyes. "You're too cheeky for your own good." She took a couple of steps to him, and playfully swatted at his shoulder.

"I'll take that as a compliment," he said with a wink. One of Elvis Presley's slow ballads started to play, and he started to hum. Taking her hand in his he said, "Come on, you owe me a slow dance."

* * *

IT WASN'T easy holding Jenna in his arms as they swayed to the music. He was getting to know Jenna better than he had over the past twenty years, and he liked what he saw. Liked her a lot. Which was a problem.

She was supposed to be a means to an end.

He only wanted to date her till the New Year and then part ways. But after that explosive kiss in the park and her revelations about working with teens, he was seeing an unexpected side of her that he liked.

Shame that she wasn't interested in him or in someday having children.

That was a deal-breaker for him. Though no more so than the fact that she didn't want to get to know him.

He'd always expected that he would be a father. He liked the idea of completing a family with a child, imparting knowledge and helping them grow and develop into an adult, ready to take on the world.

Carrying his DNA wasn't as important to him, but having a family was.

Jenna wasn't maternal and wasn't interested in children. That was not a revelation.

Over the past few hours, he'd wondered if they could have a future, once their arrangement ended.

But there were too many barriers. Children. Career. Compatibility.

They were "friendly," not friends, and he needed to remind himself that a few heated kisses weren't going to change things between them. After the Clarendon Close New Year's Eve Party, they needed to find a way to "break up."

His parents would be upset, and so would Jenna's. They had loved the romance of them falling for each other, and truly believed they'd been able to let the past go and have a future together.

But Jenna was different. A few dates and steamy kisses did not mean a lifetime of happiness.

Jenna and her kisses were needed, but just to get him through the holidays. Next year, he'd start seriously dating again. There were plenty of women in Melbourne; he just needed to find the one for him.

THE DAYS PASSED in a blur of work and events. They'd attended a variety of day and night all with a Christmas theme. The bingo night had included a visit from Santa, the Friday night dinner included Christmasy foods, and then there had been high teas, talks and games nights.

Jenna had attended them all, and there had been a lot of events, and he'd enjoyed having her there as his *girlfriend*. And on occasions, she'd started helping out, like at the games night where she'd been playing cards while he had to work. He'd caught her smiling and laughing with the people on her table, and he could see she was genuinely enjoying herself.

And in between the work commitments they'd found time to be together, they'd hired bikes and cycled around Centennial Park together, and his favourite time was them walking along the coastal route between Elwood and St Kilda beaches. She'd even tasted a mouthful of icy deliciousness from his ice-cream cone. They'd talked non-stop, she'd laughed at his jokes and he loved the way she smiled at him.

He and Jenna spent so much time together, and became so comfortable in each other's company that he had to remind himself that they weren't a *real* couple. This was make-believe. But it didn't feel like it.

Every kiss, every brush of their fingers, every look. It was starting to become more than an arrangement for him, and that made him worry. He didn't want to develop feelings for her, especially as he was still dealing with Cailah's rejection. That had stung.

He needed a woman who was more like he'd thought Cailah was; sweet, honest, kind. But she'd ditched him for the ultimate bad boy, not wanting his honest happily-ever-after.

What a poor decision he'd made with Cailah. At thirty-three, he should've known better.

Running his fingers through his hair, he took a deep breath. Relationships were hard. He needed a chat with his dad to help him sort things through, even if he did have to betray Jenna and reveal the truth of their relationship.

Despite his experience, he was floundering like he was a teen, and needed some worldly advice. And who better than his father, who was kind, dependable, and still in love with his mum years later? Yep, he knew he could always depend on his father.

* * *

A FEW DAYS BEFORE CHRISTMAS, Jenna approached her mum in the kitchen. "Can I invite some people to Christmas lunch?"

Every year the families rotated the gatherings for Christmas and New Year's Eve. This year the Willamsons were hosting the lunch.

Her mum's smile turned into a frown. "How many are you inviting? I already have thirty people coming."

Jenna's tummy twisted, knowing the burden she'd placed on her family over the years. She rarely helped, leaving that to her sister, Taylor.

She liked to be the centre of attention, the princess of the ball so to speak. And it was only recently that she'd seen the imposition she'd placed on her parents, especially her mum. This year she planned to be more helpful. "Remember how I told you that I've been mentoring some girls?"

Her mum wiped her hands on a tea towel, and then turned to look at her. "Yes," she said in an exasperated voice.

"A couple have nowhere to spend Christmas," she said, still unable to believe these teenage girls were on their own.

Her mother's face darkened with concern. "Of course, they're welcome." She paused. "But why are they alone?"

"One girl, Ella, is in foster care, but her home life is awful. It's a terrible situation. She's seventeen and there are no other foster families available for her. She's run away and is making do till she's eighteen. Then she's legally an adult and can make her own decisions, and she can rent her own place." Her posture slumped remembering how difficult it had been to hear of Ella's destructive home life over the past five years.

"Where does she live?" Amy's horrified voice came out as a squeak.

"With friends, here and there." She blinked rapidly to ward off tears of disbelief. Ella was an amazing young woman, and had such potential. She needed someone to care for her and give her a break at life.

"A seventeen-year-old? On her own?" Amy's hands fisted, visibly distressed. "I need to talk to your father, but perhaps she can stay in Taylor's room till she's eighteen? And then we'll help her find somewhere to live?"

"Really, Mum?" She threw her arms around her mother's neck. "You'd do that for Ella?"

"I trust that you wouldn't invite some *undesirable* to this house." Her mum gave her a stern look. "But we can give her some help till she gets on her feet."

"Mum, that would be amazing. She's such a great girl, and has the potential to shine. She just needs a helping hand. By living here, she can get a job, she'll have a permanent address."

"She's left school?" Her mum frowned.

"Yes, but I'm encouraging her to study at nights next year," Jenna said, with a reassuring voice. She had total trust in Ella, and believed she'd do well if given the right encouragement and support.

Amy gave her daughter a comforting smile. "Let me talk to Dad tonight, and we'll work out something."

"You are the best, thanks." She hugged her mum hard, even if she did tower over her in height. "And I promise to help more than I have in the past. You'll need it with the lunch."

Amy stood back but gave Jenna a sceptical look, wondering if she really would help. "I will. The weather is supposed to be warm so I thought we'd eat outside in the garden. Perhaps make it like a picnic?"

Jenna smiled with delight. "Great idea. Why don't you give me a list of what you need done and I'll get started? Ella can help me. We'll go and get the seafood and veggies from the markets."

Amy stood back, leaning against the counter, staring at her daughter. "I must say, I do like this new and improved version of you."

She threw her hands in the air. "I know, I know. I've been a cow when it comes to these family things. I'm trying harder, okay?" she confessed with a sincere voice. And that was genuine, she honestly meant it.

"Could it have something to do with a certain man you're seeing?" Amy pointed to her heart, giving her a knowing look.

"Leo?" She gasped. "No." Certainly not. This was about her, not about Leo.

Amy shook her head. "Since you two have been dating, you've changed."

Jenna rolled her eyes in exasperation. Now was not the time to tell her mum that her relationship with Leo was a sham. Besides, just because they were also seeing each other outside of the Mono Melbourne events didn't mean anything. Right?

A few nights ago, they'd gone together to a movie marathon, where everyone had to dress up, which was just fun. It wasn't a date or anything. They'd both wanted to go. It didn't mean anything.

Amy gave her a look that said that she didn't believe her. "I would never have guessed you and Leo together, but it works."

Curiosity got the better of her, and she asked. "What do you mean?" She nibbled her lip, pretending she wasn't interested in what her mother had to say.

"You're both career-driven, but he's more family-oriented than you. You're the louder of the two, and despite him being more reserved, you balance each other out." She paused. "I see the way you look at each other, I've never seen you look at a guy like that."

"Mum!" She squirmed in embarrassment.

"You walk around in underwear in front of strangers, and yet you can't talk to me, *your mother*, about your relationships?" She waved her hand dismissively in front of her face, the skin around her jawline was tight with annoyance.

Her lips pressed together before she blurted out. "I'm sorry that I'm not perfect like Taylor."

Her mother's jaw dropped with shock and she stood ramrod straight, looking at her daughter. "Don't be ridiculous."

"Taylor's the perfect one. She's the one who always helps you around the house, heck she even married Luca, *boy wonder*. I mean she's always been the dutiful daughter who looked after children and helped at these family functions."

A long silence hung between the two of them.

"You two are so different," her mum said. "But that doesn't mean that we love Taylor more. Look at you," she stepped back and gazed at her. "You're gorgeous. You're a successful model. You've achieved success, but in different ways than your sister. Her talents do not revolve around business. But you've worked hard and saved. Your apartment is stunning with its impressive views, and you're only living here because a builder swindled you all and used cheap cladding. This is just a blip. Once it's all fixed, you'll move back in."

Jenna felt her eyes widen with surprise at her mum's heartfelt words.

"And you're mentoring these teens, starting a business to represent talented models, and studying at night," she continued. "You're an achiever. Dad and I are really proud of you. Yes, we'd love you to help us more, but you're very driven and we love seeing you achieve your goals. We love you so much. You know that."

Jenna's breathing grew rapid, and her heart pumped

hard against her ribs. All this time she'd stupidly believed that Taylor was the golden child, and she'd carried a bitter chip on her shoulder. She knew her parents, they were awesome, but sometime over the past ten years, she'd forgotten that.

"Sorry, Mum, for acting like a teen brat," she confessed, stupidity threaded through her veins at the realisation of her childlike behaviour.

Amy sighed. "I've got your back, always. And if you want to talk, just come and speak to me." She paused. "These girls that you're mentoring, Dad and I think it's a good idea. You're still beautiful, but you're thirty-one now, you're old for a model. We're not saying you can't do it, but we like that you're diversifying your brand."

"Thanks, Mum." She stopped. "It sounds silly but it is easier prancing around in next to nothing on a stage, because I'm acting. Sharing feelings, talking from the heart. . .it's not really me."

Amy gave her an all-knowing look. "I know you. I raised you. Have you forgotten that? You've been the same since you could walk."

Her heart lifted at her mum's words and she gave her a hug.

Stepping back, Jenna said, "You and Dad have always believed in me. I'm sorry that I just acted so selfish."

And wasn't that a lightbulb moment for Jenna? How had she forgotten that success came in different shapes and sizes?

Taylor had been supporting her for years, and she hadn't even seen it. How many times did her sister help her parents because she had an audition or some event to attend?

She sagged against the kitchen top, remembering all the times her sister had been there, and she'd never realised. And now she was living overseas with husband, Luca, and how many times had she called? Hardly ever. She should've been more supportive to her as she'd migrated to a new country and had to make friends.

Too late for regrets now. She'd make the effort to call by adding a reminder to her diary.

"Are you home for dinner tonight?" Amy asked, breaking her thoughts.

"No, Leo and I are hosting a Christmas end-of-year party for *my girls*. We're going to the Melbourne Star Observation Wheel, and then a fun taco place after. They do all unusual tacos, and a range of flavoured non-alcoholic margaritas."

"Leo's going, too?" Amy lifted her brow questioningly.

"Um, yes, he's met them and the girls wanted him there," she clarified. "I've attended all his work functions, so he's attending mine."

"Okay, have fun." She paused. "I'll write up the list and you can go on Saturday to get me everything. It would really help. Do you think Leo can help Dad set up the back yard?"

"Sure," she said, her heart filled with love and happiness.

*L*ater that night, at the Docklands waterfront precinct, Leo directed them to a separate entrance at the Melbourne Star. "I've organised a surprise," he spoke softly in her ear, so the others wouldn't hear.

The Melbourne Star was like a giant Ferris wheel, except you were in enclosed glass pods. Slow turning, it took an hour for each pod to travel the 360 degrees, providing incredible panoramic views of the city.

Within minutes, their group was separated into two lots of ten people and the first group of girls walked into the first cabin and started squealing. Curious, she made her way forward and saw the cabin had been decked out with pillows and beanbags, and there was hot chocolate and cookies. The informal vibe with its quirky designs and loud colours had the girls snapping endless pics.

The second car arrived and the remaining girls all piled in, also squealing, delighted at the special treatment they were receiving.

Jenna stepped on the slow-moving cabin and Leo took

and held her hand. Turning to him, he gave her a warm smile that made her insides warm.

She looked around, and like the teens, was drawn in by the trendy furnishings that had heightened their experience. Usually, each cabin was bare. Turning to Leo in awe, she said, "You did this?"

He leaned in and said, "I wanted to do something special for them. . .and for you."

Giddy, she pressed a hand against her heart as her knees grew weak, astounded at what he'd organised for her and the girls. "I don't know what to say."

"Just say thanks," he said, his finger touching the tip of her nose.

"Thank you, Leo," she said with complete honesty, still dazzled by the surprise. Leaning towards him, she brushed her lips against his cheek.

They stood to the side, as the wheel slowly moved, giving them a view of the city, and then the Melbourne sprawl. The space was filled with excitement, giggles, and the teens directing each other on taking photos and selfies.

Jenna stood to the side admiring the view with Leo. "This is really special. I know this must've cost a lot."

"They deserve it," he said. Leaning forward to whisper in her ear. "As do you."

Her tummy went into freefall, and it had nothing to do with being sky-high above Melbourne.

"We started the month as friends, and for me, things have changed. I want us to keep seeing each other after our arrangement has ended," he whispered in her ear, obviously not wanting the girls to hear. They wouldn't have. They were oblivious to the *adults* talking.

Jenna cleared her throat, full of emotion, surprised at Leo's declaration. Staring at him she said, "I don't know what to say."

"Say 'yes Leo, I want the same,'" he said in a raw, husky voice.

Her breath caught in her throat, the words were stuck there.

"We've spent a lot of time together, not just at work, and I like being with you," he said. "Surprisingly. I just. . . I want to continue seeing you, because I want to, not because I have to," he admitted.

She wasn't sure when their relationship had shifted for her. Perhaps at the Bergmans' Chanukah party when they'd danced, and he'd held her close. But things had changed, and they'd realised they had a lot more in common then she'd believed.

Dressing up for a movie marathon. Attending talks and reading biographies. Bike riding, and going for long walks. She'd also enjoyed their time together, and couldn't remember a time she'd laughed so much.

Leaning against one of the floor-to-ceiling windows, she looked at Leo's face. The high cheekbones, the soft full lips, and the brown eyes. He was shockingly handsome, and she berated herself for never noticing till recently.

"I don't think that's a good idea," she said reluctantly, her heart aching as she said the words.

"Why?" the skin on his forehead creased with upset and disbelief.

Her heart grew heavy with remorse. "Because we're at an age where you date to get married, and I can't marry you or even consider it." She gulped down some much-needed air. "We're too different. Relationships are about acceptance not change. I don't want a baby and I certainly don't want a toddler. I know this is important to you, but I can't change. I'm sorry. I know this is what you want, a family. I can't give you that. I don't want us to date and then this barrier comes up. It's there now. We need to accept that it just won't work between us." The heartfelt, emotional words tumbled from her lips.

"You're not going to try?" His voice was filled with regret and hurt.

"We're in our thirties, we both know what we want in life." She paused. "If I said yes but we'll never have children, how would you feel?"

His face whitened, and his eyes darkened.

"You see. That's important to you. I won't change, just like you won't. It's better now than later when things. . ." She stopped unable to say what she wanted to say. That she'd fallen for him, big time. Look at what he'd organised for them tonight, something wonderful that was age-appropriate. He was considerate, kind and awesome. Everything she'd want in a guy, and she had it. "I want to be honest and upfront with you."

He nodded, but didn't say anything. Because there was nothing to say. "I don't want to hold on to you with promises that I know I can't keep." She took a steadying breath. "I wish we could resolve this between us, but I can't see how."

"You're right. And it's probably better that we talk about this now," he agreed with a lift of his chin.

She could see the hurt in his eyes, and remorse threaded along her spine.

They stood together looking out at the view, as the circle spun slowly around, but warm tears blurred her vision.

If only she could be more like her sister. But she wasn't, she reflected with a heavy sigh. They barely spoke after that, but simply stood side-by-side.

Finally, the hour-long trip ended and everyone, except her and Leo, groaned with disappointment at the conclusion.

The space was filled with chatter.

"That was so much fun."

"The best"

"I loved it."

"Thanks."

They assembled down below, on the pedestrian walkway, and Jenna did a quick headcount to ensure everyone was accounted for. They were.

"I'm sorry ladies, an urgent work matter has come up. I can't stay for dinner," Leo announced to the group.

"Oh no," the disappointed voices remarked.

"I'll see you all soon." He brushed his lips against Jenna's cheek. "Goodbye."

Her heart ached, knowing it was likely a final goodbye to their relationship. It had ended before they'd had time to develop it more. He was saying goodbye to what had barely begun, and she just wanted to collapse on a nearby bench and cry.

But she couldn't. She had eighteen girls to look after.

Straightening her shoulders, she went into acting mode. "Bye, Leo, thanks for the treats you organised, it was brilliant." She looked out. "Everyone, thank Leo for the amazing surprise."

After many thanks, he left, and Jenna, with her heavy heart, walked to the restaurant pretending everything was fine.

THE DAYS DRAGGED by as Ella moved into Taylor's old room at home. The only reprieve she got from the sadness that weighed her down, after their break-up, was focussing on Ella.

By turning her attention to the young woman, she was able to purposely push aside the pain in her heart.

She missed Leo that much.

She missed his text messages and his calls that made her heart lift with joy. In hindsight, she couldn't believe she thought of him as uninteresting. With his quirky humour and ability to make her laugh, he was the most charming and funny man that she knew. In fact, she'd probably laughed more in the last few weeks than she had over the past ten years.

Had she just made the biggest mistake of her life in letting him go?

Was it better that she was upfront with him?

There were moments when she considered lying to him, pretending that she'd love to create the family he so wanted. But she couldn't. That would be unfair to both of them.

The hurt lingered on, and she wondered when she would wake up and be able to be happy again, and not reminisce about Leo, and her own regrets.

Happily, Ella's skin was looking brighter and clearer now that she was settled, sleeping in a bed and eating well each day. Jenna's mum, Amy, fussed over her like a daughter and Jenna was surprised to see Ella thriving under the attention. She'd been expecting tantrums or sulkiness, but Ella seemed to love the firm discipline and boundaries that Amy had set.

The family love that she'd been raised under was definitely good for Ella. And even though these were early days and they may have issues later on, Jenna was proud of her young protégé.

Whilst out on Saturday, buying all the ingredients her mother needed, Jenna turned to her young charge. "You know you can trust me, don't you?"

The young girl nodded. "Yes."

Jenna knew it wasn't easy for her to trust. Having been abandoned by her own parents and moved around in the foster system, Ella was surprisingly open and candid about her feelings.

"We're not going to let you down. We'll be here for you,"

she said to the younger woman. "I'm sure it's hard to trust, but I hope you can." She gave Ella a reassuring smile.

"You're all very different from the families I've lived with over the past few years. I know I am lucky to have you, and even if I only get to spend a few months here till I'm eighteen and legally an adult, I've learned so much already. Amy is teaching me how to cook, and how to clean. And you're helping me with my career and finances." The young woman said, her face filled with appreciation and gratefulness. "I don't know what I did to deserve you looking after me after I ran away from my foster family, but thank you for taking a chance on me."

"Just because you had a bad start in life doesn't mean it has to end poorly." Jenna took a steadying breath. "My family and I are giving you a chance. A chance to better yourself. Don't look back, look forward. That's the best advice I can give you."

"But, I, um. . ." Ella's face was filled with remorse and concern.

Stopped at a red light, Jenna turned to Ella. "I know you got into trouble with the law over the years, and you've been remanded, but take this opportunity to better yourself. Once you turn eighteen, your juvenile record will be closed."

Ella's eyes widened with surprise. "Really?"

"Yes, but you need to be a good citizen from now on. It will be harder to get a job if you have a police record. Okay?"

Ella nodded with enthusiasm. "I will."

Jenna high fived Ella as the traffic light turned green and she started to drive.

"Your parents are so nice. You're so lucky to have them," Ella confessed.

Jenna's heart ached for the pain Ella had to deal with. So unfair for someone so young. "I know, but I didn't realise how lucky I was till I met you," Jenna confessed.

"Really?" There was genuine surprise across the girl's face.

"Yes, really. I took it all for granted," she admitted with reluctance.

"I want to be like you. I want to have the modelling success you've had, and then get an amazing boyfriend like Leo. You're so lucky. You have everything," Ella gushed in admiration, as teens do.

Jenna opened her mouth then shut it. She wasn't sure what to say. Her life wasn't perfect, but to an impressionable teen it seemed so.

She continued to drive, pretending to focus on that instead of talking.

At the market, they bought boxes of fresh vegetables and fruit. And then collected the seafood her mum had ordered.

There were people everywhere getting ready for Christmas, either rushing around or smiling. The day was warm but not unseasonably hot, and Jenna noticed a number of young men admiring Ella. In a pretty sundress, hat and sandals, she looked effortlessly beautiful. But being beautiful wasn't enough in her industry; you had to be hardworking and disciplined. Jenna would help Ella achieve her goals. She deserved it.

And then she'd ensure Ella didn't flitter her earnings away, but rather saved and invested her money wisely. Modelling jobs came and went, and there wasn't always consistency with the work available. She'd help Ella budget and set money aside for the days or weeks when she didn't have work.

They returned home, and Jenna was surprised to hear voices, loud voices, coming from the kitchen. Walking into the kitchen, her jaw dropped seeing her younger sister, Taylor.

"Surprise," she sang out to Jenna.

Rushing over, Jenna hugged Taylor. "How dare you surprise Mum and Dad, and not tell me."

After Ella was introduced, they sat around chatting over tea and cookies.

"Where's Luca?" Jenna asked.

"He couldn't make it. He needed to work, and is using his leave for when we go to London next month for Amber's wedding."

"Who's Amber?" Ella asked.

"My bestie. She's marrying an English guy, Darcy, and the wedding is at the end of January. After the wedding, we're going to Bath and do sightseeing," Taylor said. "I can't wait."

"Brrr, who wants to get married in the middle of an English winter?" Ella pretended to shiver and rub her arms as though she were cold.

"They're having a low-key wedding, marrying at their local church, and then an afternoon tea in the Church hall," Taylor said. "Darcy is taking Amber to Greece and Italy for their honeymoon. They'll sightsee and then have a few days on a Greek island relaxing."

"Sounds amazing, lucky Amber," Ella said. "Wish I could go."

"She is lucky," Taylor said wistfully.

Ella turned to Jenna. "Are you taking Leo?"

Taylor's eyes widened at the word Leo. Her head turned dizzyingly quick to send an accusatory look at her older sister. "Are you seeing Leo, as in Leo Turner?"

Jenna felt her cheeks warm, which had nothing to do with the warmth of the day. "Um, yes, I am."

"You never told me?" Taylor fired at her.

"Really? I was sure I had," she lied with clarity. Of course, she hadn't told Taylor as she hadn't been expecting her to fly out to surprise the family for Christmas.

Taylor's eyes narrowed. "I'm sure you hadn't." Her gaze flew to her mother. "You didn't tell me about Leo."

"I thought Jenna would tell you. We're so happy about it. We caught them kissing a couple of weeks ago when we came home from the movies," Amy confessed.

"Imagine that," Taylor said giving her sister a look that told her that she was going to quiz her later.

"Leo's so dreamy," Ella cooed. "I want a boyfriend like him. But not as old as him, of course," she said, as the other women chuckled at her candidness.

LATER THAT AFTERNOON when Taylor and Jenna were alone, her younger sister said. "Okay, spill. Tell me everything. I can't believe it. You and Leo?"

The sisters were in the back garden, a large market umbrella protected and shaded them from the hot afternoon sun.

Jenna sipped from her glass of iced water. The cold water did little to assuage the dryness in her throat. She needed advice from Taylor, but it would mean betraying Leo. She'd promised not to tell anyone about their arrangement.

"Will you promise not to tell Mum and Dad what I'm about to say?" she asked with a strained voice.

Taylor crossed her heart, like she used to do when they were kids. "Promise."

Chewing the inside of her cheek, she gripped her hands in her lap. "You know how things have been between Leo and me."

"You've taunted him for years, providing the entertainment for us." She lifted a perfectly groomed eyebrow at her older sister.

"I know," she clarified before playing with the condensation on her glass.

"Stop it," she pointed to the glass. "What is it that you're not telling me, or you want to ask. No one is around, so ask me." Taylor said, her gaze meeting Jenna's.

Taking a deep breath and ignoring the jumpiness in her tummy. "Remember when I caught you and Luca kissing?"

Taylor groaned theatrically. "How could I not? You brat. You told everyone."

"I'd always known you'd had a crush on him, but he didn't know it. What happened after you kissed? Things would've changed, yes?" Jenna leaned forward interested to hear what Taylor had to say.

"Yes, he never knew. We were just friends. And you're right. The kiss changed everything," Taylor admitted. "But forget about me. Let's talk about you. Did you have a secret crush on Leo?" Her voice lifted with excitement.

"Hardly," she said with a mocking voice. "We have this arrangement." She looked around, even though she knew they were alone in the garden. "He needed a fake girlfriend for the holidays."

"Really? Leo? He's so nice." Taylor's voice was filled with awe.

"His girlfriend, Cailah, recently dumped him and so he asked me to stand in," she admitted with reluctance.

"And?"

"And he offered me money–"

"What? Ewwww." Taylor's nose crinkled with disgust.

"No, I mean, he knew I was cash-strapped, and he said he would pay me to be a fake girlfriend. But I didn't accept the money," she clarified, feeling her cheeks burn. "Anyway, only kissing is included. . .when needed," she said, feeling flustered and embarrassed about telling her sister about the deal.

"And?"

"He knows how to kiss, I mean, really kiss,"

Taylor fanned herself with her hand. "*Oh la la.*"

"We've kissed. . .a lot. And we've spent time together, and. . .I really like him. I mean, I think I've fallen for him, big time."

Taylor's eyes lit up with excitement. "And what's the problem with that?"

"He wants a family, and I don't." She paused. "You know me, I'm allergic to baby poo and spew." She shuddered. "A family is important to him. I'm not like you. You love cuddling babies, I don't."

Taylor leaned forward to take her sister's hand. "I'm so sorry. He's such a great guy. It's a shame you can't find a middle ground to agree on."

Jenna shrugged. "It's probably for the best. We've only been together for a short time, at least we now know that it wouldn't work." She sounded comfortable with her decision, but it was fake. She wasn't. She almost wished she could pretend to like the little ankle-biters, just to keep Leo. But she couldn't do that. She couldn't hold on to him with false pretences.

"What are you going to do?" Taylor nibbled her lip.

Jenna shrugged, defeat weighed heavily on her shoulders. "What can I do? You can't just resolve it like that." She clicked her fingers in the air. "And it's not fair that either of us has to change for the other."

"You're right. This is important for couples to agree on." Her younger, obviously wiser and married sister said, nodding in agreement.

Jenna sagged against her seat with defeat. "I just can't see how to resolve it."

"If there wasn't the baby/family thing between you two," Taylor pointed her finger at her sister and drew a horizontal line in the air. "What would you do?"

"I'd hold on to him for forever," she said in a low voice, surprised at her reply. Had she just admitted that? Until now, she'd never thought about her and Leo being together past New Year's Eve. The issues between them seemed too difficult to navigate through.

"This is the first time I think you've ever been in love," her sister said confidently before placing her hand over her heart.

She felt lightheaded as apprehension tormented her. Her, in love? Really?

"Being in love is awesome," Taylor said brightly.

Jenna groaned. "No, it's not. He's going to break my heart."

"At least you have a heart." Taylor gave her a cheeky grin. "Some say you don't."

Jenna gave her sister a mock death stare before she burst out laughing. "Thanks for listening."

"Any time," Taylor said giving her sister a warm smile.

Jenna's heart ached, reflecting on the number of occasions she'd tormented her sister for the fun of it. She really hadn't been sisterly over the years. The realisation had only now come to her, now that Taylor lived far away, in America. Sure, they could speak on the phone, but she'd missed seeing Taylor and Luca while they created a new life away from them. Birthdays, anniversaries, holidays. They would be apart. Her heart ached.

This is what Leo wanted. Leo wanted a family, and children. He wanted all of this, and she'd rejected him over it. Now she understood. She may not like the baby ewww-ness, and dealing with little ones, but perhaps they could create their own family? A family unit so they could be together?

She closed her eyes and thought about Leo, and how he made her feel. She loved being with him, spending time together, talking to him, and, of course, kissing him.

Was there a compromise they could find?

"Whatever you're thinking about," her sister's voice broke

her thoughts. "Do it. You have this stupid grin on your face and you're thinking about Leo. Just do it, okay?"

Jenna opened her eyes. "I'm the older sister, and the bossy one, you can't tell me what to do."

"I'm happily married, and madly in love with Luca. So yes, I can tell you what to do." Taylor gave her sister a grin. "If you want advice, you know where to come to." She rubbed her hands theatrically. "I'm so glad I'm here for Christmas and get to see my glamorous sister grovel for the first time. . .ever."

"I'm not going to grovel. And if I do, you won't be around to see it." She stood, hands on her hips. "Your *glamorous sister* is too glamorous for that," she said in an all-knowing voice.

CHAPTER 7

*I*t was Christmas Day and the four women were in the kitchen early getting ready for the lunch. It was their turn, this year, to host the lunch for the families that lived in Clarendon Close.

"Ella, dear, can you help Jason set up the picnic rugs in the back yard?" Amy asked.

"Sure, I'm on it." Ella gave her a salute before walking out.

Amy turned to her older daughter, giving her a satisfied smile. "She's changed in the short time that she's been here. You've done a good job."

Jenna stopped cutting the vegetables, her lungs inflated with pride. "It's thanks to you and Dad. You opened your home to her," she said with an all-knowing grin.

"Yeah, and I lost my room. Thanks for nothing," Taylor said.

Jenna spun around facing her sister. "You get to stay with your mother-in-law, who does *everything* for you."

Taylor lifted her eyebrow. "What can I say? She loves me."

Who wouldn't? Jenna wanted to fire at her. But said nothing. The "old" Jenna would've made disparaging remarks. But the "new" Jenna wasn't going to. She preferred the new way of being funny without hurting people's feelings. All thanks to. . .Leo? She scratched her chin with wonder.

Taylor had always bonded well with Sofia Bianchi, Luca's mother, so it was a perfect fit now that they were mother and daughter-in-law.

"Has Sofia given you her gnocchi recipe yet? Your favourite?" Jenna leaned against the benchtop, giving her sister a smug smirk.

Taylor blushed, even her ears turned red. "Not yet. I um, am getting it when we have a baby."

Jenna gasped with surprise, unable to believe Sofia would withhold Taylor's favourite gnocchi in the hope of becoming a *Nona*.

Amy's eyes widened with excitement as the realisation dawned on her. "Do you. . .is there something you want to tell us?"

Jenna could see all the hope in her mum's eyes that her daughter may be pregnant.

Taylor sighed and her arms went limp, hanging by her side. "Not you as well. Give us a break. I've moved countries, it hasn't been easy."

"I know that, but there's something you're not telling me," Amy said with one hand on her hip, and the other hand in the air as she waggled a finger, reprimanding her youngest. But it was all for show. The girls knew their mum all too well.

Taylor bit her lip as though contemplating what to say, before throwing her arms in the air. "We're going to start trying for a baby after Amber's wedding." Her voice was filled with excitement and elation.

The three of them squealed in unison at the *secret* news.

"I'm going to be a grandmother," Amy announced before throwing her arms around Taylor.

"I'm going to be an aunty," Jenna cried. "Group hug." She drew her mum and sister into her embrace.

The women snuggled, and Jenna leaned in, loving this moment. Something they hadn't done for a long time. And not just because Taylor was overseas, but because she didn't normally do all this family mushy stuff.

But now she was doing it, and loved it.

Her heart sank as she realised there would be no announcement from her. No squeals of joy from her mum in anticipation of being a grannie.

But at least they could get joy from Taylor. Taylor was the maternal sister, the good sister who helped around the house.

After all, she was the glamorous one, the international model, Jenna, reassured herself.

LATER THAT DAY, the families arrived, excited to spend another Christmas Day together. Everyone helped with the catering, and the lunch was a hit. Once everyone had eaten to bursting point and the food taken inside so it wouldn't spoil under the summer sun, everyone relaxed.

Unlike the Bianchis who had a pool, the Williamsons didn't. And since the weather was perfect, a game of back-yard cricket was organised between the men and children, whilst the women "supervised," in between chatting.

Jenna was on-edge, surprised that Leo had attended as she'd not been expecting him. But here he was, looking oh-so-good in tailored shorts and a casual shirt. Dark sunglasses and a trendy straw hat completed his look, and her hungry gaze took in his effortless style.

Excusing herself from the other women and the lively discussion on potty training, and nursery schools, Jenna made her way to the kitchen and used her time to cover the left-overs and place them in the fridge.

A noise startled her and she turned to see Leo against the doorway watching her.

"You surprised me," she said, her hand pressed against her heart.

Leo approached her, and she stood and followed him to the lounge room.

"Merry Christmas, Jenna," he said, brushing his lips against her cheek.

She breathed in his masculine scent of citrus tinged with coconut. The beachy coconut waft was likely from the sunscreen he'd applied to his strong arms. She'd watched. She'd admired. She'd been paying attention.

"Merry Christmas, Leo." She smiled warmly at him, her gaze feasting on how well his short-sleeved shirt fit him, and how muscular his forearms were. Her insides quivered, thinking about how good it felt to have his arms around her.

"You look beautiful, as always, today."

His compliment made her feel all warm and gooey on the inside. "Thank you," she said. "You weren't needed at work, today?" She'd masked her surprise when he'd arrived with his parents for the lunch. She'd been expecting him to miss it and work.

"I was, but I wanted to see you. There's a dinner tonight at the Home," he paused. "Will you come with me?" he asked in a low voice.

"Because you want me there?" She smiled wistfully.

"I want you there," he said in a low voice, before taking a deep breath.

His longing matched her own, and a deep ache robbed her of her breath. She missed him.

With her throat dry and parched, she nodded in reply, unable to speak.

The noise of happy children and adults playing outside filled the room. "Can we go for a walk?" he asked. "I want to talk to you alone."

"Sure, I'll be a moment." She was happy to get away from the festivities and be with Leo. Since the night at the Melbourne Star ride, their conversation had been strained and awkward. She wanted to fix things between them. In seconds she'd made it to her room, grabbed a pair of sandals, and added a large brimmed hat to her head.

She walked out of the house and found him waiting for her in the street. Being Christmas Day, there were few people around, and all the residents of Clarendon Close were at the Williamsons enjoying a family get-together.

They walked in silence to the nearby park, and there he motioned for her to sit on the bench beside him.

Her mind went back to that night of the Chanukah party when he'd kissed her. Kissed her until she'd begged him to make love to her. It seemed so long ago, yet it seemed like yesterday.

"I've been thinking." He reached out, and moved some of her hair so it was behind her ear.

"Me too," she said.

"Do you want to go first?" He shifted his bottom so he was closer to her.

"No, you go," she said with a strained voice, feeling silly at not being able to articulate herself well and overthinking the situation. As her mother said, she was able to walk half-naked around strangers, surely she could express her feelings to Leo. Apparently not. She swallowed a lump of annoyance at herself for being so apprehensive.

Taking her hand in his, his thumb massaged the pulse point at her wrist. "We've only been dating a short time, but I know what I want. I want you. No more pretending, I want us to be honest, and be together–"

"But how?" she interrupted. Her insides had warmed at his inner thoughts, but she couldn't understand how they could have a future when they wanted such different things.

"Since the other night, I've been thinking, a lot. I thought Cailah was the perfect woman for me, but she wasn't. The right one was there, living only a few houses away," he said with desperate longing.

"You don't live with your parents," she said with a cheeky grin.

"It's an analogy, now stop interrupting." He brushed his lips across hers, making her shiver with need.

"You're beautiful, but there's more to you than that. I love your sense of humour, and the way we have fun together. We both like the same kind of movies and books. We both work hard, and want to achieve well in our professions. We get on, and you're the one I want to be with." He paused. "I'm thirty-three and I know what I want."

"But–"

"Let me finish. . .please." He took both of her hands in his, then kissed the knuckles on her left hand. "I spoke to my parents, and told them *everything*."

"No. Really?" She felt dizzy with shock.

"I had to," he said with a reassuring tone. "I had to know how to work out my feelings for you, and the issues between us. And they were really understanding, and gave me worthwhile advice."

"I don't want regrets between us," she said with conviction. Removing a hand from his loose grasp, she trailed her fingers down the side of his face. "But it's a big issue, you wanting a family, and me not feeling the same way."

Nerves threaded their way up and down her spine, in anticipation of what he was going to say to her.

"My parents reminded me that families come in different shapes and sizes. And I know that you won't change your mind on having a baby the traditional way, and I'm not going to ask you to do something you don't want to do. A baby is a lifetime commitment. It's hard work. So, I have a compromise. Can you consider adopting or fostering a teen? But we'll be doing it *together*. Not now. But maybe in a few years?"

She gasped, having never considered adopting or even fostering an older child.

"I've seen how you've been with Ella, you're amazing. She's so lucky to have you." He paused. "I was thinking of other children in the foster care system, and how they are unlikely to be taken in by a family because of their ages. We can help an older child." He stopped and raised his hand. "But, I've decided that if you say no, that's okay. Children grow up and live their own lives. I look at my parents, and yours. They're still happily married, and do so much *together*. I want that with you."

She sucked in a sharp breath, still unable to believe he was saying this.

"Honestly, I would rather have you in my life than miss out. You brighten my day with your smile, and I love your wittiness and outrageous humour. I don't want to lose you."

Disbelief and uncertainty tingled in her chest. Could they assuage her concerns and his so easily? "I don't know what to say." Was it possible?

"You're speechless, that's a first." He chuckled, before kissing the tip of her nose. "Just say yes."

"If we don't end up adopting, will you resent me? I don't want that," she declared with resignation.

"I've seen how incredibly maternal you've been with the young women, you have so much to give. We can foster together or we can just mentor the models, as you've been doing over the past year." He paused. "And if that's all we have, I'll be glad to have that with you. I have a demanding job, wonderful parents, real friends. I feel blessed with every-thing I have."

She looked at him, expecting to see doubt or even defeat in his eyes, but there was none.

"I can't believe you're saying that. My head's spinning, this is all happening so quickly," she said with a sceptical sigh.

"Jenna, we're in our thirties now. We know what we want, and I'm not wasting time. I want you in my life always," he affirmed with certainty.

"That sounds very serious and like a marriage proposal." She pressed her lips into a fine line, confused on many levels.

He removed his sunglasses and gazed at her in assurance. "I may have spoken with your parents recently about them gaining a second son soon."

"What?" Her jaw dropped with surprise. "You've spoken with them?" A stupid question since he'd just said it, but she couldn't believe he'd spoken to her parents about *them*.

"They're delighted, they love me." He tilted back his head and smiled with confidence.

"Who wouldn't?"

"What do you say? You and me?" He gave her a cheeky grin.

"I say, yes," she said with delight, throwing her arms around his neck and kissing him hard.

He opened his mouth, welcoming her kisses which became more heated with every sigh, and every touch.

Breaking away, his breathing was erratic. "We're in a park, with a kids' play area over there. We have to stop."

Sitting on his lap, she gave him a cheeky smile before whispering in his ear. "Do you think everyone back home will miss us if we do a quick detour to your place?"

"There'll be nothing *quick* about you, my beautiful. I'm

going to spend all afternoon kissing you, and showing you how much I love you." His voice was filled with longing.

"Oh, yes, please," she sighed, her body throbbing with anticipation.

"I think you forgot to tell me something," he murmured, as he pressed kisses to the skin behind her ear.

"Um, no, I don't think so," she said playfully, having fun at his expense.

His hands cupped her cheeks and he kissed her till they were both breathless and panting in need.

"What did you need to tell me?" He reminded her with a smug raise of his eyebrows.

With an upturned face, she brightly said, "I love you, Leo. You are the sexiest *bore* I know. I love spending time with you, and I can't wait to spend my life with you." She paused. "I love your compromise, and I promise to make you happy for choosing me. . .and will mercilessly tease you every day."

"I wouldn't expect anything less from you." He beamed at her. "Come on, my beautiful." He took her hand and stood. "I want some *alone* time with you."

"Skip the party at Mum and Dad's?" She pouted, pretending she'd rather be there than alone with him. She was bursting with excitement and couldn't wait to get back to his place.

"Yep, and tonight. We're staying there till tomorrow?" He announced with supreme confidence.

Her heartbeat raced with euphoria. "If it's a sleep-over, I'll need a nightie."

"You can sleep naked," he said in a low voice that made her shiver in anticipation.

"My toothbrush?"

"You can borrow mine."

"A dress so I don't have to do the *walk of shame* tomorrow?"

He smacked her bottom. "You have five minutes to pack and then we're going. You can tell your parents you're with me."

"The dinner tonight, at Mono?"

"I'd rather be alone with you, and besides they've seen us at many functions," he said with a husky voice.

She smiled. "I'm with you." She faced him, put her arms around his neck and kissed him. "I love you, Leo Turner. I'm so glad you picked me to be your fake girlfriend, who is now your real girlfriend."

"I love you, Jenna Williamson, my now real girlfriend," he said with pride before kissing her yet again.

Four weeks later, in London

"I can't believe Amber and Darcy are marrying in winter." Jenna stamped her feet to warm them up. "I'm freezing," she said, huddling in her warm coat, beanie, and gloves.

"Stop complaining. We've got one week's vacation here in London, and I'm loving this time with you." Leo said. "Okay, here we are." They stopped walking and Leo pointed to the structure in front of them.

Jenna looked up. "The London Eye? This should be fun."

He led her to a priority queue, and soon they were in their own private cabin, the sprawl of the great city before them.

"This is incredible. You booked a private tour for us?" she gushed, excited to be a tourist in London, with the man she loved.

"Of course." He gestured to the champagne and chocolates on the side, waiting for them. "Best bit, I get to eat all the chocolates."

She pouted with disappointment. "I've been thinking about that. . . I may have one," she teased.

He swept her into his arms. "You keep telling me that you can't eat desserts and you won't eat chocolate for your figure. Personally, I'd be happy for you to eat them." He reassured her before squeezing her bottom. "I'll still love you whether you eat chocolate or not. And once you finish studying, you'll have more time to visit me at work, and we get to play *bingo* together." He waggled his eyebrows at her.

"We had sex on your desk after bingo," she said, her breathing growing fast as she remembered how incredibly exciting their lovemaking had been that night. After playing bingo, and casting looks at each other, for the hour, they each knew what they wanted. Alone time. As soon as they could, they'd made their excuses and in record time ran to his office. There they'd locked the door before clawing at each other, desperate to be one. They'd had sex against the wall, and then again on his desk. Her skin warmed just thinking how satisfied she'd been and how he'd kissed her non-stop, the only way to silence her so the residents didn't hear what they'd been getting up to in his office.

"Bingo is fun. . .but pleasuring you is even better," he said in a low voice.

His confession made her skin tingle all over. "You're the life of the party." She recalled his enthusiasm when working with the older residents, at their events. He genuinely loved being involved with their activities.

"What can I say? It's more than a job."

"I know. I love your commitment to the Home, and the residents," she said with honesty. She caressed the back of his neck with her fingers.

"We are a great team. We've come a long way in such a short time," he said.

"Oh, I forgot to tell you that the builder is settling the

class action, and I'll be able to rent out my apartment soon," she said.

"That's good news," he kissed her nose. "And a relief to you."

"Not that I need to worry. I love your apartment, and living near the beach," she said.

"Well. . .I'm hoping you'll move in *permanently*. In case you hadn't guessed from all the romance I organised, I wanted to make our team of two official with a proposal." He took her hands in his. "Jenna Williamson, the woman who makes me smile, makes me laugh and is incredibly sexy, would you do me the honour of being my wife, my bingo life partner? I want us to spend lazy weekends playing board games, going on picnics, and walks, making dinners together, and more importantly, spending hours in bed. I want to travel with you, and make you happy always."

Pure joy fluttered in her belly. "How could I say no to that?" She threw her arms around him. "Yes, yes, yes. I want to be with you always. I can't wait to marry you. I've got some great ideas for games, but only for you and me," she said in a low voice in his ear, before nibbling the lobe.

"That sounds better than bingo." He inhaled deeply.

"Oh, it will be. We'll go back to the hotel *now* and I'll show you." Warmth flooded her belly, and she didn't care about missing some sightseeing; all she wanted to do was be with Leo.

"I'm loving the sound of that," he said brightly. "But we'll have to wait till after lunch. In one hour, we're meeting your parents, Taylor, Luca, Amber, Darcy, Darcy's family and Ella for lunch," he said in a matter-of-fact voice.

"Are you joking?" Shock made her jaw drop. The whole family knew about this?

"Not at all, they're all waiting for us." He removed a small box from his jacket. "I have this for you, but if you don't like it, you can change it." His face reddened, even his ears.

The solitary diamond on a platinum band, that he'd chosen fit perfectly on her finger and she gushed at its beauty.

"I'm so happy that we're together, and I can't wait to spend the rest of my life with you," he said, holding her close.

"Me too, Leo, me too," she said before kissing him hard on the lips.

THE END

ACKNOWLEDGMENTS

Dear Reader

I do love writing books that have connected characters. When I was looking to write this year's Christmas romance, I gravitated to Jenna, Taylor's annoying sister from Christmas Kiss, New Year's Wish.

Not only is Jenna a supermodel, talented, and gorgeous, she's also opinionated, headstrong, and can be insensitive.

So now I had my heroine for this book, but who would I pair her up with?

Leo, of course. She's been ribbing him for years, and making jokes at his expense, so it was only natural that I would concoct some fun and get these two kissing.

Writing may be a solitary occupation, but I'm lucky that my life is full of friendships and I'm grateful that I can connect with my readers and my author friends via the Internet. They enrich my work life, and I'm never lonely. Thank you!

Thanks, as always, to my editor, Jena O'Connor, my proof-reader Janice Owen, and talented cover artist Erin Cawood.

And a special thanks to my ever-supportive husband and cheeky boys who are my biggest fans. . .even if I do write about that yucky "kissy-kissy" stuff.

Merry Christmas and Happy holidays, Joanne xo

PS – I'm often asked where I get my ideas. The issue of cladding on buildings in Melbourne has received a lot of attention. It's been a difficult issue, not just here in Australia but also overseas. If you're interested, here is an article from The Financial Review https://www.afr.com/real-estate/court-case-shows-cladding-is-an-apartment-owners-nightmare-20180829-h14ogb

ABOUT THE AUTHOR

Joanne Dannon has been living in the world of romance for as long as she can remember. From doodling hearts on her school notebooks to regularly reading romances, Joanne's world has always been filled with the excitement of love stories. So it was just a natural for Joanne to begin writing the genre she's always loved.

Formerly a policy writer by day and romance writer by night, Joanne now works full time writing the books she adores. Creating heroes for readers to fall in love with and heroines to cheer on, her characters are people readers can identify with.

Joanne writes to give her readers the experience she still loves to savour—indulging in a sigh-worthy happily-ever-after, being swept away from the everyday by diving into a delicious romance novel.

Joanne Dannon is a happily married mother of two heroes-in-training who loves spending time with friends and family. She can be found on Facebook and her website www.joannedannon.com chatting about reading, writing, cooking, vintage-inspired dresses and all things romantic. She loves to hear from readers.

Sign up to her newsletter and to say thanks, Joanne will send you a free copy of Bidding on Love. Go to www.joannedannon.com
www.joannedannon.com
joanne@joannedannon.com

- facebook.com/joannedannonwrites
- instagram.com/joannedannon_writes
- amazon.com/author/joannedannon
- bookbub.com/authors/joanne-dannon

MORE FROM JOANNE DANNON

*D*id you know that I write both sweet, and sexy books?

SWEET – my sweet reads are generally my holiday romances which focuses on the emotional journey of the hero and heroine. There are usually no bedroom scenes but if there is, it is closed doors (you, as the reader do not "see" these scenes)

Sexy/steamy – my sexy reads have a heat level of 3 out of 5. There will be a couple of love making scenes, the bedroom door is open (meaning, you read the scene) but the journey of the hero and heroine is emotional not sexual.

ON MY WEBSITE, I've noted the heat level against each of my books to help you know if the read is sweet or sexy.

* * *

SIGN up to my newsletter where I share news on my latest books, insights in to my writing and recommend romances I've read; and to say thanks I'll send you a free e-copy of **Bidding on Love**.

https://joannedannon.com/free-offer-for-bidding-on-love/

FINDING LOVE

ear Reader

ALL THE BOOKS in the Finding Love series are standalone reads but have interconnecting characters.

Book 1 Want You If you love the movie, *Notting Hill*, and friends to lovers romances, then you'll love Want You.

Book 2 Marry You If you love the movie, *What Happens in Vegas*, and fake marriage romances, then you'll love Marry You.

Book 3 – Meet You If you love the movie *Love at First Bark*, and friends to lovers romances, then you'll love Meet You.

Book 4 – Need You If you love secret baby romances, second chance romances, and rockstars, then you'll love Need You.

Check out my website for all the news and updates of this fab series, and also my other books.

HOLIDAY ROMANCES

*I*f you love the Hallmark channel, and books focussing on love, family, community, with a splash of faith, then these sets are for you -

Dreaming of Christmas

Dreaming of Hanukah

Christmas Kiss series

THE KISSING DOWN UNDER SERIES

Book 1 **Kissing under the Spotlight**
- Can a superstar singer croon his way into the heart of an ordinary girl?

Book 2 Kissing like she means it
- The plan was not to fall in love. Can friends with benefits have a happily ever after?

Book 3 Kissing her brother's best friend
- Should she lie to her brother and kiss his best friend?

Book 4 Kissing him at last
- It's never a good idea to fall for your best friend's brother... or so they say.

THE KISSING DOWN Under series has been designed so you don't have to read them in order. They are each standalone romances with no cliff hangers.

However, you will most likely enjoy reading them in order.

Happy reading, Joanne x

BACHELOR DOWN UNDER SERIES

*I*f you love romances with characters that are flawed or broken, dealing with issues such as fidelity, and drug/alcohol abuse, then these romances are for you.

Note. These books have swear words, unlike my other romances.

FALLING **for the Best Man**

Not your average romance. *When the love of his life is his brother's bride-to-be...*

When he's asked to be the best man at their wedding, should he speak up, or forever hold his peace?

FALLING **for Miss Write**

A complex romance where both the hero and heroine are struggling to overcome their past mistakes.

STANDALONE ROMANCES

*D*on't have the time to commit to a series? Check out these sparkling, standalone romances with believable characters, all with a guaranteed happily ever after.

My Best Friend's **Brother** (sweet romance)

Can a single mum have a HEA with her best friend's brother?

Forever Mine (sexy romance)

She's in love with her brother's best friend. He just wants to protect her from his toxic family.

Off Limits: **Her Handsome Boss** (sweet romance)

A social media fiasco forces Jessica to hide out at a tropical retreat with her brother's best friend. Cocktails and a

private beach fan the flames of a long-simmering crush...
what could go wrong?

AN UNEXPECTED FOREVER (sweet romance)

If you love forbidden, sweet romance where the hero and
heroine have a clash of cultures, then this is the book for you.

ALWAYS YOU (SEXY romance)

If love second chance romance, then this is the book
for you.

FALLING for Mr Wrong (sexy romance)

Love fun romance, with twists and turns, then this is the
book for you.

BIDDING ON LOVE (sexy romance)

If you love forbidden, sexy romance where the hero and
heroine have a clash of cultures, then this is the book for you.

BOXED SET ROMANCES

*L*ove to read? Need more romances? Then check out these boxed sets with hours of blissful reading.

DREAMING **Of Christmas** (sweet romance)
Dreaming of Hanukah (sweet romance)
Dreaming of Desert Love (sweet and sexy romance)
Kissing Down Under (sexy romance)
New York Romance (sweet romance)

www.ingramcontent.com/pod-product-compliance
Lightning Source LLC
Chambersburg PA
CBHW031052260626
47172CB00001B/34